HOUSE ON THE HARBOR

A BIRCH HARBOR NOVEL

ELIZABETH BROMKE

PUBLISHING IN THE PINES
White Mountains, Arizona

ONE

KATE

A light breeze curled in from the window. On it, the scent of lavender. Faint but sweet.

In front of each window in her suburban Michigan home, Kate Hannigan had strategically positioned fragrant plants of many varieties.

When the weather was just right, Kate would throw open the windows and revel in the aroma like a newly appointed florist.

It was a trick her mother had taught her four daughters. *Why use candles when you have flowers and a breeze?* Nora Hannigan had often chided her daughters.

Kate happened to love candles as much as she loved taking in the earthy smell of Mother Nature. But still. It was a good thought. A good reminder of her mother. A happy one.

She smiled to herself, swept up the last pot—the one at her bedside window—and carried it downstairs, where her sisters waited.

"Last one?" Megan asked, tugging at a stiff, black pencil skirt.

"Last one," Kate replied, handing the lavender to her.

Megan transferred the purple-budded flower to a long, narrow folding table that stretched in front of the sitting room window.

Every single one of Kate's little potted plants was now re-situated tastefully for the reception. Kate was good at that sort of thing. Adding the perfect touch to a space. Bringing it *to life*.

And yet, together, in the front room, all of that lavender and jasmine and gardenia achieved more of a funeral parlor effect than that of a florist shop. Though appropriate, it didn't sit well with Kate. For, this event was meant to be less *funereal* and more *floral*. Even if it *was* a funeral.

She frowned.

Clara stole a cube of cheese and popped it into her mouth. "I'm starving," the youngest Hannigan sister mumbled through a mouthful.

Kate snapped her fingers. "I know." She strode to the window, unlatched the levers, and slid it wide open.

The cool morning breeze lifted her blonde, shoulder-length tresses up off her neck and blew in some much-needed fresh air.

"Good call," Amelia said. "It was feeling a little... "

"A little *funeral-y*?" Megan read Kate's mind. Of the four sisters, Kate and Megan resembled each other the least, in part because Megan insisted on dying her hair to match her wardrobe: black. But they shared one important commonality: a critical nature. It was a trait passed down from Nora, no doubt.

Amelia, the second oldest, was something of a silly heart, even as she ascended in age. The lighthearted nature was a characteristic that originated with their father and one that only Amelia had been gifted.

Kate was more like Megan (and Nora), discerning—though less morbid and more grounded.

Clara was neither silly nor critical. She fell somewhere in between. Anxious and, well, young.

Presently, Clara grinned at Megan's morbid joke. Then Amelia chuckled. Soon enough all four of them were laughing together. And then, crying.

Again.

"Will we *ever* get over this?" Clara asked, pushing her thumbs along her lower lash line to clear away remnants of the spontaneous sob session.

Kate smiled at her and pulled her in for a hug. "No, we won't," she replied, locking eyes with Amelia, whose smooth pale face was scrunching again into a fresh round of tears. "But," Kate went on, "that doesn't mean we'll never laugh again. Or be happy again."

Clara nodded into Kate's shoulder and lifted her head. "I'm fine," she said. "*We're* fine."

"True," Megan replied, tugging Clara onto the love seat with her and leaning back into the pillowy cushions. "We're fine. It was her time. Oh, boy, was it her time, you know?"

Kate eyed Megan.

After a brief sigh, Megan brushed a black strand of hair out of her eyes and offered an explanation. "She was going downhill. Deteriorating, even." She stopped and smiled, a sentimental, weepy smile, her green eyes turning glassy. "For all we know, the poor thing was driving herself mad. I'd imagine the disease does that, right? Anyway, I don't think Nora would have wanted to be what she was becoming."

Megan had called their mother by her first name since Megan was a teenager, and Nora had long given up the fight against it. It no longer felt disrespectful, in fact. Just one of those quirks a family had.

Regardless of the name matter, Megan was right.

It was their mom's *time*.

And it was also time for the reception to begin. Kate and her sisters had left the burial ahead of everyone by a mere ten minutes. All they had to do when they got to her house was set up the food and flowers. Relatives had agreed to handle everything else.

Kate wasn't sold on the paper products and plastic utensils, but the others overruled her, arguing that the last thing they needed after Mom's funeral was to do dishes.

Kate would argue that dishes would be the exact sort of thing she'd need.

Cleaning, to Kate, was therapy.

She checked her wristwatch, a thin leather strap with a silver face. "They'll be here soon," she announced and glanced around the room, anxious.

On the folding table, now framed perfectly by two sentinel lavender plants, sat orderly trays of cold cuts and cheese, a platter of fruits and vegetables, and a bald spot at the far end dedicated for everything else due to arrive with their aunts and cousins.

Amelia fussed with the memorial setting, which she had first established on a second square folding table, only to move it to the coffee table, and then finally to the back of the upright piano that took up the far corner of the room. "Does this work?" she wondered aloud.

Kate joined her and tweaked the centerpiece—a glass frame, behind which preened their mother in a formal portrait.

No husband sat next to Nora.

No daughters crowded in behind Nora.

Just Nora.

And that sort of photograph was perfect, because it was *Nora's* day, Kate had reminded her sisters.

Not theirs.

Only Amelia had argued, but now she seemed pleased enough. "I remember when Mom had that photo taken," she murmured.

Kate felt her throat close up a bit but swallowed it down.

The crying was supposed to end with the funeral. She promised herself that, as hostess and eldest daughter, it was her duty to see to the perfect reception. A light, happy affair.

In fact, it would be the last event she would have in her home. Because soon she'd be moving. Though to where, exactly, was still unclear.

"I'm not trying to gossip, but did any of you see Matt Fiorillo's date at the service last night?" Amelia asked, pushing a strand of her long brown hair back into position behind her ear as she went for a cheese cube, too.

Matt Fiorillo was, if recent reports were accurate, a local property investor. Also, an old family friend. An old flame, too. One who Kate hoped would stay squarely in her past. But there he was, at the funeral. Typical.

Megan chimed in next. "She might be a prostitute."

Kate shook her head and glared. "Enough, you two," she threatened through a tight voice, then pressed her fingers to her shoulders, ensuring her bra straps were in position squarely beneath the black fabric of her chiffon dress.

Kate hated chiffon.

But her mother had loved it.

It was important to make sacrifices for family. Even chiffon-loving ones. Even dead ones, too.

Kate shook the thought just as the doorbell rang.

"They're here," Amelia announced, her face morphing into a Picasso painting, yet again.

"Keep it together," Kate hissed, holding up her palm. "We can do this." She nodded at the three women, each of whom was on the brink of hysterics.

Kate willed herself to stay sane in the face of grief.

Smoothing her dress and taking in a deep, calming breath, she answered the door.

IN POURED a steady stream of well-wishers, many of whom had attended the wake the evening prior, some who'd also shown up for the burial that morning.

Both the wake and the burial had been formal affairs, drawing oversized attention from Birch Harbor locals. The usual suspects, really. Those of the Actons—their father's side—who were still alive and then Nora's own strained relations.

The strain had begun years back, when Nora refused to take (or give) her husband's last name. Apparently when she'd married, the Hannigans and relatives hoped to shake her loose and prevent the black sheep that Nora was from soiling a good family name.

They were unsuccessful.

In addition to the Actons and Hannigans, Megan's daughter and Kate's sons were also there. Grandchildren were better capable of handling funerals. They were young and distracted. Full of hope. Far separated from the reaching hands of death, to be sure. They'd been catching up together in the backyard, like old times, and Kate had left them to do just that.

Nora was survived by her country club cronies and church friends, too. And other, more anonymous men and women, clad in dutiful black, their expressions appropriately ashen, arrived for the service and would leave after tight goodbyes with Kate and her sisters.

Even Birch Harbor's mayor made a somber (if opportunistic) appearance, bringing with her several members of the town council, the same town council their mother had frequently come to blows with over any number of local dramas.

Others showed up, as well. Local business owners and shopkeepers, like Matt Fiorillo's extended family. And, Nora's lawyer, Michael Matuszewski and entourage.

They drove in a slow convoy all the way to Kate's house out on Apple Tree Hill. It was a solid forty-five-minute drive inland, away from the harbor and closer to Detroit.

Kate was impressed.

She ushered them in politely, accepting rehearsed lines at the front door while Megan lingered behind her, ready to help if Kate faltered.

Megan was a good sister that way. Austere, sure. But stable. Helpful.

Clara had disappeared into the kitchen as soon as the first group arrived, no doubt hiding. Clara was something of a hider. Kate chalked that up to her relative immaturity. She was sixteen years younger than Kate, after all, and only now in her twenties.

Kate watched in amusement as Amelia, predictably, played the receiving widow. Or widower. Or... orphan?

Whatever her label, the chestnut-haired actress shined in the role, greeting each visitor with grace and gratitude, blinking away tears at the very mention of their mom. The tears were surely genuine, but Amelia's earnest nods at every memory each of the near-strangers tried to evoke was an act. She was a good person to have on hand.

The reception began easily, with extended family taking on the role of hosting, more or less.

"Matt's here." Clara had reappeared at Kate's side, her attention now entirely fixed on any opportunity for distraction. All four sisters stood together on the threshold between the foyer and the parlor. It was the perfect people-watching position.

"Are you going to talk to him?" Amelia asked.

Kate shook her head and narrowed her eyes. "I haven't talked to him in years. Now's not the time for a reunion." The sisters gazed together across the room. Kate gestured discreetly with her drink. "There he is. By Mom's picture."

"Why is he wearing a turtleneck in May?" Clara asked.

"I like turtlenecks," Megan replied, taking up for him.

Kate scoffed. "He never had good fashion sense."

"It's not the turtleneck," Clara whispered conspiratorially.

The three others leaned in closer.

Clara went on. "It's the *woman*."

Kate bit the insides of her cheeks and caught Amelia nodding gravely. "Yes, I saw her, too."

Finally, Kate broke. "Where?" She lowered her plastic cup of lemonade and scanned the room.

Amelia lifted an eyebrow and thrust her chin to the far corner, just behind where Matt stood.

Kate took in the woman, and she was surprised to see her sisters' estimations proved valid. Clad in a black spaghetti-string top, black jeans, and black flip-flops, the poor thing was decidedly out of place.

"I suppose a black outfit isn't enough to fit in at a funeral," Megan mused behind them, her voice appropriately lifeless.

Kate narrowed her eyes on the woman, a realization hitting her. "That's not even a *woman*," she hissed, turning away and facing her sisters out of mortification. "It's a *teenager*."

"Teenager?" Clara craned her neck around Kate. "Oh my word, you're right. She must be in eighth or ninth grade!" Clara, Megan, and Amelia's eyes grew wide.

"Sh, *sh!* It's not his *girlfriend*. It's got to be his *daughter*."

Again, Kate's three sisters looked past her with sharp affects.

Finally, Clara relaxed back into position and sipped her lemonade. "You're right. That girl is no older than fourteen. Maybe even thirteen now that I'm looking. She must go to St. Mary's. I've never seen her at school."

"What is he even doing here?" Amelia asked, breathing deeply, for Kate's benefit, probably.

Megan shook her head. "Everyone wants a piece of the pie."

At that, Kate snorted. "Come on. As *if*. Matt doesn't care about money, anyway. At least, he didn't when *I* knew him."

"Maybe Matt has a heart of gold. But look around you, Kate." Megan lifted her plastic cup in appraisal of the packed room. "As far as the locals know, Nora Hannigan was the Queen of Birch Harbor, a glittery benefactor, primed to dole out her estate to anyone who so much as waved at her. As far as they know, Mom was rich. And generous, too."

Kate swallowed Megan's words, her eyes lingering on Matt. Down deep inside, she wanted to go to him. She wanted to ask why he showed up. Who his little girl was. Where he'd been.

But she knew. He'd been right there. In Birch Harbor. Matt, unlike Kate, wasn't one to run from the past.

TWO

AMELIA

One week later.

Amelia-Ann Hannigan stood in front of her foggy bathroom mirror and patted her face dry. Raw skin glowed back at her. It had taken far too long to scrub away every last bit of rouge and kohl she'd painstakingly applied for the wrap party the night before.

No, she wasn't the star of the show. Or even a supporting player. But Amelia considered herself to be a professional. And despite her pitifully tiny role as an extra in Little City Theatre's production of *Oklahoma!* she wanted to prove to her director that she had potential. Even at the ripe old age of forty-something. Hah.

Anyway, the makeup helped to conceal the bags beneath her eyes from traveling to and from Birch Harbor for her mother's funeral.

Still, it shouldn't take nearly half an hour of washcloth-rubbing to get rid of her "face."

Quietly, she promised herself to scale back a little on the makeup, even for rehearsals and performances and wrap parties. Amelia really wasn't old enough to "put on her face" for any event.

Maybe she should lose five or ten pounds. Then, the struggling actress wouldn't have to obsess over adding hollows to her cheeks with shadowy browns and angles to her cheekbones with shimmery highlighter crayons.

Amelia was too young for a full face but too old for trying to look twenty.

It was a hard spot to be in. Part of her wished to age enough to nab those "north-of-fifty" roles, part of her contemplated premature plastic surgery to better achieve the fresh-out-of-college-cover-girl roles.

Fat chance.

Amelia was due back in Birch Harbor that evening. Instead of flying this time, she planned to drive. Jimmy, her boyfriend of six months, was supposed to stay at her apartment and watch after Dobi, Amelia's paunchy Weiner dog.

She'd half-heartedly considered bringing both of them. Ever since the funeral, Amelia could not shake the longing in the pit of her stomach.

Loneliness.

The realization that Amelia was entering middle age with little to show for it. No husband. No children (save for Dobi). No mortgage.

And now, no mother.

Losing her mom was hard as hell. Really, it was.

Plus, the whole thing was made harder by Amelia's stark realization that she was bound on the same journey as sweet-and-spicy Nora, a wacky spinster whose closest friends were more often her most poisonous enemies.

And that just wasn't Amelia-Ann Hannigan. She was not a wacky spinster. Even more than that, she had friends. *Real* ones, who weren't *also* her enemies—that was important to note, a big difference between Amelia and her mother. Nora may have put on a show for the public, but her actress-daughter was the real deal. A good friend. Not a fake.

So, maybe no husband, children, mortgage, or mother... but Amelia *did* have friends. And a boyfriend, hapless though he may be. And a furbaby. And sisters.

And, hopefully—if her recent on-Broadway meet-and-greet was well-received, she might just have an exciting gig, to boot.

"Making it" in New York had been even harder than she thought it would be. Twenty years of working her way toward The Big Apple, one small-town community theatre at a time, had resulted in a demotion, actually.

Bit parts in off-Broadway productions that were poorly attended. So poorly attended, that she had to make ends meet elsewhere.

Waiting tables sucked. Plain and simple.

Who wanted to be a forty-year-old waitress? Much less, an over-forty waitress who was trying desperately to break into the ingénue-favoring theatre world?

Well, maybe *some* people. But not *Amelia-Ann*.

Now, as she felt herself pulled right and left by what she did not have and what she *did* have, she tucked away every last jar, tube, can, and palette of her makeup set and kept out *only* her mascara.

Three swipes. That's all she allowed herself. Three quick swipes before popping the brush back in its tube and the tube in her bag and zipping it with finality.

Less is more, Amelia-Ann, the voice in her head trilled.

"When you going?"

It was Jimmy, leaning shirtless in the doorway.

He had absolutely no reason to be shirtless. He'd just

arrived minutes earlier—fully clothed. Amelia had given him zero reason to undress. And there he was, an almost-six pack bulging beneath his shaved chest. Completely unnecessary.

But that was Jimmy.

"Now," she answered, pecking him on the cheek before squeezing past to hunt down Dobi for a goodbye cuddle.

"I've always wanted to go to Michigan, you know." Jimmy crossed his arms over his chest, flexing his pecs involuntarily.

That pang—that longing from the week before grew heavy in her stomach.

Her sisters would hate Jimmy. Amelia was sure of that. And Clara's tiny little apartment had no room for a fledgling couple. It would be weird to invite him. If Amelia didn't realize this before, she did now.

She bit down on her lip and raised her eyebrows at her brooding, out-of-work, *younger* boyfriend.

She sighed. "Jimmy, I would love for you to come... " she started, suddenly feeling torn all over again.

"You would?" he asked, the corners of his mouth curling up in a lazy grin.

"Well, of course," she replied, scooping Dobi into her arms and scratching beneath his collar. "But Clara only has a fold-out sofa."

"I bet we can fit," he answered, his voice dropping an octave as he uncrossed his arms and strode to her.

Amelia closed her eyes, her heart racing in her chest. She opened her eyes and lifted one palm against him. "I'm so sorry. Clara is super prim and proper. It's a no. It's such a no, and I'm *so* sad about it." She put on a pout. Dobi let out a low growl.

He took a step back and raised his hands in surrender. "All right. I get it."

"Oh, Jimmy, honey," Amelia set Dobi on the overstuffed armchair and reached for her roll-on suitcase. "I *want* you to come. But you'd be bored. I'll be with the probate attorney and my *sisters*, and—"

"I get it," he answered, letting her hug his torso as he gazed off.

"I've got an idea!" Amelia's eyes flashed open. The perfect solution occurred to her. A light at the end of the tunnel. A way for her to quell the pit in her stomach with a little hope. "Why don't you come down this *weekend*? We can play tourist for my last day in Birch Harbor. You could rent a car and drive to the lake. That way you don't have to be around for the lawyer stuff, but you can still meet my sisters, maybe, and see my hometown. We'll ride back to the city together. A mini-vacay. What do you think?"

He smirked. "Yeah, maybe."

Amelia smiled and threw one more look at Dobi, the one she really wanted to take. But she knew this was for the best. Her attention could be on all the legal stuff that would no doubt be confusing and stressful.

Then, when it was over—she'd enjoy the reward of reuniting with Dobi and put on her docent hat for Jimmy. Maybe, just maybe, seeing him outside the city would do her good, anyway. Give her some perspective. An answer. Maybe it would show her whether he was commitment-worthy or just another unemployed construction worker looking for love. Or, lust.

Maybe Jimmy could even help, in some way.

Her boyfriend was a bit of a project, but Amelia was not afraid of a project.

She bid them both goodbye and trotted down four flights of stairs and out onto the busy thoroughfare.

She took a cab to the car rental place and accepted their cheapest offering: a smoky, puke-smelling sedan that, with any luck, would take her directly to the car rental hub nearest Birch Harbor where she could deposit it and be whisked away by Clara, who, naturally, drove a cute little VW Bug. One that didn't smell like an ashtray or a vomit bag.

"AMELIA!"

Amelia whipped around just as she passed the single key over the counter to the car rental guy. It was Clara, waving wildly from the curb.

She smiled and waved back, thanking the clerk and wheeling her luggage through the greasy doors and out into the warm Michigan afternoon.

Clara rounded her car and squeezed Amelia in a tight hug. "I'm so glad you're here," she gushed.

Amelia hugged back, hard. "*I'm* so glad I'm here. I forget that New York sort of has a smell to it. Until I leave."

"You mean to tell me that place doesn't have a smell to it?" Clara pointed behind her toward the boxy, dated building that was once a fast-food joint.

"Touché," Amelia replied. "But out here? It's... *nice*." She hugged Clara again, and they drove together back into Birch Harbor.

"How was your week?" Clara asked, adjusting her grip on the steering wheel.

"Busy. We wrapped *Oklahoma!* I packed to come back. Dobi is with Jimmy. I should have just brought him."

"Jimmy or Dobi?"

"Dobi," Amelia replied pointedly.

Clara grinned. "How's that going, anyway?"

"You mean with Jimmy?"

"Yeah. Isn't he... *younger?*" Clara lifted an eyebrow at her older sister.

Amelia blew out a sigh and tugged her ponytail loose, letting her warm chestnut waves fall around her shoulders. "Jimmy is... a good guy."

"When did you two start dating again?" Clara's voice was light, but her words were heavy.

"Um, December? It was right after we got Mom's diagnosis."

"Oh, yeah." Clara brought a second hand to the steering wheel and switched lanes after checking over her shoulder.

"How'd you meet?"

Amelia frowned. Clara wasn't the type to put twenty questions to her older sisters. "At a bar. I was... I was there with Mia. Actually, it was the exact day I found out. I remember now. I drove here the next morning. But the night before, well. I was a wreck. Mia tried to distract me. And, we met Jimmy. He got my number."

Clara didn't respond, instead maneuvering off the highway and down toward the water.

Birch Harbor. A tourist community on Lake Huron known for its small-town feel, ocean-like beaches, and quaint lakeside eateries.

Just before they pulled up to Clara's digs, The Bunga-lows—a group of four ground-level units, owned by the Hannigan family trust—Amelia's phone buzzed with a new text.

She opened it up and saw two faces looking back at her: Jimmy and Dobi, posing in front of the very same car rental agency where she'd been just hours before. Jimmy stood there, grinning from ear to ear, dangling a single key above little Dobi's worried face.

A caption below the attached image read: *The tourists are on their way!*

THREE
CLARA

"It's tiny. I'm sorry." Clara winced at Amelia as she opened the door to her one-bedroom apartment. "If you decide you want to stay out of town at Kate's or even Megan's... "

Clara watched her sister's expression closely, looking for signs of disgust or, worse, disinterest.

Amelia walked around like she was shopping for houses, inspecting the insides of drawers and touching the curtains, testing their heft. "I love this place. You know that," she cooed at last. "But... "

Clara frowned. "But?"

"I just got a text from Jimmy. He's on his *way*."

"On his way? *Here?*"

Now it was Amelia's turn to cringe. "Yep." She strolled back to where Clara stood in the center of the modest living space, just feet away from the breakfast bar—the only eating area the little bungalow offered. "I'll get a hotel room. I know Kate and Megan would never invite him either." She laughed lightly before adding, "Don't worry."

But it wasn't Jimmy that bothered Clara. In fact, Clara

was excited to meet Jimmy. He was super attractive (from the photos she'd seen) and the way Amelia described him, he sounded *fun*.

He was not what bothered her.

It was that Amelia was happy to make different plans. After all that scrubbing and bleaching and sheet-changing and... *prepping*, she was going to stay somewhere else. Clara's face fell.

"I'm so sorry, Clara. I did *not* invite him. I promise."

"Why doesn't he stay here, too?" Clara suggested, crossing her arms over her tunic. "You can sleep in my room with me. He can have the sofa."

"I'd hate to impose him on you like that," Amelia whined. "Ugh. I'm just, I don't know, *trapped* with this guy. I mean, I like Jimmy. I really do, but... "

"It's completely fine by me. You can share my bed, unless you two... " Clara raised her eyebrows to her sister. She felt her neck grow warm at the thought of housing a total stranger. It nearly ruined the day. Clara could just imagine cleaning the toilet after a sloppy New York construction worker type. And what did he sleep in? Boxers? She shuddered involuntarily.

"You know what? I didn't *invite* Jimmy. Neither did you. He can get a room at the motel." Amelia smirked. "What about Dobi though?"

"Pets welcome! Dobi can stay here, of course," Clara answered, feeling her excitement return. "There's a court-yard out back. I think another resident has a little Chihuahua, in fact."

"Okay." Amelia let out a breath and clapped her hands together. "Let's do it. I'll tell Jimmy to book a room because I promised I was staying *with you*, which is true. And your place is too small for him, which is also true."

Clara nodded vigorously. "Yes, it'll be great."

"It's settled, then," Amelia added with a mock-serious expression.

Clara beamed up at her older sister. "Wonderful. All right, back to the tour?"

"Yes." Amelia smiled. "Back to the tour."

AFTER SHOWING Amelia her bedroom and bathroom, the tiny kitchen, and then how to pull out the sofa into a bed, they went over an itinerary Clara had put together.

"We meet with the attorney tomorrow at eight. Kate said to expect to be there for two hours, max. It will be the first meeting, and there could be several more," Clara explained.

Amelia nodded along as she sipped from a can of Diet Coke at the breakfast bar. "Kate said we might be able to get a few meetings set up over the course of this week. That way I don't have to drive back and forth. That's why I'm staying through Saturday. I'll find out this week if I got *Lady Macbeth*. I had a pseudo audition, you see. If I do—fingers crossed—then rehearsals will *probably* start next Monday." She grinned excitedly.

Clara squealed for Amelia. "*Macbeth*? That's like, *huge*, Amelia."

Amelia nodded and bit down on her lower lip. "I know. We'll see." Her face fell a little. "Regardless, Mario only gave me this week off from The Bread Basket. He won't hold my job after Saturday. Or so he *says*. Anyway, I'm hoping we settle everything *now*."

Clara shrugged. "Maybe. But that only works if the attorney can meet after three. I mean, at least, for *me*. I have to work every day, remember? My principal got a sub for tomorrow morning, but beyond that I risk going over my paid leave. If we can push any future meetings to June, that'd be really great. I'll be out of school by then, you know. But I think Kate is hoping to settle it sooner."

"We could probably have video calls, worst case scenario. And if something needs to be signed—well, it's the twenty-first century. The internet, you know."

Taking a sip of her own Diet Coke, Clara blinked. "Yeah. That's true. I just... I just want it to be all done, too. You know?"

Her older sister smiled and draped her arm across Clara's shoulders. "Me, too. We'll do whatever we can. And besides, Kate says Mom had everything in place. There shouldn't be any surprises. Equal division, then we go our separate ways. Full freedom to follow our dreams."

An itchy feeling crept up Clara's spine. She already *was* following her dream. What her sister had said felt tacky. Morbid. Tasteless, even. She pushed away her soda can and pulled out her phone to pretend to check for messages. "Yeah. It'll be fine," she muttered petulantly. Clara never had been good at confronting her older sisters.

She felt Amelia study her. "So, do you like teaching?"

Putting the phone to sleep, Clara blinked and met her sister's gaze. "I love it. Love the kids. Love summer vacation. It's really great." An involuntary smile lifted her cheeks. Her back stopped itching. She waited for another question about her career.

But Amelia lifted her chin and changed the line of questioning. "Are you dating?"

Clara shook her head, flushing. "No." She pulled the soda can back and took a small sip, but Amelia was still watching her, an eyebrow poised high on her forehead, willing her little sister to go on.

Clara took the hint and shook her head again. "It's *Birch Harbor*, Amelia. No one here is single. And if they are single, then they're tourists. Dating doesn't exist in Birch Harbor. Not for me, at least."

It was true. Clara had gone out a couple of times, thanks to her friends making a profile for her on a dating app. But each date had been with a guy who lived in or near Detroit. It was painfully awkward when she had to ask that they meet halfway between. Nothing had ever materialized. Which was fine by Clara. She had her career. And, up until recently, she had her mother to care for. Lingering sadness crawled up her throat and threatened to spill out, but she stalled it, swallowing hard.

"I didn't believe in marriage, you know," Amelia said quietly.

"What?" Clara was confused. Amelia never let a week go by without securing a boyfriend for herself—or nurturing a useless relationship. "You love men."

Amelia broke into a cackle. "I 'love men'? What does *that* mean?"

Clara blushed. "I mean, you always have a boyfriend. And when you don't, you're looking for one."

"Like I said, I *used* to not believe. I think that's changing now. With Mom, and... age, I guess. I spent many years thinking commitment could look different."

"It *can* look different. Marriage isn't the only way to commit." As the words formed on her tongue, Clara knew they'd bounce out as disingenuously as they felt. For Clara, it would be marriage or bust. She was no floozy.

But Amelia shook her head. "I don't buy that anymore, Clara. I don't know. Maybe I'm getting a little more... " She searched for the right word, but Clara knew where she was going.

"A little more like *me*?"

This time, they shared the laugh. "Yes. A little more traditional. Like my millennial kid sister, ironically."

"I want to be married one day, that's true. But I'm not in a rush. I've got my job. And my sisters." Clara knew she sounded lame, but she didn't care. It was the truth. The furthest thing from her mind was dating around. "Do you think you'll marry Jimmy?"

Amelia made a face. "No."

"Then why are you staying with him?" Clara asked. An honest question.

After a beat, her sister took another sip and stood up. "Maybe I will, I guess. If things change, maybe I will."

Clara left the conversation alone and joined Amelia in a little stretch.

"So what's next?" the older one asked.

"According to my itinerary, we are walking into town for an early dinner." Clara paused then flicked a glance up at Amelia. "Do you think we should, um, *wait*? For Jimmy?"

Amelia seemed to consider the question carefully, narrowing her eyes and running a finger over her lower lip. "No. Let's make it a sisters' thing. In fact, I'll text him the address to the motel now."

MOMENTS LATER, Clara had dutifully locked her front door and secured her handbag evenly along her shoulder.

Though Clara enjoyed playing tour guide, Amelia knew Birch Harbor well, if not better.

A warm breeze joined them as they walked and talked,

revisiting memories from when Amelia was still at home, living in the big house on the harbor.

Growing up, Clara was less Kate, Amelia, and Megan's younger sister and more the baby of the family. Literally.

Thirteen years as Amelia's junior had set them far apart, though not as distant in age as Clara was with Kate—sixteen years. And while Clara was only ten years younger than Megan, the two were the least close with one another. Clara felt most aligned with Kate—they were both conservative, neat... some might even say *uptight*.

But Clara enjoyed Amelia's company the most. Amelia was fun-loving and easy-going. If Clara worried about something, Amelia would wash it away like sand on the beach.

She'd always been told she was a happy surprise, but Clara's recollections of her youth weren't always so happy. Having an older mother and a long-lost father had thrust Clara into a complicated family dynamic. She knew this.

"It smells like childhood here," Amelia mused, twirling in a circle as they neared Birch Village, a cozy loop of lakeside shops and eateries situated just up from the marina.

Birch Harbor, though small in its year-round population, stretched some miles up and down Lake Huron. Informally, it was divided in two by the broad dock, the harbor the town was named for. South of it, swayed a modest thicket of white Birch trees.

Sometime in the forties, when Birch Harbor gained momentum as a tourist destination, locals dubbed the northwest side of the marina Birch Beach. And surely, it was a lovely beach, attracting daily visitors to spread out on the warm sand, books and bottles of sunscreen tossed casually into the corners of oversized terry cloth towels.

One afternoon at that beach and you'd think you washed ashore at some resort on the Atlantic coast. Show tunes wafted from storefronts along a small boardwalk and the buzz of jet skis and speed boats were just enough to lull you into a lazy nap.

The southeast side of the marina, which saw less economic and tourist activity, took on the moniker Heirloom Cove. Decidedly quieter and less peopled, water from the lake crossed a craggier shoreline and splashed up against rocky outcroppings there. It was a curve of land that offered less beach. In fact, the only beach property there was private. It belonged to the Heirloom Cove homes. A smattering of old teetering waterfront houses. The houses that had once belonged to Birch Harbor settlers. Like, for instance, the Hannigans and the Actons.

Clara followed Amelia's gaze south, toward the cove. "I think my childhood smelled different from yours," Clara murmured. It wasn't meant to be sad or melodramatic, but that's how it came out.

Amelia stopped and tore her eyes away from the house on the harbor. "Was it lonely?"

Clara frowned. "What? You mean growing up there without you?" She studied their old home, the one Clara had left the day after graduating from high school.

"Yeah. Is that what you mean? Your childhood 'smelled different.'" A wry smile curled across Amelia's lips, and Clara grew aware she was being teased.

She laughed at herself a little. "Well, I don't know if I was *lonely*. But there sure was a lot of cleaning. I felt like that's all we did. All *I* did. Your childhood smelled like summer on the lake. Mine smelled like furniture polish."

Amelia didn't laugh.

Instead, they stood together in silence, admiring the old Hannigan house. The one with a dock that sank like a ramp into the lake. The one obscured by sinewy, gray tree trunks and vibrant green leaves. From where they stood, at the crest of a slight hill from which they could tumble into Birch Harbor Bakehouse, the old Hannigan house looked normal. Beautiful, even.

But Clara knew better.

FOUR

MEGAN

Megan had planned to drive into Birch Harbor early the next morning.

But Megan Stevenson was *not* a morning person.

And, more to the point, Brian had the day off. And he was there, in their house. Still refusing to move out. Still sleeping in the guest room. Still in a stand-off about *who* was getting *what*.

The lawyers—his and hers—how cute—were waiting on him to commit to a settlement. Either he put up alimony and child support or Megan got the house.

It was as fair as the snow was white.

But Megan *knew* Brian. Well. His line of business was volatile. Investing in and mining cryptocurrency carried high highs and low lows. It was in Brian's best interest to have *something* stable. The house would be the stability he'd need.

Yet, Megan had stayed in that house for years in her official capacity as the homemaker. *See?* She literally *made* the home. How could he *not* give it to her?

Besides, Megan had no resume, no college degree, and

no useful way to earn a living. Sure, Megan had *interests*. She secretly loved romance books and tearjerker movies, though less for the romance and more for the high drama.

She couldn't get enough trashy reality television shows, especially the matchmaking-type. Megan had even been known to personally set up other suburban couples. Some had told her she ought to open a matchmaking business. What a pipe dream.

Unfortunately, romance and *casual* matchmaking among her girlfriends didn't bring in cash.

Therefore, with zero career prospects, Megan needed the house *more* than Brian. Or at least, she needed enough of a monthly stipend to cover the mortgage on a *new* house while she chipped away at figuring out what the heck it was she was going to do with her life. Part-time, dead-end jobs were not calling her name.

For now, having to share space with ol' Brian was physically painful for her. So, she figured she would take the opportunity to bunk up with Clara and Amelia.

A little sisterly surprise. They all needed that, really.

With Sarah securely planted at a friend's house for a last minute-sleepover, Megan drove to Birch Harbor one night early, scrolling through radio stations for most of the drive. Finally, twenty minutes out from her destination, she settled on an audio book.

Meditation in the Car.

It kind of worked.

By the time she rolled into the parking lot of The Bungalows, Clara's four-plex, Megan was so annoyed with trying to hold her breath for extended intervals that she'd nearly forgotten about her messy almost-divorce.

She grabbed her overnight bag from her passenger seat

and pushed out of the car and up the cobblestone path toward Unit Two.

Three sets of three sharp raps later, Megan set her bag down and withdrew her phone.

Clara answered on the first ring, predictably. "Megan?" Surprise filled her voice.

"The one-and-only."

Clara let out a sigh. "Is everything okay?"

"Other than the fact that I'm literally living with the person who should, by now, be my EX-husband, everything is perfect. Oh, and... where *are* you?"

Clara answered loudly over a throb of fuzzy background noise. "We're at Fiorillo's in Birch Village. Amelia's here, too."

Megan smiled. Fiorillo's was one of her favorite restaurants in the whole world. It was fate. "Pull up a third chair. I'm less than a mile away."

———

"I SEE you finally took off your ring," Amelia pointed out through a mouthful of buttery garlic bread.

Megan smiled wryly and wiggled her fingers at Amelia and Clara as she took a sip of her Syrah. "I know. Took me long enough."

"Did you get a new phone?" Amelia was staring at Megan's small, white device.

She shook her head. "No. Same old model I've had for, what, five years now? Is that really pathetic?"

"I hope not." Amelia chuckled. "It looks exactly like mine and I just got this thing a month ago." She waved her own sleek-faced iPhone at the girls who oohed and ahhed appropriately. "A present from Jimmy," Amelia declared proudly.

Megan thought she saw Clara make a face. She spoke up. "This Jimmy guy, is he the real deal?"

"More to the point," Clara interrupted. "How did he afford *that* if he doesn't have a job?"

Amelia's face reddened, and Megan frowned.

"Well, he has a little income stream from an uncle or something. I don't really know the details. But he is *trying* to be the real deal."

"Oh?" Megan asked, lifting an eyebrow.

"He's coming to Birch Harbor. Or, actually, he's *here*. At a motel. Waiting for me."

Clara and Amelia exchanged a look, more of a grimace than a grin, Megan thought.

"Why?" Megan asked, her tone sharp.

"I'm sorry." Amelia shifted in her seat and took a sip of wine. "I just texted him and told him to drop Dobi off later tonight. But he's staying at the motel. Don't worry about him barging in on us." She flicked a glance to Clara. "I think he's bored in the city. And, Jimmy really does love me." Again she wagged the phone in her hand.

"Sounds like a dead end to me," Megan murmured over the top of her wine glass.

Amelia opened her mouth to protest, but Clara held up a hand. "Can we... *not*? Can we just... enjoy each other? For one night? I never get quality time with my sisters."

Megan changed the conversation. Who wanted to talk about relationships, anyway? They were together in their hometown for their mother's death. That was rough enough. "So, how's work, you two?" She pasted a smile onto her face and took another swig.

Though she wasn't quite ready to admit it, Megan was champing at the bit for a career. Something to give her purpose now that her marriage was over and her daughter was approaching graduation.

A black-clad waiter arrived with their plates. Shrimp scampi for Amelia. Fettuccine Alfredo for Megan. And a Caesar salad—dry—for Clara.

"Tell me that's a joke," Amelia pointed a dark gray-tipped nail at Clara's dinner.

"I'm trying to lose seven pounds." Clara avoided their gazes and took another sip of iced tea.

Megan shrugged. "Aren't we all?" Then she pinched her fork in one hand, spoon in the other, and commenced with twirling and shoveling creamy knots of pasta into her mouth.

"*So*, about work... since you asked." Amelia dabbed her napkin along her lips. "I'm waiting to hear back on a role." She bit her lip and lowered her fork to eye Megan's reaction.

Megan swallowed. "Oh? Do tell."

"Lady Macbeth in *Macbeth*. I mean, that's my goal. I think the audition went well. It wasn't a *formal* audition, but I got to have dinner with the director. During appetizers, I put on my Scottish accent, and apart from a couple awkward slips, I nailed it, frankly. But if they offer me another 'Lady in Waiting Number Seven' I might have a public meltdown, so... there's that."

Clara giggled. Megan smiled and shook her head. "You're no Lady in Waiting; that's true. I can't believe you did an accent at dinner."

"I can believe it," Clara cut in, laughing. The three giggled together then grew silent as they worked on their meals.

After some moments, Clara cleared her throat and spoke again. "But Amelia, what *will* you do if you don't get something big?" It was a sober question, which was why Clara asked it and not Megan. Clara was a sober type of girl who asked sobering types of questions, made even more sober by the fact that she was drinking iced tea (no sweetener) and eating dressing-free, gluten-free salad while her sisters indulged in high-carb dishes and full-bodied reds.

Megan might wear dark clothes and carry a chip on her shoulder, but she was less of a dream crusher than her bright, bouncy, blonde baby sister.

Amelia, for her part, was ready for the question. "If I don't get Lady Macbeth or, at the *minimum*, one of the witches, well... I *will* do something drastic."

Clara gasped. "Like *what*?"

Megan couldn't help but smile. It was nice to be part of someone else's drama, rather than her own.

"That's a good question," Amelia replied, dabbing her mouth again with her napkin and staring out through the window at the lake. Megan followed her gaze.

The sun was setting and coloring the water a brilliant orange. Homesickness swelled in her stomach, as it sometimes did. She looked back to Amelia, curious. "Would you move back here?"

Clara and Amelia both fell silent, as though the question were too big. Too much. Too soon.

The three sisters looked at each other around the table, alternating eye contact until a smile spread between them. Amelia answered at last. "I might."

———

DINNER HAD FINISHED on a high note, and soon they were giggling back up to Clara's apartment in a line along the sidewalk that ran parallel to Harbor Avenue.

Amelia had walked out of Fiorillo's *with* her wine glass, and it was Clara who caught her, grabbed it, and set it on a low-profile wall just outside the back patio. Clara claimed she'd been humiliated, but she, too, was giggling now.

It occurred to Megan that she hadn't laughed as much in ages. Part of her wanted to blame Brian.

Mostly, though, she blamed herself.

When a person stopped being happy, she ought to do two things: look outside first. Declutter that space. Then, she ought to look inside herself. And clean her own house. And once everything was clean, it would be up to her to choose happiness, rather than blame unhappiness on others.

Megan had often chosen to blame others.

She'd decided not to be happy years earlier, when Brian left software development for the crypto world against her wishes. She decided then that she was not happy, but even worse? She decided to *stay* not happy.

Of course, that unhappiness grew like a fungus in their marriage. Both, in the end, shouldered some of the blame. Brian, for continuing to ignore Megan's desire to *do* something with her life, namely, open a business of some sort. And Megan, for leaving the marriage years earlier— emotionally, at least.

Presently, as her sisters marched ahead of her on the cobblestone steps and into Clara's small apartment, Megan pulled her phone out of her back pocket to check her messages.

Sarah had wished her goodnight.

Brian had replied with a yellow thumbs up emoji (she couldn't shake the habit of telling him she'd made it to town).

And yet, another miniature notification glowed at the

top of the screen. Its little white envelope sitting there like a delicious dessert.

It was one she'd save for later.

"I'm taking a shower. And whoever is sharing my bed is taking a shower, too," Clara announced once they were all inside.

Megan glanced up, her face reddening, and she slid the phone back into her jeans and smiled. "I'll take the sofa. But I'm also showering."

Amelia pouted. "I shower in the morning. Come on, Clara. Why does it matter?"

Clara bristled. "I just cleaned my sheets. I want to savor the fresh smell for as long as possible between washes, and I'm positive that your feet stink. You can go first, Amelia. Go on." Clara shooed her down the short hallway but not before Amelia dropped her purse onto the floor by the breakfast bar. A few items tumbled out, but she didn't notice.

Clara bent down and snatched up the purse, setting Amelia's phone on the counter for her.

Megan felt a wave of exhaustion climb up her neck and take root in the base of her head.

"Maybe I *won't* shower." She yawned and perched unsteadily on the arm of the sofa.

"Suit yourself," Clara answered, sweeping two empty cans of Diet Coke off the counter and into the trash before plugging her phone into its charger. "Let's get your bed ready," she suggested to Megan.

Megan stood and stretched, then helped.

Soon enough, Amelia had returned from the shower and Megan had unpacked her essentials—night cream, phone, phone charger, and Kindle—on the counter and was pouring herself a glass of water from a smart looking water pitcher in the fridge.

Amelia reached for her phone, waved half-heartedly, bid Megan goodnight, and saw herself to bed.

Minutes later, as Megan was climbing beneath the sheets with her precious e-Reader, she heard Amelia and Clara in the back of the apartment, their voices raised excitedly.

She tried to ignore the commotion, since a dull headache was taking shape in the center of her forehead. But it was futile, because Amelia came barging down the hall and into the living room, Clara hot on her heels.

"Oh. My. Goodness," Amelia gushed.

Megan craned her neck up to see a broad smile on her sister's face. Then Clara joined, with the opposite expression.

"Oh my goodness is *right*," Clara added, anger flashing in her eyes.

"What's going *on*," Megan demanded, sitting up and rubbing her neck.

"I accidentally grabbed your phone," Amelia sang back, holding out the white-trimmed cellular right in front of Megan's squinting eyes. Amelia jabbered on, amused as could be, "And I'll be darned if this isn't a *dating app*."

FIVE
KATE

Rain had begun to fall just *after* Kate tucked herself into Michael Matuszewski's office.

Stupidly, she'd left her umbrella in her car, wedged neatly in the space between her seat and the console.

Rain is a good sign, she reminded herself as she forced a smile for the receptionist.

"You must be... Katherine Hannigan?" the woman greeted.

Kate nodded. "Call me Kate, please. And that would make you Sharon?"

The woman rose and stretched out a small hand. Kate offered hers, and instead of a handshake, Sharon gave her a warm squeeze. "It's nice to formally meet you, Kate. I'm terribly sorry about your mom. You were busy, so I didn't want to pester you, but I came to the wake. You know," Sharon went on chattily, "Nora was in here more than once, squirrelling away money for you girls, no doubt—"

Kate cut the woman off with a terse *thank you* and asked if Michael was ready. It's not that she didn't appreciate Sharon's kindness. It was that kindness made Kate want to cry. And, well... she wasn't too certain she could regain her footing if the floodgates were opened.

Regardless, that day was not a crying day. It was a business day.

"Oh, right. Well, you *are* ten minutes early," Sharon chirped, her merry attitude never faltering. "But I'll let him know you've arrived."

Kate settled into a chair and selected a three-year-old copy of *Martha Stewart* to peruse as Sharon bustled around, poking into Michael's office in the back then watering the plants until finally lowering back behind the mahogany reception desk.

Aware of Sharon's boredom and her own looming anxiety at the fact that her sisters had yet to arrive, Kate cleared her throat. "Thank you for coming to the funeral, Sharon," she said quietly.

"Oh, honey. It was the most beautiful wake I've ever attended. And I've been to my share, I'll have you know. Such tasteful music selections. The floral arrangements... *my*," Sharon gasped. Kate smiled at that and built up enough courage to meet her eyes as she went on, describing elements of the event that Kate had put grief-stricken energy into but didn't quite have the luxury to enjoy, since, well...

"Kate." Michael appeared, his trim, tall build a reassuring presence and his good looks a nice distraction. "I have everything ready. Would you like to come back?" He waved a gentlemanly hand down the hall, and Kate rose from her seat, her back straight as an arrow.

"My sisters are on their way, I'm sure. Should we wait?"

"Sharon will show them in. Right, Sharon?" He flashed a broad grin to his receptionist who nearly melted right there on the spot. Instead, though, she nodded meekly. Kate could relate. Michael was perfection. Always had been. Tanned and toned. Focused and smart. And, successful. He'd make a perfect match for Kate, people had always said.

She didn't agree.

Kate never intended to date again. *But*, if she *did*, it wouldn't be someone like Michael Matuszewski.

It would be someone who laughed at the wrong moments and overslept and wore mismatched socks. Someone who would not remind her of Paul. Someone she could snuggle on the sofa with and who would go for a lazy stroll rather than sign her up for marathons.

It would be someone... softer, who could smooth Kate's rough edges instead of sharpening them into blades.

Michael was a sharpener. He belonged with a woman who craved structure. A woman who needed it.

Kate already had that, and in too much supply.

Moments later they were sitting in his office. Wood and leather everywhere, in typical male fashion. When Kate finally moved from Apple Tree Hill, she would limit the dark and dense in favor of white and light. It was a personal vow.

"How've you been?" Michael asked, lacing his fingers on top of his desk.

Several thick binders lined the edge of the wood, and she wondered exactly what the day would bring. What her mom had in store for them.

Surely, no surprises. Surely it was all as Nora had promised her daughters: an even split. Two paid-off houses, one rental property, and a square slab of farmland. Something for each daughter.

"Knock, knock." Amelia's voice echoed at the doorway. Kate whipped her head around to take in the sorry sight of three, sleepy-eyed younger sisters. A flashback hit—high school. The morning after prom. Kate and Amelia trudging down the stairs to join Nora in the kitchen. A fresh pot of coffee percolating rhythmically, as their mother waited as though she knew. Embarrassment had colored Kate's teenage cheeks. Excitement colored Amelia's.

But Amelia hadn't been a tattletale. Not then or ever.

Now, Kate reminded herself that she was *not* her mother. She smiled at her sisters, realizing Megan happened to come to town the night before, after all.

"Michael, you remember Amelia, Megan, and Clara?" Kate asked.

He stood and adjusted his tie along his flat abdomen. Kate glanced away, only to catch Amelia's eyes narrowing.

"Michael," Amelia answered airily. She didn't sound like herself.

Megan and Clara hung by the door as Amelia rolled her shoulders back and took the seat at the other end of the semi-circle, nearest Michael's desk.

Michael, oblivious, gestured to the two empty seats.

Kate pressed a hand to her head and tried to refocus them. "Megan, Clara, come sit." They did as they were told, and Kate waved Michael on, granting him permission to begin.

Before he sat back down, Michael picked up the folders and passed one to each sister.

Kate ran her hand over the leather, her index finger tracing the gold-embossed *MM* in the center.

Inside each binder was a packet of legalese—jargon about probate proceedings and estate affairs and case law *this* and precedent *that*. Nothing personal to Nora's accounts or plans.

Michael rambled on about usual procedure as the

women shuffled through pages that read, to them, like stereo instructions.

Megan interrupted. "Any chance you can cut to the chase, Michael?"

He looked up, no doubt unaware that four lives sat there before him.

A woman whose husband died and who had no more money to cover the mortgage.

A woman with no real job and a vapid life in a city she hardly called home.

A woman in the throes of divorce with a child at home still.

And a young woman whose life had yet to really begin.

Kate glanced at Clara to see how she was doing. She seemed okay, so Kate helped soften Megan's blow by addressing Michael softly. "We're tired and sad. And, maybe anxious." She glanced more pointedly at her sisters.

Megan sighed.

Amelia, too.

Michael cleared his throat. "Of course, of course. Again, I'm so sorry for your loss. I'll get down to it, I suppose."

Kate leaned forward slightly. Clara did the same.

"In your mother's last will and testament, she determined Katherine Acton Hannigan would act as executor. In the event that Katherine, or Kate," he looked up briefly at Kate and smiled, "is unable to fulfill the duties, the role of executor falls to Amelia-Ann Hannigan. And then, to Megan Beth Hannigan." He paused again, and the women nodded.

Clara kept mum.

"Nora Katherine Hannigan signed and sealed her last will and testament recently, I'd like to add."

Amelia lifted an eyebrow. "Had she become a frequent flier in here?"

He shook his head. "She visited from time to time, yes. Chatting with Sharon out there," he paused to nod toward the waiting room warmly before going on, "but in terms of formal changes, she handled the last one with a former associate of mine. Zack Durbin worked here for a short time and handled your mother's estate." He shifted in his seat, and Kate sensed a nervousness, though why she couldn't imagine.

Megan added, "I didn't know she updated it at all. Didn't she settle this back in the nineties after Clara was born?"

Kate shushed everyone. "Michael clearly has this information right in front of him," she said to her sisters.

"I want to caution you all," Michael answered. Kate blinked. Amelia frowned. He went on, "Many families enter these meetings with an idea of how things will go. Sometimes, the decedent has been crystal clear, and there are no hiccups. More often than not, however, the survivors don't always know *everything*." Both his words and tone were ominous, but it didn't quite reach Kate. As though she were stuck in a trance—a belief—that her mother had done precisely what she'd told them she would do, she batted his warning away.

"I'm sure it's fine. Go ahead, Michael. *Please.*"

SIX

CLARA

One Year Earlier.

"She's over seventy now, and, from the sounds of it, her symptoms started years ago. So, no. It's not early onset," the doctor replied. Clara watched Kate nod in response. She watched her keep it together, her eyes dry, her gaze steady.

Then, Clara looked at her mom, whose face was blank.

"So," Clara inserted herself through trembled speech, "what does the prognosis look like?"

The doctor cleared his throat and laced his fingers on his desk. Glimmering windows of other high-rise buildings shone like the broad sides of diamonds behind him.

Clara hated the city. Even more now. Big cities meant bad news.

"It varies," he answered Clara, then turned to speak directly to her mom. "Mrs. Hannigan—"

"It's *Miz*," Nora corrected, her voice a sheet of ice.

He flushed, Clara was certain. She couldn't help but smile. It was the exact sort of thing to level the tension.

Clara glanced at Kate and they shared the sentiment, silently. Some relief.

"Excuse me. *Miz* Hannigan. To answer your question, this disease looks different for different people. For all we know, you could live a normal life for another twenty years."

Clara could have sworn Kate sucked in a sharp breath.

The doctor went on. "Or, it could progress quickly. The best we can do is schedule regular appointments. Keep up with the meds. Eat well. Stay active. The whole bit." He raised his palms and smiled. White teeth glowed back at them. Clara's own smile fell away. Doctors liked to use "we" as though they had any control over the diseases they diagnosed or the patients they treated.

Little did this one know, Nora Hannigan would not be controlled. By his treatment plan, the medications, good nutrition, or anything else.

But, again, their mom didn't seem to react at all. The only moment that perked her up was when the doctor accused her of being married.

"What's next?" Kate asked, poising her pen above a notepad trimmed in a floral pattern.

"Truthfully?" he asked, now frowning and pulling his rimless glasses down his nose and folding them neatly. Kate and Clara nodded together on either side of their mother. He went on. "Make the most of your time together. Keep her healthy," he pointed his forehead toward the older woman, speaking—once again—about her rather than to her. "And," he added, his voice dropping an octave, "start making preparations."

"MOM, you said hardly a word in there," Clara pointed out as they ushered her into Kate's Navigator.

Nora clicked her tongue. "Do you believe even one word that man said?" she hissed, pulling herself into the front seat with Clara's help.

"What's not to believe, Mom?" Kate asked. "And also, are we still going to Fiorillo's for lunch?"

Clara frowned at her older sister. "How can you think about eating right now?"

"I'll tell you how," Kate answered, bristling as she launched into a classic Kate lecture. "Nothing has changed. Absolutely nothing has changed. People go to the doctor and learn something new then let that *news* disrupt their lives. We won't. Right, Mom?"

Nora came to life. She spoke lucidly and with focus. "I agree with Kate. Just because he confirmed what you two suspected doesn't mean I'm going to walk into Lake Huron with rocks in my coat pockets. Fiorillo's is perfect. We need wine. If you want to know my mind, well, I think doctors see people like me and haven't a clue what to think. What they ought to do is put in a prescription for a bottle of wine. The good stuff. It'd save us all money and time and headaches."

Clara smiled in the backseat and shook her head, catching Kate's amused face in the rearview mirror. "Well, *wine* won't save you a headache, but I do see your point."

Their mom twisted to face Clara, her hand gripping the console to keep her body in its awkward position. Clara's eyes hung on the baubles clacking between Nora's knobby knuckles. Glinting silvers and golds that made the woman who she was. A glamour girl. A Titaness.

A small-town queen crashing into her golden years like she was late to her own party.

But beneath the gems lay paper-thin, age-spotted skin. Prematurely bruised. Arthritic. The product of a life built on hard work rather than precious jewels and luxury. The latter two were the result of a cutthroat attitude and decades of ruthless business building. *The spoils of war*, their mom often sang out as she swung a glimmering fist across her chest.

"A wine headache is different than a bad news headache," the woman murmured with a wink before turning back around and directing Kate where to go, unnecessarily.

LUNCH WAS A FAST AFFAIR. Salad all around. Basket of garlic bread untouched.

"Doggy-bag these," Nora directed the waiter.

Clara offered a smile after her mother and thanked him discreetly. "*Mom*," she began, only to think better of reprimanding the poor woman for her typically absent manners. It wouldn't be productive.

"What? Trudy loves scraps."

"You shouldn't feed Trudy people food, Mom. You know that," Kate replied, slipping her card out of the check holder and tucking it back into her leather wallet. "She's already overweight."

Nora ignored Kate and took the box from the waiter, adding a syrupy thank you, after all.

Clara wondered about that. Not the boxed garlic bread destined for a cruel, fat-bellied Chihuahua, but about her mom's insincerity, swinging from overweening demands to gushing supplication in the blink of an eye.

Had the woman *always* been disingenuous? Or was it a

recent development? Clara couldn't tell anymore. It was as if her own memory had turned fuzzy, too.

"Where to next, ladies?" Clara asked with a yawn, checking her wristwatch. She had papers to grade and a kitchen to clean. Both responsibilities she'd no doubt put off when she actually arrived back home.

She'd once read somewhere that true perfectionists were also procrastinators. They hated to tackle a chore for fear of, well, imperfect execution. Maybe Clara ought to lower her personal standards.

It might pay off in more ways than she knew.

"Home. Right, Mom?" Kate asked once they were situated in the SUV.

Nora pointed up the hill toward Main Street. "No, take me to see Michael."

Clara flashed a glance to the rearview, locking eyes with Kate. They frowned at each other. "Michael? As in, Michael Matuszewski?" Kate replied.

Their mom nodded. "Yes. He's my lawyer."

"I know that, Mom. Why do you want to see him?"

"I have to fix something. Sign something. He called the other day and wanted to go over a document. Just stop complaining and take me there, goldarn it, Kate."

Kate's eyes grew wide in the mirror and Clara let out a sigh.

They arrived at the attorney's office, and Nora let herself out of the SUV. Kate and Clara opened their doors too, but the old woman held up a hand and stopped them. "I'll be five minutes. Just stay there," she commanded.

Again, the sisters exchanged a look. Clara shook her head. "We have to go with her, right?"

Kate nodded. "Mom, we're coming with you."

"Five minutes!" Nora screeched as she tugged the door open and waddled inside before they could stop her.

True to her word, Nora emerged at the door again in just five minutes. This time, with a plump, cheery-looking woman gabbing away at her side who waved boisterously at Kate and Clara.

She walked Nora to the Navigator and said *hello* and *nice day out* and all the things chatty types couldn't help but eject despite the circumstances.

"Everything go okay in there, Mom?" Kate helped Nora buckle her seatbelt then waited for an answer. The air conditioning hummed softly around them.

"It went well." Nora stared straight ahead. Her jaw slack, her breathing heavy for such a short excursion. "I just had to drop something off."

Clara's skin prickled. "You said you were signing a document."

"Did I?"

"Yes, Mom," Kate answered.

"Well, no. I had to drop something off. I don't want to talk about it. I need to rest now." Nora's flame had started to flicker. It was the emerging normal. A full day of high energy and feisty bossiness that eventually, come early afternoon, waned into a sludge.

As they crested the hill back down Harbor Avenue, Nora lifted a wobbly finger out toward Heirloom Cove. "Have you watered the flowers lately, Kate?" she asked quietly.

Kate glanced at Clara before replying. "Clara does that now, Mom. Remember? She's the one who takes care of the old house."

Nora lifted a painted eyebrow then lowered it. "Oh,

right. Well, Clara?" she twisted in her seat part of the way and dropped her chin. "Have you?"

"Yep. I was there Tuesday. Speaking of which," Clara took a risk. It was something she and Kate and even Amelia and Megan had been arguing about for ages. It was something they'd better settle sooner rather than later. "What are we doing with the house, Mom?"

"What do you mean?"

Kate looked over at Nora.

Clara forged ahead. "I mean, when are we going to start clearing it out?"

The old house on the harbor had all but turned into a museum by that point.

"You can handle it after I'm dead," their mom replied, flatly.

Clara's pulse quickened and she unbuckled from the middle seat in the back, feeling suddenly like a little girl all over again. An eavesdropper on a conversation that didn't belong to her.

But it did.

"Mom. *Not* okay," Clara reprimanded.

The woman batted her hand weakly. "You can sort through everything then. Right, Kate?"

Both Kate and Clara drew back at the question. Clara waited for Kate to say something—anything—to diminish the morbid thought and also take back the reins.

Kate blew out a sigh. "Oh, Mom. Do you have any idea how much work that will be? And how difficult? We will already be sad, then we have to face all of your *things*? Your belongings? We really should start *now* while—"

"While I'm alive and you're still irritated with me instead of when I'm dead and you feel guilty about pestering me." Nora coughed into her fist, a dry, phony cough.

Clara rolled her eyes. "Whatever."

Kate let out a short laugh. "Something like that," she answered, laying her hand over their mother's on the console.

They rolled past the old place, and Nora leaned forward in her seat, craning her neck around Kate to get a better view.

"Do you want to go there now, Mom?" Clara asked from between the two front seats, her voice soft.

The SUV heaved forward as Kate took her foot off the brake and checked her rearview mirror, this time looking beyond Clara.

Nora fell back into her seat and crossed her arms like a petulant child. "No. Keep driving, Katherine. I will never step a foot in that haunted place again."

"Mom, whoa. *Haunted?*" Clara asked, confused by the woman's sudden shift.

"I don't want to talk about it. With either one of you. Don't take me there. Don't bury me there. Don't even drag my casket into the front parlor there."

Clara and Kate fell quiet. All of their lives, Nora loved the old house on Heirloom Cove. As far as they knew, that's why Nora kept it instead of selling or renting.

But, her words stuck. As addled as Nora's mind may have been, Clara and Kate solemnly and silently vowed to fulfill her wish.

Nora Hannigan would never go back to the house on the harbor.

And Clara began to wonder why.

SEVEN

AMELIA

Tucking a strand of her dark hair behind her ear, Amelia leaned in toward Michael, ready to devour every word.

Though there was nothing specific Amelia hoped to have *earned* from her mother's estate, she was very interested in how things worked out. Who got what. As a middle child, she had always been acutely aware of discrepancies.

Inequities.

Imbalances.

Now, Amelia knew, those things would be revealed in full.

Her phone buzzed in her purse on the floor. Jimmy, no doubt. She'd told him they could meet for lunch in the Village, and it was his own fault if he couldn't entertain himself in the meantime.

Although, Amelia figured he'd find *something* to do. Jimmy was that type. He made friends easily. Didn't mind putting himself out there. He should have been a car salesman, probably, rather than a construction worker. He loved meeting new people and getting into trouble. Two things that had drawn Amelia to him to begin with.

The friendly bad boy, Megan had once dubbed Amelia's "type."

She pushed her bag with her toe to muffle the buzzing and returned her attention to the lawyer.

Michael cleared his throat. "We'll begin with your mother's personal effects. Then, I'll share her wishes regarding real estate." When no one reacted, he read on, quoting their mom. "'To Katherine, I leave twenty-three flowerpots, my dining room table, the front hall runner, my wedding china, Wendell Acton's wristwatch, and my Sunday wardrobe.'"

Amelia leaned back, studying her older sister's face and then glancing to catch Megan and Clara's reactions.

Kate's throat bobbed in a swallow and her chest rose and fell.

Clara blinked and tucked her lips inside her teeth.

Megan shrugged.

Pausing, Michael lowered the page from which he read, perhaps waiting for the inevitable. An argument. A passive aggressive sigh. Anything.

"I didn't know she named her clothes by the day of the week," Kate answered softly.

A small giggle erupted among the girls. Amelia knew if their mom was there, she'd snap at them for making fun. But a little laughter was just what the doctor ordered. The whole affair had become too tense. Too awkward.

Amelia added, "I hope I get Saturday."

Again, they laughed together in front of poor Michael, who appeared unsure how to react.

"Go ahead, keep reading," Kate said at last, wiping away happy tears. Or maybe sad. Amelia couldn't tell which anymore.

He held the paper back up to his face and answered,

"That concludes Kate's inheritance of Nora's personal effects."

Amelia blinked and raised her eyebrows at her older sister. But Kate simply smiled. "Right. I expected as much."

Michael continued. "Shall I go on?"

All four sisters nodded urgently, and so he did.

"'To Amelia,'" he began. Amelia leaned forward again and narrowed her eyes on Michael's full lips behind the thick, white page. "'I leave the upstairs chaise, my patio furniture, Wendell Acton's Smith and Wesson snub nose, Aunt Ida's tiger's eye necklace, and... '" Amelia sucked in a breath. "'My furs.'"

"*Furs?*" Clara cried out.

Amelia sank back, oddly disappointed, though not necessarily in her mother's fashion choices.

Michael stopped reading and set the page down.

Kate murmured that she didn't know Nora *had* any furs and that she figured any guns were long gone.

Clara carried on about how they ought to donate any fur—if, in fact, Nora owned any *real* fur— to animal shelters to be used as beds. "Fur is beyond passé. It's unethical," she added, clicking her tongue in disgust.

Megan yawned.

"Donate them," Amelia spat. "I don't want fur coats. And why does she refer to Dad by his full name?" She crossed her arms and shook her head before adding, "I'm sorry, Michael. Go ahead with the will. I just—"

"You had different expectations," he answered patiently. It's understandable. Amelia bit her lower lip and glanced up at him to catch a look. An unreadable, un-lawyerly *look*.

"Yes. Silly, really. Just go ahead."

The women sighed collectively, and he did as he was told.

"'To Megan, I leave my silver Tiffany's collection, my wedding band, Wendell Acton's wedding band, the desktop computer, and our marital bed.'"

"I guess we know who the favorite is," Amelia muttered, lifting a conspiratorial eyebrow to Clara, who ignored her.

"Her 'desktop computer'?" Megan turned her head sharply to Amelia. "As in the 'new' one she got in 2000 once she was convinced Y2K 'killed' her old one?" Megan rolled her eyes.

Clara made a face. "What does she mean by *marital* bed?"

Michael offered a sympathetic smile, but it was Kate who answered. "Obviously the king bed that was in her bedroom."

"Why did she have to use the word *marital*?" Clara asked again, but it was Amelia this time who added a dose of maturity.

"Mom was trying to be specific, no doubt. Go ahead, Michael." Amelia bit down on her thumbnail, anxiety creeping in.

Michael lifted his eyebrows, waiting for permission to read. Amelia rolled her hand in a wide circle to get him going again.

"'The balance of my personal possessions is to be divided evenly under the supervision of my eldest daughter, Katherine.'"

Four jaws dropped.

It was a bombshell.

An error.

An oversight.

Kate spoke immediately. "What about Clara?" she asked, glancing wildly from her sisters to Michael.

He shook his head. "No personal items were specifically designated to Clara Hannigan."

"Is there more?" Amelia asked, trying to be helpful.

"Yes, her properties and a personal letter."

"Okay, then go ahead," Amelia prompted. Kate nodded her head, and Megan and Clara did the same, all four of them frowning deeply.

"All right," he answered. "'Real estate and land, including owned and leased properties, businesses, and accounts related thereto,'" Michael continued, holding a new page crisply between himself and the women. His eyes danced down to Nora's own words, and he read, "'As for my rental properties, including the Birch Creek Cottage, The Bungalows, and the undeveloped parcel inland, I would ask they be evenly divided between Katherine, Amelia, and Megan.'"

Amelia felt her stomach twist with stress.

She glanced over at Clara, expecting a fresh round of tears. Anger. The exact feelings that Amelia had felt many times over during the course of her own upbringing.

But Clara's face was expressionless. Calm.

Clara and Kate exchanged their own glance, and that's when Amelia realized why Clara wasn't having a tantrum right then and there.

The house.

The house on the harbor.

EIGHT

MEGAN

Megan wasn't easily rattled.

But something didn't sit right.

Nora had updated her will recently. So why wasn't Clara named? And why wasn't the house included?

The scowl on Amelia's face suggested exactly what Megan was thinking, but there wasn't a chance. It was their family home. The place they'd grown up in. No way would their own mother leave the whole thing to Clara.

Then again, knowing Nora, perhaps it *did* make sense.

"Is she getting the house?" Megan asked point blank, her finger aimed directly at the youngest of the group, Megan's black nail polish providing a sort of morbid costume effect in the context of the probate meeting.

Michael opened his mouth to answer but Clara beat him to the punch. "I certainly hope so. Don't you think it would be nice if she thought I was worth *something*?" She brushed her blonde hair back over her shoulder, and Megan saw a flush creeping up her youngest sister's neck, blossoming into her cheeks.

Clara was such a child. Still.

"It wouldn't be fair for you to get the Heirloom house, Clara. Surely you can see that," Megan hissed, feeling herself lose control.

The whole meeting had been a disappointment. An uncomfortable, awkward disappointment, peppered only by brief moments of humor that were quickly washed away by the revelation that Nora Hannigan hand-selected her oldest daughter to play Mom and divvy out scraps to the others. And for *Clara* to get the *house?* Unconscionable.

Kate raised a flat palm. "Enough. We have no idea what becomes of the Heirloom house, because Michael hasn't gotten that far. And if Clara *doesn't* get it, then we still have an issue."

"What issue?" Amelia piped up. Megan nodded sagely in agreement over the question.

"What *issue?* The issue of one of us being left out of the will, obviously," Kate answered. "Especially the one who has been caretaker to both Mom and the house, itself, for years now. *Years,*" she emphasized, "while you, you, and even *I* have been out living our lives beyond the borders of Birch Harbor, I might remind you." Kate thrust a bare index finger first at Megan then at Amelia and finally at herself as she rounded out her argument.

Megan dropped her gaze. Amelia kept mum. Michael cleared his throat for what felt like the millionth time. If Megan had to hear him do it again then she was leaving. Her mother and father's marital bed was not worth all this. Especially considering their father had *left* them.

"Nora included a separate declaration for the Heirloom Cove property," Michael said at last, his voice as even and earnest as could be. "Her final wish."

The women looked with interest at him, each sitting tightly on the edge of her seat.

"Is this the part she updated recently?"

"Yes and no," Michael admitted at last, pressing his lips into a line before adding, "The last time Nora was here was for a separate matter. A... *private* matter." His eyes darted up to Kate, who seemed confused. "But she did have the opportunity to confirm the plans for her personal effects and various properties."

Amelia pushed air through her lips, and Megan clapped her hands on her thighs. "Classic Nora," she snorted, rising and tugging her handbag onto her shoulder.

"Megan, *please*," Kate whispered.

But Megan couldn't take it. Not after all they'd been through. Not after the reading of the will and the notable favoritism apparent between Nora and Kate, and now probably Clara, too.

Amelia reached for Megan and rested her hand on her arm, pulling her gently back to her seat. "Megan, it's fine. We have no idea what's in there. We're in this together, remember?" The two locked eyes and Megan felt a sob crawl up her throat.

Her own divorce. Nora's death. It was all too much.

But Amelia was right.

They were sisters.

Kate, Amelia, Megan, and Clara.

They were sisters.

No matter what happened, they'd make things right.

Even if eccentric, bitter, game-playing Nora Hannigan had set things wrong.

NINE
KATE

"'Regarding 131 Harbor Avenue, the property and land situated on Heirloom Cove and the private beach included in said parcel,'" Michael read, his voice clear and even, as though whatever might be wrapped up in their mother's written words needed a stable platform, a firm channel. Kate felt her breaths grow quick and shallow. She glanced at her sisters, each on the edge of her seat. "'Upon my death, I leave the deed to be transferred to Katherine Nora Hannigan, Amelia Ann Hannigan, and Megan Beth Stevenson.'"

Kate gasped.

Their mother's language was crisp and precise. The content of her final wish relevant and painfully recent. As recent as Megan's wedding, at the very least. As recent as Nora's eventual acceptance that Megan chose to take Brian's last name, in an inflammatory act of daughterly defiance.

Michael set the page down.

No one said a word.

The silence continued on for some moments. Uncomfortable and suffocating.

Clara was the next to emit a stifled sound. A soft sob.

Kate glanced at Amelia and Megan, who were dutifully confused. Respectfully quiet.

"Are you serious?" Amelia whispered to Michael.

He nodded.

Kate stood. "Let me see, please." She stretched a hand out as Amelia and Megan reached over to their littlest sister.

Michael lowered his voice. "Kate," he said, "it would be best if you and I meet privately. I have one more item for you to go over as the executor. But we need to look at it alone." He glanced beyond her to the others.

Kate nodded and turned.

"Let's take a break first," she suggested, exhaustion pooling at the base of her neck. She pushed a finger to each temple.

The others rose and paused as if to thank Michael. But it was hard to show gratitude on the heels of bad news.

Michael stood to walk the ladies out of the office. He stopped in the hall when Kate turned to address him one last time for that morning.

"When should I come back?" she asked plainly.

"I have no obligations for the rest of the day. I knew the Hannigan Estate—your mother's estate—would be... "

"A challenge?" she finished his sentence.

Nodding gravely, he added, "All estates present obstacles. Death is hard. And handling the affairs of the deceased amplifies that. Nora, of course, had a lot to decide. That's never easy. Not even for a sharp-witted, good woman like your mom."

His words should have hit the right notes. They should have reassured her.

But Kate knew her own mother too well. She thanked

Michael and followed her sisters outside into the warmth of the early summer sun.

Humidity hadn't yet set in, or perhaps, hadn't yet made its way to their position inland.

"What are we going to do?" Amelia asked, her face scrunched in fret.

Megan replied, "Do you mean about the will or—?"

"Of course I mean the will. What else?" the former snapped.

Clara shook her head sadly, blinking against the rays of late morning light that cut across the parking lot. Kate pulled her sunglasses from her handbag and took over. "Lunch. The Harbor Deli. We'll talk there. In the meantime, just let it settle. Clara, why don't you ride with me?"

"I drove them here," Clara whined, hooking a thumb at Amelia and Megan as though they were aggravating teenagers to be trucked from activity to activity.

Kate considered the next best route. She'd have to return to Michael's office and intended to do so sooner rather than later. But she didn't want Amelia or Megan to get into Clara's head.

Or, worse, spill any beans.

Lord knew there were plenty to spill.

Kate assumed that Nora had spent extra time at Michael's because she was taking care to arrange her affairs tightly and without issue. The woman never once asked for help. She never once suggested anything would be... unexpected.

Yet there they were, four sisters. Four properties. But only three claims.

It was like a sick and twisted nursery rhyme. A riddle. One Kate couldn't solve.

Or, more likely, *refused* to solve.

Because the only explanation was the truth.

And the truth, the Hannigan truth, would change everything.

AMELIA AND MEGAN ended up riding with Kate. Clara drove alone. They met at the deli and each ordered some version of a turkey sandwich. Iced teas all around.

The lake lapped up against the boats in the marina, just yards away from their bistro table on the patio. Kate wanted nothing more than to sit there and enjoy the view she'd given up years back, when she decided to become a suburban housewife. A mom with a backyard that was many miles away from the threat of an open body of water.

"What's the deal?" Amelia asked, once they had all settled in with their sandwiches and clinking glasses of amber beverage.

Kate let out a deep sigh and leaned forward on her elbows. "The deal is that Mom obviously went senile earlier than we realized."

Megan lifted a dark eyebrow and took a small bite of her lunch, covering her mouth with a napkin as she held Kate's gaze.

"Right?" Kate asked. A heavy frown set on her mouth, pulling the skin of her cheeks with it. She propped her face in her hands and could feel her age, pooling there, where her jawline was starting to become jowls. She felt old. Old and stupid. And, alone. Even among her sisters.

Perhaps, especially among her sisters.

Megan looked away. Amelia kept quiet.

Kate felt her stomach clench, and she set her sandwich down. "Clara, what time do you have to get back to work?"

"I have a substitute until lunch. So, soon. Half an hour. Tops," she replied, studying her wristwatch for an extra beat.

"Right, well. Here's the plan." Kate rubbed her fingertips into a clean paper napkin and took a sip of tea for courage. "I'll go back to the office—Michael's office—and see about filing an appeal, or whatever it is you do.

"To contest the will?" Megan chimed in.

"Yes, to contest the will. Do you all agree?"

Clara buried her face in her hands and nodded her head.

Amelia and Megan murmured their agreement.

"Good. It's settled. This is clearly a case of a woman gone mad. I'm sure our biggest obstacle will be Michael, himself. Clearly he didn't put two-and-two together sooner and *guide* Mom."

"Woman gone mad," Amelia muttered into the wind as she stared out across the water below them.

Just on the other side of the marina sat the house. Heirloom Cove, with its rocky shoreline and long shadows, stood darkly against the glimmering water. The small figure of the old house, its red paint glowing from between white birch trees, taunted them.

Kate looked at Clara, who was also staring at the house.

She spoke, at last. "I don't know how I'll ever go back there," Clara whispered.

Megan snorted. "I don't blame you."

"Let's just leave it be. Mom made a mistake. That much is clear."

"No," Clara replied. "I have a feeling she didn't make a mistake. I think she made a point."

TEN

AMELIA

Like the leftovers of a strong perfume, Clara's fear hung in the air long after she had excused herself to return to work.

The others remained on the patio as the sun drifted up as high in the sky as it would go.

Amelia traced doodles into the condensation on her iced tea. Megan scrolled through her phone. Kate stared off —at the lake or the house, Amelia wasn't sure.

"It was a mistake," the oldest one said at last.

Amelia and Megan looked at each other, and Amelia saw something flicker behind Megan's eyes. Sympathy? Or, the opposite?

As Amelia opened her mouth to reply that, no, it clearly was *not* a mistake, something else caught her attention. A figure, tall and lean, striding comfortably beneath the easy layer of a graphic tee-shirt and khaki shorts—the exact opposite of what one would expect a construction worker to wear —toward the patio. His thick blonde hair bounced with style on his head.

Jimmy.

Amelia closed her eyes and pressed her hand into her forehead, but it was too late.

"Amelia!" he called loudly and waved.

Megan pulled her sunglasses down her nose and narrowed her gaze on him. Kate turned and covered her eyes with her hand, squinting into the wash of sunlight that spread beyond their bistro umbrella. "Who's that?" she asked.

Amelia plastered a fake smile on her face, stood, smoothed her shirt, and opened her hands. "Jimmy?" she feigned pleasant surprise. "What are you *doing* here?"

"Babe," he cooed, smiling at the other deli patrons as he strolled past slowly. When he arrived at their table, Amelia felt herself sway back slightly. But he slipped his hands around her waist and pulled her to him in a deep hug. The type of hug that had, months earlier, persuaded her to start seeing him.

The type that got her into trouble.

He pressed a wet kiss on her cheek and spun her around to face her sisters. "Lunch, right?" Jimmy said, dipping his chin in a pout. "But I see you started without me."

"Is this the construction boyfriend?" Megan asked.

Amelia flushed and her eyes grew wide. "Megan," she hissed. "Do you have an ounce of tact?"

But Jimmy didn't care. He loved it. "I *am* the construction boyfriend," he answered with a broad smile. "Jimmy Baker, at your service. I dabble in a little bit of everything. Framing, electric, plumbing. If I had a card, I'd give you one." He stuck out a strong, smooth hand—the sort of hand that did not belong to a *successful* laborer. Amelia knew this deep inside, and she winced.

Kate hesitated a second too long before offering her

hand to Jimmy in return. But, still, she offered it, and he ignored the delay. "Kate?" he asked.

"That's right," she answered.

It occurred to Amelia just then that Jimmy thought of himself as a charmer, a suave playboy type able to win over any woman, anywhere. It had worked on her, after all.

But he hadn't met Amelia's sisters.

"And that's Megan," Amelia pointed across the table, willing him to disappear inside, where he could order a decaf coffee and chat up the sandwich maker for half an hour.

After nodding and even bowing slightly toward the farthest seated sister, he lingered. "Am I interrupting anything?"

Amelia felt her heart tug a little, and she smiled. "Well," she began, looking at Kate for guidance.

"No," Kate answered, surprising them all. "No, Jimmy. Please, sit. You'll be a good distraction, actually." She offered a warm, motherly smile, and Amelia wondered if she was wrong about Jimmy. He meant well, after all.

And he was fun.

And sweet.

And hot.

Too hot, probably.

Jimmy pulled Amelia's chair out and gestured for her to take a seat before easing himself into Clara's empty spot.

"This town is great," he began, before launching into a full-blown review of all he'd seen. "It doesn't smell like fish guts or bird poop, unlike the lake in the town where I grew up."

The women relaxed, Kate even letting a short laugh escape her mouth. "Oh yeah?"

"Oh yeah," he replied. "And here," he waved a hand

around Birch Village, "not too many people but enough to make it interesting. And there's a beach. Who knew you could find ocean-front property in Michigan?"

He went on and on, complimenting the variety of eateries and shops for their quaint effect, the motel for how clean the bathroom was, and asking, at last, what the plan was for the day.

"Well," Amelia started, genuinely sorry to break the bad news to him. "We aren't sure yet. There's been a hang-up."

"With the will?" Jimmy asked, his tone thickening.

Kate straightened her back and took a long sip of tea. Megan set her phone down for the first time in ten minutes.

"Yeah," Amelia replied, unsure how much to reveal or what information to protect. "It's regarding the house."

"What house?" Jimmy asked.

Kate gave Amelia a sharp look, but it was too late. Megan had thrown her finger across the marina toward the cove. "*Our* house," she answered. "The one on the harbor."

LUNCH WAS LONG OVER. Kate had excused herself to return to Michael, leaving Amelia and Megan to flounder about. Clara had given Amelia her house key so they could go back to her place—which they would do, at least for a while to let Dobi out and freshen up—but after that?

Wait for Kate to finish her super-secret-exclusive-executor-attorney meeting?

Apparently.

Jimmy trailed behind the two remaining women as they strolled slowly around the village, playing tourist and gossiping, a ritual of any tightly bonded sisters. Or even loosely bonded sisters.

Megan didn't bother to lower her voice when she began to ask about Amelia's relationship. "Construction worker? He looks more like a model. Acts like one, too," she remarked when they emerged from White Birch Soaps and Sundries.

Jimmy stepped out just after, and, having missed Megan's question, swooped in beside Amelia and slid an arm around her waist. "Ice cream anyone? I saw a place between the clothing boutique and the hair salon."

Megan twisted her lips into a knowing smirk, but Amelia wasn't sure if her judgment was for his use of the word "boutique" or his utter inability to read a situation.

Or, his ability to read a situation perfectly well and play it off like he was a dopey interloper.

"Sure, yeah," Amelia answered brightly. "Ice cream. Then we need to check on Dobi."

Jimmy flashed a grin. "You two go grab a couple of seats. I'll get us the good stuff. What's your poison, Megs?" he asked, shooting a finger gun at her.

To Amelia's surprise, her younger, ruthless sister recovered quickly from the unwelcome nickname, shaking her head and finally replying, "Vanilla bean on a waffle cone."

He nodded then aimed his finger to Amelia. "Babe?"

Amelia gave him a look. "You know my favorite."

He drew his hand to his mouth in a philosophical pose. "For my beautiful actress? Has to be... mint chocolate chip, which is also my favorite. Great minds think alike, right?"

"Oh my Lord," Megan murmured beside Amelia, and the latter swatted her sister's shoulder.

"Rocky road, please," Amelia said at last, tugging Megan in the opposite direction, toward a common area deck. Jimmy danced away with another goofy smile.

"You just can't help yourself but to be rude?" she

snarled to Megan as they found a set of Adirondack chairs on the wooden platform that stretched out from the village.

"Amelia, be real. You two don't go together. What do you see in him?"

A long pause gave it away. "I think Kate likes him?" was all Amelia could respond with, at first. But she quickly added, "Clara says he's nice."

"They haven't had the chance to knock you upside the head, yet. I do. Dump that guy. Sooner rather than later. What is he even doing here, Amelia?"

She shrugged. "He's like a puppy dog. He's out of work but he's trying really hard to find something."

"None of that makes sense. He looks like he'd grab a screwdriver if you asked for a hammer. Don't you see any of this?"

Amelia nodded sadly. "Yes, I totally do. But, he's good to me. And he's so... *sexy*."

Megan recoiled. "Please never use that word again, first of all. Second of all, your standards are too low. I need to set you up with a quality person. That's your problem, Amelia. You don't know how to pick."

"I pick just fine, thank you."

"No. If you were a good picker, you'd be married with five kids, happily holed up in a three-bedroom in the suburbs of Detroit with someone like... like... I don't know. Like Michael Matuszewski. Instead, you have a chubby Weiner dog in a studio warehouse of an apartment in New York, where you wait tables and line up for auditions, accepting crappy roles when you could be making it big somewhere else. With *someone* else."

Amelia swallowed and turned her head to her sister. Tears welled in her eyes. "Are you seriously doing this right now?"

"Seriously doing what? Telling you what you need to hear? Yeah, I am."

Closing her eyes tightly, Amelia willed away the urge to cry before finding a smooth, calm answer. "You just told me to raise my standards. Now, you're saying I should drop everything and leave New York and take up a post as an unhappy housewife who's next in line for a divorce?" She had no idea where it came from. Amelia had never been good at snappy retorts. She'd make a terrible lawyer or sketch comedienne. Improv was not her area of expertise.

But there she was, shooting Megan's own admonitions right back at her.

Megan shifted in her chair, her voice softening. She didn't quite react to the brutal comeback, but there was a change in her tone. "Amelia, listen. Jimmy seems fun. And, he is handsome. Really handsome. Maybe he's good with his hands, too," she paused and lowered her chin, and Amelia couldn't suppress the childish grin that formed across her mouth. Megan went on, "Who knows? If the house needs a few repairs, he might just be our guy."

Amelia raised her eyes to Megan, listening carefully.

"I know you see my life and think that what I have is misery. Sometimes it is. I want a job. A passion. I want to lose Brian and get out from a boring marriage, sure. But," Megan blinked, and Amelia could have sworn she saw the reflection of a tear along her sister's lash line. "Just trust me on this, Amelia. I think you could do better."

"What about you?" Amelia replied. "Is that why you're divorcing Brian? Because you could do better? Because you could find some guy on your little dating app who ticks off one of the boxes that Brian doesn't?"

The tear found its way over the edge of Megan's kohl-lined lower eyelid and trailed down her cheek until she raised her hand and wiped it away. "I'm not looking for anyone," Megan spat back. Glancing over her shoulder. "I'm—"

"I think you need to reconsider the divorce."

There. Amelia had said it. The thing that had been on her mind since Megan revealed she was filing. The thing that had been on all their minds. It was a fool's move. Brian wasn't perfect, and neither was their marriage, no doubt.

But Megan seemed to be... searching. However, Amelia didn't entirely believe her younger sister was searching for a *new man*. Just a new chapter, maybe.

Megan frowned deeper and shook her head, anger pooling in her eyes.

But Amelia was on a roll. "You don't need a divorce, *Megs*," she said, her lips curling into a smile as she looked out over the marina at the house. *Their* house. "You need a *project*."

ELEVEN

MEGAN

Amelia didn't know squat about love or life. That much was clear.

But, Megan did like the idea of a project. A distraction. Something to pull her out of the rut she'd fallen into.

The house on the harbor *could* be that project. But it *wouldn't*. They were selling. Splitting it three ways (four if they contested effectively) and selling.

If she was honest with herself, Megan knew Nora's final wish was unfair. Clara deserved as much or more than the rest of them.

So then why was the poor thing excluded with such finality?

Megan knew the truth. They all knew the truth—except for Clara.

Maybe they could simply agree to give Clara The Bungalows? Maybe there was a better way to find a fair solution than rewriting Nora's last will and testament?

If the sisters had the chance to split the house three ways and keep even just two of the properties functioning as income, that'd leave enough money for Megan to move out on Brian, buy a whole *new* house, pay for Sarah's college tuition, *and* follow the secret dream she had. Opening her business. A small-town matchmaking enterprise. Maybe, she'd even do it in Birch Harbor.

But probably not.

Too close to her sisters.

Too close to their drama.

Jimmy returned with the ice cream, and Megan took her time working away at the chunky sweet edges while Amelia bit down through the top, her lips smacking around the cream loudly.

Megan laughed at the sight and sound.

"Sorry," Amelia said as she swallowed the massive bite. She held a hand over her lips to cover the mess. "Like Clara, I've been dieting off and on. I'm starving. Didn't you see? I had a spinach wrap. For God's sake, who substitutes spinach for bread? Me, I guess. I'm trying to lose ten for Lady Macbeth. But I can't resist sweets."

"Ten pounds in a week?"

Jimmy guffawed. "I know, right? She's perfect just the way she is."

As he said it, a group of college-aged girls in string bikinis trickled past toward the dock.

Megan watched in morbid fascination as Jimmy nearly dropped his cone onto the grass. He legitimately could not tear his eyes away from the grotesque scene of tanned butt cheeks peeking beneath bright bottoms and pointy shoulder blades wedged high and tight along slender backs.

She couldn't help it. Megan raised her hand and snapped her fingers in front of his face, more for her own benefit than Amelia's.

Jimmy raised his eyebrows and fumbled his hands,

catching his ice cream cone flat on one palm, green sludge dripping faster than he could lick it away.

Megan shook her head, pointed her finger sternly at Amelia, and said, "I guess *you* already *have* a project."

Together, they burst out giggling as Jimmy apologized awkwardly and left, muttering some lame excuse about finding napkins.

AFTER ICE CREAM, Amelia had suggested that Jimmy head back to New York. Instead, he doubled down on his dumbery and said he'd wait it out at the motel.

"You might need my help this week," he offered weakly, his tail halfway between his legs by then.

"Even if we need you, we won't *want* you," Megan answered. Amelia stared daggers at her, but she didn't care. It had to be said. Jimmy, in all his sweet-talking, hot-stuff-walking glory, was a sleaze. And Megan would take a computer nerd over a sleaze any day of the week.

The whole scene had made her seriously, and painfully, reconsider everything she had ever known about her marriage. Especially about Brian's role in it. She began to question if Sarah was an ally or a victim, after all. If, maybe, awfully, Megan had poisoned her teenage daughter's brain, setting the stage for the girl to consider her own father a dope.

Megan's stomach started cramping as she reflected on it all.

Brian wasn't a dope. In fact, in his younger years, he'd rivaled Jimmy for good looks and toned abs. Sure, he'd hit middle age. But hadn't Megan, for that matter? Hadn't everyone?

But no matter that, she reminded herself, she hadn't entered into filing for a divorce lightly. It had come after years of neglect. Between them both. They were *both* to blame for a failed marriage. And who could fix a failed marriage?

SOON ENOUGH, the two sisters found themselves trudging back along Harbor Avenue toward The Bungalows. Jimmy had convinced Amelia to let him stay in town. They even had dinner plans. It was nauseating, but Megan had more important things to worry about.

The conversation about Clara and the house was on the tip of her tongue, but Amelia seemed distracted by her own problems.

Still, they were in Birch Harbor to handle Nora's aftermath. Or, rather, the aftermath of Nora.

"What do you think about the house?" Megan asked Amelia at last.

The older one turned to her just as they walked through the waist-high picket fence that ran along the front of the little complex.

"Do you mean the harbor one? Or the cottage, because I've been thinking about the cottage, too. I mean, is that where everything *is*? Or did Mom leave a lot at the house on the harbor?"

Megan shrugged. "I'm not sure. When we went to the cottage before the funeral, it seemed like everything was sort of... I don't know *in order*. Like she had made plans for an easy turn-over. Like she was checking out of a hotel rather than dying."

Amelia paused when they reached Clara's unit. "I

haven't been back to the harbor house in months. Clara's been the one keeping it up. She'd know better."

"Speaking of which," Megan answered, capitalizing. "Are we really going to split that place three ways? What about Clara? What do *you* think about the will?"

"I think it's awful, sure. But Kate is there now, reading some private paperwork. So maybe there's another heirloom for Clara, you know? Maybe Mom put together the will, then later added a letter that indicated Clara should actually keep The Bungalows or the cottage or the land. Or maybe there was cash left. Michael didn't tell us about her liquid assets, right?"

All good points, and all reasonable assumptions.

"If Mom left Clara out of the will, Amelia—" Megan went on, as Amelia thrust the brass key into the lock and turned it, spurring Dobi into a feverish barking barrage.

Amelia answered before Megan could finish. "We don't know what the letter says, Megan. Mom was kooky, but she wasn't evil. I'm positive she left *something* substantial for Clara, too."

"But what if she didn't?" Megan pressed.

Amelia scooped Dobi into her arms and attached a thin leash to the dog's collar before frowning at her younger sister. "Why *wouldn't* she?"

Megan crossed her arms. "You know *exactly* why."

TWELVE

CLARA

Clara unlocked the door at the end of her hallway, effectively sneaking in during the tail end of the lunch period.

Any moment now, stinky pubescent pre-teens and teenagers would be tumbling into the hall, lining up outside one of the four classrooms, anxious to collapse into a plastic desk chair where they would spend the next fifty-five minutes complaining, peeking at their phones, and generally doing anything other than learning.

It was Clara's burden to bring them back on board. One she relished. One she was good at. Her kids, as she called her students both affectionately and sometimes aggravatedly, had become her world. Even before her mother died, Clara wrapped up all of her hopes and dreams in her classes. Their test scores were her test scores. Their spelling errors were her spelling errors. Their engagement in the lesson was hers. And their bad moods were hers, too. It was a symbiotic relationship of the highest order.

They taught each other.

And today's lesson was going to fail everyone. Especially Clara.

She propped the heavy wooden door, the same one that the old school was built around in the early twentieth century, the one that sequestered her with hormonal seventh and eighth graders.

"Miss Hannigan?" a small voice echoed from the doorway as Clara tucked her handbag into the bottom drawer of the filing cabinet.

She turned on a sensible clog heel to see Mercy Hennings standing there, her hands clutching her backpack straps at the shoulders. Mercy Hennings was possibly the prettiest girl at Birch Harbor Secondary, even when compared against the makeup-faced seniors. And, surprisingly, Mercy was by far the kindest.

She was Clara's favorite, actually. Yes. Teachers had favorite students.

"Hi, Mercy," Clara answered. "Is everything okay?" They glanced up at the clock at the same time, budgeting how many minutes they had for whatever private conversation the girl was hoping to start.

"You weren't here this morning," Mercy pointed out.

Clara nodded. "I know. Did things go well with the sub? I had a family matter to handle."

The girl shrugged. "It went okay. I just wanted to pass in my homework to you instead of to the substitute."

Clara smiled. This was classic Mercy. Anxious. Worrisome. "Thanks, Mercy. I'll take it." She reached out as the girl handed over a neatly typed page.

After glancing at it, Clara frowned. "I think this is the wrong paper, sweetheart."

Mercy had given her a science report rather than the literature analysis she'd assigned the week before. The girl winced and began shuffling furiously through her backpack.

"Mercy, don't worry about it. You can bring it in tomorrow."

"No, no. I'll find it. I promise. I don't want to use my homework pass—"

Clara held up a hand. "You don't have to. Just bring it tomorrow. No problem, okay?"

But Mercy would not accept the exception, apologizing again before zipping her backpack in disappointment and muttering that she'd run home after school and bring it back by four o'clock.

Frowning and sighing, Clara again redirected her. "I won't be here, Mercy. I have some things going on that I have to see to after school."

The bell rang, and Mercy muttered a final apology then scurried off through the halls just before fifth period piled up by the doorway.

"Good afternoon!" Clara sang out as cheerfully as she could muster.

Typically, a day at work could distract Clara from bad news that seemed to take a regular hold on her personal life. She could sink her fears into Robert Frost or Edgar Allan Poe and find herself deep in the enchantment of bringing to life the old stuff for the new set of emerging readers. Emerging literarians, as she often called her students to their half-hearted scoffs.

But not today. All through her grammar lesson she kept stealing glances at her phone, waiting for a text from Kate. Some indication that the will was phony or wrong.

Anything.

But it never came.

Fifth hour slogged along. Then sixth. By seventh hour, Clara's planning period, she was ready to ask Mrs. Adamski if she could leave before the final bell.

She shuffled the papers on her desk into tidy piles, turned her computer off, and collected her handbag. Just as she opened the door to leave, her phone buzzed loudly.

Scrambling for it, Clara nearly missed the call. It was Kate.

"I don't have much news," her older sister admitted, as Clara hesitated to leave her classroom.

Feeling the threat of tears, Clara thought better of heading to the principal's office. Instead, she slid into a student desk and asked Kate to explain.

"Well," Kate started, "I talked to Michael, and he thinks we have a case for protesting the will."

"Protesting?"

"Right," Kate answered. Clara could hear traffic in the background. "You should have a claim. The fact that you were totally left out is unconscionable. Michael agreed, but... "

"But what?" Clara dropped her purse on the desk and stood, pacing now. A renewed energy coursed through her veins. Anger, probably. Anxiety, too.

"There's a complication," Kate said at last.

Clara shook her head. "What complication? That Mom was losing her mind? I fed her. I gave her sponge baths, Kate. I was there with her in the cottage every single day until the end. How could she do this?"

Kate's voice shook as she replied, "Mom wasn't well. But, that's not the complication, Clara."

"Then what is the complication?"

A pause filled their phone call, and a million things ran through Clara's mind. The unfairness. The bizarreness.

Something did *not* add up.

Especially when Kate said, "Just, you know. Something

funky. A complication. Clara, I have to go. Let's get together later tonight. We'll talk it through, okay?"

But Clara didn't have a chance to agree. Kate had already hung up.

Kate slid into her car and pressed her fingers to her throbbing temples. She had two choices. Read the letter now, or read it with Amelia and Megan, people who knew the truth and could support her if the letter was upsetting.

But that was just the issue. What was *in* the letter? Was it something she'd prefer to keep private?

Who knew?

She'd share it with Amelia and Megan. They'd figure everything out together and *then* bring Clara in. They'd fight the will, the properties *and* the furniture and heirlooms inside of the properties would be split evenly, and they'd all move on. Back to normal.

Kate would find an affordable, smaller house. Maybe closer to the boys. Clara would keep teaching and carry on as Birch Harbor's pretty hermit. Maybe, Clara would even take on the family membership plan at the Country Club and start hosting stilted dinner affairs where she flitted from catered table to catered table.

Doubtful, but at least Clara could start to love her life for once.

Amelia would land an acting gig and never talk to them again once she found that fame she'd been searching for. And Megan would get a divorce and stay put in her three-bedroom two-story in the suburbs, doing whatever it was she did with her free time. Scrolling through her phone with a permanent scowl, probably.

With the plan firmly in mind, Kate dialed Amelia and threw her car into reverse.

Her sister answered on the first ring. "Hey, how'd it go?"

Kate replied quickly, her breath shallow. "Meet me at the house on the harbor. I'm on my way there now. Bring Megan."

KATE STOOD on the street side of the house. Harbor Avenue stretched like an artery from the south side of the marina up through to the village, but it forked off into something of a frontage road, offering private access to the strip of homes that dotted the lake.

Each of the houses along that narrow side street was immaculately maintained. The Hannigan home, however, less so. Clara had done all she could, no doubt, but she—unlike the couples and families who summered in Birch Harbor—didn't quite have the motivation or even the means to hire a landscaper or a handyman to come and regularly help with upkeep. Plus, Nora had refused to budget for it.

In Nora's years of tending to various rental properties, she relied, as she often said in a put-on Blanche DuBois drawl, *on the kindness of strangers.*

That wasn't entirely true, since there were few strangers among those who lived in Birch Harbor year-round. However, Nora was a woman who got her way.

A sweet smile to the custodian at Birch Harbor Secondary set her up with an emergency contact for water leaks or power outages.

The right compliment to the groundskeeper at the Country Club resulted in a lifetime of monthly hedge trims and brush-and-bulky hauls.

As for nearly everything else, well, Nora had figured it out herself. Applying her father's knowledge and her mother's intellect, she came to be able to fight her way to fix or update anything all by herself. No hired man necessary. Just a second trip to the salon to touch up her manicure.

Still, it was curious that, when Nora decided she was abandoning the big house for her creek-side cottage, she also abandoned her hard work there. And with that, the helpful friends who no longer found their paycheck in the enigmatic smile and home-baked goods of their patroness. Those gentlemen, who'd aged along with Nora, found other ways to spend their time.

Unsurprisingly, Nora allowed her daughters to pick up the slack, much of which fell to Clara. She grew tired of it, or so was Kate's observation of the matter. But it was an observation she refused to share, since she wasn't helping much herself.

But, Kate helped in another way. She managed The Bungalows, offering robust contracts that stipulated far-reaching responsibilities of the tenants. But even that was growing tenuous.

Soon, she'd need a real property manager, someone who could make the bigger repairs that Kate had begun to pay out of pocket years earlier. Mentally, she added that task to her to-do list: find a handyman tenant who would take care of the place better than Clara, who didn't grow up the same as her older sisters or mother, with the expectation of corralling the troops for a weekend of scraping hard water off of swamp cooler panels.

Presently, Kate stood on the sidewalk, just inches from a short, white picket fence, the same style Nora had erected at The Bungalows. Beyond the fence glowed a thick, shaggy green lawn, in desperate need of a mow. Bushes and flowers grew wild along the terraces that crisscrossed prettily beneath the front porch. And behind the untamed yard loomed the house. Two stories. Three if one counted the attic. Four, even, if one counted the basement, which Kate always had as a child.

Back then, growing up and even well after her college years, Kate took great pride in living in that house. She and her sisters pitched in the year their mother decided to paint it a warm, rich red. It took them all summer just to get the front of the first floor coated once. That was when Nora agreed to hire out. A rare occurrence, indeed.

As the years wore on, Kate became aware of flaws and attributes that weren't previously apparent.

The red paint had long begun to peel and, in some places, curl up and chip off.

The weathered shutters had presented shabby chic potential, but they now threatened to pull away from their hinges. Kate imagined them breaking loose and sailing out to the lake like miniature wooden barges on a waveless sea.

She unlatched the squat fence gate and stepped across the invisible line that divided Birch Harbor from the old Hannigan family home and its previous inhabitants.

As Kate neared the house, she noticed one quality that had been nagging her lately—just how close the property was to the harbor. Less than a stone's throw to Birch Village and the marina.

Without a doubt, it would sell. It would sell, and Kate

and her sisters would get everything in order. Between proceeds from the sale and income from the investment properties, as long as they could agree to split things fairly, Kate saw a future in which she could, for once, have some peace. No worrying about bills. Not her mom's. Not her own.

"Get off my lawn!"

Kate spun on a heel, her face flushing and her pulse tripling in the time it took her to locate the person yelling at her.

Her eyes bobbed wildly before landing on two women, walking in long strides from up the sidewalk.

Megan and Amelia.

The latter waved her arm in a wide half circle. "I said get off my lawn!" she hollered again, her voice deep, disguised. Megan laughed beside her, and Kate smiled at last.

"You scared me," she called back. "Sounds like your voice lessons are paying off, though. That's a good baritone."

Amelia recovered from her own laughter. "I haven't taken voice in years. I gave up any chance of musicals long ago."

Kate walked back to the gate and opened it for them, and they gathered together on the lawn, examining the house again.

Megan sighed. "What has Clara been *doing* all this time?"

Defensiveness wrapped around Kate like a blanket, seizing her in paralysis for a moment before she answered honestly, deflated. "The bare minimum. It's all she *can* do, really."

Amelia and Megan glanced at each other, frowning in

tandem. But Kate just shrugged, adding, "We haven't been here to help."

"She could have hired someone. Mom had an income stream, right?"

"A *limited* income stream," Kate answered.

"What do you mean 'limited?'" Megan pressed, crossing her arms over her chest. "The Bungalows are fully rented. Clara aside, we should be pulling in good money from three tenants, right?"

"Yes and no," Kate admitted. "Three tenants, yes. Two of them are long term people. They signed a contract back in the nineties, if you can believe that. They aren't paying much, and Mom never raised their rent. The third pays something more reasonable, but it's still not much. And I have to use some of that income to cover maintenance. Clara dips into whatever is left over to pay electric, gas, and water here." Kate waved a hand at the house. "And, we pay utilities for the cottage. And taxes on all four properties, the land included."

"You mean that farmland out west?" Amelia asked.

Kate nodded.

"It's exactly why we need to be smart about how we handle this. If we play our cards right and make good decisions, we will come out ahead, I promise," Kate pleaded to her sisters' impassive faces.

But they weren't having it. Megan cleared her throat. "So what about Clara? Why isn't she here?"

FOURTEEN
AMELIA

Amelia didn't quite share Megan's harsh agitation over how well—or how poorly—Clara had kept the place. Amelia understood Clara was just getting by. Each of them, after all, was just getting by. Megan with her divorce. Kate with her widowhood. And she, herself, with her wreck of a life.

Following Kate and Megan up to the porch, Amelia took in the place, admiring its stateliness and wondering, selfishly, if they might not make a buck. Something to help cover New York rent. Something to pay for a little Botox. *Something,* Amelia thought, to help her make more of her life than the depressing audition-rejection-waitressing cycle she'd found herself caught inside of like a hamster in a plastic wheel.

She watched as Kate pushed the spare key into the heavy brass key plate, turning the tarnished key and the knob below in tandem. But it didn't budge. She pushed the key farther to the left, then tried the knob again, rattling it. It gave a little, but Kate had to press her shoulder into the door to jostle the wood free. Amelia winced. She hadn't been back to the house in long enough that she felt like all three of them were trespassing somehow.

With one quick pop, Kate fell into the foyer, and a thick warmth sucked Amelia and Megan in behind her.

The air of the house hung still.

Amelia shut the door behind them by pushing her back against it.

Just across from the entryway unfurled the wide wooden staircase, rolling up to the second story landing like an architectural centerpiece. Ample floor space spread around it, original hardwood floors tracking back toward the kitchen, right toward the front hall—as their mother called it —and left toward the parlor.

Amelia took a tentative step into the front hall. Every piece of furniture was covered in heavy white sheets. An outline of a piano and that of a set of sofas confirmed that, actually, nothing much had changed other than a few years' worth of age settling into the room.

She turned and joined Megan and Kate, who began their tour in the opposite direction, through the parlor. Similarly, there, the sitting chairs and side tables stood draped. Dust had been slow to collect on top of the fabric, but Megan ran her finger along one cloth and held it up to reveal a gray oval.

Kate bit her lip. Megan dipped her chin to Amelia.

They moved into the kitchen. It was there that it occurred to Amelia how valuable the house just may be.

Rustic wooden countertops cut utilitarian angles around an ample island. Beneath the window, the porcelain farmhouse sink, complete with an apron, presented itself like a solitaire popping up from a thick, corroding gold band.

The fridge, a narrow, white piece from the mid-nineties,

was the exact same one Amelia had used when she lived there. From it, she'd fetch milk for cereal in the mornings and a glass tray of butter for dinner rolls each night.

The kitchen table waited beneath yet another heavy tent. Consenting to an urge that tugged at her from the moment she saw all the drop cloths, Amelia gripped the edges of the one on the table and tugged hard, flourishing the fabric back like a matador.

The dust turned to an aerosol, blasting all three of their faces and tickling their throats into coughing fits.

"Gee, thanks, Amelia," Megan choked out at the end of a final wheeze.

"Don't be so dramatic," Amelia replied, grinning, and wiped her hands along her jeans. "I had to do it. The temptation was too strong."

Beneath the sheet was the same farmhouse-style table they'd used as children. It was an heirloom, from the Hannigan ancestors. One of many, to be sure.

The sisters stared at the wooden piece before moving on through the pantry and into a small dining room, one they'd never used with any regularity.

From there, they looped back to the staircase and split off. Kate and Amelia turned up the stairs, and Megan walked past, to the basement door which opened just between the kitchen and the foyer at the backside of the staircase.

As they explored, Amelia and Kate murmured remembrances about years gone past. Sliding down the banister and nearly cracking their heads open. Helping their mom strip, buff, stain, and wax the hardwood by hand, one room at a time. For as much work as they had all put into the house, it now felt like a waste.

Amelia broke away from Kate at the second landing and

opted to take the narrow staircase at the far end of the hall, up to the attic.

It had been her space, as a child. A space where she put on her puppet shows and rehearsed for dance recitals—the dance recitals she presented for her mother and whatever friends were visiting for the evening.

When she made it up the stairs and through the narrow door, she came to a stop, unable to move beyond the few feet just inside the door. Towers of boxes blocked her access. Stacked in dense rows across the attic floor, they were entirely unfamiliar.

Pushing out a sigh, she turned and descended, rejoining Kate in the hallway.

Kate offered a weak smile. "Sheets everywhere. Otherwise, it's the same. Frozen in time, I guess."

Amelia nodded. "Let's find Megan."

THEY SAT at the kitchen table; their three handbags propped by their feet. Megan picked at her chipping nail polish. Amelia flicked a glance to Kate, who held an envelope on top of the table, squarely in front of her.

Amelia shifted in her seat. "Wow," she began, attempting to break the ice. "A private document for the executor, or a private letter for *you*." She lifted an eyebrow and pretended to scrutinize her older sister. The effect seemed to agitate Kate, and Amelia laughed lightly. "I'm kidding. But what's inside?"

"And why is it a secret?" Megan added, dropping her hands to her lap. "And why isn't Clara here?"

Kate looked up at them, and Amelia thought she saw a tear form in her eye. But it was gone in a flash as the woman launched into what could only be called an appeal.

"First of all, I'm not inviting Clara to join us until we come to an agreement. I haven't opened this letter yet, and I'm not going to just yet. Regardless of what's inside, we have to make a decision about what we're going to do. And it has to be the *right* decision."

Amelia leaned back, taking in Megan's initial reaction. She tugged either side of her black hair behind her ears and looked back at Amelia, who shrugged.

"Go on," Amelia answered, propping her elbows on the table.

Kate licked her lips. "Clara belongs in the will."

Amelia sucked in a breath. "Well, obviously."

Megan cut in. "So then why isn't she?"

"We know why she isn't," Kate hissed.

"Because Mom was a mean old woman?" Megan replied.

Amelia shook her head and held her hands up in sharp angles. "No name-calling. No bitchiness." She felt the others narrow their eyes on her, so she went on. "Fact: Clara was left *nothing*. Fact: Clara should have gotten *something*."

"Fact," Megan inserted herself, her tone one of mockery, "it doesn't matter who was in the will if Kate is right about all these *bills*." The last word rolled off her tongue like poison.

"Okay, calm down," Kate answered. "I am *right* about the bills. But that doesn't change that we each get a piece of the pie. And it shouldn't change the fact that Mom made a mistake. We can fight this. We have to fight this for Clara. She doesn't deserve to be left out."

Amelia's face softened. She agreed with Kate. Clara

deserved one-fourth. Each of them deserved exactly one-fourth. No matter their history.

"So can we agree to fight it?" Kate pressed. "Can we agree to contest the will on the grounds that Mom made an error?"

Amelia nodded right away.

Megan shrugged. "Sure. Yeah. Obviously it's not fair. Go ahead. Contest it. She's our *sister*, right?"

Kate frowned deeply. "Thank you. And anyway, maybe this letter explains things. If the house was not designated for one of us, then we'll have to share it anyway. I still don't think that's fair enough, though. Regardless I'll go back to Michael's office first thing in the morning and file an appeal."

"For the love of all that is good in this world, *open* the *letter*," Amelia demanded, softly pounding her fist on the top of the table.

Kate opened her mouth to reply, but she was thwarted by a deep, intrusive chime.

The doorbell.

FIFTEEN
MEGAN

Megan strode to the front of the house in a huff, convinced it was a local busybody snooping for some sort of belated gossip.

She was wrong.

"Oh," she murmured, after tugging the door hard enough to nearly pull a muscle in her shoulder. "Hi."

Matt Fiorillo stood haplessly on the porch. He was dressed like he was about to go golfing—at a par 3 out in the sticks. A frumpy polo, untucked, above the most casual of khaki shorts. Ankle socks and clean white sneakers gave way to tanned, muscular legs.

He raised a hand and scratched his dark hair as he met Megan's gaze. "Megan?" he asked.

Megan had always liked Matt. Even after he and her sister broke up. She'd liked him in the way a girl admires a handsome distant relative. Perhaps, an uncle by marriage or a second cousin, twice removed—with fascination and a dose of envy.

If she was honest, Megan used Matt as a template, of

sorts. He was the type of guy she wanted to marry. She'd always said that to herself.

And, in many ways, she was successful. Brian, too, was something of a puppy-dog type. Friendly and frumpy. Kind eyes. Gentle words. Brian, however, was more of an intellectual, preferring computers over cars and phone apps over fixer-uppers.

Of all the people in Birch Harbor who Megan had ever heard gossip about, Matt was not among them. Nor were any of the Fiorillos, really. It was a nice family. A lovable one.

"Matt? What are you doing here?" Megan glanced behind her, waiting for Kate and Amelia to appear at any moment.

He dropped his hand from his hair and tucked it into his front pocket. A deep sadness took hold of his face. "Megan, I'm so sorry to hear about your mom. I was at the funeral, but—"

"We were busy," Megan replied on his behalf. "It's okay. Thank you for coming, though."

Just then, Megan felt the air change behind her. Matt's eyes lifted.

She turned. Kate and Amelia stood there, both sets of their eyes frozen on him.

"Matt. Hi." The voice belonged to Kate, but Megan didn't recognize it. Her words came out pinched and high.

Megan cleared her throat and stepped aside. "Amelia, let's go to the parlor and leave these two alone."

Kate shook her head and pinned Megan with a look before glancing back to Matt. "No, no. It's fine. Matt, come in."

He thanked them and followed as Kate escorted

everyone to the back porch, which was hitherto uncharted territory.

Megan was glad for the change of scenery, but even more, she was glad to be in on this little reunion, of sorts.

Things had not ended well with Kate and Matt. Megan was only in grade school when it happened, but she could remember the whole fiasco like the back of her hand. Kate's sobs. Matt's angry helplessness.

They'd both put up a good fight. One they thought no one had borne witness to.

But Megan had.

Twelve-year-olds were good at that sort of thing. Sneaking around and eavesdropping on their older sisters. Especially when a boy was involved.

But then, that memory extended far past the emotional night that pushed Matt away indefinitely.

That was the summer they went on *vacation*. All of them. Like a happy family. Their aunt's house in Arizona. Far away from Michigan. Far away from everyone.

The walk to the backyard felt long. Megan had flash-backs to when they lived there, Amelia and Kate always striding ahead of her and Megan doing her best to catch up. She didn't like to miss anything. And, usually, she didn't have to.

However, now was not a good time to meddle. Standing and facing the lake added to the discomfort Megan sensed. Amelia must have felt it, too, because she tugged Megan's arm lightly. "Come on. You were right. Why don't we let these two catch up? You and I can walk the grounds. I haven't been down to the lake in forever."

Megan, again, felt Kate's eyes bore a hole, but Matt smiled easily.

"Ten minutes," Kate called after Megan and Amelia. "Just give us ten minutes."

Amelia chuckled once they were on the far side of the lawn, stepping through the white wooden gate of the seawall and down to the little beach.

"What's funny?" Megan asked.

As if guided by muscle memory, they both kicked their shoes off and stepped into the warm sand. It curled up between Megan's toes, and she realized how much she missed it. The last time she'd sat out on the lake was years prior. Even then, when she had found herself on the shore, she hadn't taken her shoes off. She hadn't felt the sand on the bottom of her feet or sliding overtop. If she closed her eyes now, she could transport herself to Rehoboth or La Jolla.

Or, even better, she could transport herself to her childhood.

"This whole thing," Amelia spread her arms out wide and twirled in a circle. "Being home. Like, *home*, home. Mom. The weird-as-hell will. Matt," she lifted her chin up toward the porch. They were far enough away to be out of earshot, but Megan only stole a quick look.

"It's not that funny," Megan pointed out.

"Oh, it's funny. Life is funny, Megan."

They walked to the shoreline. Directly back from the property, a wide thatch of grass halted at the seawall. From there, lay a pristine sandy beach. But just yards off, in the direction of the harbor, spread a rocky outcropping. Though the waves of Lake Huron weren't the crashing kind, every so often a boat would zoom past and push water up against the rocks. The resulting splash turned the cove and the marina beyond into more than a community by the lake; Birch Harbor became a small town *on the water*.

Megan stared out and up the shore, beyond the marina. Miles north, past the tourist fanfare, stood one of Lake Huron's many lighthouses. Thoughts of her father and his parents washed over her—the grandparents that the Hannigan girls cuddled with, the ones who took them to the Detroit Zoo and the county fair. The ones who maintained the rickety old tower and the house beneath. She wondered who was running it currently. It still worked, after all.

"Why are you with Jimmy, Amelia?" It fell out of Megan's mouth before she could swallow it back. Megan felt now was the time to nail it down. She knew her sister deserved better than Jimmy, but she needed *Amelia* to see it, too. For her own good.

By the seawall at the far corner of the property there sat a small wooden shed, its boards dead and gray.

Amelia pointed to it. "Let's grab chairs and sit. They might be longer than ten minutes."

Soon enough, the two middle sisters were sitting with their feet in the water, idly lifting the shore on their toes and splashing it gently back out to the lake.

"Jimmy is... " Amelia began with a sigh.

Megan felt compelled to finish her sentence, but she refrained, trying to accept that it was far better for Amelia to find the truth on her own than for anyone else to thrust it at her.

After a beat, Amelia lifted her hands and slapped them back down on the arms of the chair. Megan winced. "Don't get a splinter." The wood of the chairs was sun-bleached and brittle.

A rumble of laughter caught in Amelia's throat and spread across to Megan. They giggled together. It felt good.

"Jimmy is your boyfriend," Megan said, her tone impartial as could be.

"Jimmy is my boyfriend, yes." Amelia stopped for a minute and furrowed her eyebrows. "Wow. Boyfriend. Am I fifteen?"

Again, they laughed, but this time it wasn't as light.

Megan kept quiet and picked at her nail polish. Little black flakes lifted up and carried off on the breeze. She glanced back toward the house. Kate and Matt weren't standing there anymore. Maybe they'd gone in.

"What do you think they're talking about?" Amelia asked.

Megan shrugged. "I doubt much. Kate isn't going to rehash the past. She's too focused on what's happening with the will."

"Clara deserves more," Amelia answered, her voice flattening. "You know that, right, Megan?"

Megan frowned. "Yes, I know that. But something doesn't add up."

Amelia didn't answer. Instead, she changed the conversation. "Have you talked to Brian since you've been here?"

Another breeze, a stronger breeze, whipped across their faces. Though it was getting later, and the air was turning cooler, the sun still hung in the sky behind them, casting their shadows onto the water. Megan stood abruptly and kicked water at hers, but it reappeared quickly, like a long, lifeless blob. Not quite a reflection. Still, it was her own image, stretching out into the lake from her feet, indelibly attached. "No," she answered.

"Does he know you're on that app?"

Megan turned sharply to her sister and narrowed her eyes. "I'm not on the app. I mean I'm on it, but—it's not what you think," she replied. Her breath turned sour and her mouth grew dry. It was an internal struggle that she should be able to share with Amelia. With anyone, really.

But she was too scared things might not pan out. She was scared it was a dead end. And then she'd look the fool.

"It's not what I think? Then tell me, what should I think?" Amelia replied. Her voice was soft, but her words pushed Megan to the brink of revealing her little secret.

No. Another week or two. Then things might materialize. She might be able to share. It might be different. And anyway, they weren't together in Birch Harbor for Amelia or anyone else to pick apart Megan's life decisions. "I'm getting a *divorce*. And, actually, the dating app has nothing to do with it," she spat back.

But as she walked away from Amelia and back toward the house, Megan felt a knot form in her throat. She couldn't swallow past it. It stayed there, thickening, until she began to wonder if her plan was a joke. Who was Megan Stevenson to pursue her dreams?

As she crossed through the gate and up the sidewalk, Megan's phone vibrated in her back pocket.

For the first time in forever, she hoped it was him.

Not any of the men whose in-app messages she'd always ignored.

She hoped it was *him*. Hers.

Brian.

But it wasn't.

SIXTEEN

KATE

Kate hadn't spoken to Matt Fiorillo in years. Even at the funeral, they successfully avoided each other. At the time, his presence had even felt... voyeuristic.

"Why'd you come, Matt?" she asked as he followed her through to the kitchen, where she landed behind a chair. She felt a little naked in front of him. She hadn't brought her most fashionable outfits or all of her makeup and hair products. He was seeing her plainly, as she was.

"Mainly to see if you are okay."

"Really?" She frowned. Kate had no reason to be angry with Matt. And, she wasn't. But still, she couldn't quite trust him, interrupting her and her sisters like that.

He dropped his voice. "Really. Are you?"

"Am I what?"

"Are you okay?"

Her eyes fell to his hands, work worn and bigger than she remembered. "I guess."

In a moment, he was next to her. "Is there anything I can do?"

Shaking her head, Kate blinked away a tear. She wanted

to ask him about himself, but it wasn't the time. Maybe it never would be.

"I'm here for you. Whatever you need. I can run errands. I can give you money—whatever you need."

She looked up at him. "We don't need your help, Matt. Thanks, but we will be okay."

"And," he replied, pausing momentarily. "Your *sisters*? How are they?"

Kate looked up sharply. "Fine. They're fine. There are some complications, but we'll make it work."

He inhaled deeply and took a step back before waving his hand around. "What are you doing with this place?"

A shrug was all Kate could offer in reply. "We don't know. My mom wasn't very clear, unfortunately. Or, if she was, then we haven't found out yet."

"It is staying in the family, right? You four will get it, though?"

She frowned. "I hope so."

Matt stepped back toward her, tucked the edge of his fingers under her chin and said, "Please let me know if I can *help*. Do you promise, Kate?"

A single tear spilled over her lash line and onto his hand. Kate sniffled and pulled away. "Of course. Thanks." He started to walk out, but Kate called after him. "Matt."

"Yes?"

"If, for some reason, we can't keep this place—" she started.

He cut her off. "I'll buy it. Name your price, and I'll buy it."

SEVENTEEN

CLARA

"Megan?"

Her sister answered the phone just before Clara suspected she was about to be hit with a voicemail greeting.

"Hey, Clara," Megan replied. She sounded tired. Deflated. Disappointed, even?

"Where are you? Where are Kate and Amelia?"

"We're here. At the house."

Clara was about to untuck herself from her car, but waited instead. "You mean the Heirloom house?"

"Yep," Megan answered.

Muffled barks floated through the walls of her unit down to her parking space at The Bungalows. Clara had always wanted a dog. But not a dog like Dobi, insecure and anxious. Always barking. Always wondering where Amelia was, no doubt.

Dobi was like a sweeter and more neurotic version of Trudy, Nora's late Chihuahua. Trudy, the demon pup, as Clara had nicknamed her. The white miniature beast hated everyone except Nora. It was definitely for the best that the poor thing preceded her mistress in death, because Trudy would have been the one remnant of her mother's estate that no one would fight for. Then again, that wasn't true. In reality, Clara would have accepted Trudy with open arms. She'd be like a little version of Nora, terrorizing the town by day and stealing table scraps at night. Though, unlike Nora, Trudy didn't mind an extra pound here or there.

Clara forced an errant sob back down her throat.

She wasn't sure what her next move ought to be. Ask to talk to Kate and rip into her for hanging up? Pretend nothing was happening and just show up at the house. *Surprise! Face me! Face the one who was left out of the will!*

Instead, she closed her eyes and leaned into her seat back, waiting.

Megan murmured something to someone in the background, and Clara could have sworn she'd overheard a man's voice. "Who's that?" she asked, her eyes shut in the still, warm air of her car.

Her sister came back on the line. "Matt Fiorillo. He came by to ask about the house, actually."

"What?" Clara's eyes shot open. "What do you mean he asked about the house?"

"He wants to put an offer in, I guess. He and Kate chatted for a while and—"

Megan's voice was cut in half, and then Kate's replaced it. "Clara?"

Clara scowled. "You hung up on me."

"Listen, I'm sorry. Why don't you come over here, okay? To the Harbor Avenue house."

"Fine," Clara snapped, tapping her phone off. She was about to start the engine again but guilt nagged at her, and she went inside, clipped Dobi's leash to his collar, and led him to the courtyard instead. It was a break for both of them and a moment for Clara to compose her thoughts and think about what it was she really wanted.

Because the time had come for her to ask for it.

"HE SAID HE'D MAKE AN OFFER." Kate avoided Clara's gaze.

"*That's* why he came over?" Amelia asked, her eyes bulging. "He didn't want to, like, *talk?*"

Clara watched as Amelia and Kate exchanged an unreadable expression.

"You called me over to tell me someone wants to buy the house? Are you also going to clue me in on the secret?" Clara stood in the doorway to the kitchen as her sisters sat at the table. Only Kate offered her a supplicating look.

"What secret?" Megan asked. "There is no secret. Mom left you out of the will because she was losing it."

"Megan," Kate hissed.

"It's as much as we know, actually." Amelia straightened in her seat and ran her hands down her thighs.

Evening had set over Birch Harbor, and the lake outside the kitchen windows glimmered in the backdrop.

Clara's stomach started cramping. "So, then what's the plan?" she asked at last, her hands clasped tightly below her waist.

"The plan is this," Kate answered. As she spoke, Clara detected a delicacy in her words. A hesitancy, even. "We are going—well, *I* am going to Michael Matuszewski's office first thing in the morning and filing an appeal."

A heavy sigh filled Clara's mouth and she pushed it out, nodding in agreement. "That's great." Her hands relaxed and she shoved each into her back pockets and leaned against the doorframe.

"And," Kate went on, "once we get that in place, we'll talk to Matt again. See if he's serious and if he can make a reasonable offer."

"What about the other properties?" Clara asked, drawing a fingernail to her lips and chewing distractedly. "And are we *positive* we want to sell?"

It was Megan who answered this time. She spoke softly, warmly even. It was a breath of fresh air after what felt like ages of attitude, like a flip had switched. "Hopefully, Clara, the appeal will result in an even split. I think our goal is one of two things, and that's why you're here."

Lifting an eyebrow, Clara studied each of her sisters in turn. They seemed... sad. Anxious.

"Okay?" Clara asked, feeling all of her youth at that moment. Familiar anxiety bobbed at the surface of her mind, and she thought back to Mercy Hennings. Sweet Mercy who made a special trip to turn in her paper, on the brink of tears, praying to not get marked down. On her way out, Clara had all but bumped head on into Mercy's dad as he was searching for the front door of the building. When Clara asked him if he was dropping something off, he must have realized she suspected his delivery was meant for her.

They exchanged a quick introduction, and Clara apologized that she couldn't chat longer, promising him an extended conference at the end of the school year. He'd thanked her profusely, and she'd felt gratified to be in the presence of a supportive parent. In fact, the whole thing had been the highlight of her day.

"We have a proposal." Amelia cut into Clara's reverie, and she snapped out of it, listening now with acute focus. Amelia looked at Kate, who took over.

"Originally, it appeared that we'd have to liquidate in order to split everything evenly and adhere to the demands of the estate. That, or rent out and split the income. The second option would allow you to stay on at The Bungalows."

"Right," Clara interjected, unsure if she was following as well as she ought to be.

"But that's our question for you, Clara," Megan said. "Do you want to stay on at The Bungalows? Where do you see yourself?"

Clara frowned. She'd never once considered leaving her little one-bedroom by the Birch Harbor Bridge. It was a central location, and it was... actually, no. It wasn't quite home. She opened her mouth, about to claim that she'd love to have the house. The one in which they currently met.

But that wasn't true either.

Clara felt a disconnect from the house on the harbor. She tolerated life in Unit 2. Being relatively asocial and particularly disinterested in the regular maintenance and management that her position as property manager demanded, Clara realized she'd been living someone else's life for a while.

A long while.

She'd been living the life Nora had assigned her to. Keeper of her mother. Middleman to her out-of-town sisters. Single, youthful spinster whose only real escape was *work*, of all things.

"I don't want The Bungalows. And I don't want this place either," she answered, startling herself as much as the others.

"So what do you want, Clara?" Kate asked, cocking her head.

Clara swallowed and furrowed her brows as she stared

off into the inky lake in the distance, the lake she swam alone in as a girl. The lake that boasted loud tourists on their weekender Jet Skis.

She thought of school and her students. The pile of papers to be graded each night. The literature-rich lessons she'd pored over every weekend.

Mostly, she thought of her last days with their mother and the quiet time they shared, the private moments. Tending to Nora alone was hard. But it was an experience Clara wouldn't give up—even if she had known what she knew now, about the will. And yet, it never provided the insight that they now desperately needed to solve the puzzle. Spending day after day at the cottage—night after night for weeks and then months had resulted in nothing but exhaustion. And now, confusion.

Mustering the energy to reply, Clara gave her sisters the truth. "I have no idea what I want."

EIGHTEEN

KATE

There was no returning home. Not until the estate was settled and a firm plan was in place. And, although Kate could have either stayed at the house on the harbor *or* the cottage, she chose to bunk up with Megan on the pull-out sofa in Clara's bungalow.

It was like a sleepover, and the meeting they'd had the night before softened the hardship of an extended stay in town. Then again, Kate had to admit that being back in Birch Harbor was more good than bad.

They'd wrapped up their meeting at the house and stopped by Fiorillo's for a glass of wine. Clara had asked about Matt's connection to the restaurant, which prompted Kate, Amelia, and Megan to question the girl's knowledge of her own town.

Unwilling to discuss Matt Fiorillo one second longer, she'd batted away the topic, explaining to Clara that the owners were his folks. End of story. Nothing to see there.

Now, they were all tucked into their respective beds, Dobi whipping through the house like a maniac as Amelia and Clara giggled in the back bedroom like little girls.

"See what I have to put up with?" Megan asked Kate once the lights were out.

Kate nodded in the darkness and turned to face her sister. "Do you miss her?" she whispered to Megan, feeling sad all of a sudden.

"Who? Mom?"

"Yeah." Kate tried to focus on Megan's face, tried to assess her reaction. Her features. Her expression. But it was too dark. Megan was lying on her back, staring straight ahead, unmoving, as far as Kate could tell.

"Yeah. Of course. Just because things got bad at the end doesn't mean I don't miss her. She's our mom. I love her. Loved her. *Love* her. Jeez. How do you talk about someone who's dead, Katie?"

Kate smiled at the nickname. No one had called her Katie in years. Decades. "I know." She let out a sigh and shifted under the covers, mirroring Megan and facing the ceiling. The shape of a modest ceiling fan whirred above, blowing Kate's hair in ticklish wisps across her forehead. She hunkered down deeper in the covers.

"Do you miss her?"

Kate blinked at the question. "Mom? Of course."

"Yeah, but... your relationship was... different. We all know that. At least, Amelia and I do."

Considering this, Kate hesitated before answering. No matter what she said in response, she would never come close to articulating her real feelings, which were as complicated as the estate itself. And even if she offered a decent response, it would result in a lifting of the floodgates. Memories from the hardest years would pour out, and Kate would get no sleep.

"I loved Mom. Always will." It was a simple answer. It should have been enough to end the conversation that Kate regretted ever opening. But it wasn't, and Megan pressed on.

"Did you open the letter yet?"

Kate shook her head and pushed her tongue to the roof of her mouth hard, willing away the tears that had climbed up the back of her throat.

Moments passed, and the tongue trick didn't work. She gave in to quiet crying and pressed the heels of her hands as deep into her eyes as she could bear.

The bed creaked and dipped beneath Kate's body, and she nearly fell into the middle toward Megan, who was wiggling closer. "It's okay," Megan whispered, slipping her arms around Kate and squeezing her shaking, sobbing body close. "It's okay, sis."

———

MEGAN HAD FALLEN ASLEEP SOMEWHERE around ten or eleven. Kate waited until two in the morning until she gave up on any shuteye and snuck out of bed and to her purse.

She wasn't quite sure what she was waiting for. A moment alone? A chance to breathe? Or, most likely, courage?

As Kate pulled the envelope from her purse, her heart pounded in her chest. Her mom could have said anything. It could be an apology. It could be a chastisement. It could be nothing, even. After all, in the past couple months, Nora's downward spiral knew no bounds. She might have repackaged her electric bill, for all Kate knew.

She glanced back to ensure Megan was still asleep, then stole away through the backdoor and onto the quaint porch. There, propping her phone like a flashlight, she studied the white envelope, trying to make sense of the past day.

But she came up empty.

Quietly and delicately, Kate slid a finger beneath the far corner of the sealed flap, tugging the glue free in a smooth drag.

The letter was not, actually, a letter.

It was not an electric bill, either.

It was the torn page of a notebook or journal of some sort—unlined, beige, its edge revealing a hasty rip rather than a clean tear.

Kate frowned, her eyes dancing back and forth to make sense of what it was Nora had seen fit to leave.

But there was no puzzle in the handwriting. No evidence of delirium. Kate could see plainly what it was.

Nora's personal diary. No more. No less.

A single-page entry wrought by the hand of a woman who made a decision, a decision that would change everything. And there it was, in all its glory, to push Kate over the edge of grief and confusion. To surprise her.

To ruin everything.

NINETEEN
AMELIA

Clara had left for work. Kate was nowhere to be found. It felt like they were back to the drawing board with plans.

That would be all well and good if Amelia didn't need to get back to New York. She had tips to earn and, maybe, a part to prepare for. The whole estate thing was turning into a bigger project than she'd have liked.

And now, with Clara acting despondent... the immediate future did not look bright.

Megan agreed, complaining in no uncertain terms that morning over coffee.

"Do you think she wants the cottage?" Megan asked, narrowing her eyes on Amelia suspiciously.

Amelia took a sip, and it scalded her tongue. She winced. "I have no idea. I think she just wants... normalcy. Right? I mean, don't we all?"

Megan rolled her eyes. "I don't see normalcy in our immediate future. We've only just begun uncovering issues with all this."

Amelia considered her sister's suggestion. "What do you mean 'all this'?"

"Mom's estate. Clara and Kate teaming up. Our past. All of it. We don't even know what else is going to turn up from here on out. That lawyer acted like his four leather binders would answer everything. No. Too pat. Too neat. Especially for Nora."

A defensive prickle climbed up Amelia's spine, though she wasn't sure who to defend. Poor handsome Michael? The man with his life together who was just trying to do his job? Or their mom, for weaving a web of secrets and promptly dying before a final showdown. "Michael's just trying to help," she started, trying again on her coffee, this time with more success. "And Mom was from a different time. A different era. She didn't live her life online for the whole world to see. Of course we have to claw through some cobwebs." Amelia involuntarily rested her gaze on Megan's phone.

Tucking it away into her sweater pocket, Megan answered smoothly, "I beg to differ."

"Oh?" Amelia replied, slurping down half her mug. She was going to need at least three more pots to make it through that day. Jimmy's insistent presence. A problem with the estate. And now Megan, dredging up old wounds.

"When a woman puts her kids to work on her income projects while she flounces about at a country club for the weekend, I think it's safe to say she is living out loud. Or... *was*, as the case may be."

Shaking her head, Amelia couldn't help but grin. "Touché."

Kate and Megan carried hard feelings over how much they had to work growing up. Amelia, however, had enjoyed it. Perhaps, she was afraid to admit she was a little more like their mother. A little more interested in a publicly glamorous life, the same kind that Nora made happen. Did she pull it off by slave-driving her daughters?

Yes.

Did Amelia mind?

No.

Work hard, play hard. It was the adage Amelia had looked forward to most about growing up. Whenever that time came.

"I GOT A TEXT FROM KATE." Megan reappeared from the bathroom, her face scrubbed clean of the usual black eyeliner and pallid setting powder. She looked, for once, *alive*. Vulnerable, even.

Amelia smiled at her. "What did she say?"

"She had to run an errand. Something to do with Matt." The two grinned at each other. "She said for us to go to Michael's office and get the ball rolling with the appeal."

"Can we do that without her?" Amelia asked, unhooking the leash from Dobi's collar and letting him race free throughout the small living room. She'd never seen him as energetic as he'd been in Birch Harbor. Lakeside living suited him. Even in a little bungalow.

"I don't know, but I'm not sitting around here waiting. If we aren't moving on this, then I'm going back home. Sarah has been texting me nonstop. Brian can't cook to save his life, and she's stuck there alone with him."

"I could think of worse people to be stuck alone with," Amelia replied, grabbing her purse off the counter.

Megan frowned. "Oh, yeah? Like Jimmy?"

A cackle erupted out of Amelia's mouth, and she

quickly quelled it, bewildered by the outburst. "Sorry. I—I have no idea where that came from."

"I made a joke. A sort of mean joke. You laughed. That's where it came from."

Amelia shook her head and started toward the door. "Yeah, thanks. I get it. I just meant—"

"Oh, no. I know what you meant. You meant that you didn't want to laugh at Jimmy and your joke of a relationship." Amelia whipped around, ready to start a fight, but Megan held her hands up in apology. "Sorry. I'm sorry. That was harsh. True, but harsh."

"No, I understand, actually. All of you hate Jimmy. Even Dobi hates Jimmy. I'm embarrassed now that I left the poor guy with him. But... "

"Oh, here we go. More excuses. Amelia, girl. Own it. If you're going to stay with him, then stop apologizing for him. Stop giving credit to *our* feelings and start giving credit to *yours*. Yes, we don't like him. We think you should end it. But if you won't end it, then at least stand up for him. Fight for him. Make us *like* him."

Taken aback that Megan was, in some bizarre way, validating Jimmy (or, at least, Amelia's stick-to-itiveness with Jimmy), Amelia cracked a grin. "I think I know where this is coming from," she answered as they left Clara's house and headed to Megan's SUV.

"Oh yeah? Where?"

"Your dirty little secret," Amelia replied, pinning Megan with a meaningful look.

Megan shook her head. "I don't have any dirty secrets. I'm honest as they come."

"Okay, then spill. What are you doing with the dating app?"

Megan shook her black hair back off her shoulders and

pointed her key fob at the vehicle. But Amelia wasn't going to take a beep for an answer. She didn't get in on the passenger side. Instead, she stood in front of the SUV with her arms crossed.

Hesitating at the driver's side door, Megan cocked her head. "Nothing. That's what."

With that, the raven-haired Hannigan hopped in the front seat and revved the engine.

Amelia wasn't intimidated by this menacing show of force. Yet, she believed Megan. Her sisters might be imperfect and oddball. But they were honest.

Which, by all accounts, set them apart from their mother.

The late, great Nora Hannigan. Queen of the Country Club. Mother of Girls. Manipulator Extraordinaire.

That was Nora. But that was not her daughters.

THEY PULLED up outside the family law offices, and Megan threw the SUV into park.

"I really don't think we're going to make any headway without Kate. She's the executor," Amelia protested as she chewed on a hangnail.

Megan shrugged. "We'll try. If we get nowhere, then I'll send Kate an emergency text."

With that, they headed in together, Megan in front, pumping her arms purposefully into the quaint building as Amelia strode behind.

"Oh, it's the Hannigan sisters," the secretary cooed from her perch down below a tall reception desk.

Megan answered first. "Stevenson. Megan Stevenson."

Sharon made a face at Megan's correction. "Sorry about that. I didn't mean to overstep."

"She'll be back to Hannigan soon, anyway," Amelia added helpfully, but Megan threw her a look. "What?" Amelia asked her sister before stage-whispering to the secretary, "She's getting a divorce."

"Now that's a darn shame." The woman stood behind the desk and wrung her hands in front of her ample bosom. "I'm terribly sorry to hear it. Divorce is worse than death, they say. I wouldn't know. My Harry and I have been together since the war."

Amelia stifled a giggle. Whatever war that woman could possibly be talking about made no sense. And even if it did, using war as a context for the birth of a marriage felt morbid, at best.

She cut in, trying to divert the conversation appropriately. "Ma'am, we're hoping to see Mr. Matuszewski."

Michael Matuszewski wasn't originally from Birch Harbor. His family, however, was. Amelia wondered why he'd come to Birch Harbor at all. Was Detroit overrun with lawyers? Did this guy spend every weekend at the lake? Amelia wondered quite a lot about him.

"Ladies, hello." His familiar, warm voice boomed at the edge of the hallway. Amelia and Megan looked up.

"Hi," Megan said, waving a rigid hand.

Amelia smiled. "Hi, Michael." She could have sworn his eyes lingered on her a moment longer than was appropriate, for their particular circumstances or any, really. Between veritable strangers, a lingering look was almost always indecent. What mattered was whether it was welcome.

Amelia decided it was.

"I was expecting Kate this morning. Are you here waiting for her?"

Megan glanced back at Amelia, and they turned to him together, Megan taking the lead. "Yes and no. Kate sent us ahead of her to reopen the conversation."

"Come on back. I expected as much." He waved them toward his office, more casually than the day before. Now, despite the early hour, Michael wore his sleeves rolled up to his elbows. His hair was a little less gelled and a little messier. Still, however, he radiated power and control. Two things Amelia had never known a man to possess. After all, she was reared by a strong woman. Their dad had left the picture before Amelia even got to high school.

"Clara," he began, once they were seated orderly around his desk.

Amelia frowned and glanced at Megan. "Pardon?" she asked.

"You're going to contest on Clara's behalf, I presume?"

"Yes," Megan answered this time, her posture rigid and voice assured. "We'd like to discuss rearranging some things based on the fact that she was entirely left out. And, well, she *was* Nora's daughter, I mean."

Michael arched an eyebrow but answered evenly. "Sure. I understand. With Kate's blessing, we can move to arrange the proper paperwork in contest against the terms of the estate. Is she on her way, or...?"

Megan and Amelia looked at each other. "She will be, yes," Amelia replied as Megan pulled her phone from her pocket and tapped away on a text message.

"Should we come back?" Amelia asked, her eyes on Michael now, studying his features, his sharp, lawyerly jaw. His deep gray eyes. He *looked* like a lawyer. But not, maybe, a small-town lawyer.

"No, no. I am free this morning. Other than an after-noon meeting with the town council, I'm all yours." There it was. Amelia was positive. He was examining her just as she was examining him. She suddenly felt aware of her crow's feet. Her bare face and flat hair. Digging in her purse for her lip gloss would be an obvious maneuver. One only an insecure woman would enact.

Her heart thudded in her chest as Megan fumbled with the phone just inches away, but Amelia reached into the deepest recesses of everything she knew about acting and pulled out the confidence of a starlet. A top-billed actress. A Lady Macbeth, even.

"Michael, tell me. What brought you to Birch Harbor originally?" She pricked up the corner of her lip and dipped her chin only just, glaring through her naked, dark eyelashes.

He faltered a bit, and Amelia felt good. Better than she'd ever felt with Jimmy. "My family," he answered, anchoring his jaw in his hand on top of his desk. She had his full attention.

Amelia's eyes fell on the lower half of his face. The stubble and full lips. White teeth. "Your parents... or?"

"Yes. This practice was my grandfather's, actually. My dad moved away and never looked back. But, well, I was curious, and I love the history of the place."

He was about to carry on, and Amelia was entirely enraptured, but Megan broke in.

"Amelia," she said, her voice ice cold. "Kate wrote back. She can't come. She, um—" Megan flicked her eyes up at Michael before staring hard at her sister. "We need to go. Now."

The doctor just left.

The girls are fine. That's as much as I'll say there.

As for Wendell, well... Wendell is... accepting. He's accepting, though I don't know why. I feel angry. Everything was perfect before. Now this. I could punch a hole in the wall, I could. Where was I?

It's like a recurring dream, but the faces are different.

It's my fault. I had control and lost it. I let it slip through my fingertips. I was distracted, admittedly. All the work. And all the play. Wendell is mad at me, probably. He should be. I deserve it. IT. Now it's become a monster. I can't allow that. It is not an it. Oh! He? She?

Wendell says leave "it" alone. Let go and let God! He's fine with embracing the natural course of events. He loves me. He loves the girls. To him, there's nothing more. No reason for a big, bad change. But he has not been down this road before. Not like me.

Lord, Your will is what got us here. I hate to even write this, but I can't bear it, Lord. You've slapped me in the face.

It's unacceptable. Unsustainable. Unfair. Un-everything, Lord.

And yet, I trust You.

Besides! I'm Nora Hannigan, and You made me a planner, and so I have a plan.

Arizona, where Roberta lives. She's my sister. She'll help. I haven't spoken with her yet, because Wendell won't go. I'm not sure he'll want us to go, either. He says if I go and take the girls then he'll stay with his parents. It feels like a threat, but it's not. He refuses to be alone, of course. He hates to be alone. Maybe that's why he doesn't mind this little surprise, this little intrusion. The more the merrier. It's something Wendell says.

I would say it, too, if I hadn't already been down this dark and deathly road. I would say it if it were true! But these things never turn out merrily. You know it as well as I do. That's why it's a commandment, right, Lord? That's why you punished me before.

But I can't stay. Not now. I might come back. If things fall into place, I might come back and resume this life, if Wendell won't mind if I change the story. I have to change the story.

But if I don't change the story, what will I do? Or what if Roberta won't have us? Should we even be traveling? That's a question for the doctor.

Maybe I'll buy another place. Something away from town, inland. A farm or something. Or, I could go to Arizona, after all. I could do both! My God, we have the money now. I could do both! Wendell won't mind a new project. He loves it. He loves us. He wants us to be happy. No, he probably doesn't care about the shame, but I care. I care for us.

TWENTY-ONE
MEGAN

Sweeping Amelia out of the office and into the sunny Michigan morning, Megan spoke in hushed tones.

"Kate opened the letter. And *that's* why she's with Matt."

Amelia's eyes grew wide. "What was in the letter? How do you know?"

"Well, I don't know for *sure*. But why else would she skip the meeting? I think it's obviously about Clara. And, that's where we are going. Kate said to meet her at Matt's house."

Shaking her head, Amelia spit a few curses. "Why couldn't Mom just add Clara to the will? What was the problem with that?"

"I don't know," Megan replied. "Hopefully we're about to find out."

HEADING to Matt's house was no easy task. He lived on Heirloom Island, a tiny chunk of land that floated southeast of town, adjacent to Heirloom Cove. They'd first have to go to the ferry, then sit there and grow nauseous for the next half an hour until spilling onto shore amid smells of the ferryman's sweat-slicked sunscreen and the flapping fumes of a variety of lake birds. The Birch Harbor Ferry wasn't known for its glamour. It could probably use a makeover, Megan thought to herself.

But as she sat there, next to Amelia, chewing on her thumbnail and imagining the sort of news that Kate was unwilling to reveal on the phone or via text—the sort of news that demanded they take a damn *ferry*, Megan thought of something else.

There were a *ton* of people in town. For May, the number seemed significant. Tourists by the droves. Cute bikini-clad girls and handsome tanned guys vying for attention from each other. Some in groups laughing, some paired off, canoodling in the far corners of the boat. It was fascinating. Megan felt like she was a fly on the wall of *The Bachelor* on location at Lake Huron, Michigan.

Once the ferry docked, Megan and Amelia hung back, waiting for the crowd to thin before them.

Amelia gripped Megan's hand. "Should we have called Clara?"

"No," Megan answered, firm. "Let's wait to see what Kate says. Maybe something *good* happened." Megan wasn't usually the optimistic type, but who knew? Kate and Matt out on the island instead of holed up in that mahogany and leather office? Maybe something good *had* happened.

They strode along the deck and up to the parking lot, where Kate said she'd meet them. Sure enough, the figure of a slender woman stood erect at the crest of the slight hill, her hand casting a shadow over her face so as to ease the reflection of the sun from off the water.

Kate waved, her fingers flashing up in a lackluster cascade. "Hey," she said once they were close. "Matt's house is just up the shore." She pointed back toward a pretty Victorian.

"Wow," Megan replied. "I didn't know he lived on the island."

"Moved here a few years back. After his divorce."

Megan and Amelia raised their eyebrows to one another before following Kate on foot less than a mile to his home. Kate didn't turn around, preferring instead to walk quietly in front of them.

Once there, Megan noticed Matt, pacing his front porch, one hand pushed through his hair, the other gripping a cell phone against his head.

"Is everything okay?" Megan asked, a feeling of alarm clenching her gut.

Kate stopped at the front lawn and waited for them to catch up before answering. "Yes and no. Everyone is fine. But there's been... a revelation."

"And Matt is in on this?" Amelia asked, hooking a finger toward him.

Nodding solemnly, Kate let out a sigh. "Yep. Now you two will be. I had to come to him first. I hope... I hope you'll understand."

Megan didn't, really. Her sisters were her blood. Not this local islander single dad who'd written off the Hannigans just as soon as they'd returned to Birch Harbor after their extended desert vacation.

At least, that was Megan's thirteen-year-old impression of things at the time.

The women strode to the porch, joining Matt as he thanked the person on the other end of the line before hanging up. "Hi, Megan. Amelia." He nodded his head to each in turn, and they said hello back.

"What's going on?" Amelia asked. Kate pressed her palms to her eyes and shook her head.

Matt stepped to her and set a hand on her shoulder awkwardly. Megan would have cringed at the gesture, if the situation didn't seem so dire.

"Let's go inside," he suggested, waving a hand back through a yawning front door.

They filed in and each found a spot at an industrial-style kitchen table—all wood and metal and screws beneath the rustic knotty top.

The next words out of Kate's mouth stunned Megan into silence.

"We can't contest the will."

The news had rocked the family. Their father had fallen quiet. Their mother turned to ice. Kate had no idea what her parents' private conversation consisted of.

All she knew is what happened next, a drawn-out succession of events. The last-minute road trip after a hushed phone call with their family doctor. The summer in Arizona with Aunt Roberta. A girls' summer, their mom had called it. That much proved true.

And of course, before all of that, the breakup with Matt: a tear-stained conversation where they went back and forth and back and forth, both pleading and pushing and blaming. Teen angst at its finest.

But none of that was the worst thing that happened that summer.

The worst thing was losing their dad. It made for a second secret. They returned home, the new baby having fussed and pooped and spat up the whole, long journey back, and he was gone.

At the time, Kate and her sisters believed their mother.

They believed that he just... left, that the events of the summer pushed him over the edge.

But the thing of it was, Kate never read such a response in her father's reaction. She never saw hate or anger. Fear, maybe. But Nora had herded them so quickly out of there, that Kate had no clue what the poor man thought about it all.

Upon their return, there were meetings—important ones. She remembered that part as well as anything else. Nora had visited the Actons. The Actons had been in touch with authorities. Everyone settled on a loose agreement: that Wendell Acton took off. Nora eventually painted him a deadbeat, but Kate never felt the woman had believed that. It didn't make sense, for one, that Nora Hannigan would marry a deadbeat, and, for two, that Nora Hannigan believed her husband had, all of a sudden, turned into a deadbeat. Whatever happened to Wendell Acton rested deep in the heart of Birch Harbor lore. And there it would stay.

Kate never did decide if her father's fate was related to their vacation. She didn't think her mother capable of—or interested in—anything insidious. But the timing was too odd. Or, too perfect. He wasn't *that* mad. Not to Kate or anyone else.

After the whole thing, the Actons dismissed Nora and her daughters entirely. Holing up in their house, the old, antiquated Birch Harbor lighthouse on the lake, like recluses, until their dying days years later. Kate suspected that her grandparents held her mom accountable. Even Kate sort of held her mom accountable. Amelia and Megan cast blame, too.

But, with time, the town forgot about it. Accepting that

some men just leave. And, Wendell Acton was one such man.

Yet, there was a hole in the theory, a detail the investigators and the family didn't piece together then and maybe never would.

It wasn't just Wendell who went missing, it was some of his belongings, too.

Things the Hannigans wouldn't know were missing until years later, when Kate was rummaging around in the basement of the house on the harbor, laying claim to the treasures left to her by their late mother's estate. An estate so finely tuned, that no one had questioned its flaws. Its inaccuracies.

Kate never would find her father's wristwatch.

TWENTY-THREE
AMELIA

"Are you going to show us?" Amelia asked, her voice so quiet she didn't think Kate had heard her.

Matt pushed the envelope across the table, his eyes on Kate, who nodded.

Megan leaned in, and Amelia carefully slid out a thin, narrow page from the envelope.

"Is this her...?"

"Her diary, yes," Kate answered. "At least, I think so."

Together, Amelia and Megan read the slanted, even script—their mother's careful handwriting, handwriting she'd taken seriously in her years of grammar school. Handwriting she had flaunted during Country Club fundraisers when they asked *who will make the sign?* and at town council meetings when they asked *will anyone put together thank-you notes?*

Amelia's eyes moved across the words, but none of them made sense. If what she was reading was true, then they had lived a lie, and for what? If what that journal said was true, then the will *was* valid. Precluding the date of the Heirloom house, of course.

Her pulse quickened and her breath caught in her throat as she finished and looked up at Kate, first. Then, Matt. Finally, Megan.

It was Megan who spoke next. "Is this *real?*"

Kate shrugged then dropped her head to her chest.

Matt answered. "As far as we know, yes. We called the county recorder's office here and in Arizona. I just got off the phone when you two showed up. I talked to the record keeper at Birch Harbor Unified, too."

"And what do they say?" Amelia asked, floored, still.

Kate lifted her head. Lines crossed each other above her head. The hollows beneath her eyes sat deep and sallow. "They didn't know about anything. Mom lied to me. To us."

"That's what they said?" Amelia asked, bewildered.

"No, that isn't what they said." Matt reached his hand out and covered Kate's. Amelia shifted in her seat, unable to tear her eyes away from the equally familiar and foreign display of modest affection.

"So what did they say? Get to the point." Megan's neck glowed red and splotchy. Amelia shook her head sorrowfully.

"They said," Kate began to answer, searching Matt's face. "They said the truth. Somehow, we just never found out."

TWENTY-FOUR

CLARA

Teaching all day was exactly what Clara needed. It would distract her from the business of contesting the will.

It would also give her a chance to be away from her sisters and really think about their question. *What did she want?*

First period was a blur, a mess of papers and excuses for not having papers and following up on the sub's notes. By the time second period began, Clara finally had a chance to sit at her desk, check emails, and sip coffee.

Her students sat quietly, completing their bell work, and Clara knocked out a flurry of housekeeping messages; there would be an assembly on Friday; tardy lunch students were being rerouted to the library; ticket prices for the promotion dance were going up, up, up! *Get yours today!*

It reminded Clara of her own middle school experience. The hope of being asked to a dance. The nervousness about starting high school.

Most kids who had older siblings, enjoyed something of a paved road—for better or worse. Amelia had it harder. Teachers had loved Kate. Or at least, that was Clara's impression. To follow in her footsteps was to succeed a lovable queen to the throne. But then Amelia, with her creative energy and free spirit, set the bar low for Megan. Megan, more Type A but less lovable, simply enjoyed the experience of knowing almost everyone who was in the upper grades. It offered her a buffer. A reputation.

Then came Clara, twelve years younger than Megan. Most of her sisters' teachers were retired or long gone by then, and no students had ever heard of a Hannigan child. They only knew about the Hannigan family. The earliest settlers of the area. The name was more like a story than an identifier of real people. It had turned Clara into an only child with a history. An odd thing to be.

Now, as she sat at her computer, finished with emails, neat stacks of papers to grade towering to the left of her keyboard, she felt an itch.

A list-making itch. Not the pros/cons type. More like the goal-setting type of list she'd forced her churlish students to compose months back at the start of the second semester.

She pushed her keyboard aside and pulled open the small notebook she kept for her personal notes. Shuffling through a few pages of shopping lists and one to-do list, she landed on a blank page with thin pink lines running orderly across.

At the top, Clara titled it: *Personal Goals*.

Beneath that, she pushed the tip of her Ticonderoga onto the start of a new line—a new word... a new sentence... *anything*.

But nothing came.

She flipped the page. On the next blank sheet, she added a different title: *Hannigan Estate*.

Beneath that, she found her rhythm, jotting down each

of the four properties and even some of the belongings she recalled from the reading of the will. Lastly, she added a few mementos she had wanted to keep for herself, such as her grandmother's afghans and a hope chest that she once heard about but never did see with her own two eyes.

Beside each item, she listed who she felt best matched with each property. To Clara, it didn't make sense to sell the house on the harbor. At least, not yet. It was too important. Too historic. But also, too much work. Perhaps Kate was a good fit? She needed to move anyway. Of course, she'd wanted to downsize, but that was just because of the mortgage payment. If she had the house, then Ben and Will could visit. Megan's daughter, Sarah, too.

Clara didn't know what made sense for Megan. She was on the verge of divorce. Maybe she'd be better off with the house? Amelia was least likely to handle it. But she could handle *something*. She could handle low-maintenance rentals... like The Bungalows.

Would anyone want the cottage?

Clara thought back to what she knew of the cottage's modest beginnings. Apparently, it was something that her mother and father began working on in the months leading up to Clara's birth.

From what Kate had told her, Clara knew that Nora had asked Wendell to find, purchase, and break ground on a new home inland, something lower maintenance. And, he did. Of course, his project went unfinished, but Nora forged ahead, hiring people here and there and chipping in herself to pull off completion of the modest, pretty three-bedroom, two-bath that sat next to Birch Creek.

Then, nothing. With Wendell's absence, the cottage sat there, collecting dust and overflowing clothes and furniture for a long time, until Nora decided to move in herself, leaving the place on the lake for one with easier daily upkeep, apparently.

It was a short walk to the school. So short, indeed, that sometimes Clara would steal away inside the cottage by herself and snuggle into the single iron frame bed that made its way there. In that bed, Clara would read and drift in and out of sleep until nighttime drew near, at which point she'd hurry home to an almost empty house.

Clara snapped to attention, inhaling sharply.

Yes. The cottage.

That's what Clara needed.

The cottage with the afghans and the iron bed. The cottage that had been her hideaway for so long.

The cottage that was denied to her when Nora wanted her to live at The Bungalows and play property manager.

She needed the cottage.

It was settled.

After a quick set of directions to her students to put away their grammar textbooks and take out their journals, Clara tapped out a text message to the group chat with her sisters. She knew she'd be interrupting their meeting with Michael, but they had to have the information. They had to know to give her the cottage. Nothing else. Just the cottage.

All Clara needed was the cottage. If she could get that, then she wouldn't necessarily have what she *wanted*, but she could figure it out. Clara Hannigan could solve the world's problems in that little place on the creek. She did as a kid. She would do it as an adult.

Clara would move to the cottage on the creek, and that is where she would figure out her life—away from the big house, away from the four-plex, away from the loud lake and the tourists and the noise of town. In her own little cottage.

Where maybe she could find that hope chest.

TWENTY-FIVE
KATE

Kate had always thought her life was defined squarely by two phases: before she had children and after. This is what everyone had led her to believe, and it's what she indeed knew to be true.

After all, giving birth and taking on the role of motherhood was life changing.

Once Ben and Will were born and Kate and Paul had found their new normal—their lasting normal, by all accounts—phase two finally began in earnest. Kate took solace in raising her little family, and found the chance to part with Nora, Amelia, Megan, and even sweet little Clara to be easier than she'd ever imagined.

Living all the way up on Apple Tree Hill, away from Birch Harbor, didn't hurt, either. There, she'd made a new life. She paid bills, changed diapers, and organized mother meetings in her front room. There, she washed the dishes every night and sorted and stowed fresh laundry each morning. Then, once the boys left for college, life tipped again. She was still, of course, their mom. And at that point, she was also still a wife.

New normal became book club and floral arrangements and gardening. Then, eventually, Kate discovered the working world. First with a secretarial position at the sanitation company Paul managed. Then as an underling at an upstart realty company. Currently, she was still very much an underling, since during Paul's sickness and subsequent death she was forced to take so much time off that she had to start over again from the beginning when she'd finally grieved enough to return.

Kate had always predicted she'd one day become a comfortable widow far down the road and well into old age. Comfortable financially, thanks to wise investments and helpful children. Comfortable in her new town, which always somehow felt like a new town. Never a hometown.

But she was stripped of that luxury. No comfort. Too young. Too mired in debt from *poor* investments and expensive college tuition times two. Of course, Ben and Will were worth every penny. But she'd like to have some money to spare. Some to cover the mortgage on the house the boys had grown up in, for starters.

Then again, even that felt wrong. Kate didn't actually want to stay in that beautiful house with casement windows and high ceilings and a lush garden. She wanted soul.

She wanted a home. And, in fact, Birch Harbor was the only home she'd ever known, even if it came with the heartache that a true home often knew.

The two phases of her life—before children and after—weren't the full story. It would appear that there was about to be a third phase: The Great Unknown. The preview to her golden years, should she be lucky enough to enjoy them. And, the handling of her mother's death and her needful sisters. But God didn't stop there, no sir. He had to throw in a monkey wrench. A twist. A problem.

Kate's biggest worry for the moment was not, in fact, sharing the truth with Clara.

It was whether Amelia and Megan were going to cooperate in light of that truth.

Then again, perhaps the letter, that sweet, sickening letter, meant they wouldn't have to. Maybe, just maybe, there was another way out.

Presently, she and her sisters sat at Matt's table, their lips in tight lines and eyebrows furrowed heavily.

Kate spoke. "I'll take the cottage. We'll split the house, since it wasn't mentioned. You two can fight over The Bungalows and the land. That's the plan, okay?" She started to pull her hand away from Matt, but something stopped her. "Speaking of which," she continued, slipping her hand out from his and returning it primly to her lap. "What did you plan to offer for the house, Matt?"

She felt Amelia's and Megan's eyes bore a hole in her, and she caught Matt's uncomfortable reaction. But this was down to brass tacks. The will—and Clara's exclusion from it —was irrelevant if they could fetch a pretty penny on the sale of the house. Or, at least, find another option that would provide Clara with *something*.

He cleared his throat. "Kate," he started, holding up his hands defensively. "I'm not sure now is the time to discuss that. Are you sure you want to sell it?"

"You showed up there, right?" Megan pressed, suddenly on Kate's side.

He nodded. "Yes, but, I didn't... I didn't realize things were sticky. I would never want to intrude. If I can help, then I will help. But I'm not about to come between you three—or, um... you *four*. And that place is a legend. I mean... " He was rambling, and it made Kate smile. He always used to ramble, even as a teenager, a fumbling teenager who asked permission to so much as kiss Kate on the cheek.

"Listen, I'd be happy if we sell it. I'm in New York now, and—" Amelia was on the precipice of launching into some well-meaning lecture about her unavailability and big dreams and high hopes, but Megan cut her off.

"Oh, please. Amelia, you haven't had a real part since you left Lincoln, Nebraska. Nothing is keeping you in New York, and you know it."

Kate's eyes widened in horror as her sisters opened the same argument that they'd gone rounds with since the funeral.

Amelia put up a good fight. "I have Jimmy. And Dobi. And a great studio apartment," she protested.

Megan rolled her eyes, landing them squarely on Kate. "Are you hearing what I'm hearing? She actually plans to stay in the city?"

Kate shook her head. "I never thought she was *leaving* the city. And why do *you* care, Ms. Suburbia?"

Megan clicked her tongue. "I'm not sticking around there. Not unless I get the house, and even then... well, I'll probably sell it."

"So you're coming back to Birch Harbor?" Kate pressed.

"Maybe," Megan replied. "Maybe I'll take the cottage. It's the right size for Sarah and me, and then... just me, once Sarah graduates."

"You're not taking the cottage," Kate answered, her eyes narrowing on Megan, her spine lengthening into a rod.

Matt held his palms up at the three of them. "Ladies, come on. We have bigger fish to fry than who gets what, right?" His eyebrows twisted up and he looked at Kate. She swallowed and her body relaxed.

But he was wrong. Nora's letter, the revelation, the truth, and the will—all it came down to was *who* was getting *what*.

And Matt was now part of the puzzle, but he didn't seem to realize it.

TWENTY-SIX

NORA

Wendell phoned yesterday. Or should I say I phoned him. He found a little house on Birch Creek. It's a fix-it-upper, he says. He also says it's full of charm and that it reminds him of me. It's incomplete, though. It has a back building, a barn I think. Lots more construction to become whole, I guess.

I'm not sure that he'll make an offer, but I hope so. I'm in no state to make big decisions. That much is true.

If we get the house on the creek, then I'll feel better. I'll feel like we have options when we return. The girls can stay at the cottage while things blow over. Maybe all the moving and shaking will distract everyone and paint us as eccentrics. I always wanted to be an eccentric, until I married Wendell. I could have been Miss Havisham herself if it weren't for my loving husband and wayward children.

I told Wendell what I thought was best regarding our family's little situation. He didn't seem to understand. He didn't see "what the big deal" was. Wendell's heart knows no shame. I envy him for that.

All I have ever known are the scales of shame. My life has always been weighed on them.

I am going to live through this, and I will do it right. I won't be ashamed, not of the situation. In fact, no matter how hard it is, this will all be a blessing. A blessing. I'm sure of it.

The lunch bell rang at the same time Clara's phone buzzed against the metal pencil tray in her desk drawer.

She'd forced herself to keep her focus on her classes. She'd forced herself to ignore the background drama of the estate.

Now, it seemed, she'd get some news.

Mercy Hennings was dawdling at her desk, and Clara hated to shoo the nervous little thing out, but she had to answer the call.

"Mercy," she began, her phone crooked at the ready in her hand, "are you staying in here for lunch... or?"

"Oh, no, Miss Hannigan. I just wanted to let you know that my dad said thanks for meeting him in the parking lot yesterday. And, well, I suppose I wanted to say thanks, too."

"It was no problem. We just happened to bump into each other is all," Clara replied warmly as the incoming phone call went to voicemail. "Well, have a nice lunch, Mercy."

"Thanks. You too." The child smiled sadly, and Clara's teacher instinct kicked into overdrive.

"Mercy, is everything okay?"

The girl turned on her heel and bit her lower lip. "Oh, yeah. Kind of." She kept her eyes on the hardwood planks of the classroom floor.

"Oh, sweetheart, come here. Sit down. What's bothering you?" Clara waved a hand to the student chair next to her desk, and Mercy eased down into it, her backpack sliding off her shoulder.

Clara eyed the backpack, then her phone and asked Mercy for a moment to send a text. She quickly wrote to Kate explaining she'd be in touch in five minutes. Just five minutes to solve the problems of the world for a middle-schooler. Guilt tugged at Clara's heart.

"It's just that high school is coming up, and I'm scared."

Relaxing into her own seat, Clara smiled. "What are you scared about, Mercy?"

"The other kids, mostly." Mercy fell into a hunch and crossed her arms over her chest.

Clara replied with some confusion. "What do you mean? You know almost everyone who will be in your freshman class."

Mercy sighed a deep, adolescent sigh, her upper lip catching briefly on her braces.

Clara suppressed a grin.

"I mean the private school kids from the island."

Nodding knowingly, Clara answered with a wise, "Ahh. Yes." On Heirloom Island, just southeast of the house Clara had grown up in, stretched a small water-locked chunk of earth, complete with its own private school. An island with a private school made for special circumstances. Of those children who lived on the island, there were two types who opted out of St. Mary's: too poor to stay and pay for the Catholic school or too heathen to have any interest in applying for a scholarship. And as for those children who lived on the mainland, there were also two types of children: normal and just heathen enough to beg off the ferry ride to school or Catholic and rich enough to afford and even enjoy the exclusive day trip to get an education on an *island*.

But that trouble only lasted through eighth grade. So far, the Catholic school on the island didn't offer grades nine through twelve. This meant that all those little private school teens would flood Birch Harbor High.

"I get it," Clara went on. And she did. "Tell you what, Mercy. If you get to ninth grade and start having friend trouble, you come tell me. I'll help, okay?"

Mercy nodded gratefully and collected her backpack. *Problem solved.*

"Okay, Miss Hannigan. Thank you."

The girl hesitated at the door, just as Clara was about to hit CALL on Kate's contact details. "Yes, Mercy?"

Mercy ran her tongue over her lower lip, freeing it from another catch on her braces. "My dad said you're really pretty."

AMELIA ANSWERED KATE'S PHONE. "HEY," she said, her voice betraying some sense that things were not going according to plan.

"Hey," Clara echoed. "How's it going?"

"Well, we aren't at Michael's office."

"Oh?" Clara asked, a pit growing in the bottom of her stomach and washing away a smile from the compliment she'd just received.

Amelia cleared her throat and waited a beat before

answering. "Everything is totally fine, though. Something came up, but it's actually okay. Seriously."

Clara felt flushed, and she stood to pace the rows of student desks as she pressed Amelia for details. "What did the lawyer say? Do we have grounds to contest still? We do, right?"

"Like I said, Clara. Something came up. The appeal... ah... well, we are shifting direction."

"Can I talk to Kate?" Clara asked, her voice pinched as she held her breath, waiting for her oldest sister, her most grown-up one.

"Hi, Clara," Kate's voice came on the phone, smooth and reassuring. "Listen, we can't contest the will anymore. But we're all here talking and we realize that we do need to get some clarification on what we can do with mom's property. Everything is going to be fine. I don't want you to worry, but let's plan to meet at the house on the harbor after you're done with school. I'll have Matt order a pizza, okay?"

Clara frowned. "Matt? Matt who?"

"Oh, right," Kate answered, murmuring something away from the line before coming back on. "Matt Fiorillo. Um, he's here, too."

Before Clara could ask why, Kate had passed the phone off to Megan like they were playing a long-distance game of hot potato.

"Can *you* tell me what's going on?" Clara asked Megan, her tone revealing her anxiety and impatience. She felt so left out and in the dark. It was like their childhood all over again. Clara so much younger, so much different, so much apart from her older sisters. Part of her wished Mercy had stayed behind to have lunch in the classroom. Then, at least, Clara wouldn't feel so lonely.

"All I can say," Megan answered, "is that Kate is fighting for you."

Clara figured Megan meant it as a kindness, that Kate was "fighting" for her. But then, did it also imply that Amelia and Megan... were not?

TWENTY-EIGHT

AMELIA

"We have a couple of hours. What do we need to do to get everything in order?" Amelia asked earnestly after Matt cleared away their glasses of iced tea. Tensions had cooled, but there was a lot left to do and discuss. And, even minor issues awaited them back on the mainland. For Amelia, those included Dobi's potty break and Jimmy's looming existence. He'd texted her throughout the morning, commenting on where he was and what he was up to. Somehow, he'd made his way to the house on the harbor, though he promised her he'd stick to Birch Village until she was back at the house.

Megan, too, was fighting against urgency. Sarah needed her to return home that night. Although, Amelia wondered if that was true or if Megan *wanted* to return home. Or, at least, return to her daughter and husband.

Kate seemed distracted more than ever. Amelia felt for her. Here Kate was, in control of their mom's affairs on the heels of her own personal tragedy—losing Paul not too long before. Plus, Amelia knew Kate's financial situation was not much better than her own. Or Megan's for that matter. The only one who enjoyed any degree of stability at the present was Clara, of all people.

The financial pressure along with an extended run-in with Kate's high school sweetheart only added to their drama. Being sequestered in Birch Harbor until they hammered out the details felt like bunking up in a crucible. Something—or someone—was about to burst.

A thought occurred to Amelia, an off-topic detail, altogether, but one that perhaps mattered. "Do you live here alone?" she asked Matt, staring around the walls. "Or do you have a roommate?" She fixed her gaze on Megan, who caught on to her line of reasoning.

"I live here with my daughter," he answered.

Kate cocked her head at Amelia as if to say *see? No scandal.*

Amelia smiled. "How old is your daughter? What's her name?"

"She's fourteen. Viviana." He plucked a photo from his fridge and showed it to them. Each sister cooed in turn.

"She's beautiful. Does she live with you full-time?" Kate asked.

Matt nodded. "Yep. Her mom moved to Detroit chasing some big-city gig. She's very successful. She visits often."

"If you died today," Amelia went on, narrowing down to her main point and question—they had figured he had a daughter, that was no big mystery, "who would get this place?"

"Viviana," he answered easily. "Why?"

"Well," Amelia replied, her emerging claim surfacing on her lips like she was morphing into some sort of intellectual detective, "what about your ex? And your parents? Would they get in the way at all?"

He laughed derisively. "No, of course not. Everything would go to Viviana... or—" his voice fell away, and he looked at Kate.

TWENTY-NINE
KATE

Her face softened at Matt. Kate didn't know Viviana. She'd only ever seen the girl at the funeral, and, while she knew Matt had moved on from their adolescent romance, his new life was a hard pill to swallow. Then again, hadn't Kate moved on, too?

Yes.

Kate had moved on. She'd married and had two sons and lived a whole new life, worlds away.

So then, why did her pulse quicken when Matt covered her hand with his? Why did she go to him first, before her sisters?

There was no rule demanding that Kate seek out Matthew Fiorillo. Her mother hadn't left such a stipulation in her diary entry, after all.

But there they were, in his kitchen on Heirloom Island, like old friends. Perhaps that's exactly why she'd gone to him. Amelia and Megan were too removed from Birch Harbor. Matt, having stayed on there and experienced the waves of time in the small lakeside town, was a rock. More so than Kate's own sisters, apparently.

"Matt," she said, changing the conversation. "What have we missed?"

"What do you mean?" he asked.

Megan and Amelia had left the table and were currently wandering around in front of the house, giving Kate and Matt space to talk.

"I mean what has gone on in Birch Harbor all these years? What have you seen and heard?"

"What have I seen and heard about your mom and Clara?" he asked earnestly.

Kate blinked. "Well," she began, swallowing a growing lump in her throat. "Yeah."

He breathed in through his nose and pushed the air out of his mouth as he leaned back in his chair, a reflective glaze coating his stare. "Same old, same old, I suppose. I've seen your mom do her country club thing. I've seen her at the village. I've heard she's made her rounds at parties and big town events, sponsoring this or showing up for that." He lowered his voice for what he said next. "I've seen her with men."

Kate paled at his implication. Her heart hurt. Her body even hurt. She was supposed to be back home by now, packing her house and preparing to put it on the market. She was supposed to be sad and depressed that her mother was gone, not angry that her mother left something of a mess behind.

Inhaling sharply, she nodded in response. "And Clara? Do you ever see Clara?"

He shook his head sadly. "No. I think she keeps to herself."

Kate nodded again, this time more thoughtfully. "I'm sorry I dragged you into this, Matt. I'm sure you weren't expecting your high school girlfriend to rush in asking you to save her."

They locked eyes, and Matt leaned forward in his seat. He was the same boy she'd fallen in love with all those years ago, but now a man. His kind eyes sat inside of crow's feet and his chin and cheeks were shadowed by handsome stubble. And, Matt's mouth. A full mouth that had lived a lifetime away from hers. Back then, she'd have hated to think that Matt would belong to anyone but her.

But, he had. And not just romantically. His lips had no doubt kissed his own frail mother. His... daughter. Kate had missed all those moments with him. Were there more women, too? Was there someone... now?

"Matt," Kate whispered again. Just as she was about to apologize a second time, his jaw set and his eyes lowered to her lips.

"No," he whispered back. "I'm sorry. I'm sorry I didn't fight harder for you." A tear welled along her lower lash line. He lifted his thumb and reached across the table to brush it away. "Is it too late?"

SHE SWALLOWED. It wasn't too late. But the timing was bad. She shook her head at Matt and blinked away the tears and thirty-some years' worth of regret. "We need to get ready to go. Clara will be done with school soon. I want to have a plan in place for this meeting." Kate stood abruptly from the table, and the air sucked out from between them, leaving in its wake a chill. "What do you have going on this afternoon? Do you have to pick up, um, Viviana from school, or...?"

"Or am I bringing pizza to the meeting of the minds?" he finished her sentence in a half-joke, and it successfully lightened the mood.

Kate grinned. "I did say that, didn't I?"

He nodded. "I can bring the pizza. Viviana walks home. She goes to St. Mary's just up the road. I'll leave a note for her. But, Kate—"

Folding her lips in between her teeth, she dipped her chin toward him. "Yes?"

"Are you sure I should come? This is a... this is awkward. It's a big conversation. Maybe a private one, even."

Kate glanced out the front window, her gaze falling on her younger sisters. She contemplated his point, mulling it over like she was smoothing a jagged rock in a tumbler.

Matt was right. The conversation was serious. It would be upsetting. It would be uncomfortable and confusing.

Two things needed to happen. And they needed to happen soon, so that the women could get back on with their lives. They needed to tell Clara the truth. And they needed to decide who was getting what.

And those conversations were inseparable, tied together in history and in the present, by all four of them. Matt belonged there, too. And if Clara were Amelia, who reveled in high drama and theatrics, then Kate would maybe bring him.

But Clara wasn't Amelia. She wasn't dramatic. She wasn't Megan either—tough and steel-willed. No. She was most like Kate, quiet, reserved, and generally serious. Mostly, Clara was still just a girl.

"Will you bring the pizza but wait outside? Perhaps in the back porch?" she asked Matt.

"Of course," he answered. "I'm good at that."

She cocked an eyebrow for clarification. "Good at what?"

He replied through a mischievous smile. "Waiting."

THIRTY

NORA

OCTOBER 4, 1992

With Wendell gone, I don't have the courage to be the woman I once was. My strength has left me. My neck seems to hurt every morning when I wake up. I'm sleeping on my stomach again, because I have no one to hold me at night.

There's only one way to honor Wendell, and it's done. Well, there was nothing technically "to do." And that's what Wendell wanted. For me to leave it alone.

So now here we are, with angry in-laws living up north, an unfinished cottage, an empty lot, the four-plex, a new baby, and this big old house that Wendell couldn't stomach to stay in alone.

I don't blame him.

There are secrets here, and they kissed our lives. He knew that, and I do. The girls probably sense it. But secrets can make things better.

Oh. Oh my. I just had an idea! I suppose writing in this old thing pays off after all.

Amelia left the back yard and walked down to the shore to take a phone call—from Jimmy, no doubt.

Megan felt empty, lonely, too. She hadn't spoken to Sarah or Brian since she'd been in Birch Harbor, and she missed at least one of them.

Sarah didn't answer. She was still in class. Megan left a message asking her daughter to return her call. She needed to hear someone else's voice.

Before clicking off her phone, she rubbed her thumb up the screen, revealing Brian's name.

Without a second thought, Megan tapped it.

It rang. Anxiety crept up her arms, settling into her neck. Reluctantly, and yet, with a degree of giddiness, she pressed the device to her ear and waited.

Three rings later, his voice came on.

"Yeah," he said. Not a question. Not a greeting. Just a yeah.

"Um, hi. It's me." Megan waited a beat before adding, "Megan."

"I know," he replied. His tone matched the prickliness of his voice, and she immediately regretted calling.

Fumbling around for what to say next, she defaulted to what had become the most common topic of conversation. "I'm calling to check in on the settlement."

He sighed. "We're selling the house."

"What?" she asked, alarms filling her head. "What are you talking about? I thought either you or I would get it?"

"Lawyers think it's a dumb idea. We sell and split the profit, if there is any. Fresh slate. We can go our separate ways. You can follow your dream, for once."

"That's it?" She kicked herself for the way she'd asked it. She sounded weak and desperate. Like she *wanted* the fight to go on.

Maybe she did.

"Listen, Megan. It's a win-win for you. You get to buy a new house, and I'll pay child support and alimony. The whole shebang. It's everything you wanted, right?"

Silently, she shook her head. "So, what happens next?" she asked, eyeing Amelia who was returning up to the lawn.

"Next, we sign off on this. No mediation is a good thing. It can go straight through. I guess then the divorce can be finalized." His voice dropped off on the last sentence as though it was hard for him to say. Almost, as though he hated to say it at all.

Megan wondered if she hated to hear it, too.

The next thing, he whispered. Like an afterthought. An allowance. "Megan," Brian said. "I'm tired of this, okay? If you don't want to sell, then you can have the house. You can take it all. I just... " His voice broke, and Megan's eyes began to brim with tears. "I just want you to be happy."

THIRTY-TWO

CLARA

Clara had never been one to rush out of school after the final bell, much less *before it*, but here she was, on day two of finding her attention indelibly ripped from the only constant in her life.

Instead of asking permission from the principal to leave early yet again, she slipped away twenty seconds before dismissal, scurrying to her car and easing out of the parking lot and toward the house on the harbor. Her sisters weren't expecting her for another fifteen minutes at least, but Clara could not wait. She had to know. She had to be part of the mess, as much as she hated it. Her future—her ability to sculpt out a future for herself—depended on it.

As Clara turned right onto the easement just past Harbor Avenue, she spotted just Megan's vehicle. A sliver of jealousy wedged its way into her chest. The thought of her sisters carpooling around town, sipping mimosas at Fiorillo's, and bouncing in and out of shops in the village with little paper bags of souvenirs made her feel unreasonably angry.

She tried hard to push it aside, focusing instead on what

she would say. "I'll take the cottage, if you don't mind." Or maybe: "I'd like to have the cottage, regardless of what I've been left. I won't bother you for anything else. All I want is the cottage." No matter what words she practiced in her head, she sounded like a baby.

Now, Clara turned her attention to the narrow street in front of the house. Just as her eyes focused, a flash of black dashed in front of her car. A squirrel or a bird—no. It was a bigger animal. Not big, but bigger than a bird, for sure. And four-legged.

Slamming her foot on the brake, Clara's heart pounded in her chest. She threw the car into park and tore out of it and around to the front, where she was positive she would find small animal carnage.

A voice cried out from across the street. "He's okay; he's okay!"

Clara glanced up to see an attractive stranger jog toward her. Ignoring him momentarily, she searched the pavement until her eyes landed on a little dog, splayed on its back in submission, his needle-shaped tail wagging like a windshield wiper across the ground.

"Dobi?" Clara asked, bending down and tickling the chubby pup's belly.

"Sorry about that," the man said as he neared. Clara looked up, squinting through the eastern-facing sun behind him.

"Jimmy?" she asked, shielding the rays to make sense of his features.

"At your service." He grinned cockily and joined her on the steaming asphalt.

"I thought I hit him," Clara murmured as she gave Dobi's slick potbelly one final pat before rising and smoothing her dress.

Jimmy hooked the leash clip on the dog's collar and faced the house, gawking in admiration. "Wow. I can't believe you grew up here," he commented, raising his eyebrows to Clara.

She shrugged. "Yeah. I guess."

"Everything okay?" he asked, dipping his chin. "I mean now that we've established Mr. Dobi here is alive to tell the tale of his near-death experience."

Clara began to reply that she was tired, but Jimmy held up a hand, his eyes growing wide.

"Wait, wait. You probably heard, huh?"

"Heard what?" Clara answered quickly, desperate for any crumb of information she could wrap her brain around.

Aloof, Jimmy answered easily. "Well, I mean I just got off the phone with Amelia. She didn't want me to come down here, but things sounded pretty serious, so I figured I'd better check in on all of you girls. This Matt guy seems like he's up to no good."

"Matt?" Clara played dumb as she noticed movement behind one of the windows of the house. "You mean Matt... *Fiorillo*?" she lowered her voice.

"I think so. Yeah, well Kate took the... whatdoyoucallit? The barge? Or ferry or whatever—she took it to his place and then some drama went down, you know. I guess there's a question about him and your mom, maybe? Amelia didn't tell me *everything*, but I put two and two together. This Matt guy, I guess, has lived here forever. He even showed up to your mom's funeral? And then he came to the house earlier today to 'check on things.'" Jimmy threw up air quotes. Clara hated air quotes.

She scrunched her face. "What do you mean Matt and my mom?"

"And *you*," Jimmy replied, pointing an accusatory finger

at Clara. "I mean, Matt being your real dad, right? That's the big scandal, right?" Clara felt her face grow hot and her heart thud against her chest wall at Jimmy's words. But he kept talking, stupidly. "Small towns, I tell you. I'm glad I'm from the city. We don't keep anything quiet there. If you have a crazy family, you know about it from *day one*."

CLARA BURST through the front door fuming. "Kate!" She screamed across the foyer and towards the kitchen.

Kate's face appeared in the doorframe. Behind her, Matt Fiorillo.

"Is it true?" Clara wailed, glaring venomously at both of them.

Megan stepped in from the parlor, grabbing Clara's arm before she had a chance to peel off down the hall. "Clara, what is going on?"

"Is he... my... my *father*?" Clara pointed her finger at the man.

The reaction that smacked across both Kate's and Matt's faces told her all she needed to know.

Stupid Jimmy, the interloping tourist-boyfriend, was right. She spun around to see him amble in behind her, little Dobi cuddled into his arms. Clara threw a hand back towards him. "He told me *everything*."

Amelia appeared behind Megan, bewilderment on her face.

Clara had no idea what *they* had to be confused about. *They* knew the truth all along. *They* were the secret keepers.

Amelia joined Clara at the door then reached for and grabbed Dobi out of Jimmy's hands. "Whatever you said, get out. Leave," she spat.

Jimmy started to protest, but Megan opened the door and reiterated Amelia's command. "Leave, Jimmy."

He did.

Clara's breathing had slowed only marginally. The left-over breaths now available to her were turning into tears and pricking at the corners of her eyes. "Is it *true*?" she asked everyone and no one, her eyes searching her sisters and avoiding Matt's hardened stare.

She didn't even know Matt. All she knew about Matt Fiorillo was that he was Kate's boyfriend before Clara was even born. She'd rarely seen him around town. Even when she saw his supposed daughter at the funeral, they seemed wholly unfamiliar.

Except for one shadowy memory. Something she hadn't recognized until that very moment. Except in that memory, they were in opposite positions.

She was there, in the kitchen doorway. Matt was where she now stood, in the foyer, looking floppy but cute. Cute for an older guy, Clara distinctly recalled.

He'd shown up one day randomly, when Clara was perhaps ten or so. Her mother greeted him coldly and made him wait in the foyer until she'd retrieved a sweater. After that, they'd left together. Curious, Clara had flown to the windows in the parlor, peeking out and listening hard through the lavender plant that stretched in its pot just beyond the cracked window.

But she hadn't caught any of their conversation. And the only other part of the memory that she now recalled was her mother returning into the house and warning Clara that she had better never talk to that Fiorillo boy ever.

Easy enough for Clara.

She didn't talk to anyone.

Amelia pressed her hand to her heart, willing it to slow down. Jimmy was such an *idiot*. A freaking *idiot*.

He'd gotten it wrong. Almost all wrong. Implying that Clara was the product of some affair between their mom and Matt?

Gross.

And, wrong.

Jimmy and all his false bravado about helping repair the house and enjoying some romantic interlude while they were in town was a hilarious fantasy. Not even a fantasy. A joke. He was a joke! Their relationship was a joke. Especially in contrast to the very real family situation that lay before them now.

She bounced Jimmy from her mind and wrapped a protective arm around Clara. "He doesn't know what he's talking about," she whispered, regretting ever mentioning anything to that halfwit.

"Please," Kate interrupted. "Will everyone give us some privacy?" Amelia's older sister pierced Megan, Amelia, and then Matt each with a glare.

"Okay," Amelia answered, giving Clara one last hug and nodding Megan and Matt through to the back porch.

———

ONCE THEY WERE OUTSIDE, Amelia couldn't bear the burden of being separated from the secret that Kate was about to reveal inside the house. It was almost painful, the keep-awayness of it all. But the truth was not Amelia's to handle.

Matt blew out a sigh, shoved his hands in his pockets, and—without a word—walked down to the beach, not bothering to glance behind.

Amelia started after him, but Megan interceded. "Let him go, Amelia."

She turned and faced Megan. "Shouldn't he be in there?"

Megan shrugged. "It's not our call. Let's just mind our own business for now. I'm sure Kate will call us in when she's ready."

Amelia set Dobi down in the grass and unhooked his leash. He dashed away, leery enough of the sea wall to stay near.

"I can't stand this," Amelia whispered, stretching her arms in a wide circle above her head. "I can't stand it!"

Megan answered, "Let's get our minds off of it. Talk about something else."

"Like what? What could we possibly have to talk about while they are in there dealing with this?" Amelia drew a dramatic circle around the property, as though it was the pit of the big drama.

"Jimmy, for starters," Megan replied, a tired smile curling her mouth.

"Nothing to talk about there. He made a fool out of himself. Case closed."

"Are you going to break up with him finally?" Megan pressed.

"Are you going to divorce Brian?" Amelia shot back, an attitude edging into her voice, though from where it came was beyond her.

Megan glanced at her phone then clicked it off. Amelia had an opportunity and an instinct, and she went for it, snatching the phone from Megan's hand and turning her back sharply as she turned the screen on and shuffled through Megan's apps as she wailed behind Amelia, clawing her back.

Amelia deftly avoided giving up the device long enough to open the dating app. As she began scrolling through the unfamiliar interface, it occurred to her that Megan had stopped protesting all together. Instead, the younger, darker Hannigan sister now stood a couple of feet away, her arms crossed and her lower lip trembling.

"Megan," Amelia said, her voice low. She dropped the phone and held it out. "I'm sorry. I was just joking. I shouldn't have—"

Megan wiped an errant tear from her cheek and took the phone before tapping quickly and flashing the phone up to Amelia's face. "See?"

Amelia leaned forward and squinted. A digital inbox glowed back at her. She wasn't sure what she was supposed to see, so she shook her head helplessly back.

"Look," Megan pressed the phone back at Amelia, forcing her to take it and study it closer. "I don't know why I'm being weird about it. Just look, if you're so curious."

Four messages fell beneath what appeared to be Megan's "profile," which offered the shadow of a head instead of Megan's photo and a semi-anonymous handle, *meg_2020.*

Amelia glanced up at Megan, whose eyes were now dry and, curiously, even smiled back. A... nervous smile?

"*Mark47* says, 'can i get a pic?'" Amelia read aloud.

Megan lifted an eyebrow and nodded her on.

Amelia went to the next. "*TheBigMichigander* says, 'Hi. How are you?'"

This time, Megan shrugged.

"You didn't answer them," Amelia pointed out, reading on to find that the next two messages were also vague and unreturned. "So, you're testing the water?" Amelia prompted, completely absorbed by the unfolding circumstances despite everything else going on just yards away in the house.

"In a way," Megan replied. She shook her head and rubbed her thumbs beneath her eyes as if to clear the threat of more tears.

"What's going on?" Amelia asked, confused by Megan's veiled hints and moodiness.

A deep sigh lifted Megan's chest. She glanced up at the house then fixed her gaze back on Amelia. "I'm not on that thing to meet men."

Amelia stole another look at the phone, trying to discern something—*anything.* She came up empty. "I don't understand."

"It's embarrassing, I guess. I don't know. I didn't want to say anything until I worked it out."

"So you *are* seeing someone?"

"No," Megan answered, her eyes drifting off until they landed on Matt in the distance. Amelia followed her stare. Sadness tugged at her heart. There were so many answers for them to uncover, and time was of the essence. At least, if

Amelia wanted to return to the city in time to resume her waitress gig and prep for Lady Macbeth.

"Then what, Megan? Spell it out, for the love of God. Spell. It. Out."

"I applied to work for them," Megan answered, covering her mouth as she said it.

Amelia frowned. "What?"

"I applied to work for the app. The matchmaking app. Just before Mom's funeral. I haven't heard back yet, but I wanted to get an idea of what it was like. You know?"

"So *that's* it? *That's* what you've been keeping from us?" Amelia laughed.

A sheepish smile took hold of Megan's mouth. "It's... look, I haven't even heard back yet. I don't have the tech skills, probably. And what matchmaking company would hire someone who's in the middle of a divorce?"

Grinning broadly now, Amelia rushed Megan in a hug, burying her face in her sister's shoulder. "I'm so proud of you," she whispered.

Megan laughed in reply. "Your standards must be low. You're proud of me for applying for a *job* and keeping it a secret?"

"No," Amelia replied. "I'm proud of you for following *your dream.*"

THIRTY-FOUR
KATE

They sat at the table together in silence, the two blonde-haired Hannigans. The house felt bigger, and in it, Kate felt more vulnerable.

She swallowed hard and stared out through the window, watching on as Amelia and Megan pounced on each other in the grass like obnoxious children. Kate envied them. Amelia and Megan had always been safe, removed. Separated and shielded. *Free.*

Not Kate. She was smack dab in the middle of it. Kate was the *cause* of it.

Matt's shape reappeared in the distance. Her heart ached. For him. For *them*. For all the years that had filled up like an ocean. Mostly, Kate's heart ached for Clara, who should have been none the wiser.

Kate thought about the will and wondered what her mother was thinking when she left the house out? And even more than that, why didn't Michael Matuszewski ask?

"I'm not sure how to start," Kate whispered, returning her attention to Clara. It was maybe the first time in years Kate had looked upon her like she did now—*differently.*

Clara's eyes, bright and blue, took on a milky effect. Darkened hollows framed them, adding to her tired face. Her hair, tied back at the top with a barrette, tugged free at her temples in brittle flyaways. Clara's skin, devoid of much makeup, drew down in red splotches along her chin—hormonal acne she was too young to kick.

Kate wondered what it would have been like to have a daughter.

"I just want to know why," Clara replied, taking in a deep breath and letting it out slowly through parted lips.

"Mom didn't mean to leave you out of the will," Kate answered. "She just didn't update it."

"Why didn't she?" Clara shot back, her brows furrowing toward the bridge of her nose.

"You came so much later, and—" Kate stopped short, unwilling to reveal the next thing. The big thing.

"Mom was in Michael Matuszewski's office," Clara responded, her tone pleading, even desperate. "Why wouldn't she think to?"

"Well, in a way she *did* make an adjustment," Kate replied at last, reaching into her purse which sat slumped on the floor.

Clara's face lifted. Hope.

Kate pressed the envelope onto the table beneath her palms, securing it there for the time. "She had a diary, I guess you could say. And she left an entry for us, or me, specifically," Kate said at last, her eyes welling up.

Her eyes widening, Clara shook her head. "A *diary entry?*"

"Yes. She tore it out. Maybe there are other entries, but I'm not sure. It seems like she left this one as part of... her will or something. I think... " A sob escaped Kate's lips. "I think she was confused. But, Clara, she meant well."

Tears streamed down Clara's ruddy cheeks. Her neck blossomed in red patches—evidence of grief and relief and shock.

"But that's not all," Kate whispered.

Clara's crying paused momentarily as she locked eyes with Kate. "Then, what?"

"You," Kate began, her voice trembling uncontrollably against the weight of the truth. "Clara, you... " They looked at each other, and Kate could feel Clara's heart pounding in her own chest wall. Nausea churned in her gut.

"What?" Clara whimpered back.

"Clara, you are not our sister."

THIRTY-FIVE

CLARA

A panic attack.

Clara was officially experiencing a panic attack. Her entire life flashed before her eyes. Little moments here. Big memories there. Her feeling left out for all her childhood. Her hard work. The cleaning. The life of lonesomeness. Her chest began heaving. Her neck grew tight. No tears. Just panic.

"Calm down. Clara, calm down."

Clara could hear the words, but Kate's face became blurry. Foggy. Like a pencil eraser had been rubbed across her features. "What are you—what are you—" She repeated the same three words over and over again, trying to steady herself against the failing vision and cramping muscles.

Kate rose from her chair and knelt next to Clara, her hands pressed against Clara's cheeks, leveling her jaw. "Clara, shh. Listen to me. Calm down, okay?"

One deep breath later, and Clara could see again. The tears came now. Frightful tears. "What are you talking about, *Kate*," she hissed between sobs.

"Clara, when I was in high school, I got pregnant."

The sobs halted abruptly. Clara *knew* she misheard. Or misunderstood. She sniffled and rubbed her fist beneath her nose, smearing away a mishmash of fluids from her face. "You never told me you had a baby," Clara answered, lamely. How could she not know that her older sister was a teen mom? "What happened?" Clara asked, feeling her heartbeat return to normal.

Kate blinked and frowned but went on, answering in slow, looping words like Clara was a toddler. "Matt and I... " Kate glanced out the window behind her, as if she hoped he'd appear at the door. Clara was glad he didn't. "We were in love. But that's no excuse, I guess. I'd tell you it was a mistake, but I'd be lying. I got pregnant. That's why we went to Arizona. Mom was mortified. She didn't know how to handle it, I guess." Kate stopped, shaking her head. Fresh tears budding along her lower lash line.

"So what did you do with it?"

Kate offered a half smile, wiping away the wetness from her cheeks. "The baby?"

Clara nodded back.

"Well, we didn't know what to do. Mom was so worried about people in town finding out. It was... uncomfortable."

"What about Dad?" Clara asked.

Kate let out a small laugh. "That's the funny thing. He wasn't mad. He was okay with it, I guess. I mean, not *okay* with it. But he just figured we'd deal with it. That's why he started building the cottage."

"What do you mean?"

"Mom figured she could hide me away there. With the baby, I mean. We could keep it a secret."

"Is that what happened? Did you move into the cottage? What happened to the baby?" Clara's panic returned, as she began conducting some simple calculations in her head.

But before she had a chance to finish doing the math, Kate answered, quelling her questions for the moment. "Mom decided to adopt the baby."

Clara's head bobbed and her vision grew blurry again.

Kate grabbed her hands, squeezing them, and whispered through tears, "Clara, *you were the baby.*"

THE NEXT SEVERAL minutes were a blur. Clara had already put two and two together in the course of Kate's story. But the confirmation of what she suspected slid across her like an avalanche.

Her panic attack took hold once again, paralyzing her muscles and launching her stomach into full-blown nausea. She rose from her chair and stumbled to the kitchen sink, retching until Kate ran out to the back and hollered for the others to come inside.

Three women rushed in behind Clara as she lifted her head from the porcelain. She turned the faucet on, scooping tap water into her mouth and swishing. It was the most normal thing she could do.

Amelia and Megan twittered behind, shushing her and patting her back. Clara felt Kate's presence nearest her, murmuring assurances and rubbing Clara's neck.

"She must be in shock. Let's have her lie down." The voice, calm and deep, was a stranger's. And, apparently, her father's. Another wave of nausea filled her throat and she heaved again into the sink.

Kate continued rubbing her neck then directed orders to the others. "Get a glass for water. See if there's ice in the freezer. Pack it in a dish towel. Clear the parlor sofa."

It was an emergency. An actual emergency. "Take me to

the hospital," Clara wheezed from the sink. "Take me away from here. Away from all of you," she wheezed between heaves. Dramatics be damned, she couldn't handle the pain in her heart.

But the others just kept on shushing her, treating her like the baby she was. The baby she had always been.

MINUTES LATER, minutes that felt like hours, Clara lay prone on the sofa, alone now. Dust motes floated past her blank stare and down beneath her slack jaw, settling onto her blouse. A blouse she'd selected for its conservativeness and comfort. The perfect teacher's uniform. Boring and trusty. Just like Clara.

"Clara?" Kate's face appeared, cutting off rays of the setting sun as they pierced the parlor windows and cut across the younger one, allowing for her view of the twirling, whirling dust.

Clara blinked. "What?"

Kate squeezed herself onto the cushion. "Can we talk?"

"I don't know what to say."

"Well," Kate went on, her voice still trembly, "you must have some questions, right? Do you want to go over anything, or—"

At that, Clara tugged the ice-packed dish towel from her forehead and pulled herself to a sitting position. "You're my *mother*." It wasn't a question. Just a statement. But Clara wanted to test out the words. See how they felt. She swallowed and took in Kate's features. Her own features, in many ways. The blonde hair—kept up by highlights nowadays—the blue eyes and petite, aquiline features. Features that were also inherited from Nora. But now, Nora was dead. Her inheritance didn't matter anymore.

Kate nodded silently.

Clara glanced past her, toward the foyer. "Did Matt leave?"

"No. He's waiting."

"For what? To talk to me? Where has he been all these years, Kate? What happened between you two?" For some reason, their relationship felt more pertinent than their parenthood.

"Mom made us end it, of course. Clara, it was a major scandal. It was as big of a deal then as it feels to you now. You know? A shock?"

Clara's face softened. She sat up and crossed her legs beneath her, and Kate moved deeper into the sofa. A stale smell tickled Clara's nose, and she felt a sneeze coming on.

"God bless you," Kate said in reply to Clara's gaped mouth and subsequent spasm.

Clara couldn't help but giggle. Kate smiled.

"Kate, I'm so sorry," she whispered.

"Are you kidding? You have nothing to apologize for. That would be me. I'm the one who ought to say I'm sorry."

"But for what?" Clara answered.

Her older sister—or whoever Kate was to Clara—hesitated for a moment, gathering her thoughts before replying, it appeared. "Clara, I bent to Mom's will very easily. Especially back then. I felt like I didn't have a choice. Coming back here as a mother would have been hard. And, even if I was up to the task, things might have been different for all of us, you know?"

"How?" Clara pressed, desperate to know anything else that would help her paint a truer picture of her childhood—the one that felt so much less like a childhood. If Kate had raised her, would she have had playmates? Would Ben and Will be obnoxious little brothers she shooed away from her bedroom? "Oh," Clara added, upon finishing the thought.

"I would have had nothing to offer you. Matt and I couldn't have made it work, not financially. And... I never would have met Paul, probably." Kate closed her eyes for a moment.

Clara interrupted. "I still can't believe it. It feels... *unreal*." She lifted a hand and pressed it to Kate's arm. Her sister—*her mother*—felt older beneath her fingers. Her skin felt different. She even seemed to smell different. Everything, in the blink of an eye, had changed. "It still doesn't explain the will," Clara said flatly. "If Mom—er, *Nora*, I guess, *adopted* me, then I should still get one-fourth. Just like I always thought. I should still be her daughter, right?"

Kate swallowed hard, her eyebrows falling low and her voice dropping. "I think you need to read the diary entry."

December 1992

I lied to my daughters.

There, I've written it. I can't say it. I won't say it. I will never say it.

I was not going to commit to paper the events of the past year. I was dedicated to keeping the secret. Let me be clear: I am still dedicated to this secret. But you know how secrets go! They fester like blisters, desperate for someone to come along and poke at them until they bleed.

I won't let anyone poke, but I have to confess somewhere. To someone.

I did not file the paperwork.
I did not adopt Baby Clara.

THIRTY-SEVEN

KATE

They were all together, sitting at a large weather-worn table on the back porch, sipping from glasses of lukewarm soda. Two boxes of delivered pizza flapped open and closed to the rhythm of the breeze. Kate studied her glass. It was one of the many she'd known as a child, growing up among the heirlooms left to them in the house on the harbor. Hannigan heirlooms.

Amelia and Megan were the only two with any appetite left, but it was with deference that they nibbled on their slices, chatting quietly to themselves while Matt and Clara cracked open the lengthy process of getting to know each other.

Their words were stilted, to be sure, awkward, even. But Kate saw the flecks of hope in Matt's eyes, flecks she'd seen when she'd first told him she was pregnant. Flecks that died off when Nora had turned him away, time and again, from their door in the days and weeks—and then even years—after the news.

Did Kate and Matt ever meet in secret? No.

They never met again, in fact. It was too painful. That

she carried his child when she and Matt were both only children was too much for the teenage girl to bear.

Instead, Kate finished school, graduating quietly among the rest of her class then heading to college where she would meet Paul; safe, dependable Paul. From there, life settled into place, happy distractions cropping up one after another as if to reassure Kate that she had moved on. That she *could* move on.

But Kate Hannigan *never did* move on. Yes, she grew accustomed to knowing Clara as her sister, but it was always and painfully an act, a fact that she had to force herself to digest and learn and apply, much like a newly wedded woman must digest and learn and apply her married name. And yet, Kate wasn't a newly wedded woman, excited to change her name. She was a mother thwarted. Jilted, even.

Now, she knew that that's exactly what Nora had left Kate in her will—a silent inheritance—a jilting.

At first, back when they were still inside on the sofa together, once Clara came around, Kate thought it best that everyone go home and call it a day. They could address the remainder of the estate and the fallout from the news another time, when they'd be better able to handle it.

Clara had protested, however. She had no one to talk to, after all. She needed her *sisters*, she'd claimed.

And that's when they agreed that Wendell Acton had always been right. They could still be sisters. They could leave it alone. Let go and let God.

So, there they sat, Kate, Amelia, Megan, and Clara. Still sisters. Nothing more. Nothing less.

AFTER ANOTHER SLEEPOVER in Clara's cramped

quarters at The Bungalows, Kate awoke early, much earlier than the others. The predawn morning hummed outside Clara's window.

Kate admired the place. It had the charm of the 1920s and the comfort of living in community among others. She knew that Clara wasn't very social, much like her.

Quietly, she poured herself a chilled glass of water and slipped out onto the back patio and tucked herself onto the wicker seat. The courtyard needed a little work. Flowers. A good raking. But Kate wasn't bothered. She wasn't upset with Clara. She knew that Clara had long been living under a state of oppression, and it was time that she did a better job of helping her.

All three of them could do a better job. So, Kate decided they'd have a final family meeting. At the house on the harbor again, this time without Matt.

Yet, Kate had to see him again. She couldn't sleep the night before. She couldn't move on without some sort of closure... or *something* with Matt.

Nervous, she pulled her phone from her pajama pocket where she'd slipped it first thing when she rolled out of bed.

She moved to her text messages and shuffled into her exchange with Matt. So far in the past day, their messages were terse and business oriented.

It was early, very early, but she couldn't wait. And if it woke him, oh well. Tapping out another terse, brief message, Kate asked if Matt could meet her and hit send, drawing her finger to her mouth and nibbling on a sharp hangnail as she slid the phone back into her pocket.

Mentally, she began preparing for the meeting they would have as sisters. The "Who Gets What" meeting that had been dangling over them for going on two weeks now, in effect. Kate had a sense of what she'd like to see happen, but then again it was not quite her place to dictate the matter.

A vibration tickled her thigh. Like a cowgirl, Kate whipped the phone out and held the screen to her face.

Matt.

Her heart skipped a beat.

She tapped the message open and read and reread his words. He hadn't slept either. He'd love to meet. She could name the place and time, and he would be there.

Swallowing, she responded with the location and the time. *The house on the harbor. Now.*

THERE WERE NO FERRIES, but Matt had a boat. He could have docked it at the house, if the Hannigan dock were in any decent shape, which it was not.

Once Kate arrived at the house, she immediately regretted it. Thinking that, instead, she could have walked to the marina.

Hesitating at the front door, it occurred to her that she still had time. She could walk there. Surprise him. Then, they could walk back to the house—or even wherever they wanted to go. Anywhere in Birch Harbor.

She spun on a heel and, for the first time in a long time, followed her heart instead of her brain.

Morning was settling over the harbor, and the warm glow of the sun thawed Kate's hardness. A smile even pulled at her face when she saw Matt, there at his slip, tying off his boat and carousing with the few others who were on the dock so early.

It was hard to avoid drinking in the sight of him. Khaki shorts gave way to tanned, taut calves. His polo hung loose around his torso, but with each jerk of the rope, his shoulder blades cut through the light fabric, revealing a fit upper half.

Kate tucked a strand of her hair behind her ear and ran her tongue across her lips. She'd been limited in primping, but she felt good about herself. Healthy. Plain but pretty. It's how she felt when she was in Birch Harbor. Like herself.

She felt like a spy, watching him from a close distance without his consent. But then, as he strode up the dock, his sun-kissed face turning away from the men he'd just waved to, he saw her.

A broad grin spread across his face. Kate thought she saw the shape of her name part his lips.

"Matt," she whispered, slowly striding toward him. "Hi," she said once they met on the sidewalk that would carry them up and down Harbor Avenue.

"Hi," he replied, scratching the back of his head, his hair flopping over his forehead in a boyish mop. "Good morning," he added, smiling again.

"Good morning. Thanks for meeting me."

"How's Clara?" His face turned solemn and he dipped his chin, searching her eyes for a good answer. The right answer.

But there was no right or wrong anymore. Not since the truth came out. There was only *now*. "We talked a lot last night," she answered him. "She's... hurt. She doesn't understand why we never told her. I'm starting to wonder the same thing myself."

He nodded then said, "Let's go for a walk, okay?" She agreed and they strode side by side in the direction of the house on the harbor. "You know, Kate," he went on. "Lots of families have secrets. Some of them are way worse than yours."

Intrigued by his attempt to reassure her, Kate glanced Matt's way. "Oh yeah? Do the Fiorillos have skeletons in their closets, too?"

Chuckling, he replied, "Maybe. Well, yes. I do. My family doesn't know about Clara, for one. Not even Viviana." He slowed to a stop and licked his lips, his hands shoved deep in his pockets.

Frowning, Kate stopped too and faced him. "I'm sorry," she said. "I'm sorry about that."

Matt shrugged half-heartedly. "Can I tell them now?"

Caught off guard by this, she blinked. "Do you *want* to?"

He pushed air out of his mouth and shook his head. "It's *all* I've wanted to do. Do you know how hard it is to live in the same town as your daughter and never... " He faltered, searching for words that she could have filled in for him.

And, she did. "You mean do I know hard it is to live in the same *house* as your daughter and be forced to pretend that I didn't give birth to her? Why, yes. I know that feeling quite well."

Matt flushed a deep red, his jaw working as he licked his lip and twisted his head side to side slowly, uncomfortably. "Kate," he whispered, pulling his hands from his pockets and running his fingers through his hair before pinning her with a sad look. "I'm sorry. I didn't mean—"

"It's fine," she replied, compassion filling her voice. "I shouldn't have thrown it back in your face like that." She regretted being harsh with him. Swallowing, she jutted her chin back up the road. He took her cue and they resumed their stroll. "I guess we both know what it feels like."

"You're the one who carried her," he pointed out.

"You're the one who stayed here," she shot back as they neared the house.

Matt's eyebrows drew together above the bridge of his nose and, catching her entirely by surprise, he grabbed Kate's hand in his and squeezed it hard. They now stood on the other side of the stout, white fence. Kate suddenly couldn't tell if she was fifteen again or not.

He cleared his throat. "Are *you* going to stay this time, Kate?"

She fell away from him half a step, dizziness clouding her vision. It was a thought she'd considered for some time. Returning to Birch Harbor. To her sisters.

To... Matt?

"I'm not sure," she answered, finding her footing and straightening. "Maybe. I don't know what we're doing with the properties." As she said it, she remembered his initial interest. The notion of Matt Fiorillo buying her family home had felt sour before, but now it didn't. Now, it made sense. It was a way for him to connect with Clara. And, with Kate. "Did you... did you still want to buy this?" She waved a hand up at the towering home.

He shook his head. "I don't think so. I have other projects going on, and I'm away from Vivi enough. Mostly, I was curious. I figured I'd see what you all planned to do. What would happen, you know?"

"Matt," Kate asked, crossing her arms over her chest. "Did you know that our mom was going to reveal the secret or something? Is that why you poked your head in?" She said it with a smile, but the accusation hung in the morning air like a missile.

"No, no, no." Matt held his hands up in defense. "I never knew she'd tell you. I figured she *wouldn't*. Your *dad* on the other hand... "

Kate's eyes grew wide. "What do you mean my *dad*?"

He muttered a swear and bit down on his lower lip.

"Listen, no. I mean, I took your dad as the type who might have said something. I tried to talk to both of them, Kate. When you were in Arizona, I went to your dad. But he didn't know what to say to me. That's the impression I got. He was confused, I guess. He didn't know how to handle the whole thing. Especially your mom."

Propping her hands on her hips, Kate frowned. "He didn't know how to handle my mom?"

"Yeah, I mean... your dad was a nice guy. I didn't want to come between them or interfere with the 'plan,'" he threw up air quotes.

"What 'plan?'" Kate mimicked him.

"To keep your secret. To keep the town from knowing that Nora Hannigan's daughter got pregnant by some Italian kid." He laughed nervously.

Kate frowned. "You think my parents didn't like your family?"

Matt blew out a sigh, rubbing his eyes with his fists. "Your mom didn't like that you got pregnant. And I'm the one who did that to you. I think she saw me as a... perpetrator or something. The bad guy."

Shaking her head, Kate replied, "She didn't think you were a bad guy. She thought I was an embarrassment."

"It was a hard thing," Matt agreed at last. "Your dad went easy on me though. I remember coming here" he lifted his chin up to the house. "I knocked. I was so nervous about what he'd say. If he'd punch me in the face or what. But he wasn't even home. I ran into him at the hardware store a day later and he shook my hand and *apologized*. He *apologized*, Kate."

"Why?" she asked, her face crumpling at the memory Matt offered. The memory someone had of her father. The father who left them in the midst of their tragedy, never to be heard from again. His whole existence and disappearance shrouded in some horrid small-town mystery.

"I'm not sure. He just said he felt bad about how things were unfolding. He said he knew what I was going through. But you know what else he said?"

"What?" she whispered, a breeze brushing her hair across her face.

"He told me not to give up."

A sob escaped Kate's mouth and her shoulders rounded in. He caught her and pulled her into him, holding her tightly in place. Keeping her together.

She felt Matt's lips press against her head, and she took him in and everything he said. That her father was rooting for them. That her father was the sort of guy who would have loved Kate no matter what happened. That whatever happened to Wendell Acton was not a reflection of Kate's pregnancy or Clara's birth.

And, she realized that Matt made good on his word.

He hadn't given up, and he never would.

"I'm going to stay, too," she murmured into his neck.

Matt gently pushed her away, searching her face earnestly. "In Birch Harbor?" he asked.

Fresh tears dried along her cheeks as she nodded. "Yes. Somewhere here. In Birch Harbor. Near Clara. Near *you*."

THIRTY-EIGHT
CLARA

After coffee, Amelia, Megan and Clara walked down the road to meet Kate at the house. Wednesdays were late starts for teaching planning and meetings, but Clara had nothing scheduled, and so it was her prerogative to spend the morning tending to her family business.

Kate had texted that she was meeting Matt. Their reunion felt odd to Clara, but she was glad they might come to some sort of resolution. Closure, maybe.

Then again, closure wasn't exactly the result when someone broke open a long-held secret. In fact, quite the opposite. Now that Clara knew what she knew, they all needed a fresh start. A place to begin again, rather than a place to end.

A safe place.

Itching to get out of the apartment and away from her sisters, Clara nearly asked to spend the morning alone. But that wouldn't do. She was torn between needing privacy and support. Mostly, she wanted answers. Always the planner, Clara needed to know *what would happen next*.

They walked in silence. Amelia and Megan offered

their respect by withholding their casual observations and general flightiness.

Once to the house, Clara's stomach churned in unrest.

She glanced around, attempting to locate evidence that Kate and Matt had engaged in some sort of indecency there. It was all she could picture: the woman formerly known as her sister with the man formerly known as a stranger. But once the trio passed through the gate and headed toward the house, Kate appeared in its doorway, alone, her face awash in morning light.

"Let's grab breakfast. I think we'll handle this better with a healthy dose of carbs by the dock. Sound good?" Kate was all but beaming. It was hard not to catch her happiness, even in light of the hard days behind them.

Amelia and Megan looked at Clara, clearly deferring to her judgment. She grinned back. "Sounds great."

"DO WE NEED THE LAWYER HERE?" Amelia asked, lifting an eyebrow at the others as they sipped on fresh brewed coffee from the deli while awaiting their toasted bagels.

Clara looked at Kate for the answer. The latter lifted her shoulders. "I think we need to decide who wants what, first. Then, we can take that to Michael and contest the estate. Or, if we can all agree on something else, then maybe... oh, jeez. I really don't know."

Clara was hoping to save time where she could in order to make it to first period on time. "I printed these out," she said, passing around a neat page that listed each property, the items indicated by the will, and other significant mementos she'd like to address.

The others took a minute to study her handout.

Finally, Megan lifted her head. "The biggest thing is the house on the harbor. It's not in the will, so it should be liquidated and split among the three of us, technically. But if we contest, we split the proceeds among all four. We can still contest, right, Kate? On the grounds that we were under the belief that Clara was adopted?" Megan didn't mince words, and Clara found herself to be glad of that.

Kate nodded. "From what I read online, we can contest and might have a case. The diary entry would be proof, and Michael himself was witness to it. Plus, Matt can testify—is that the right word? Well, he can *testify* that he signed off on some document about giving up parental rights just like I did. We didn't know she never took those documents anywhere. We didn't know that she shredded them up, or whatever. We were just kids."

"Right," Amelia replied, taking a deep breath.

The bagels arrived, but each woman set hers aside in favor of the business at hand.

"So, do we sell the house on the harbor?" Megan asked again, this time eyeing each sister in turn.

Amelia shrugged.

Clara swallowed.

Kate answered, "No. I don't think so. I know it needs some work, but there's too much history there. We have to keep it."

"Who's going to take care of it?" Megan asked.

Kate lifted a hand. "I will. I'll take care of it."

"You don't live here, Kate," Amelia reasoned. "It'll just fall to Clara again."

A thin line formed on Clara's mouth. "I'm sorry," she interjected defensively.

"No, no," Amelia replied. "I don't mean to say you can't

handle it. I mean it's not fair that we always default to you. It's time you get your way a little here, girl. We all agree that you've been Mom's punching bag for way too long. Don't you see that, too?"

Warmth flooded Clara's chest, and she nodded. "Yes. Actually, yes. I think I'd like to have my way." A small laugh followed, and Kate reached over and squeezed her shoulder.

"Okay then. So, Kate. If you don't live here, we need to seriously consider another option. I mean if I were to move back to Birch Harbor—which I'm not—I wouldn't want it. It's huge and *so* not me."

"You're thinking about moving back here, aren't you?" Megan deadpanned.

Amelia seemed to hem and haw, finally throwing her hands up. "I don't know! Maybe. But even if I do. I won't live there. Too creepy." She looked past them towards the house on the harbor.

"Megan," Clara said, "you like creepy stuff. Do you want the house?"

Megan shook her head. "No. I want to downsize, if anything. You know, simplify. Streamline. All that."

"Then?" Clara replied, looking at Kate, finally.

"I'll take it." Kate said at last. "I'll take care of it. I'll move here, and I'll take care of it."

The three others glanced at each other.

Megan spoke first. "But how do we split it evenly, then?"

Kate cleared her throat, an answer already appearing to form on her tongue. Clara leaned forward.

"Mom left one property for each of the three of us, right? The Bungalows, the farmland, and the cottage. And now, we have the house on the harbor to split. I think each of us gets one property. The house is easily the most valuable. We can discuss ways for me to pay each of you out. The Bungalows brings in income, though. The farmland, of course, is undeveloped. We might have to get creative, but a starting point is to assign a property to each one of us."

A silence filled the table. Clara looked down, furrowing her eyebrows nervously as she picked the skin around her nails. She wasn't included in the will. She was at their mercy.

"I think Clara picks first," Megan said at last.

The other three whipped their heads to Megan.

Amelia nodded slowly, her eyes lighting up. "Clara has had the short end of the stick all of her life. She had to deal with Mom alone the longest. And she has had to deal with the trauma of being left out. I agree. Clara picks first."

Clara's heart pounded against her chest wall. Her cheeks felt warm. She began bobbing her knee up and down beneath the table as she looked at Kate.

Kate smiled. "That works for me. Clara, what do *you* want?"

After a beat, Clara answered, "I'd like to have the cottage, if that's okay?"

She glanced around. Something passed between Amelia and Megan, something unreadable.

Kate cleared her throat. "I'm fine with that. What about you two?"

Amelia licked her lips. Megan looked away then back.

"I'll take the land, then," Amelia replied, furrowing her brow.

"What are you going to do with farmland?" Megan asked, scoffing.

"What is any one of us going to do with anything? That's the real question," Kate piped in.

Amelia answered, "Are you getting the house or is Brian? I feel like that's relevant here."

Megan winced and took a sip of her coffee. "I don't technically need a place to live. Brian said I can have the house if I want it. Either that or we sell and split the profits. Kind of like in this scenario."

Clara cringed. It was starting to feel like life was a series of transactions. Negotiations. Agreements where two or more people split a candy bar in half down the middle. But when they got to see their half, it was less than they wanted to begin with. So, no one really got their way.

"Sorry, Megan," Clara whispered. "I bet that's hard."

Megan shrugged. "Yeah. It is. I'm not sure what to do. Either way, you can have the cottage, Clara. You deserve it." Megan reached across the table and covered Clara's hand in hers.

Kate broke in. "What about The Bungalows? Megan, would you want them? Then you have a place to stay, you know, if you need one?"

Megan shook her head. "I'm not a fix-it-upper type. I'm more like Clara that way." She winked at Clara, who was starting to wonder if her "sisters" weren't as distant as she'd always known them to be. Were they acting more like aunts? Had they always acted like aunts? Clara shook the thought, instead focusing on what she knew to be true: they were sisters. Always had been. Always would be.

"How about you, Amelia? You might be good at being a landlady," Kate suggested.

Amelia flashed a smile. "I've got Lady Macbeth," she replied, lifting her palms and her shoulders in a flourish.

"Do you?" Megan asked.

"Well, I certainly hope so. And if I don't, then... "

"Then what?" This time it was Clara who pressed.

Clara looked up to Amelia, often enamored of and amazed by her flawless people skills. Her aptitude with audiences and her boisterous, pleasant demeanor at any hour of the day or night.

Amelia considered Clara's question, pressing a finger to her lips and thinking. "If I don't get the role, then I don't know what I'll do. But it won't be living in a four-plex, patching drywall and planting flowers. That's not me," she answered at last.

"Okay," Kate reasoned. "No one has to live there I guess... "

"Wait a minute," Amelia interjected, her eyes lighting up. The others looked at her with hesitant interest. "I... if it comes down to who is getting what, well then... I might like to have a place to stay when I come here, you know?"

"So you want to have a unit available for you as a, what? Vacation rental?" Megan asked, throwing a sidelong glance at Amelia.

Amelia started to protest but Kate shushed her, waving her hand over the food. "Wait a second, wait a second. That's a great idea. We *should* all have a place to stay when we visit. Or, I guess when *you* visit, since it seems Clara and I will be locals." She lifted one corner of her mouth conspiratorially at Clara, who was a little lost. Clara was content to host any of her sisters wherever she lived. Why add a complication?

Kate continued. "We have enough property to offer something more. We could become a business in town. We could have space for Amelia and Megan, and Ben and Will, and Sarah... even Jimmy if we ever decide to let him come back," she added as a joke.

But the others didn't laugh. Their eyes widened at the prospect. A Hannigan sister enterprise. Clara could see the idea percolating in their eyes. Still, Clara didn't want any part of it, really.

"I'm not sure. I don't think I'd make much of a hostess," she offered lamely.

"You've got the cottage. You can just stick to that. But what if... what if Amelia, you take The Bungalows. It can pay for you to keep—to keep doing whatever it is you're doing in New York. I can help manage it here, and you can come to town when you're free to work on more major issues. It'd be a great project for you," Kate added in a sing-song voice.

Megan and Kate exchanged a knowing look, and Clara had the distinct feeling they were in cahoots on something, though what, she did not know.

Amelia frowned and chewed on a nail before replying. "How about this, if I don't get Lady Macbeth, then I'll take The Bungalows. It can be my consolation prize. I'll get to quit The Bread Basket, maybe. It could work," she said, a wry smile crossing her face.

"And Megan, what about you?" Clara offered, worried that things weren't turning out as fair.

"I'll take the land. Worst case scenario, I can sell it for a little profit. But it sounds like Brian is going to be more flexible than I first thought."

"Well," Kate jumped in. "I have an idea that will help all of us moneywise. Separate from The Bungalows' rental income."

"Okay?" Clara asked, feeling outside of their plan still.

"The house on the harbor. We can open a bed and breakfast. I'll run it. I'll keep a room open for whenever you two come to town—or anyone else we want to put up."

"Are you sure?" Megan asked.

Amelia echoed the sentiment. "That's a lot to offer, Kate. Is this all as fair and square as we'd like?"

"Clara gets the cottage and is relieved of her property management duties. I get the house and turn it into an... an inn! And share profits. They won't be much, so don't get too excited. The Bungalows, that's the only piece of the puzzle that's missing. It's a lot of work for me to take that on without getting paid... "

Clara let out a sigh. Nothing felt manageable—*or* fair, she realized. She needed to step up and help. "I don't need the cottage yet. I can stay at The Bungalows for as long as it takes to settle this," she offered helpfully.

Amelia smiled at her, but her face quickly fell into a frown.

"What's wrong?" Clara asked.

Setting her bagel down, she tugged her phone free from her purse. "My phone is buzzing. If it's Jimmy, I swear I'm going—" She stopped abruptly, her frown deepening as she studied the caller ID.

Clara stared on, but Kate rustled next to her, digging her phone out, too. Kate whispered to Clara, "Oh crap, look. I missed a call from Michael."

After briefly glancing at Kate's phone, Clara turned her attention to Amelia, who was now talking to someone in hushed, serious tones.

A moment later she hung up, her eyes flashing across the table. "It was the lawyer. Michael. He tried to call you, Kate," she fumbled a little, nervous for some reason.

"I know. I missed it. What did he say?" Kate pressed.

"He says there's something he needs to discuss with us. There's been a... an oversight."

THIRTY-NINE

KATE

"I'm terribly sorry. Terribly sorry. I don't know how this slipped by." Sharon stood in Michael's office, wringing her hands safely behind the protection of her receptionist's desk.

Michael, with his hands shoved in his pockets, faced the four of them in the waiting area.

"It's nothing legal. Nothing that can formally alter the conditions of the will like a contesting of the will," Michael warned them, his voice even. "I expect you'll still contest on Clara's behalf, correct?"

Kate waved a hand. "Yes, but... well, there's been an oversight there, too," she admitted, glancing at her sisters.

He cocked his head. "How so?"

Wondering if she should start or if she should press him to reveal his news, she looked to the others for help.

Amelia cleared her throat. "You go first, Michael."

He reached toward Sharon who fussed herself nearly into a fit, grabbing a generic yellow legal envelope. "Here. I just can't imagine the confusion you've suffered," she whined, her attention squarely on Clara.

Michael accepted the envelope and reached his hand inside. "You see, your mother left *four* notes, not just one." He winced a little as he said it and read over each page. "Won't you come back?"

Anxious now, and even excited, Kate motioned her sisters, and they followed Michael to his office, where just a couple days ago they'd first met as one big group. So much had seemed to happen in the interim. Stress and strife. Anxiety and the depths of pain and confusion.

And there was always the answer, there in the darn lawyer's office.

Then again, Kate felt certain that nothing they were about to see would rival the news from her own note.

"Honestly," Michael began, smoothing his tie as he lowered into his seat. "What happened was that Nora had left that yellow envelope with Sharon about a year ago. Apparently, your mother told Sharon to add the contents to her will without reading what was inside. You see," Michael shifted in his seat and cleared his throat.

Kate felt her hands gripping the arms of the chair unnecessarily. It was just paper. Just a note. Surely, there would be nothing *else* to say?

"You see," Michael repeated, fixing his stare on the envelope in his hand. "Sharon had removed just the one page—the one I gave you, Kate," he flicked a glance to Kate. "Since your mom never saw me or asked to open her estate and formally publish a revision, I figured it was a personal note that could be read by you," he looked at her again before his gaze wandered to the others.

They all nodded eagerly, desperate for what was to come.

"Before she threw out the envelope, Sharon dug inside and found three more notes, or pages, what you will." With that, he finally slid his hand out and with it, just as he'd claimed, three more pages—identical to the one Kate had read for herself. Her pulse slowed, and her jaw fell slack. Something like disappointment curled around her heart, but she pushed that down in order to tend to her excitement at what else could be lurking in their mother's private notes. Michael cleared his throat again. "Sharon had forgotten to give the other ones to me, because I was out of the office the day she found them. Well, today she happened to sort through her files and found them again." Michael passed the thin stack to Kate.

Not a single one was addressed to any of them, and no added notes appeared anywhere.

Kate swallowed and looked down the line of her sisters. "Here," she said, handing one page to each sister to read. Kate figured she'd had her own. Now it was their turn.

Forcing patience upon herself, she simply studied each sister, waiting. Waiting. Waiting for an expression of shock or heartbreak or realization, maybe.

Megan lifted her eyes first. "It's another diary entry all right," Megan declared. "Here, listen."

May 24, 1973

I DIDN'T THINK I'd be back here, writing in you. I figured my diary days ended when I was a teenager.

You'll be interested to know I've met someone. Well, I didn't just "meet" him. I was set up on a date, if you can believe that! You turn 24 and people start to wonder about you, I suppose. Yes, my mother arranged for me to have a picnic with Wendell Acton. His family is from Birch Harbor, too. But they keep to themselves. Wendell went to the Catholic school, not Birch Harbor High. I've seen him at church but nowhere else, really. His father runs the light-house up north of town. They're a little odd, but that's okay with me.

So, the picnic. Let me tell you about the picnic. It was pretty well perfect. We set out on the lake in Wendell's wooden boat, and he brought sandwiches and a thermos of cider to share. I have to confess, I figured I'd never meet a man I could tolerate.

Boy, can I tolerate Wendell. More than tolerate, in fact.

The real question is, how did my own mother figure Wendell for me? He isn't the sort she would have "pinned" for a daughter of hers. I'm not sure my father knows. Either way, supposedly she bumped into him when he was oiling the pews in the parish hall, and one thing led to another, and there I was, in a wooden rowboat on Lake Huron with this poor boy from the outskirts of town. It was like a scene from a storybook.

When we got back to land, we went for a walk into the woods. He held my hand. I'll never forget this, but we saw fireflies! Yes! The first of the season, right there in this little clearing.

And then, he asked me then and there to be his girlfriend. He said the fireflies were a "sign." I believe in signs, so I had to say yes.

Now here I am, a twenty-something with a beau. We'll see where this goes. Stay tuned!

MEGAN DROPPED the sheet to her lap, tears wedging

themselves into the corners of her eyes. "Did she ever tell us how they met?"

Kate shook her head. "Not that I remember. That's so sweet. She wanted us to have that." Each of them, now, was dabbing at their eyes over the innocent words of their mother. Words that had nothing to do with the will, but that she had to share with them, somehow, even in the throes of her disease.

"Did she tell Sharon why she dropped these off?" Kate asked Michael, gesturing to the other women and their pages.

He shook his head and lifted his palms. "I'm sorry, I don't think so. She was a little... a little confused, if memory serves."

A sadness washed over Kate, but she pushed it down, lifting her chin to Clara, instead.

"What does yours say, Clara?"

The youngest, who'd long ago begrudgingly called into work and requested sub coverage, cleared her throat. "This one seems more recent but there's no date, just a month. It seems like she was trying to... plan ahead or change the will. It's confusing. You're right, Michael. She seems... confused." Clara licked her lips and read through a trembling voice.

April

I'M PLANNING to visit the law offices today to make some changes and plans for the future. I don't know the law, and there's a good chance Clara will be left out entirely if I don't give them this here note that I'm writing.

Legally, no, I guess Clara is supposed to get nothing. Oh, the ways of the world. A girl cares for you and loves you and calls you mother and that means nothing to the powers that be.

Well, here I am to tell you, Mr. Lawyer, that you can rewrite the law. Give Clara whatever she wants. She can decide, okay? She's spent her whole life without that chance. I'm even the one to suggest she get her teaching credentials, after all.

Okay, now that we have that squared away, I'd like to add some other provisions. Please change it so the girls can't sell off the properties. I'd like to see them keep the four-plex as rental income. And they can build on the land and have a new home here. Maybe one of the girls needs a fresh start and I'm too busy to see which. Well whoever that is, grant it.

The harbor house must remain as it IS. But for the love of all things holy, don't turn it into a museum. I'd be humiliated to have people rummaging around in my childhood home like no one ever really lived there. That's what happens to these "homes" that turn into museums, you see. The visitors forget what they were truly meant to be. The House on the Harbor was meant to be slept in. With beds and a fridge full of food and a sink full of dishes. I'd have stayed there to keep it alive if it weren't for Wendell leaving us. After a while, a woman can't bear to live with her husband's ghost. So that's why I left for the cottage. I need privacy. I needed to be away from that burden and from the prying eyes of other people who carried their suppositions and held them over my head.

So I left that house.

But you better not, Hannigan girls.

Keep it occupied, dear girls. Please and THANK YOU!

That's not to say I like the idea of a museum, just not MY house.

One other item of business then I'll end. Matt Fiorillo came by the cottage yesterday. Truth be told that's why I decided to make this change at all. He asked me what would become of Clara, if you can believe that. Well, I suppose I can. Matt may be the boy who threw my life into chaos, but he's a good boy. He loves Clara, and he doesn't even know her. I suppose that means something.

So, anyway, here I am, at the behest of that meddling Matt Fiorillo, rewriting my will. I already did, though! I met that other lawyer, the one who left town, and I told him please be sure ALL OF MY DAUGHTERS are IN MY WILL!!! It was a big job, because I didn't have time to go over names and socials. He had to look it up himself. Who can trust these lawyers? Not me. So that's why I've penned this ADDENDUM. To see to it that my girls get their come-uppance, no thanks to you, MATT FIORILLO for your snarky suggestion.

KATE BELTED out a laugh at the final sentence. "I'm sorry," she said through tears. "I can't help it, but she never did like Matt. And only because of the pregnancy. She thought he did it on purpose or something." After a sniffle, Kate added, "It sounds like Mom was more confused than we realized."

Clara, Megan, and Amelia were weeping, but a few laughs made their way through. "It sounds like Matt wanted me to get something," Clara said at last, staring at Kate for an answer.

Kate nodded, shutting her eyes briefly and wiping the

rest of the wetness from her cheeks. "Of course he did. He's always loved you, Clara. Even when he couldn't show you."

Warmth seemed to return to Clara's cheeks, and Kate knew in that moment that it was all Clara needed. That slip of paper wrought by their mother's well-meaning hand. It was all the little one needed to feel safe in her family.

And, the note provided some more guidance. A plea from beyond the grave that would help them nail down everything they were struggling with.

"It sounds like our plan is on track with what Mom wanted," Kate pointed out, as the others composed themselves. Michael kept quiet, a soft smile filling his face.

"What is your plan?" he asked quietly.

"For starters, it seems like we need to fill that big heirloom on the harbor with people, don't you think, girls?" Kate asked her sisters, wondering if they agreed.

Each one nodded enthusiastically, but it was Clara who answered. "That's it!" she cried out. "The Heirloom on the Harbor!"

"What do you mean?" Megan asked.

Clara nodded excitedly, but Kate caught on fast. "What about... *The Heirloom Inn?*"

FORTY

AMELIA

After they'd settled on the name and even began twittering about with a plan—Kate moving back and acting as innkeeper, Clara pitching in after school, Megan joining on the weekends and maybe even bringing Sarah along to help with little repairs and painting projects—Amelia had an idea.

"We could hire Jimmy, you know," she suggested, her face clear and hopeful, but her heart held hostage by *something*. Their reaction?

No.

Her own dreams?

Maybe.

"Over my dead body," Clara declared, crossing her arms over her chest.

Amelia flushed. "We could tell him exactly what to do," she added weakly.

Kate gave her a stern look. "If there's one thing we have all learned this week, it's that Jimmy is a problem, not a solution."

Sighing deeply, Amelia couldn't help but flick a glance

to Michael. Talking about Jimmy in his presence felt... perverse, somehow. Like there was a matter of loyalty, and to even mention Jimmy's name was a sin.

A buzz tickled her leg. Thankful for any distraction, Amelia reached down into her purse to check who the text or call was from.

It was a text. From her agent. Rather, Mia, who was her pseudo agent. And friend.

"Oh my God," Amelia whispered.

"What?" Kate asked. "What is it?"

Amelia looked up, embarrassed. Humiliated. Horrified.

"Is everything okay?" Michael asked.

Willing herself not to totally lose it in front of him, she simply shook her head. "I didn't get Lady Macbeth."

Silence came in reply. Kate, who sat next to her, rubbed Amelia's back and pulled her in for a hug.

Megan uttered a quiet apology. Clara did the same.

Michael, the handsome, aloof lawyer, broke the silence. "Were you auditioning for a part in New York?"

Amelia could have sworn she heard something in voice. Was he... impressed?

She nodded to him, lamely.

"I'm sorry to hear. I actually sponsor our community theatre here in Birch Harbor. The Birch Players."

Whipping her head to him, she replied, "What? There was no community theatre when I lived here."

Amelia caught Clara's eyes light up, as she added, "Yes, there is. Some of our kids from the high school are involved in their productions. I think our drama teacher is the one who founded it."

Weakening at the news, Amelia overcame the urge to cry. "That's... cool."

"If you ever move back here, I can connect you,"

Michael offered. It was a curious thing to offer, in light of Amelia's own sister claiming a solid connection to the company of thespians.

She met his gaze, and a smile formed on her lips. He seemed to grow red, and Amelia smiled broader. "Thank you. Maybe we can... maybe we can exchange phone numbers?"

He nodded dutifully then cleared his throat.

Kate broke up their moment. "Amelia, the paper. Mom's diary entry. What does *yours* say?"

It was the briefest of the notes, and, initially, Amelia wondered why Nora Hannigan had left it at all.

But as her eyes danced over the words and her lips formed full sentences aloud, she came to life with the information.

An adventure.

A project.

April

I HAD A THOUGHT TODAY, but I'm not sure if I'll have time to find the answer. It's a big project, and it demands someone who is willing to go on a bit of an adventure—someone who isn't afraid of a project.

I never did find the deed to the lighthouse. In case I don't get to it, please have one of the girls go search for it.

As far as I know, it's part of their inheritance. The lighthouse on the lake, that is.

AMELIA'S EYES flashed up at her sisters and at Michael.

No one knew what to make of it.

"The *lighthouse*?" Kate asked, perplexed.

Amelia shrugged. "It was the Acton's, right? It belonged to Dad's parents."

"And it's where Dad stayed when we went to Arizona," Megan added.

Silence spread between the three of them. Amelia frowned. They'd arrived at so many answers in such a short span of time. Megan and her peculiar obsession with her phone. The mystery of whether Amelia would be the next Lady Macbeth. Hah.

Clara's absence from the will was the most tragic. The most upsetting. Clearly, poor Nora was in worse shape than any of them knew, and the associate Michael had hired back whenever Nora had gone in to make and adjustment wasn't able to offer much help. That besides, Sharon the receptionist was all but useless. Sweet, but useless. Fortunately, the solution was at hand.

"How will this affect our plan?" Megan asked, reading Amelia's mind.

Kate answered, "It doesn't. We're going to tackle the house on the harbor together. After that, we can start chipping away at the other properties. I'll take over on managing The Bungalows. If everyone agrees, still, Clara can help me start clearing the cottage, too. And then she can move in eventually." Kate dipped her chin and looked at Michael. "Maybe you can help us make sure that's on the up and up?"

He nodded, his face serious.

Clara glanced around, nibbling on her lower lip nervously.

Megan and Amelia patted her hands on either side of

her, and Amelia whispered, "The cottage is yours. We can start dealing with the other properties. *Together*."

A smile spread around the four women. Peace, at last. After a lifetime of tepid sisterhood made more complicated by a cutthroat, domineering mother, they shared a realization in that moment. Nora wasn't trying to be some evil queen. She was tending to a secret, and that secret nearly broke her, so much so that she tried to pick it open. She tried to set things right.

She was just a little too late.

Amelia felt a sob climb up her throat despite the new, tranquil energy. Or maybe, because of it.

Michael cleared his throat. "I don't want to overstep my boundaries, here, but... I can start looking into the lighthouse, if you four would like?"

Kate let out a sigh. "It's a big project," she answered, her smile fading as she stared across her sisters. "As far as we know, our father still has a claim to it. Wherever he is."

"I could help," Amelia offered, the lump in her throat sliding back down. She winked at Megan, lifted her dark hair off her neck, rolled her shoulders back and stared directly at Michael. "No boyfriend. No Lady Macbeth. I think I could use a *project*."

Find out what happens in Birch Harbor next. Order
Lighthouse on the Lake today.

ACKNOWLEDGMENTS

House on the Harbor was a joy to write and largely because of the wonderful people who lent their expertise. Lori Clarey, thank you so much for painting a picture of Pinconning and Tawas and Michigan in general. I love that we are coworkers in more ways than one, now!

From my early childhood into my early adulthood, I spent many summers in the suburbs of Detroit on up through to Frankenmuth and Mackinac. They are some of my fondest memories because of my close relationship with the Ruthenbergs and my enchantment with a place that had rain and grass and where the houses had basements and the countryside offered cherry picking. To my parents, thank you for driving Michael and me some two thousand miles to give us a view of our nation and a summer with our cousins. I'm sorry I was an irritated teenager for most of the road trip.

Thank you so much, Nina Johns, for your critical feedback. Your honesty and competence improved my writing not just for this book but for every other I will ever write. So glad I found you.

And thank you, Judy, for your wisdom. You're a true mentor to me.

My editor Lisa Lee, who read and reread this book—thank you! I feel like God drew us together. Your notes and our conversations made this story shine. And Krissy, you are a gem. Thank you for your help in proofreading and your sweet pep-emails. Dublin soon?

Finally and ever, my husband. My supportive and loving best friend, business partner, and sweetheart: I love you so much. Thank you for *everything*.

Mr. Magoo, always for you.

CPSIA information can be obtained
at www.ICGtesting.com
Printed in the USA
LVHW090724020421
683193LV00005B/38

PRAISE FOR

INTERNATIONAL BUSINESS EXPANSION

Anthony has written an entire encyclopedia of knowledge about building an international business. Comprehensive, covering all the variables that come into play, with a very positive sense for how to be successful at it. A must for the bookshelf of every company going global.

—JAMES G. ELLIS, Dean, Marshall School of Business,
University of Southern California

Whether you are strategizing about how to grow your business globally or just seeking insights to improve your international business, this book offers advice that only someone who's been growing businesses for 30 years can offer. A veritable roadmap for success in expanding to the global marketplace. Content rich and comprehensive.

—BRIAN E. CABRERA, Senior Vice President & General Counsel,
NVIDIA Corporation

Comprehensive, professional, practical – this book will be immediately useful, chapter after chapter. Crisply written, with recommendations that come from decades of experience on the front lines of international trade, country after country.

—JOHN L. NESHEIM, Professor of Entrepreneurship, Johnson School,
Cornell University & Author of bestseller High Tech Start Up

In his brilliant new book, Anthony Gioeli offers proven methods, instructive examples and asks provocative questions that enable entrepreneurs and business leaders to successfully launch their businesses overseas. The approach and steps articulated allow readers to introduce, develop and expand their company and business outside their home market. I highly recommend this book to business leaders who are looking to expand their addressable market overseas in a step by step way.

—JULIAN FOULGER, Swiss Mergers and Acquisitions, Company Director,
Luzern, Switzerland

Evaluating markets, customers, strategies and people are the key success factors in becoming a global player. Anthony defines all those factors using many case studies in this comprehensive book.

—HYOENG S. OK, Director of global sales and marketing,
Samsung Electronics and Display Co., Ltd.

As a partner of a venture capital firm that specializes in supporting start-up companies expanding into Asia, we deal with global expansion on a daily basis. Up to now, there has been little literature that provides more than just basic principles and guidelines. Now, based on his long career as an expansion practitioner, Anthony Gioeli offers a step-by-step manual of how to think about and actually execute on international expansion. The principles are well thought out and the required actions are explained in a simple and easy to understand format. I highly recommend this book to executives and educators who may teach this subject in the classroom.

    —JAY EUM, Co-Founder and Managing Director, Translink Capital

Everything a startup CEO needs to know before starting an international operation. I strongly recommend this book.

    —BOB HAWK, investor, former CEO of US West Multimedia Communications

If you are looking for a practical book with demonstrable guidance and actionable advice from someone who has a proven track record of international business success, then this is the right book for you. Well written and straightforward, Anthony explains how each business opportunity and country requires a unique and thoughtful approach. As a well-respected Silicon Valley high-tech executive, he writes from experience, punctuating each lesson with real "behind the scenes" stories that help the reader more fully appreciate his perspectives and process.

    —G CRAIG VACHON, Angel Investor and Entrepreneur

International Business Expansion

International Business Expansion

A STEP-BY-STEP GUIDE TO LAUNCH
YOUR COMPANY INTO OTHER COUNTRIES

ANTHONY GIOELI

Editor: Rick Benzel
Art Direction: Susan Shankin & Associates
Design: Tanya Maiboroda
Illustration: Cristian Voicu
Published by Over And Above Press
Over And Above Creative Group, Los Angeles, CA
www.overandabovecreative.com

First edition
Library of Congress Control Number: 2014915700
ISBN: 978-0-9890917-4-9

Printed in the United States of America

This book is dedicated to my wife, Monica,
and children, Francesco and Stephanie.
Thank you for your patience and dedication
over all these years of my globetrotting.
It would not have been possible
without your love and support.

Contents

Introduction

⎯⎯⎯⎯ ⦿ ⎯⎯⎯⎯

OVER THE LAST 30 YEARS, ADVANCES IN TECHNOLOGY, communications, and transportation have brought the world closer together. Innovations such as the Internet, jet aircraft, and wireless telephony have significantly lowered or even removed former barriers that hindered the flow of goods, capital, ideas, and people from one country to another. This process has entered a new word in our daily vocabulary: *globalization*. Today, international trade is no longer a luxury available to only Fortune 500 corporations. Companies of all sizes can easily take advantage of globalization and quickly become multinational organizations.

The importance of international markets will continue to grow. While the United States has the largest economy in the world, today its share of global GDP is down to 22% as other nations expand trade. And while the US GDP will continue to expand, its portion of the global economy will keep on shrinking. Over the next 20 years, we can expect the US GDP to fall to only 10 to 15% of the global economy.

The message is: the future is in international trade. By not expanding internationally, you will likely severely limit your business opportunities. For a US company, ignoring international markets means overlooking between 80% and 90% of the potential economic opportunity for growth. If you are a non US-based company focused only on your domestic market, the opportunity loss is even greater!

Coupled with the increasing and more predictable global demand, the time is right for you to embrace international expansion.

Let's clarify an important distinction. An international company offers products in multiple countries but does not have a legal presence outside of its home market. A multinational company is one that has operations and a legal presence in more than one country.

To maximize your company's benefit from globalization, you must go beyond being international and become a multinational corporation. Chances are that some of your competitors are already either global today or will be within the next half decade. If you do not plan to expand to multinational operations, you run the risk of going out of business, as you may no longer have the scale to compete against larger competitors that operate across national boundaries and time zones.

Depending on both your sales opportunities and your company's core competencies, different countries may represent better opportunities than others. Personally, I favor having operations closer to my largest customers. So if your greatest opportunities for sales are in China or Russia, it is best set up sales and support offices in those markets. For example, if you are developing products for mobile phone or computer manufacturers, greater China—defined as China, Hong Kong and Taiwan—is an ideal place to set up an office as more than 50% of all electronic goods are manufactured in those markets.

For product development and back-office support, you should seek locations where there are core competencies that match your needs. For example, if you are primarily focused on software development, countries such as Bulgaria, Romania, Ukraine, Brazil and India would be very good places to set up an R&D center as those locations have an abundance of extremely talented and reasonably priced software engineers. If you manufacture simple goods, such as non-electronic household items, then Southeast Asia, Central America, and southern Africa would be good markets for expanding your manufacturing organization. For more technically challenging products, China, Mexico, and Thailand are ideal locations to create high-tech assembly operations.

By 2025, it seems likely that more than 70% of successful companies with sales greater than $10 million will be multinationals with a dedicated presence in at least one other country outside their home nation. Over 50% of multinationals will have offices in at least three of the following continents: Africa, Asia, Australia, Europe, and South America. Without a global presence, your company may end up being squeezed out of the market.

Who This Book Is For

International Business Expansion: A Step-by-Step Guide to Launch Your Company Into Other Countries is intended to help you capitalize on these future opportunities. With a little bit of planning, companies of all sizes, including start-up organizations, can quickly become multinationals. As long as you are already generating revenue at home, setting up operations in foreign countries has never been easier.

This book is thus for business leaders who want to explore the potential value of expanding their business internationally, but are not sure how best to achieve this. Whether you are proactively looking for growth or reacting to competitive pressure, it's time to do something for the long-term success of your business.

International Business Expansion will help you make intelligent, well-structured, strategic decisions as you expand your business. It provides step-by-step guidelines for:

- researching which markets to enter and when,
- setting clear and realistic goals that take into account the uniqueness of each market,
- evaluating various market entry options for both immediate and long-term expansion,
- financially modeling your international business, as ways of doing business differ by country, and

■ growing your global business long-term so you can achieve more than just a one-time increase in revenue growth.

My Background in International Business

I have over 25 years of experience managing fast growth high technology companies. My specialization is building and leading global organizations. I have served as President & CEO of three US-based technology companies: CloudTC, Inc., Atrua Technologies, Inc. and AirPrime, Inc. Two of the companies (CloudTC and AirPrime), were acquired by foreign corporations, and the third generated over 80% of its business overseas. I have also served as a division General Manager at Xircom, and as VP of Sales, Marketing and Business Development at several companies in the technology industry that were headquartered in North America, Europe and Australia. In my most current position, I am CEO of a company based in Switzerland. Earlier in my career, I worked at large multinational corporations including AT&T, Compaq Computer Corporation (acquired by Hewlett Packard) and IBM in various roles in engineering, marketing, finance, and sales.

Throughout my career, my focus has been on international business. Some of my activities have included setting up an R&D center in China; opening up sales and support offices in Belgium, Germany, Japan, Singapore, South Korea, Taiwan, and the UK; establishing joint development agreements with companies in Bulgaria, India, Romania, South Korea, and Taiwan; and forming strategic partnerships with companies in Africa, Asia, Australia, Europe, North America, and South America. My educational background consists of earning a BSEE from New York Institute of Technology and an MBA in finance from the University of Southern California.

Overview of the Chapters

International Business Expansion: A Step-by-Step Guide to Launch Your Company Into Other Countries is structured into four main parts.

While each section expands on what was previously covered, the book has been written so that you can jump to any section and be able to read it independently.

In Part 1, *Which Markets to Enter,* you will learn how to analyze each individual market. This is a critical first step, because you need to do the right research and determine which markets to enter based on facts and data, not emotions. Within this section, we will start by understanding how to size up an opportunity and recognize the unique dynamics of each market. Then we will learn about the various business climate issues you need to consider. The next chapter looks at competition: who are your competitors, how are they positioned and what are their strengths. Another key item to consider when determining which market to enter is possible partnerships you could form, as well as the state of your industry's ecosystem within that market. The final chapter of this section discusses how you can leverage your existing relationships to help you successfully enter a market.

In Part 2, *Market Entry Options,* we review the different ways you can enter a new market, and how best to evaluate these options for your business. We'll start with the most straightforward entry option and grow in complexity with each chapter of this section. For example, we'll examine the pros and cons of partnering with a master distributor to enter a market. We'll discuss hiring "local agents" in a country. Next we'll look at what it takes to set up a local sales and support office. It is important that you have a plan for not just generating sales, but supporting customers in each market.

Things get more interesting as we move on to examine how to set up an R&D center overseas. Depending on your product, this can be very tricky, especially if you have proprietary intellectual property that may need to be transferred. That chapter is followed by deciding if licensing your product or technology to enter a foreign market makes better sense. In some cases, local entities are so well entrenched that competing with them head to head may be too difficult. We conclude this section by looking at whether forming a joint venture could be your best alternative to enter a particular market.

In Part 3, *Financial Considerations*, we get down to nitty-gritty money issues, such as what are the cash implications to your business of being a multinational entity. We start by examining costs, specifically, what operating costs you should model for your international business. Each country has its own set of regulations and business practices that must be understood before you enter that market. Then we examine sales forecasting. In some markets, the sales cycle is longer than we are used to in the US, so you need to understand how to plan properly for delayed income. We then look at currency risk: how to plan for fluctuations and what contingencies to put in place. Finally, there is cash flow management. Each market operates differently and traditions are impossible to change. In some countries, for instance, customers pay up front, but in others, you may expect 90 to 120 days before payment. Receipt of payments will clearly impact your business, and so you must understand the rules before you finalize your financial model for each country.

Part 4, *Growing Your International Business*, takes off from the moment you have decided which markets to enter and how best to enter them. We discuss how to plan to maintain your growth beyond the initial success of your market entry. For example, you may need a plan to maintain visibility in a market, including having a strong personal presence. We also look at localization—such as the best ways to localize your sales and support functions given business models in other countries. For example, if you are an American company, structuring your sales and support in Japan to replicate what works for you in the US will not be successful.

Another chapter on localization addresses your products and services, focusing on any customization that might be required. Depending on your product, you may need to change its look or functionality in order to be successful in a particular country. The same goes for translating your documentation, where word-for-word is seldom enough. Finally, we talk about you—the owner, CEO or executive sponsor of internationalization—addressing what you must do to network and localize *yourself* in a given market. Regardless of the team you build locally, your image as the top person from headquarters is influential. We therefore provide suggestions for how to adapt your business style in each market in order to earn the trust of your customers and partners.

In the Conclusion, you will find a valuable set of resources and suggestions to move forward. We examine whether your planning and strategy needs to change depending on whether you are selling goods, providing services, or offering online software.

I have also included two Appendices. The first is a compilation of questions to consider from each of the chapters in the book. These "checklists" are provided so you can easily go through the entire process of analyzing and entering a foreign market. Too many times, in the rush and excitement to move forward with a plan, key factors are overlooked that greatly impact the success of a business plan. I've found using a checklist to be helpful in ensuring important considerations are not ignored. Finally, I offer you a short additional resource list that you can leverage for obtaining more detailed information about entering a specific country.

After Reading This Book

Once you have completed this book and are ready to get started, your first steps should include strategizing with your accounting and law firms. They are hopefully good resources to help you both understand the unique aspects of each country and structure your multinational intentions for maximum benefit.

In addition, I suggest you contact the trade office of your country's embassy in the nations in which you wish to establish a presence. Trade offices are a great resource to help businesses navigate and plan their initial market entry into that country. There are also many trade organizations that can be helpful. Please see my website, www.goglobalbusiness.com, for some recommendations.

You will need patience and a budget to proceed. Depending on the size of your staff and other company projects, it can take anywhere from two to six months to complete all the steps outlined in this book. Then, depending on the country you want to enter, it can take, on average, another three to six months to establish your local business.

International expansion requires some capital up front. From planning through execution, it can take anywhere from $10,000 to $100,000, depending on the amount of outside legal, accounting, and other assistance you need and the complexity of your particular business. For example, establishing a sales presence can be done in two to three months at a cost of $10,000, while setting up a full R&D center can take six to nine months at a cost of $50,000 to $100,000.

Let's Get Started

By the end of this book, you will have the tools to create the vision, build determination, and plan your successful international expansion. You will be able to:

- analyze which markets to enter,
- determine the best ways to enter each market,
- forecast the impact of global expansion on your overall business,
- and plan continued international growth.

Remember, each business and situation is different. While I aim to provide accurate and specific advice in this book, you must create your own unique international blueprint specific to your business. If properly planned and executed, your global business expansion can be very profitable!

PART 1

WHICH MARKETS TO ENTER

CHAPTER 1

Opportunity and Market Size

So you've decided that expanding your business globally is the right move for your company. You want to become either an international company or a multinational. The first step is to decide which markets to enter and how to enter them.

While there are many large population centers throughout the world, some are better suited for an initial expansion than others. Not all markets are created equal, and there are many key factors to consider when deciding where and how to expand. When evaluating various countries, you need to take into account several important factors.

The first factor to assess is the need for your product in a particular country. Not all countries need the same goods. Before selecting where to expand, you must determine where there is "natural" demand for your specific products. The more historical and factual data you have, the better decision you will make.

Let's say you are trying to export an innovative, quick drying bathing suit. The need will be greater in countries that have warmer climates and higher concentrations of people near beaches. Such swimwear will sell better in Brazil than in Russia.

The next factor to assess is the disposable income of the potential buyers of your product. Even in some higher income countries, people have less disposable income to spend than you might think. What the local population deems as non-essential items may also differ among countries with high disposable incomes. For example, while Italy has a high GDP, certain areas of the country have much less disposable funds and may not be attracted to your product. For instance, if your company has developed an inventive high-end digital recorder for TVs, many parts of the country may not see this as essential and will not spend their disposable income on such a purchase. But, on the other hand, given that mobile phones are vital in many countries, even consumers in poor nations may deem purchasing the latest smartphone as essential.

You next need to look at whether there are any unique regulations in the country that can diminish or alter your ability to sell your product. Just because you are successful in your home market does not mean your product can be sold or distributed the same way overseas. Each country has its own regulations that you need to understand before deciding whether to enter its market. For example, I ran a company that developed unique, high-end Internet phones for voice-over-IP (VoIP) telephone service. While China business users had a need for the product and the means to purchase it, the government forbids VoIP services and thus our market opportunity did not exist. By talking to industry contacts early in our evaluation process, we avoided spending time and resources on planning a market entry that would not have been successful.

The competitive landscape is another key factor to consider. Understanding the competitive environment in your target market is critical when you devise your entry strategy. And since each country is unique, they all need some customized strategy for successful entry. For instance, many products have both global and local competitors in a country. It could be that local competitors have cornered segments of the market, making it impossible to crack that country. For example, Starbucks can be found almost anywhere in the world but not in Italy, where the family-owned cafe concept has been thriving for many decades. So based on the competitive environment, you may need to alter your global attack plan.

Distribution channels can also be different from one country to another. Each market has its own way of getting goods to consumers and businesses. Some countries have a very straightforward, transparent distribution channel, while others have very complex and costly distribution channels. For example, if you want to sell product in retail outlets in Japan, there are so many 'middle men' in the supply chain that you often have to revise your pricing model. If you try to circumvent the existing distribution channels in Japan, you may find retailers and even consumers reluctant to do business with you.

Finally, you need to understand operating costs in each country. This includes everything from office space to employee benefits to regulatory compliance and taxation. Prior to finalizing a market entry strategy, it's important to understand these aspects in your prospective country. Some countries are friendly towards corporations, but others strongly favor local labor. The immediate costs and financial resources needed to ramp up your business need to be well understood, as they will impact how you decide to enter a market and your financial projections.

Some issues are highly unique to a specific country. For instance, take the process of firing an underperforming employee in France. Unlike other countries, workers there are highly protected, so it could take months and lots of paperwork compared to the same process in the United States. Having to replace an employee in France will require more expense and management time, potentially impacting your growth plans.

When you take all these factors into account, as well as others we will shortly cover, you may be surprised that the countries you thought you might be targeting are not the ones you should enter. This is why it is important to research and analyze the market opportunity for each country you are considering. To be successful, it is critical to do your research and develop a strategy for each country based on facts, not assumptions or emotions.

This research will not only help you determine which countries to enter, but also how to enter each individual market. Furthermore, it is vital that you analyze each country separately. You cannot size up Asia as a whole by combining the markets of Japan and Korea, or

Japan, Korea and China. They are just too different. Everything from people's preferences to sales channels to local competitors to regulations varies from country to country. For example, consumer criteria for selecting a dishwasher in Germany are different than for consumers choosing one in Italy. Even within some countries, there are variances from region to region, and sometimes city to city. China is a good example of this, as you might know.

The Opportunity Funnel

Here's one method to define market size and opportunity for a given country. You can't just look at the total population of a country; not everyone is a potential customer, of course. You need to narrow your focus to determine a more realistic potential for your product. The most effective method for determining a true market opportunity is the funnel approach.

The top of the funnel is very broad, but as you analyze the data, you go down the funnel until you reach the bottom where it narrows down and reflects your true potential business opportunity in

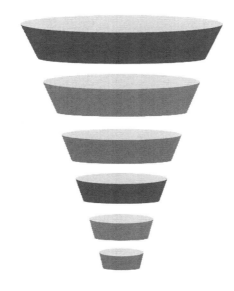

a given country. It is from this adjusted market size that you base the rest of your business planning.

So for example, if you are selling a product for consumers, the very top of the funnel typically starts with the total population of that country. Depending on your product, you reduce that audience to count only those within your primary target demographic, however you define it (based on age, gender, educational level, home-ownership status, etc.). This filtered number is a much more realistic starting point for your analysis. At this point in the funnel, we have defined what is referred to as the Total Available Market, or TAM.

Next you further refine the TAM by narrowing it down to those within your target demographic who you believe have a need or strong desire for your product. After all, you cannot count on all consumers in your demographic to purchase your product. The more you research the country, and speak to others involved in this particular market, the better you will be able to determine this number.

The next level of refinement comes by reducing this last figure to take into account any alternative or substitute products that consumers could purchase in place of yours. We are not talking about your direct competitors, but rather alternative products that can fill the need. For example, if you are selling ice cream, alternative products would be other sweets and snacks such as chocolate or cookies. In the technology world, tablets would be a substitute purchase for notebook computers.

You may not have access to real data that helps you reduce your market size in a realistic way. If so, you need to come up with your own estimates based on educated guesses and sound judgment. In the ice cream example, consumers in a cooler climate like Sweden or Norway may not be eager to purchase frozen treats during their long, cold winter, so you might need to reduce their market opportunity, due to alternative desserts, by 80 or 90% for several months of the year. In a warm climate like Ecuador, however, consumers are very comfortable eating ice cream all year round, so you might reduce the market opportunity by only 50% even if there are many viable alternatives your demographic might buy.

As you go through the calculations winding your way down the funnel, you end up with what is referred to as the "addressable" market. This is the portion of the TAM that is realistically viable for your business. We are still not talking about the impact that your direct competitors might have or on your ability to win market share. That will be covered in another chapter. This is what the funnel looks like based on the analysis we just reviewed:

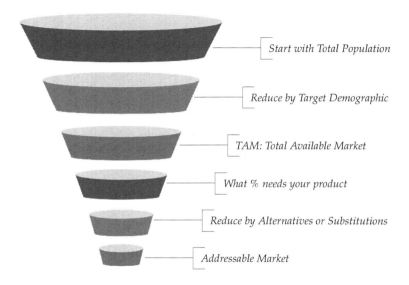

Start with Total Population

Reduce by Target Demographic

TAM: Total Available Market

What % needs your product

Reduce by Alternatives or Substitutions

Addressable Market

Examples of Addressable Market Calculations

1. You have developed an innovative, quick drying bathing suit. You are analyzing Brazil as the potential market to enter. Demographic data about Brazil is easily available via Google searches. The country has a total population of about 197 million. Since your bathing suits are somewhat revealing, your primary target demographic is the 15 to 34 year olds. They make up 35% of the population, or about 69.3 million people. This is your TAM.

Approximately 70% of the Brazilian population lives in one of its coastal states. And, as many Brazilians grow up going to the beach, we assume that 75% of that coastal population comprises regular beach goers. Taking our original 69.3 million, we reduce it by 30% to account for those not living near the coast, so we are at 48.5 million. Then reduce it again a further 25% to remove those who are not regular beach goers, and now we are down to 36.375 million.

Finally, we try to determine if there are any alternative or substitute products. In this product category in Brazil, everyone wears a bathing suit of some kind. Although you can swim with regular clothes on, we don't factor this as an alternative or substitute products. So our total addressable market remains approximately 36 million people. This is still a preliminary number, as we need to understand the impact that other factors might play, such as business climate, regulations, distribution channels and competition, all of which could impact our market opportunity.

2. This example is one I experienced with one of my companies that was making integrated circuit components for the mobile phone market. We were investigating whether we should enter China, given that the Chinese population had been the largest mobile phone market for many years in terms of subscribers and new phone sales. At that time in 2007, 190 million cell phones were sold annually in China. Since we did not sell to end customers, but provided components to manufacturers, our focus was not on the consumer population but on the number of phones sold annually.

That number, 190 million, became the top of our funnel. However, at that time, around 60% of phones sold in China came from foreign manufacturers such as Nokia and Samsung. Since we were selling only to Chinese designers of phones, we needed to exclude all foreign manufacturers. (If we had wanted to sell our component to Samsung, we would have needed to sell their designers in South

Korea, a completely different market analysis.) So 190 million x 40% = 76 million—this was our TAM for the China market.

Next, we had to factor in that our component was used only on high-end phones. This meant reducing the TAM to eliminate entry-level phones, about 70% of their market. So taking into account this fact, our opportunity was reduced to 22.8 million.

At the time, there really were not any substitute security products for mobile phones, as these other technologies were still at least three years away from mass market. So we made no adjustments for alternative products. In the end, our total addressable market was 22.8 million phones.

Just as with the Brazilian bathing suit example, this was still a preliminary number, as we needed to explore the impact that other factors would have on our market opportunity. (Note: I'll continue to build on this example throughout the rest of this book, as it touches every section and enables us to follow a real-life international expansion opportunity from inception to conclusion.)

Recommended Process for Calculating Market Size

I am often asked who should do the work of calculating the market size for each country. Based on my experience, some of this work can be outsourced but other tasks are best handled by those who know your business best. You can break down this task into three sub-tasks:

1. Create the framework for your specific funnel.
2. Research and fill in the numbers (as we did in the examples).
3. Make some final assumptions to get closer to your real addressable market.

I suggest that creating the framework of your funnel is best handled by your company management. This is the most important activity when determining your market size. If you focus on the wrong demographics, or miscalculate the assumed need or strong desire for your product, you may completely misjudge the opportunity in a country and end up basing this important decision on inaccurate facts.

The next step of researching and plugging in the numbers to your funnel is one that you can delegate to a lower level employee or even outsource to a third party. Collecting this information is not difficult, but it is often time consuming. Just be sure whoever collects the information also logs their sources. This helps you verify that the sources are credible, and allows you to revert back to the original data set to probe deeper into the numbers or get clarification.

The bottom of the funnel is the basis for starting financial modeling, so management must handle this portion. To reach the end of the funnel, you must make assumptions regarding alternate products and their impact on your potential customers. You may also need to estimate based on educated guesses or assumptions as you determine your final addressable market number. Since no one knows your business better than you and your internal team, you are the best sources to make such final determinations.

If you are not familiar with the dynamics of a potential country, you may need to find an external resource to help validate key assumptions that are part of your framework or final addressable market calculation. This is where the trade offices of your in-country embassy, as well as your industry's trade associations and councils, are good sources to reach out and ask for assistance. While they, too, may not have exact data, the discussions you have with them will likely be extremely helpful in validating hypotheses.

- As you plan for international expansion, you must start by determining the potential opportunity in a given market. This is the first step in coming up with a concrete plan for expansion.

- Not all markets are created equal, and there are many factors to consider when deciding where and how to expand including determining the need for your product, impact of disposable income, and understanding country regulations, competition, distribution channels and operating costs.

- Research is critical when deciding which international markets to enter, as you need to make decisions based on facts, not assumptions or emotions.

- You must analyze each country separately, as every country has distinct differences.

- The best way to size your market is using the funnel analysis. Start by defining your total available market (TAM) and then refine that to a realistic addressable market based on demographic scrutiny and justifiable assumptions.

SUMMARY STEPS TO DEVELOP YOUR FUNNEL

(remember, do a funnel for each country)

Step 1:   find the total population or other high-level measure

Step 2:   what percent of this total is in your primary target demographic?
▶ **RESULT:** Total Available Market (TAM)

Step 3:   what percent of your TAM has a need or strong desire for your product (you may have to estimate)

Step 4:   what percent reduction to your TAM must be taken due to alternative or substitute products (you will need to estimate)
▶ **FINAL RESULT:** Addressable Market

CHAPTER 2

Business Climate

Now that you have sized one or more target markets, it's time to learn about doing business in each country. Every country has its own unique history and ways of trade and commerce. What seems like logical for doing business in your country may be seen as illogical or inappropriate in your target country. Many local customs or procedures date back decades or even centuries, and if you do not appreciate these aspects of the target culture, you risk alienating potential employees, partners and customers.

Many of the issues in this chapter are legal or financial in nature, so make sure you consult with your attorney and accountant to guide you as you find answers to the numerous questions we will discuss. If your attorney or accountant does not have experience dealing with the country you are evaluating, they might be able to reach out to professional colleagues who can assist you. Let's take a closer look at the various business climate issues.

Get to Know the Economy

To do business in a country, you should have an understanding of its economy. Study the country's economy in detail in order to better evaluate the risks of establishing a presence in that market. Look at historical trends, current economic conditions, and the country's own projected forecasts for the next several years. Of course, you should rely on current economic conditions and projected forecasts to guide your decision on the timing of your market entry. But historical trends are also valuable because they paint a picture of what the local economy typically experiences as it undergoes various business cycles.

Specifically, look at the following three statistics:

- Economic growth rate
- GDP per capita
- Unemployment rate

A country's economic growth rate tells you if the economy is generally healthy. Check if, historically, the economy is stable or fluctuates wildly between growth and recession. Stable economies allow you to better plan and predict your expansion. Your forecast will be easier to develop, and if you are operating in the country, there will be fewer surprises. A fluctuating economy presents a challenge when forecasting, and it creates a more difficult operating environment once you establish your presence.

However, depending on your business, the opportunities in a country with a history of economic fluctuations may be so great that you accept these risks. For example, companies selling oil-drilling equipment commonly accept the turmoil in countries like Russia due to the massive market opportunity. (We see this as I write this book, after the Russian invasion of Crimea and potential occupation of eastern Ukraine, where the major oil companies still seek to do business with Russia.)

A country's current economic growth rate should be a critical part of your market entry timing. If the economy is growing, people are confident and likely to spend more money. If you find this scenario, you may want to expedite your market entry in order to take advantage of the current economic climate. Consumers and companies are more willing to buy during good times, especially from a new market entrant. On the other hand, if the local economy is in a recession, continue your planning but consider postponing the actual execution of your international expansion until the country's economy starts its recovery. As you often hear in business, timing is everything, so knowing the local economic conditions is a key factor in deciding the timetable of your market entry.

Next, look at a country's GDP per capita, as this will tell you the average income per person. Depending on your product's price, the average income in a country could impact your sales potential. If you have a high-end luxury product, it could fail to sell if GDP per capita is very low. However, if your product can replace another, more expensive product, a lower GDP per capita can work to your advantage. Many fast growing economies have lower GDP per capita, while many mature economies have a slower economic growth rate but higher GDP per capita. Depending on your product, mature economies could present better opportunities despite the slower economic growth rate.

The unemployment rate is another important factor to consider. Low unemployment is typically a positive sign about the near-term potential in a country because people who are employed have a tendency to spend more money. In contrast, if a large percentage of the population is not working, most of their purchases will be limited to necessities. If your product is more of a want than a need, unemployment can impact your sales. But as before, if your product is a lower cost alternative to what people are already buying, a higher unemployment rate can benefit you in quickly capturing market share. Note also that if you intend to set up an office in that country, a higher unemployment rate might enable you to more easily find employees and have more power in negotiating salaries.

Finally, look at the more recent economic forecast projections for the country. First, find out what is the expected growth rate of the country for the next two years. Entering a growing economy is traditionally easier than entering a market that is contracting, so a positive projection is a good signal to enter the market now. Positive projections tend to boost local morale, resulting in people spending more money. Meanwhile, the unemployment forecast is also an important factor. As mentioned, if unemployment is expected to shrink, it is a good sign because employed people have a tendency to spend more money than the unemployed. However, shrinking unemployment typically means employees have more leverage in negotiating salaries so you may need to budget higher personnel expenses.

Say you are considering entering France. For the last few years, the country's economic growth rate has been steady, between 1 and 2% per year. France's GDP per capita is approximately $43,400, which is high. Unfortunately, the unemployment rate is also high at 11%. Projections for the next two years show continued slow growth and not much change in the unemployment rate.

What does all this economic information tell you about France? It says the French have money to spend, their economy is stable but the high unemployment could impact your sales, depending on your product's price. However, if you want to set up a local office, the high unemployment rate could aid you in quickly establishing an office and hiring. Because of its general economic stability, France could be a good expansion market if the opportunity for your product and other business climate factors are positive.

Examine the Country's Infrastructure

A country's infrastructure is often overlooked. Regardless of the product you are selling, the condition of the local infrastructure can be a critical factor in determining your future success. Whether you sell technology products, consumer goods, perishable items or provide services, the infrastructure can either help you succeed or lead you to failure. Specifically, you should ask the following questions:

- Are utilities generally available or do consumers and businesses struggle to get consistent electricity, gas, and water? Are the basic necessities to conduct business always available or not? No matter what you sell, unpredictable utilities (e.g., brownouts and blackouts) can disrupt your business and cause severe financial problems.

■ Is there a robust transportation network within the country? Are the roads, railways, and ports developed enough to easily transport goods within the country? Transportation issues can impact your business even if you are not selling perishable items, as shipment delays of any type of product can alienate customers. Services businesses are also impacted by transportation issues as both employees and customers can be subject to unpredictable commutes on a daily basis.

■ Is reliable and secure high speed Internet easily available? So much commerce and research is done via the web that easily available and secure connections are now a requirement for any business, even non high-tech companies. Not having consistent access can put you at a competitive disadvantage. This also impacts voice services, as communication via the Internet is quickly becoming the main way to talk to customers and partners. Services like Skype are quickly replacing traditional telephone methods.

■ Is the country easy to reach via international travel? Once you invest in entering a market, you and your domestic employees will need to make many overseas trips to establish and support your new market presence. Impractical travel routes requiring many connections and long layovers can affect employee morale and overall business effectiveness. If you don't want to fly on small puddle-jumper aircraft, isolated regions may not be for you.

Years ago I worked for a company seeking to build its own factory overseas. We selected Penang, Malaysia, because it met all of the infrastructure requirements. We located the factory in an industrial area of the city that had many other factories run by foreign technology companies. The local government ensured that utilities were available and stable. Malaysia's transportation network was robust with high-end seaports, a good freeway system, and reliable rail lines. High-speed Internet was quite dependable, and airport travel, while far from the United States, was readily available with many convenient flight options. This choice helped the company launch its factory far more easily than some of the other locations we were considering.

Learn about the Regulatory Environment

The country's regulatory environment is important to understand in how it impacts the business climate. Not only does each country have its own set of regulations that will require conformance, but you also need to get a sense of how open the regulatory agencies are to hearing their constituents. Most countries have rigid policies, with no flexibility, but with the right local connections, you can more easily navigate through the process.

Here are some of the main questions you need to answer:

- Are prices regulated for your particular type of product within the country? If so, is there is any flexibility for you to control your pricing to your channel partners?
- Are there clear guidelines when importing and exporting? How much paperwork and red tape will be required?
- Do you need specific licenses, including industry licenses for your product to be sold?
- What is the legal system like? Is there due process? Can foreign companies succeed in the local courts?
- What about intellectual property protection? Is it respected and fairly litigated when there are infringements?

Depending on your industry, there may be many specific regulations you need to know before proceeding with an expansion into that country. It could be useful to consult with an attorney to ensure you have a full understanding of the country's regulatory environment for your products and type of business.

As I mentioned, when looking to establish my IP phone company in China, we quickly learned that voice-over-IP, the main way customers could use our phones, was forbidden by the government.

Despite its market size, we had to rule out this market. Instead, all we could do was monitor the situation, expecting that at some point in the future this restriction might be lifted and we would be eventually able to sell our product there.

Check out Employment Policies

If you are planning to hire people in the foreign country, what are the policies for hiring and terminating employees? Each country has its own regulations that are important to understand before you jump in. In some countries, such as Switzerland for example, there is a 90-day evaluation period after hiring someone. If you are not happy with the employee, terminating the employment agreement is much easier at the end of the evaluation period than for an employee who has been on the payroll much longer.

You also need to know about any government-mandated employment costs. These can range from guaranteed bonuses to retirement fund contributions. Just about every country has some form of contribution that the employer must make. For instance, in China it is mandatory to provide a 13th month of salary as a bonus, while in Singapore the employer must contribute an additional percentage of salary to the employee's retirement fund. Knowing the local requirements before you develop your financial plan can save you headaches, so consult with your attorney and accountant. Otherwise you may be surprised by additional costs that can impact your cash needs for the business.

Finally, find out if there are any local business traditions that, if you do not follow them, would put you at a disadvantage in hiring and/or retaining employees. While not government mandated, local customs are expected to be honored, so forsaking them can severely impact your business. Here's an example: in highly competitive job markets like Bangalore, India, it is customary to offer raises twice per year. If you do not provide these raises, your best employees will most likely leave for other companies who entice them with higher salaries. If you are serious about a market, make an effort to talk to local human resource organizations to learn about such employment practices and traditions.

A few years ago, I wanted to expand one of my businesses to Europe. Unfortunately, we were a small company, and the restrictive policies regarding flexibility of hiring and firing were too great. So we got creative and came up with a solution. Through my personal network, I knew of two people who had their own consulting business in Belgium. Instead of hiring them as employees, I signed a contract with their consulting firm such that they became my European sales office. They were technically independent contractors, but we put on an appearance of having them as direct company employees. They had email accounts and business cards from our company, and they participated in all company conference calls and other activities as if they were direct staff. However, since legally they were not company employees, I could freely increase or reduce my monthly fee with the consulting firm. This arrangement gave us the full flexibility to adjust our business staffing with them as appropriate.

My same company also considered entering the China market. We wanted to establish a sales and support office, as well as an engineering center. Unlike Western Europe, the regulations in China provided us a lot of flexibility. We were able to file all the paperwork to rapidly set up a subsidiary office and hire the team we needed. If our business necessitated staffing changes in the future, we had ability to act quickly. So in this particular case, we hired people to be actual employees of our company and we negotiated salaries and other benefits at the individual level.

Tax Policy

A country's tax policy and local tax laws can have a major impact on your business' profitability. Like regulatory issues, there are many items to consider, so make sure you speak with an accountant who understands international taxation in your specific target country. Questions you will need answers to include:

- How easy is it to move money in and out of the country? For example, China has strict currency restrictions so you need to plan money transfers well in advance in order to have time to get government approval.

- Are there any government withholdings when money is being transferred? This can impact money you send to your office, as well as customer payments that are made back to you. Each country is different so consult with a tax accountant.

- Are any duties assessed when you import product into the country? Depending on your product and the country in question, duties can be significant and impact your profit margins. While free trade agreements have helped reduce duties between countries, not all products are covered. Your tax accountant can guide you.

- What about export taxes if you want to ship product out of the country? Even if you have no intention to sell the product in the local market, some countries will levy a value added tax (VAT) based on the work contribution made to the product while in their country. This adds to your cost. Knowing if you will face export taxes could be important to your business model.

There are other tax matters, too. If your product will be taxed when entering the market, you need to know that amount before you determine your pricing strategy. If taxes are high, you may need to charge more to be profitable. To prevent grey market sales—defined as products being purchased in one country for use in another—it helps to have uniform pricing throughout the region. Unfortunately, that is not always possible because of taxation. For example, import duties in China and Hong Kong vary significantly for certain products. To compensate for varying product costs due to taxation, you may need to customize your product to create slight variations in different countries so that what you ship in each country is not identical. That often helps avoid grey market sales.

Here are some examples where tax policy has impacted my own businesses in the past. In one company, we found it easy to set up an office in China, but funding it and later retrieving profits was much more challenging. We faced many regulations that we and our international accounting firm needed to manage. In order to keep our R&D center working efficiently, we had to send monthly reports and make requests to the government to obtain permission to send money to our subsidiary. As long as we planned effectively, we did not run into any issues, but last minute money transfers were extremely difficult.

As for government withholdings, consider this story. About ten years ago one of my companies did a project in South Korea where, in addition to product sales, we were able to offer our engineering services for $500,000. When our customer finally made the payment, we only received $412,500. Why? Because the Korean government withholds 17.5% of engineering payments made to a foreign company. Had we known this, we would have priced our services differently, because we were a small company closely managing our cash flow. We should have consulted our accounting firm prior to making the sale as it would have netted us an additional $87,500 in funds.

Sales Channels

Before entering a market, you also need to understand the country's sales channels. Some questions you need to answer are:

- How are products like yours sold in the country?
- Can you sell directly to end customers?
- Do you have to go through a distributor?
- Can you offer your products directly to retailers?

It is critical, of course, to understand how product flows within a market before you finalize market entry strategy. Typically, the more hands that touch a product, the greater the squeeze on your margins. One way to learn is to talk to people within your industry who already do business in that particular country, as they can often guide you in understanding the channel structure.

Let's do a comparison. In the United States, most products get to market through a two-tier distribution channel. The manufacturer sells the product to a distributor, who then sells to a retailer or reseller. Of course, with the Internet, today many companies can also opt to sell directly to end-users. This has put great strain on both distributors and resellers, as a direct sales channel from manufacturer to consumer is very easy to establish. In the United States, the manufacturer has a lot of flexibility in determining how its products will reach end-users.

Japan has a different structure though, in which the distribution channel is much more complex. Most products need to go through at least four levels of intermediaries before reaching end users. This not only means it takes longer for your product to get to market, but also your profit margins are more severely impacted unless you raise your prices. Unlike the United States, you also have very little flexibility in setting up your sales channels in Japan. You can also try to sell direct to consumers, but it is more difficult in Japan as they are accustomed to purchasing through well-known, established sales channels. As a foreign entity with no track record in the country, buyers will not feel comfortable purchasing directly from you.

We will discuss sales channel options in more detail in Part 2 of this book.

Receptiveness to Foreign Products

One last item to investigate is the general receptiveness of foreign products to customers in your target country. Some nations or regions are so patriotic that your chances of gaining relevant market share may be very low. In such markets, the local products always have an advantage compared to foreign products. Two countries where I have experienced this are South Korea and France. For example, for many years it has been difficult for American companies to sell white goods, such as refrigerators and washing machines in South Korea. One reason is nationalistic pride to purchase Samsung, LG or other local Korean manufacturers.

As part of this, also find out if there are any negative biases towards your home country in a given market that can impact your ability to sell. The bias can be based on such factors as trade history, political history, war, perceived quality of products from your country, and others. For example, based on the geopolitical climate today, not all countries are receptive to American products. Even if there is no favoritism towards local products, there may be a bias against products from American companies.

The best way to research the level of receptiveness to foreign products, and specifically products from your country, is to take a trip and learn first-hand how potential customers respond to you. See what people are buying and the reactions they have towards products from your country. Talk to local people to get their point of view. This will preview the reactions you might expect if you introduce your product into the market. You will learn a lot about the attitudes potential customers have towards foreign products as you do primary research specific to your industry.

- Understanding the business climate for a target country is an important part of your analysis. As there are many legal and financial considerations when looking at business climate, this activity should be done in partnership with your attorney and accountant.

- Study the country's economic conditions, specifically the economic growth rate, GDP per capita, and unemployment rate.

- Examine the local infrastructure as it can have a major impact on your business.

- Regulatory issues can hinder your ability to do business in certain countries.

- Employment policies, including flexibility in hiring and firing, are another major consideration.

- Make sure you understand the tax policies and duty structure as these can severely impact your pricing and cash flow.

- Sales distribution channels vary by country, so learn about the sales structure in your target country.

- Visit the country to understand the receptiveness that buyers have to foreign goods.

CHAPTER 3

Competitive Landscape

EACH COUNTRY HAS ITS OWN DYNAMIC, INCLUDING ITS LOCAL competitive landscape. We've already discussed indirect competition (alternative products to yours), so in this chapter, our focus will be on direct competitors, defined as companies that offer products similar to yours. However, always keep in mind that potential customers have the ability to substitute one type of product for another.

Global Competitors

Global competitors are companies that are typically well known and have offices throughout the world. They have the broadest reach, and usually the deepest pockets. Their products are very visible not just in your target country, but also your home country. They spend the most on marketing. Because of their visibility, they are the easiest to figure out as they are the best known and you probably compete with them today.

Some of your existing strategies to compete with these global companies will carry over into the new markets, but not all. Thus, when analyzing entry into a potential country, it is worthwhile to determine if any global competitors are doing something differently in that target market. Chances are they have tried numerous sales and marketing approaches over the years, settling on what is most effective. Often they position their products differently in different countries—and you can learn from them.

For example, Toyota markets their entry-level automobiles differently in some markets than in the United States. In Argentina, for instance, their entry-level automobiles are targeted to the middle class, while in the United States these vehicles are positioned as entry-level automobiles for younger drivers.

In some instances, global competitors also modify their products to appeal to a larger customer base in a specific country. For example, P&G and Unilever sell individual use shampoo sizes in emerging markets like India. Competing with these companies in the US, you would not be aware of this local India strategy. If you were to compete in India with them, you would need to follow suit, broadening your product line to offer individual use sizes in order to attract customers just as P&G and Unilever do. Otherwise you would be at a competitive disadvantage. The bottom line is that you can learn a lot from seeing what global competitors are doing, and save yourself time and money by avoiding mistakes and missteps.

Regional Competitors

Regional competitors are companies that sell within a given continent or portion of a continent, such as in South America or Europe. They are usually well known within the region, as they do broad marketing in their target territory. However, given that they do not sell in your home region, you may have no experience competing against them. Thus, you need to learn as much as you can about such regional competitors before making decisions regarding your market entry.

Just because a competitor is regional does not mean they are passive, unknown, or lack financial resources. In fact, they typically succeed at the expense of foreign entrants who underestimate them. Many regional companies also have developed a strong emotional attachment with their customers, which is hard to break. You need to research and study the marketing strategies of such regional competitors so you can devise a successful market entry strategy for yourself.

One example of a successful regional business is the Italian company, Ferrero, with their Nutella product. For over 20 years, this product was sold primarily in Europe, (although the company has now gone global). Outside of Europe, you had to go to specialty shops that imported European food products. A generation of Europeans grew up with an emotional attachment to eating Nutella throughout their childhood. If you are now trying to sell chocolate or another gooey bread or cookie spread-like substance to many Europeans, getting them to switch products would be very difficult. Companies have tried to unseat them, even with products such as peanut butter, but Nutella easily remains the market leader in Europe.

This is an example of how it is vital to study the regional brands and their hold in a target market. People who have decades of positive experience and memories associated with buying a brand that dominates their market will be difficult to convert to your brand.

Local Competitors

Local competitors are home grown companies that are usually, but not always, smaller. In larger economies, such as Brazil and China, some local competitors are quite large with sales in the billions of dollars. This is especially true of retail brands, providers of commodities, and companies involved in the energy and telecommunications sectors. Even smaller companies can be very effective in their home markets based on their cultural understanding and historical backgrounds.

Local competitors often have the best understanding of a market. While they may not have huge marketing budgets to compete with regional and global companies, they usually do a lot of guerilla marketing and know the local needs best. Due to their local position, they also connect emotionally with customers who have grown up using their products. Like regional competitors, it would be foolish to underestimate local companies as they will be the fiercest in fighting to keep their domestic market position and often focus all their corporate resources on their home market.

However, if you have a unique product offering that complements a local competitor, a good strategy is to think about having them become a partner. Depending on your technology and the dynamics of the particular market, partnering with a local competitor can be a fast and profitable way to enter a country. Rather than going head-to-head and trying to build your own sales channel and reputation, working with a local company might quickly get you to revenue. We will discuss this topic in more detail when we look at various market entry options in the next section of this book.

Doing a Competitive Analysis

Depending on what you find among your competitors, your tactics may need to change. Here is an example I experienced competing in Taiwan when selling products to original device manufacturers (ODMs). These are companies that design device products that other companies brand under their own name. For example, all HP notebooks are designed by ODMs in Asia, but sold by HP as their own branded product.

My company, Xircom, was selling communication solutions being integrated into notebook computers. We were a mid-sized company, a global brand with offices throughout the world, doing about $400 million in annual revenue. In the Taiwanese market, we were positioned in the middle. 3Com was the multi-billion dollar big player in that space, clearly our global competitor. But we also competed with about half a dozen low-cost Taiwanese companies, some regional competitors that were strong in Asia and some local competitors only servicing customers within that country.

For the Taiwanese market, we devised a 'divide and conquer' strategy in order to become the market leader. We came up with two ways to position our company depending on the competitive situation. Many of the larger ODMs were willing to pay a premium to work with a global brand, and 3Com was the preferred vendor because of their sheer size, both in revenue as well as having a large local support team. When we were competing against 3Com, we positioned ourselves as a much more flexible vendor with a strong global reputation, able to respond faster to customer inquiries, more malleable in accommodating unique product requests, and easier to do business with in regards to contract negotiations, delivery terms and pricing.

When competing against Taiwanese competitors, our tactics had to change because they were local, faster and more flexible than us. Some were also extremely easy to do business with. So in these situations, we reversed strategy and took advantage of our position of being a well-known, global brand, able to compete with the local companies via reputation and quality. Our tactics in these sales situations changed from positioning ourselves as the smaller, faster, easier-to-work-with vendor to being the safer, more established vendor. Ultimately, we convinced many customers that despite our price premium, we were a better choice than the local competition.

If you are selling to consumers or corporate end users, with today's online capabilities, you can also implement this same "divide-and-conquer" strategy. For example, you could create multiple landing pages targeting various segments of the market so different customer sets can access and view just the product(s) you have positioned for their specific needs. You can create different messaging to promote your company at social media outlets such as Facebook (consumer focus) and LinkedIn (business focus). You can also create multiple Twitter news feeds addressing different portions of your market.

Creating a Competitive Matrix

After identifying your competitors, you need a methodology to analyze them. The method I have consistently used to provide a clear picture of where my company stands and how we should position ourselves is the competitive matrix—a grid that helps you compare yourself against competitors.

In some cases, you may need two matrices. The first compares you to your competitors at the corporate level. This impacts how you position your company in the market. From the example we just reviewed, the corporate level competitive matrix guided our positioning within the Taiwan market. The corporate level matrix is not very extensive, as you can focus on just high-level attributes such as:

- company size (global and local)
- existing market share (global and local)
- advertising/marketing expenditure (local)
- distribution channels (local)
- customer support responsiveness (local)
- lead-time in fulfilling orders (local)
- flexibility in payment terms (local)

Sometimes a second competitive matrix is necessary to compare the features and benefits of your product(s) against your competitors' offerings. This matrix is extremely useful for seeing how to position your products in all your sales and marketing activities. Whether you will be writing brochures, ads or doing sales presentations, knowing how you compare to the competition is critical to tailor the message you need to convey to outrun your competitors. You always want to position the attributes where you have an advantage as being the most important, and try to downplay the significance of your product features that are weaker than your competitors.

I create these matrices using Microsoft Excel, as you can easily add competitors, new attribute fields, and change sorting on the fly. Here is an example of a matrix my team developed to compare our upcoming product with those from our key competitors. (I've only included one part of the matrix showing the first three sections, as the full matrix is too large to put into this book.)

Competitive Landscape October 2012

Features	Our Model 1100	Comp A Model 250	Comp B Model 670
Average Street Price	$479	$399	$449
BENEFITS			
Outlook Contacts Integration	x	Contacts Sync	
CRM Integration on Phone	x		
PC Screen Sharing	coming		
FEATURES			
Mobile Contacts on Phone	x		
Open OS (Android)	2.3	2.2	2.2
Apps Market (Apps Store)	x	x	
Annuity Revenue Streams	x	x	
Touch Screen	x	x	x
Wideband Audio	x	x	x
Bluetooth	x		
USB Port	x	?	x
Lines	6	?	6
Wired Ethernet Port	x	x	x
PoE Support	x	?	x
Wi-Fi			
Video Conferencing	no	no	no
LCD Display	8.9" 1024x600 Pixels	7" 800x295 Pixels	7" 800x480 Pixels

Pricing Sources: telecomworldonline.com; hellodirect.com; ipphone-warehouse.com

In this matrix, I have highlighted what our advantages are in light grey, and disadvantages in dark grey. By looking at these highlights, it was easy to begin painting a picture of how we would position our particular product. While we were priced in the middle, the features we offered, such as a larger display, embedded Bluetooth, and CRM integration enabled us to position our product as "a high-end phone at a very competitive price." We thus marketed our product as providing the best value and feature set for a large screen device.

When you do your matrix, include only those product features that are relevant in that particular market segment as other attributes can distract from your research. Here are some of the ones you might want to include:

- Price comparison
- Feature comparisons against your product

Comp C Model F	Comp D Model 600	Comp E Model C	Comp F Model 2200
$1,900	$579	$999	$239
x	?	x	
x			
		x	x
2.2	2.2	2.2	2.3
		x	x
		x	
x	x	x	x
x	x	x	x
x		x	x
x	x	x	x
1	1	1	6
x	x	x	x
x		x	x
x	x	x	
yes	yes	yes	no
11.6" 1366x768 Pixels	7" 800x480 Pixels	7" 1024x600 eff res	4.3" 480x272 Pixels

- High level listing of key benefits
- How does the competitor position their offering?
- What kind of marketing does competitor do for this particular product?
- How do they sell their offering?
- How do they support their product (24/7 live phone? Email support? etc.)?
- Does the competitor have any unique relationships for this product that afford them an advantage, such as a distribution, financing, or technology partnership?

Your competitive matrices are living documents, and should be updated at least once per year (more often in rapidly changing markets). If a new entrant comes into the market, or new products are introduced, you should update as well. The task of developing and managing competitive matrices should fall on your marketing team, with input from your regional or country sales teams.

One final note: do not be surprised if you cannot find all the information needed to complete your matrix. The Internet is a great source of information, but not everything is readily available. Some companies do a very good job of keeping detailed data about their products hidden from competitors.

SWOT Analysis

One last exercise that has always helped me in effectively positioning my company against competitors is called the SWOT analysis. Perhaps you are familiar with it. SWOT stands for Strengths, Weaknesses, Opportunities and Threats. Strengths and weaknesses require you to do an internal analysis on your company and product(s), while opportunities and threats get you to do external analyses on your market and competitors. You should do a SWOT analysis for each country you are considering.

The next page shows a sample SWOT analysis framework. Notice that it is done on one sheet of paper so that all relevant information is clearly visible.

I create my SWOT analysis after I've developed my competitive matrices. This helps create a more in-depth SWOT because you can look at your matrices and see your internal strengths and weaknesses at both the corporate and product level. Also, the matrices often prompt you to recognize opportunities and threats that you may not think of. Your matrices do not have all the information to complete a SWOT, but they are a great starting point. If you need more details on how to perform a SWOT analysis, there are many books focused solely on this topic.

Lastly, when you have one or two main competitors in a market, I have found it extremely beneficial to put myself in their shoes and develop a SWOT analysis from their perspective. This gets you

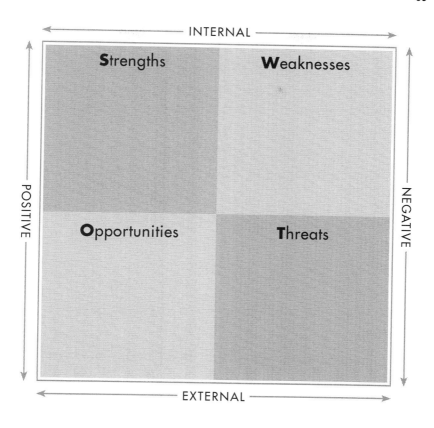

thinking about their internal strengths and weaknesses, and their market opportunities and threats. I find this exercise always reveals interesting insights you can use when approaching a market. It is also extremely helpful when you plan "divide and conquer" marketing strategies. Formulating a sense of how your competitors likely perceive a market is a great way to come up with a unique value proposition for your own business. This value proposition can then guide how you might position your company in all your sales activities and marketing collateral. It was this type of SWOT analysis that I did for 3Com and several of my Taiwanese competitors that helped me figure out how to position myself effectively at Xircom.

KEY LESSONS

- The competitive landscape for a target country can differ significantly from your home market. Understanding the uniqueness of the competition is important as you devise a sales and marketing strategy to enter a new market.

- Each country has its own unique competitive dynamic. You need to know who are the global, regional and local competitors in that market.

- Depending on whom you are competing against, your tactics may need to change.

- Develop a corporate level competitive matrix for each market you plan to enter.

- Also develop a product level competitive matrix for each market you plan to enter.

- Once your competitive matrices are done, do a SWOT analysis for your business.

- It may also be beneficial to do a SWOT analysis for your main competitors in each country.

CHAPTER 4

Possible Partners and Ecosystem

ONE OF THE EASIEST WAYS TO ENTER A FOREIGN MARKET IS either in partnership with a company who understands it well, or with partners who can help guide you in establishing your business. Partnerships can take many forms, including sales alliances, technology sharing and manufacturing relationships. At this stage of your thinking, it can be worthwhile to research and see if there might be potential partners suitable to help you move more quickly and successfully in entering your target market.

A local, well-known partner offers many benefits, including:

- providing your company instant credibility
- giving you a broader presence with more sales and support staff
- opening up access to fully developed sales channels
- helping you get a deeper understanding of the local market requirements
- providing assistance in localizing your product for your target market

As you decide which markets to enter, understanding the local marketplace and identifying potential partners should be key parts of your analysis. The more you can leverage the expertise and experience of partners, the faster you can establish a successful business in the country.

I've successfully worked with foreign partners many times in my career. The most effective partnerships provided both immediate and longer-term benefits. In the near-term, partners can help you quickly establish your office and ramp up sales. Over time, successful partnerships continue providing you market knowledge and rapid sales growth. However, to ensure success it is important that you proactively manage each relationship. Your partner's top corporate priorities are seldom yours, so you must continually promote your own priorities in order to achieve success. If you are visible with your partner, the level of support provided to your business will continue to be high. Otherwise, the partnership will never live up to your expectations.

Example of a Sales Partnership

One of my companies, Atrua, made security components for the mobile phone market. As the country that launched the most innovative mobile phones at the time, Japan was a critical market for us. We had already set up a sales office there, but without support staff or brand recognition, we were successful only with a small percentage of our target market. So we decided to find a partner.

We sought a company large enough to reach our entire target market but was not offering competing products to ours—either direct or indirect competitive solutions. We created a list of potential partners and then conducted research to learn about each one. As part of our analysis, we studied which of their product lines were the bestselling ones and which customer segments were most strategic to them. Ensuring our partner had the same strategic focus as us would be important if we wanted to succeed in the Japanese market.

From this analysis, we identified a well-respected firm, Murata, which was a multi-billion dollar manufacturer of electronic components. Their products did not compete with ours, and more importantly, their most strategic market segment was precisely our target market, mobile phones. In the majority of the phone manufacturing accounts we coveted, they were one of the top three component suppliers. Through personal contacts, we got an introduction to Murata and formed a very successful partnership that brought us a significant sales increase in Japan.

As it turned out, Murata was also looking for ways to expand its product set, and we quickly found a win-win scenario. Murata gave Atrua:

- Market credibility, as it is highly respected for its product quality and customer responsiveness. Being aligned with Murata quickly made all potential customers look at us differently. Many now saw us as a viable option because such a highly respected company validated us.
- A bigger sales and support team, with dedicated resources at each of our target accounts. Instead of having the same one or two Atrua people visiting all the target accounts, there were now fully dedicated account teams frequently going onsite at each customer.
- Access to all mobile phone manufacturers in Japan, as they were a strategic supplier to many of them with relationships at all levels in the organizations. We would not have been able to do this on our own with a small staff.
- A deep understanding of the local market, based on their years of successful sales and executive-level account relationships. Murata participated in strategic planning sessions with their customers and we benefited from these activities.

Tapping into the "Ecosystem" in a Country

Understanding the industry ecosystem in a foreign market is another good strategy to help you determine which markets to enter. My definition of the corporate ecosystem comprises all the companies that could be influential in helping your success, but are not the actual customers of your product. Often these are companies that provide products or services complementary to your product offering. While they will not buy your product, your offering makes theirs more attractive in the marketplace, which should lead to higher revenues for both parties.

Business ecosystems are everywhere. For example, a furniture company could benefit by aligning itself with building managers, interior decorators, architects, and construction contractors. The combination of these parties, along with others, would form an eco-system for the furniture company. By working together, these firms might be able to create more attractive offerings that would result in greater sales of furniture, architectural design, and decoration services.

As you evaluate expanding your business internationally, spend some time researching the ecosystem for your industry in your tar-get country and how you could possibly work within that system to increase the demand for your products.

When my company Atrua was selling security components to mobile phone manufacturers, we needed to influence other parties in order to generate interest in our solution. The ones who would most benefit were the application developers and network opera-tors. The application developers were critical because their new apps would drive demand for having our security component embedded into the phones. Without their support, there were no use cases for our solution. In return, our security component would make their applications more attractive to end-users. So we aggressively sought partnerships with application developers and assisted them in add-ing an additional layer of security to their software.

The mobile network operators were our customer's customers. They ultimately decided which mobile phones they would offer for sale to their consumers, so we needed to influence them to want our security component embedded in their selected phones. If our secu-rity component enabled the network operators to either attract new customers or upsell additional services to their existing customers, they would be interested in having it available on the devices. This was a key factor to drive our business, because unless the network operator requested a new feature, phone manufacturers were reluc-tant to include it. Often, network operators refused to pay extra for features they did not specifically request. Thus, the mobile phone manufacturers would not add the expense of a new component to their product unless their customers were willing to pay for the additional functionality.

I always referred to our sales and business development at this company as a three-legged stool. Each leg— the application developers, the phone manufacturers, and the network operators—had to be solicited in parallel. We needed to get an app developed at the same time we were selling the value of our functionality to the network operators while also working with the phone manufacturers to add our component into their next phone design. If one leg of the stool got too far ahead of the other two, the stool would collapse, meaning that the demand for our technology would not align with all three parties. If one of the three were too far behind, the sales process would stall, as the need and demand for our solution would not be apparent.

Each country you are interested in entering may have a different ecosystem, so you need to understand it before you move into that market. An example of this, sticking with the mobile phone industry, is how phones are sold in different countries. In the United States, phones are selected, branded, and subsidized by the network operators such as AT&T, Sprint and Verizon. Each of these networks carries their own choice of phones for consumers. In most other countries, phones are not subsidized and retailers play a bigger influence in the mobile phone ecosystem compared to the US. So in the UK, adding a large mobile phone retailer such as Carphone Warehouse to your ecosystem would be of significant value as they are an important part of the ecosystem influencing customers to a particular phone model.

Example of an Effective Ecosystem

Here's an example of how Atrua effectively used an ecosystem to grow our business in another country. To expand our efforts in Asia, we partnered with a company in Japan called HI Corp, which had developed a 3D user interface for mobile phones. This interface offered an intuitive, easy-to-learn way to navigate through menu items on a phone. This was well before the iPhone came out with tiles, which revolutionized the mobile phone user interface. Our touch sensor enabled users to quickly navigate through icons represented in a 3D cube.

As ecosystem partners, we worked with HI Corp so that our component would make their 3D user interface easy to use and secure. We jointly developed a 3D User Interface with built-in security that worked exclusively with the HI software with our component. Not only did we have an innovative solution, but it was also exclusive in that the two parts would work only if used together. Even though HI Corp itself would never be our customer—since they were a software interface design company, not a hardware manufacturer—we worked closely with them to develop this unique solution as it provided both of us something distinctive to offer the market.

Once the jointly developed solution was finished, my sales team went out and sold it to phone manufacturers in China and Japan. The fact that our component also offered a value-added software application impressed our potential customers. None of our competitors was able to offer anything similar, and this provided us a distinct advantage in the market. This was one of the differences that enabled us to win additional business in these two very competitive countries.

Two Strategies to Identify Partners

As you try to determine potential partners, it is useful to segment candidates into categories. Some can help improve your product offering, while others can help you reach more potential customers. The examples I've just related reflect the two key strategies that I've used to develop a partnership strategy:

- *Sales channel strategy.* Find companies that are selling into your target customer base, but are not selling competitive products.

Such companies are usually receptive to a partnership because they see your products as a way to expand their offerings and grow their business within their existing accounts. They already have strong relationships in place and would like to leverage these contacts to increase their sales revenue. The Murata example falls under this category, as our product gave them a new product line to offer their customers and quickly expand their revenue.

▪ *Product enhancement strategy.* Find companies where either your product or technology can enhance their existing offering. Such companies will see you as a value-add to their solution as you help make their product better and more attractive to potential customers. By working together, their product can either be sold for a higher price or reach new customers. The HI Corp example falls into this category, as we enhanced the value of their 3D user interface by adding our security features.

Which strategy is right for you will depend on many factors, including the maturity of your market segment, the competitive environment, and the specific ecosystem in your target country. You might deploy one strategy in one country but the other strategy in a different market. At Atrua, we actually implemented both partnership strategies in Japan. Murata was a sales channel strategy partner, while HI Corp was a product enhancement strategy partner. In other markets that Atrua entered, including South Korea, Switzerland, and the United Kingdom, we mostly implemented sales channel partnership strategies that expanded our business opportunities in those markets.

- A useful way to enter a new market is to find a local partner who can provide many of benefits, including market credibility, access to established sales channels, and a better understanding of the local market.

- Proactively manage your partners; remember, your priorities are NOT their corporate priorities.

- Evaluate your specific industry's ecosystem before entering a market, as business within your industry may be transacted differently than in your home market.

- Use one of two key strategies to find partnerships:

  - A sales channel strategy, where your partner is able to expand its product offerings through your product

  - A product enhancement strategy, where your partner's products are improved through your technology or product.

CHAPTER 5

Leveraging
Existing Relationships

Before concluding this part, we will discuss whom you should contact to help do the research and make final decisions on which markets to enter. My recommendation is that it is best to reach out to contacts that are most familiar with the market you want to enter. Given that you are unfamiliar with the market, why not leverage contacts with whom you have done business in the past and who know the country to guide you? Do not be reluctant to ask for assistance. You'll be surprised at how many contacts are willing to share their expertise and lend a hand.

While existing relationships should not be the driving factor in deciding which markets to enter, reaching out to gain a better understanding of the local market will help you make a more informed decision. Your contacts can help you size up the market, analyze the local business climate, gather competitive intelligence, categorize the local ecosystem, and identify potential partners. The more information you can gather in a short period of time, the better equipped you will be to make intelligent choices.

Who to Reach Out To?

The types of relationships I've reached out to successfully in the past include:

- *Existing partners.* Look at any current partners in your home market. If they are larger companies, chances are they are doing business globally and their remote offices can lend you a hand. Even smaller partners may be doing business in your prospective country. If they recently entered the market, what they know could be extremely valuable.

- *Suppliers.* Think of everyone who supplies your company, whether it is product components, office supplies, professional services, or anything else. If you expand your business, it should also benefit them because if you grow, your need for them will increase so they have a vested interest in helping you out.

- *Customers.* Customers are a good source of information, as satisfied clients are typically proud to share their experiences and even help. Again, if your customers include larger companies, there is a chance they may have either offices or contacts in the markets you are targeting.

- *Investors.* Investors are an excellent source of referrals, as they share in your greater success. This is especially true if you are a privately funded company. Many venture capitalists and corporate investors have expansive global networks and are at your disposal to make the proper introductions. I have found investors to be the most eager to help their portfolio companies, especially making mutual introductions when there is a possibility that two companies can help each other out.

- *Your personal network.* Go through all the business cards you have collected over the years to see if any contacts can help. In addition to reaching out to your primary contacts, you can also ask them if they have any contacts that could be beneficial to you. I also use LinkedIn as a source of potential connections as this it enables you to expand far beyond your direct personal network.

In addition to the relationships above, you can leverage several other resources. For example, get assistance from government agencies. Most countries have agencies than can help domestic companies expand overseas. In the US, agencies such as the Export-Import

Bank, the Small Business Administration, and the US Trade and Development Agency provide free assistance to companies. They provide education on both general international experience as well as specific country information for your target markets.

Next, you should reach out to any foreign trade offices that are established in your country. Many countries set up trade offices in foreign countries to help companies expand into their local markets. These organizations exist for the sole purpose of expanding trade between their country and yours. For example, Japan has a trade office called JETRO, which stands for Japan External Trade Organization. JETRO has 73 offices outside of Japan that are available to help you enter their country. Within Japan, JETRO has 40 offices that can offer assistance once you are there. Seeking their help will make your entry into the Japanese market much easier, and most likely more successful. Many other countries have similar organizations you can find through Internet searches.

Finally, there are also industry trade groups that can introduce you to all types of partners ranging from sales channel and product development partners to financial and regulatory resources needed to enter a market. For example, the Wi-Fi Alliance is a great resource for companies in the wireless Internet space looking to expand their market presence. With hundreds of member companies, this nonprofit can facilitate introductions with companies that are active in nearly every corner of the globe. Whether you are looking for a sales channel partner or product development partner, they can assist with introductions.

What Kind of Guidance Should You Seek?

Given that each company and industry is unique, you may need local experts to help you in certain areas of your business but not others. I've always found it useful to speak with as many people as possible and then use their input to come up with my own strategy. The more data points you collect, the better tactical decisions you can make. What follows are some of the main areas where I've seen companies benefiting from getting local advice in planning their market entry.

1. *Where to set up your initial in-country office.* Local experts can help you weigh the pros and cons of each city you are considering to establish your workplace. In some countries, the choice is obvious, but not so in others. In Australia, for example, should you establish your first office in Sydney, Melbourne, or Perth? Sydney is larger with a broader collection of industries, but Melbourne has a strong technology scene, while Perth has very strong technical universities. In Mexico, do you target Mexico City or Guadalajara first? Again, Mexico City is larger, but Guadalajara has a stronger technology base. Not knowing the local environment, you are more likely to select the wrong city for your initial market entry if you do not get the advice of local experts.

2. *Potential tax breaks and other benefits.* Tax breaks can be substantial so you should always look for opportunities to benefit from them. Every tax dollar you save can be invested in growing your business. Some countries, like China, have tax free zones that provide additional benefits to foreign companies who base their business there. Depending on what part of the city you set up your office can impact your tax rate and cash flow.

3. *Hiring someone to lead your local office.* How do you go about hiring local employees, especially a general manager? This is one of the most critical decisions you will make in expanding into a foreign market. Any time you hire someone, it can be hit or miss if that person is right for the job. If you are hiring someone overseas from a different culture, the risk of hiring the wrong person is even greater. You will not meet the person face-to-face every day so it can take months to realize there is a problem, and even longer to fix it. So see if your contacts can recommend the right person for the job, and if they also assist in speaking or interviewing candidates in the

local language. This helps ensure you get a better picture of whether the person is the right fit for your company.

4. *Local suppliers.* Depending on the type of presence you are planning, you may need to replicate much of what you've set up in your domestic market. This means finding local suppliers capable of supporting your specific business needs. Getting introductions to firms that can process your local payroll, do your accounting, and provide legal advice often facilitate entering a new market. Find out if your existing suppliers can support you in your new market. Even if they cannot, they may be able to recommend local firms. It is often faster and safer to work with companies recommended by your partners as opposed to finding someone on your own.

5. *Finding local office space.* Over the years, I've learned that your office is an important component in attracting and retaining top talent. You want to select office space that is attractive, both in aesthetics and location, to entice potential employees to join your company. Local employees working for a foreign company often desire a certain level of prestige in the quality of their office space. A run-down facility may turn-off potential hires and visiting customers, especially in markets where appearances are important. With traffic congestion in many major cities throughout the world, the location of your office can also be a major advantage of disadvantage for hiring prospective employees. If commutes are too long, many will simply seek employment elsewhere.

Example of Leveraging Relationships

I was running a company called AirPrime that made wireless modules for computing and handheld devices. We saw great opportunity in China, Japan and South Korea, so we quickly devised a plan to enter those markets. The China market was especially important as this was where most of our customers were manufacturing their products. We felt we needed a presence somewhere there. Being able to locally support our customers from the design integration of our module into their products all the way through their release to manufacturing was a great way for us to offer differentiated service. Our customers really appreciated our support efforts.

As they were the most advanced mobile device markets in the world, Japan and South Korea were also very important in meeting our objective of being the most cutting-edge vendor in our industry. The phones and networks in Japan were at least two years ahead of those in the US and Europe. In South Korea, the development cycles were much faster than in the West and their manufacturers often were first in releasing new features. Establishing a strong sales presence in these two countries, with powerful local executives, enabled us to quickly become the market leader.

We leveraged several relationships that introduced us to partners who helped us get established in these three very important markets:

- Our largest customer in the US helped us in China by introducing us to a local company that we hired to provide technical support our customers on a daily basis
- One of our investors helped us in Japan by introducing us to a recruiting firm that helped us hire a very good sales director in the country
- A key supplier helped us in South Korea by introducing us to a very well connected individual that we hired as a local agent

In each case, by leveraging existing relationship, we were able to establish ourselves quickly in all three markets. Would we have succeeded without their assistance? Probably, but it would have taken a lot more time and in the business world, you seldom have the luxury of time.

KEY LESSONS

- Before finalizing whether you should enter a particular country, try to leverage you contacts, along with third party agencies, to get a complete picture of the opportunity. You contacts can help you size up the market, understand the local business climate, gather competitive intelligence, lay out the local ecosystem and identify potential partners.

- Reach out to everyone in your network including existing partners, suppliers, customers, investors and your personal network to assist you.

- Get help from various government agencies, trade offices, and industry trade groups.

- Ask your relationships for help in selecting cities for your location, understanding tax breaks, hiring employees, finding suppliers, and selecting office space.

PART 2

MARKET ENTRY OPTIONS

CHAPTER 6

Master Distributor

WE HAVE REVIEWED HOW TO ANALYZE AND DECIDE ON WHICH markets to enter, and now our focus shifts on determining how to expand into each foreign country. The strategy used may need to differ based on the local environment, as well as your overall business objectives. It is common to invest differently in various parts of the world. In addition, entering some larger countries is complex, so your strategic plan may need to employ several entry options over time.

The most basic international plan involves not allocating your local resources to a foreign market, but instead to export remotely from your home base. This gives you some opportunistic sales, but it is not a complete international *strategy*. Without some sort of local presence, it is extremely difficult to build a stable and successful international business. You may generate some revenue, but you lack a solid foundation for continued success. By limiting your international expansion to exporting, potential customers may decide not to do business with you long-term due to:

- costs of shipping product on an order-by-order basis.
- lead time associated with the additional transit of goods.
- currency fluctuations, as many consumers and companies prefer to do business in their home currency.

■ support concerns if customers need assistance in the local language during their normal business hours.

This is not to discourage you from selling to customers overseas, as I've exported to countries all over the world with success. If you have these opportunities, take advantage of them. As long as you have a process to ensure getting paid from overseas customers, then there is not much downside to exporting.

However, if you are serious about being successful in a particular country, you need a strategy that shows your company has a deeper commitment. The good news is that you can start off with a commitment that does not require a huge investment of financial or people resources.

The easiest way to do this is to sign up with a Master Distributor in a country. A Master Distributor is a company that imports your product and sells it to other distributors, resellers, retailers, integrators and in some cases, end customers. They are either local or international companies that have been operating in your target country for many years. They typically have a strong sales and support infrastructure in place and are well known and trusted in the local market. Having the right Master Distributor can provide you instant market credibility. Many will invest in marketing your brand and building your reputation in the country as well.

Benefits of Master Distributors

There are many benefits to utilizing a Master Distributor. To start, they take title of the goods upon delivery, so you no longer have inventory or theft risk. While they usually pay you in your own national currency, they transact with their customers in the local currency. This means they take on the currency risk, shifting it away from you. Since your financial transactions are all with one company, invoice collecting also becomes much easier as you do not have to track down multiple customers each month to get paid.

Master Distributors also inventory your product locally, so customers can receive shipments faster at reduced shipping charges. By shipping product in bulk to a Master Distributor, your per unit transport costs are also much lower. Moreover, because you typically ship to a Master Distributor on a set schedule, you have more flexibility in selecting the method of shipment, which can further reduce costs. These are savings that can be passed along to end customers, making your product an even better buy.

Most Master Distributors are larger organizations and they can handle the first level of customer support. You train them, and they deal with most customer issues. This can save your team a substantial amount of time. Just as important, your Master Distributor can support customers in their local language, which helps put potential clients at ease when deciding to select your product. For larger customers, your Master Distributor usually has the ability to provide onsite support. Finally, since your Master Distributor is local, their team is easily accessible during normal business hours.

If you select the right Master Distributor, they usually pay on time so you can better manage your cash flow, an important factor when you establish business in a new country because it can impact your credit worthiness (see Chapter 15, Cash Flow Management). Collecting from the end customers, which can be challenging in a foreign market, becomes their responsibility, not yours. Furthermore, returns can be handled locally, giving your customers more confidence in your support capabilities. Local returns also reduce your shipping expense when exchanging products.

With regards to marketing support, Master Distributors can "localize" all your sales collateral (e.g., translating it, adapting it to local customs, and so on) and market your solution in the country. You gain the benefit of both having additional resources at your disposal plus local marketing expertise, which can often speed up your marketing efforts by at least several months. Many Master Distributors even dedicate a marketing person to not only translate your materials, but also modify them so that your messaging better resonates with the local market. If your product proves popular, they will often assign a larger team to help increase awareness.

Most Master Distributors also have large sales organizations, so there are more feet on the street promoting your products to as many potential customers as possible. In addition to prospecting to find new accounts, the sales team also has direct access to their existing customer base. It is always easier to sell into a customer base where there is an existing relationship. You will find a Master Distributor's sales people are always eager to bring on a new source of products, especially if it is in the same ecosystem as other products they sell.

Finally, your financial modeling is more predictable with a Master Distributor. You set a fixed price to sell to them, and they set the marked-up price for their customers. While they may vary that mark-up based on their sales opportunity, you at least have a predictable revenue stream based on your fixed price model. As another aid, Master Distributors usually provide sales forecasts that can help you plan your manufacturing requirements. Having a predictable revenue stream based on long-term forecasts thus helps you develop more accurate financial projections.

Example

Here's an example of how a Master Distributor helped one of my employers. More than ten years ago, I was running sales for a company called Nomadix. Nomadix made Internet Access Gateways. These are electronic boxes that enable lots of people to access the Internet simultaneously. Our main customers were hotels, airports, and apartment buildings.

We found a Master Distributor in Japan called Rikei. They were a local company with a broad reach within Japan, specializing in selling technology products to hotels and apartment complexes. They agreed to be our Master Distributor in Japan, which enabled us to quickly enter the market and our sales grew immediately. The company did all of the following for us:

- Purchased our goods in US dollars at a set price, taking all inventory and currency risk.
- Prepared all the Japanese marketing collateral.
- Marketed the product extensively within Japan.
- Provided direct customer support.
- Handled product returns and exchanges locally.
- Always paid on time.
- Provided monthly forecasts that helped us cost-effectively plan our manufacturing.

It proved to be a win-win for both companies. Nomadix became an instant market share leader in a very large market. Rikei was able to leverage its existing relationships to grow as they broadened their product offering. Japan became our largest market, and Rikei profited nicely as well.

Should You Ask for Exclusivity?

As you can see from all the services they can provide, the Master Distributor is investing a great deal of time and money in selling your product. As you can imagine, they would not want you to sign up additional distributors who take advantage of all the market momentum work they did and start offering your products at a lower price. So in most cases, they will ask for a contract to appoint them as your exclusive distributor for the country.

Most companies react negatively to a request for exclusivity. It seems that it is in your interest to have the ability to sell product to whomever you want. However, exclusivity can be a useful tool if it is negotiated correctly. Here's what I recommend.

First, you need not give blanket exclusivity. You should always ask for terms that protect you including:

- *A time period.* Give the distributor exclusivity for just 12 or 18 months, tying certain volume thresholds that must be met in order to extend the agreement. If they do not meet those volumes, they can continue as a distributor but they lose exclusivity. This time period is sufficient, as it should give the Master Distributor ample time to execute a sales and marketing plan.

■ *A volume commitment.* For exclusivity, the distributor must agree to a minimum purchase every month or quarter. If they do not make the purchase, they lose exclusivity. If a Master Distributor is not willing to make such a minimum purchase commitment, they may not be the right partner. Since you are also investing resources in this relationship, you want a partner who is confident in their ability to generate enough sales to make the relationship worthwhile.

■ *An investment commitment.* They must spend a certain budget each month promoting your product. They must also assign dedicated resources to sell and support your product. If they cannot make these investments, they should not be an exclusive Master Distributor as you need a partner that is dedicated to helping you succeed in their country.

■ *Mutual Exclusivity.* In offering them exclusivity on your product, they must agree not to sell any directly competing products. If your success in the country is dependent on them, their success should be dependent on selling your product. If they are selling a competing product, they may not always have your best interests at heart. Your competitor might even offer the Master Distributor and its sales team a bigger incentive to sell their product over yours. The loser in such a scenario is your company.

■ *Better payment terms.* If the Master Distributor wants exclusivity, insist they pay their invoices faster. For example, if the contract originally had 45-day payment terms, reduce it to 30 days. Receiving payments faster helps you improve your cash flow. As you expand into new markets, faster payments provide you more flexibility and options in running your company.

If you are considering granting exclusivity, be sure to learn about the company and speak to other vendors that do business with them. Two important points to verify are that your Master Distributor

(a) has the capability to generate the volume that you are modeling in your financials , and (b) has the same sales volume expectations that you have. If a small company offers to be your Master Distributor in a large country, they will likely not have the staff to maximize your sales potential. They may also run into problems paying you on time. With Master Distributors, your success is governed by their capabilities, so make sure they have the resources to meet your objectives.

Moreover, both parties must have the same goals as to what sales volumes will be reached within a set period of time. Even if the contractual volume commitment is lower, both parties should agree on a set revenue target. Do not assume that your partner shares your vision, especially if your two cultures are different. In some cultures, such as Japan, silence on an issue means no agreement has been made. So if you do not explicitly agree to a target, you may be surprised to learn that your expectations were not aligned. It can happen that your partner may believe they are being successful for you, while you feel extremely disappointed. Worse, they will keep doing only what they are currently doing even as your frustration grows since you expected more of them.

Finally, one other thing to learn about a Master distributor is what other products they carry. If they represent many different products, their priorities may be swayed from time to time. Other vendors might run promotions that provide additional bonuses to distributors if they reach certain sales targets in a given month or quarter. If your master distributor is offered many of these promotions, your products may be neglected regardless of the contractual agreement you have in place. It's simply worthwhile for the Master Distributor to put their time into selling the other products.

As with any partner, you must be proactive in managing the relationship if you want to reap the benefits you envisioned when you first signed the contract. In our case with Rikei in Japan, we had a very motivated partner. However, we still flew to Japan every month to be visible. Not only did we have good sharing of the minds but our distributor and their customers' saw that we were vigilant and committed to growing our business.

Occasions to Be Flexible on Exclusivity

If a prospective master distributor in a country that was not one of your main targets approaches you, it can be worthwhile to be more lenient on the exclusivity terms. Given that this market was not at the top of your international expansion list, as long as they agree to market your product, support it, and pay on time, you may have little to lose. Sometimes it can be surprising how well your product will do in countries that were not your top priority. Nevertheless, just make sure your expectations line up with the Master Distributor's.

For example, with my IP telephone business, we had a potential Master Distributor in South Africa approach us. As the product category was new, they were unsure of the volumes the product would generate in their country. Instead of one-year exclusivity, they asked for a two-year term, saying they needed time to build up demand in their market. Given that South Africa was not on our list of near-term expansion targets and the firm was willing to dedicate marketing and support resources, there was no negative impact on agreeing to their terms. We signed an agreement and I dealt with them on a purchase order basis, with payment of invoices in advance of product shipment. Although they did not become a large revenue generator for my business, they were a profitable partner.

- Exporting products based on purchase orders may be good for your business in the short-term, but it is not an international strategy.

- The fastest way to enter a country is in partnership with a Master Distributor, a company that imports your product and sells it to other distributors, resellers, retailers, integrators and in some cases, end customers.

- Master distributors provide many benefits including taking on currency and inventory risk, marketing and selling of your product, providing customer support and exchanges, and paying on time.

- Exclusivity works well with a master distributor if negotiated correctly. An exclusivity agreement includes a time period, volume commitment, resource investment, applies to both parties and provides better payment terms.

- Verify you are in agreement on sales volume and revenue targets though.

- In non-strategic markets, being flexible on your exclusivity terms is good business.

CHAPTER 7

Local Agents

————◦❖◦————

Y OU MAY SELECT MARKETS WHERE YOU DO NOT WANT TO commit to a master distributor, or there is no major master distribution partner. Or, you may want a more dedicated resource—someone who acts and is seen as an employee—but you are not ready or financially able to make a commitment to set up an office in your target country. In these cases, the solution is to hire a local agent within that market. (Sometimes they are also called manufacturer's representatives.) Local agents represent one or more manufacturers and focus on sales. They can be viewed as extensions of your team in a country, so you are seen as being more committed to the market than signing up a Master Distributor.

Some local agents are independent individuals operating alone, but others work for a firm with several people. In my experience, whether they work solo or are part of a team is not important. The abilities, experience, and energy level of the person working as your agent are most significant. Hiring a local agent is almost like hiring an employee: you must be selective to ensure the person can do the job and is a good fit with the rest of your organization.

Attributes of a Good Local Agent

The best local agents come from within your industry. They have either worked for a local competitor, large target customer, or a sales channel partner. If they worked for a local competitor, they know a lot about your market's competition and have a Rolodex full of customer contacts. If they worked at a large target customer, they know how to position your product to solve a customer's problems. If they worked at a sales channel partner, they will have a good understanding of which partners will best help you get products to end customers. With any of these backgrounds, a local agent will likely have good industry connections and can create sales opportunities much faster for you.

I've always preferred selecting a local person rather than a foreigner in that country to serve as my local agent. Why? First, they fully understand the culture and language. I believe it is vital that a sales representative be able to communicate effectively and not alienate potential customers. Second, they can guide you on how to finalize business in the country because they know local customs and the current business climate. Third, local people have a lifetime of connections that can come in handy. As selling is often relationship based, the more people your agent has strong relationships with, the greater success you will have. For example, the person's university and even high school connections can turn out to be a great source of referrals or business itself, as most people are loyal to their schools and fellow classmates. If your agent did not attend these institutions locally, all those potential connections are lost.

Great communication skills in your language are also important. The reasons for being able to speak the local language are obvious, as just discussed. But just as important is your agent's ability to speak your language. If your customers do not speak your language, agents are your main interface to them. The agent must be able to effectively interpret what the customer wants and explain it to you clearly in your language. This extends beyond doing a literal translation, as the agent must be able to successfully convey any nuances of the situation. Your agent must be able to express the state of affairs clearly, both on conference calls and via written reports, to you and the rest of the company.

The last attribute to assess is educational background. If you provide a technical product, having an agent with a technical degree or experience is critical to build credibility with target customers. This is especially true if you sell your product to technical customers like design engineers. A representative who cannot explain the workings of a product will have your company's credibility questioned. This can affect your ability to sell. If you find a good local agent with a great track record but the person is non-technical, insist that he work with a technical associate who can be involved in making customer visits, conducting technical presentations, and assisting customers with engineering-type questions.

Example of Hiring a Local Agent

One of my companies, Atrua, made security components for the mobile phone market. You may recall from prior chapters that we successfully set up a subsidiary in China, hired full-time employees through a consulting firm in Europe and formed a successful partnership in Japan with Murata. China, Japan and northern Europe were key markets to us, but they were not the only strategic markets we were targeting.

South Korea was another of our high priority markets, because two of the top five mobile phone manufacturers at the time were based there. In addition, the phones sold in South Korea were some of the most innovative in the world. While we eventually wanted to establish an office in Seoul, we did not initially have the funds to do so. So through one of our venture capital investors, we were introduced to a senior person at a firm called JayWave, a local agent or rep firm with about 10 employees focused on technology products, primarily for the mobile phone market.

The person we interfaced with was a Korean national with over thirty years of experience in the electronics and mobile phone markets. Based in Seoul, he had recently taken an early retirement package from an American company providing components for mobile phones. He was very energetic and eager to assist in building a new business. We decided to hire both him and the firm. With his industry connections, we were quickly introduced to the decision makers not only at the two biggest manufacturers, but also three additional manufacturers who were making several million phones per year. His expertise in the local market and industry connections proved invaluable in helping us enter the Korean market.

JayWave provided us many benefits that we would not have been able to obtain on our own, including:

- immediate access to decision makers at all our target customers
- access to executives at all the mobile operators in South Korea, which helped us build out our ecosystem,
- a team of three highly experienced, well-connected people: a senior manager, a sales person, and a technical person. All were Koreans who spoke and wrote English very well.

We closely managed our relationship, with either myself or someone from my team flying to Seoul every month in order to work with our local agents and target customers. We built up a very strong relationship.

Payment to Agents

What payment arrangement is best to make with local agents? Unlike distributors to whom you sell a product and they make their profit on the resale, agents do not purchase your product. Instead, there are two ways to pay an agent: monthly retainer and/or commission on sales.

Actually, most agents will ask for a monthly retainer plus a commission. The monthly retainer is a set fee paid regardless of success. I've tried to avoid paying retainers as much as possible, because there may be less motivation for the agent to close sales. I'll gladly pay a higher percentage commission instead of providing a retainer.

This way, your interest and the agent's interest are perfectly aligned. So I recommend that you aim to pay only a commission—even if it is a higher percentage.

Commissions can be based on a one-time payment for the initial sale or continuous, as long as the customer keeps buying. While some companies insist on only paying one time for the initial sale, I'm comfortable paying on a continuous basis if the agent remains involved in managing the customer. A win-win situation occurs when the customer continues to receive good service from your local agent, and the continuous commissions keep the agent motivated to manage and grow the business within the account.

Regardless of the commission structure you implement, make sure your commissions are only paid out after you've collected from your customers. Otherwise you risk paying out cash and not being able to collect for sold product. You need to ensure your agents are held accountable for the ability of their customers to pay.

Hiring Multiple Agents

Whether or not to hire multiple agents in one country depends on the particular situation, as there are cases where multiple agents make good sense. For example, if you have multiple product lines that are so diverse that the target customers are different, then having multiple agents is a good idea because you want agents who have existing connections with these target customers. Let's say you make a module that is integrated into a product, but you also sell an end product directly to consumers. These are different product lines and your target markets are not the same, so having different agents is a better choice to maximize your sales potential for each product line.

Another case when you might want multiple agents is when you have a product that is valuable to different vertical markets. For example, let's say you have a wireless module that can be beneficial to computer manufacturers, makers of household appliances, and automobile companies. These are three very different markets, and you most likely will not find one agent who understands all three market segments or has the right connections for all three. Multiple agents will be necessary in this situation to maximize your sales in each vertical.

You might also take on different agents when you have certain geographic considerations. It can be especially helpful in very large countries, or countries where there are two or three rival cities. China, for instance, is an enormous market for some products, so getting one agent to cover the entire country may not be in your best interest. Instead, finding agents in each of the key cities—such as Beijing, Shanghai and Shenzhen—is a much more prudent strategy. Another example is Spain, where an agent from Madrid may not be warmly received in Barcelona. Having a second agent to cover Barcelona would be a better strategy. In many cases, having local agents in the main cities where you want to do business can also be advantageous, since they will be able to spend more face time with customers and have a better understanding of the local competitive environment.

Maintaining Communication with Agents

One final consideration: be sure to set up a clear communications plan with your local agents. For one, the agent must constantly inform you on what is going on in the country, specifically as it pertains to customer feedback and competitor activities. Not obtaining timely customer feedback prohibits you from making changes that impact your success. All feedback, both positive and negative, should be provided to you.

Likewise, not being up to date on competitor activities can put you at a major disadvantage in the market. As soon as your agent learns that your competition is doing anything unique with its products, pricing, or promotions, you need to know so you can respond in a timely fashion. Getting one report at the end of the quarter is too late.

The best communications plans with local agents include:

- Weekly conference calls, where you can discuss the latest opportunities, customer feedback, competitor activities and local market conditions. This is also the right forum for you to update local agents on company successes in other countries, new products, or features and upcoming company activities. Typically, these calls are scheduled for one hour per week, and the information that is shared in both directions is well worth the time.
- Written status reports, summarizing everything neatly. In these reports, all account activity should be reported, including a summary of next steps and action items that need headquarters assistance. The reports should also include an updated sales forecast that reflects the latest expectations. If you have weekly conference calls, the written status reports can be monthly or twice per month. If you do not have weekly conference calls, then these reports must be provided weekly.
- Visits to the country to see customers and potential customers with your agent. The more face time you or your executives spend in the country with prospective customers, the more successful you will be. The visits are also the best way to verify that the information being communicated back to you is accurate and the sales forecast is achievable. Frequency of visits depends on the revenue potential and strategic nature of the local market. Sometimes monthly visits are required, and sometimes just two or three times per year will suffice.

- If there is no ideal master distribution partner or you want a more dedicated resource, but are not ready to make a commitment to an office, hiring a local agent is a good solution.

- Local agents provide a more dedicated in-country resource than a master distributor, and less of a financial commitment than setting up your own sales office.

- Look for agents who are local people, have experience in your industry, and have great communication skills in the local language and your language.

- If you have a technical product, be sure the agent has technical degree or background, or has a technical assistant.

- Determine how the agent gets paid: commission-only is best and, remember, only pay commissions after you get paid!

- Decide whether you should hire multiple agents – it depends on your product lines, target vertical markets, and geographic needs.

- Set up a strong communication plan with the agent via regular weekly teleconferences, written reports, and site visits.

CHAPTER 8

Sales and Support Office

AS YOU ANALYZED WHICH MARKETS TO ENTER, SOME PRESENTED better opportunities than others. Weighing the potential rewards against the risks and costs associated with entering a market, you may decide that going all in, and establishing a permanent presence is your wisest choice. This way you have direct control over the destiny of your business expansion and you can hire employees who are 100% dedicated to your business.

If so, deciding to set up an office in a foreign country can be complex as each country has its own regulations for:

- establishing a legal entity
- employment policies
- taxation
- banking requirements

As you start the process of establishing an office overseas, you will probably need expert advice. You should engage with an international accounting firm that has experience setting up an office or subsidiary in your target country. They can assist you in understanding the taxation and banking requirements in your new country. In addition, you will need legal advice, especially if the country has unique requirements, so find a law firm that either has an office in your target country or has a partnership with a law firm there.

Among the many services your law firm can provide is setting up the legal entity and helping you with employment policies. Note that these items are discussed in more detail in Part 3 of this book, Financial Considerations.

Based on my experience, I recommend having your accounting firm be your primary professional services partner, especially since they charge lower rates than a law firm. If your existing accounting firm does not have an office in your new country, you can supplement them with a small local firm to handle your basic in-county accounting. With regards to your law firm, even if they are not international, they most likely have relationships with foreign firms that can assist you. Keep in mind that both your accounting and law firms have a lot of historical data regarding your company, and you do not want to lose that as part of your expansion.

Considerations in Setting up a Local Office

When setting up an office, it is important to remember that you need not just sales but also support functions there. You must support your new customers with any billing, technical, shipping, and returns issues. Depending on your product, you may be able to handle some of these issues remotely, either back at headquarters or in a regional office. However, in some cases, it is invaluable to have local staff that speak the language, understand the cultural nuances, and are available during their normal business hours.

Make sure you have a well thought-out plan before you decide to set up a local office. One of the most critical decisions is who will be the general manager or top executive in your office. I cannot emphasize enough the importance of this. Without the right person to lead your in-country team, you will not succeed. This person will set the tone of the local company including office culture, energy level, and how you deal with customers. The image you convey to your local customers and partners will be a direct result of the personality and leadership style of the general manager.

To select this person, here are some guidelines based on my experiences. First, you need to decide whether to hire someone locally or send someone from headquarters to run the office. In my career, I have always hired someone locally. Like selecting a local agent, a local general manager will fully understand the culture and language. Not only is this important when dealing with customers, but his or her familiarity is useful when it comes to hiring and leading a larger local team. If your employees clearly understand what the leadership wants, they will better execute your objectives and have a tendency to be happier and stay with your company longer.

However, sending someone from headquarters, who will be considered an ex-pat, can also be an effective strategy as long as the executive you are sending:

- Has extensively traveled and conducted business internationally. The person has to be comfortable operating in new work environments. Without having previous experience in different cultures, the executive can easily become confused and defensive. Without extensive international experience, the risk of this happening is too great.
- Is accepting that the culture will be different. This applies to not only dealing with customers and partners, but also within the office. Early in my career, I recall visiting our Japanese and German offices when I was working at Compaq, and seeing firsthand how different the office culture was from US headquarters. Local general managers ran these organizations. If a US-based executive had tried to enforce the headquarters culture, those foreign offices would have had a lot of turnover and not been successful.
- The person either speaks the local language or is willing to immerse him or herself to learn it. Although most international companies use English as their official language, to really understand what is going on, and demonstrate respect for their culture, familiarity if not fluency in the local language is critical. Office chatter is always conducted in the local language, as are many

side conversations in external business meetings. Your company will be at a disadvantage if your general manager cannot understand these side talks. Besides, both employees and customers will appreciate an executive who is making the effort to learn and speak the local language.

■ The person is a good communicator, able to explain and break things down well in both written and oral communications. When on a foreign assignment, extra effort has to be made when communicating with others. Keep in mind that at least one of the parties is translating the conversation in his/her mind in real-time, so the other must be patient and work harder to get the message across.

■ The person is a "people-person" and gets along well with others. This would seem obvious, but you'd be surprised how often it is overlooked. Many rising stars in corporate America are aggressive individuals who have not spent time nurturing relationships and coaching others. Their 'take no prisoners' approach has helped the company's bottom line but has not have endeared them to many coworkers. Such individuals, while great company contributors, are often not the right fit for opening a new international office. Instead, you need a leader you can patiently coach to develop a team of new employees in that location.

■ The executive must be agreeable to appointing a local person as a clear number two person in the office. Having a local person that the team can look up to is very important. This person is often the one that office staff will go to with issues, as they may feel more comfortable discussing confidential matters or conflicts with a fellow national in their own language. It is not a sign of disrespect to the general manager, but when issues arise, people often seek resolution from those who share more in common with them. It is a natural human tendency.

If you decide to hire locally, as I've always done in my career, conduct a broad search to find the best candidates. I've often hired a local recruiting firm, as it ensures that you get a good cross section of candidates and prospects from different pools. In addition, when the recruiting firm presents qualified candidates, ask your local contacts to interview them to provide you with their perspective. They can also compare them to any individuals they may have recommended to you.

Perhaps the most critical attribute you seek in a candidate is experience within your industry, ideally if they know your products and can bring potential customers with a big Rolodex of contacts that also includes future employees, ecosystem partners, and suppliers. In some cultures, particularly in Asia, many years of experience is highly cherished. Someone with grey hair who has spent a lot of time within your industry and is highly respected will be better able to attract talent and impress potential customers in many of these markets. Although such experienced leaders can command higher salaries, the benefit of their knowledge and connections often makes the extra cost worth it.

Next, you need to assess whether the candidate can build a strong team and develop them as time goes on. As you will not be involved day to day in the local business, a general manager with this skill set is critical. The person must be able to take ownership of recruiting and motivating the local staff. Find out if the candidate has done this before; learn if he or she has been able to retain the best performing employees over long periods of time. Although the general manager is your single most important hire, it is the expertise, motivation and stability of your team that will ultimately determine your long-term success in a country.

Finally, the candidate must have excellent verbal and written communication skills in your language. The person must be able to communicate effectively with the rest of your company across geographies and job functions. He or she also needs to clearly understand all company communications that are provided either orally or in writing. Any miscommunications can lead to poor decisions that negatively impact the company. The person has to be comfortable enough to be an active participant in company planning activities, otherwise he or she will quickly feel isolated.

One more item that is important to building out your sales and support office is the actual office space. You want to select office space that is attractive, both in aesthetics and location, to entice potential employees to join your company. Most major cities have lots of traffic congestion and in order to attract quality employees you need to take their commutes into consideration. If you can avoid it, you do not want to be outside of town away from your prospective employees. As most major cities outside of the United States have well-established mass transit systems, you should look for office space near major rail or bus lines.

Ideally, you also want office space near most of your customers so they can visit you more easily. The easier you make if for customers to reach you, the more likely they will make the attempt. The more face time you can spend with prospective customers, the better the chances they will do business with you. When customers visit your office, you also want to make sure it is in a good neighborhood, in a nice building, and well furnished. They may make judgments based on whether your company space looks professional and organized. However, sometimes having too extravagant an office can be seen as a negative if potential customers perceive you to be wasteful. Talk to local people to understand the boundaries of what is and is not acceptable in office furnishings.

Example of Opening an Office

I was running a business unit at Xircom, where we provided communication modules to PC vendors. This was in the late 1990s and many of the leading vendors were designing notebook computers in Japan. We knew that to succeed, we had to set up a sales and support office in that country. The largest potential customers expected a local team that could quickly visit them onsite if needed. They wanted the assurance that if any questions arose during their design phases, our team was always available.

Using our accounting firm, we set up a company "representative office" that allowed us to hire a local team. In Japan, a representative office gives you a legal presence to operate within the country, but not to conduct commercial transactions. We handled every aspect of the business locally, but the actual customer purchase orders were processed in the US.

In the beginning, this worked well as most of our customers were large multinationals such as Toshiba, Panasonic, NEC, and Hitachi that had lots of experience conducing financial transactions with American corporations. A few years later, as our business expanded and we dealt with smaller entities, we saw a need to form a full subsidiary in Japan that gave us the ability to process purchase orders locally in Japanese Yen.

We thus needed to build a strong, local team. I hired a recruiting firm that presented many good candidates to us. For our general manager, we selected a gentleman who had worked most of his career for American companies and sold into the same set of customers as we were targeting. He was a very effective, charismatic leader. Within the first year, he grew the team to four people, having sales, field engineering, and administrative support. This provided us a strong local base to support our new customers. In addition, every month we would send personnel from headquarters to provide further assistance. Our new customers saw that we were committed to their success providing them with both local and international resources. We were very successful, with Japan becoming our second largest market.

Interacting with Your Overseas Office

Once you set up a local sales and support office, you need to determine what day-to-day interactions you should plan and expect.

The first rule is to communicate constantly with the new office. You must make a conscious effort to interact regularly with your remote offices, even if time zone differences make it difficult. This is especially true in the first months, when they need your support and you need to know they are on the same page as the rest of the company. Besides, calling and emailing your remote employees regularly improves employee morale, making them feel they are an important part of the overall company.

I've always preferred weekly calls with each of my offices, and at times even scheduled a weekly global call for the senior managers of each foreign office to interact with each other and headquarters. These global calls proved extremely effective as all the offices were able to learn about different tactics and strategies that worked in other markets. Of course, coordinating such calls across many time zones is difficult but the gains in company cohesion and better financial results make it worthwhile. As long as the calls have a clear agenda, do not constantly repeat what was previously communicated and are focused on ways to grow the business, remote offices are happy to participate. In my view, there is no such thing as over-communicating with remote offices.

You must also give remote offices the freedom to structure and conduct business as they deem best for their markets. If you hired well, your in-country people will understand your company objectives and what it takes to succeed. But they also need the ability to adapt your business processes to maximize their success. By constantly communicating with the rest of the company, they should be in synch with the organization and the overall goals of the business. As long as there is a clear understanding of what is and is not permissible, give the local team the flexibility to conduct its own business. Of course, as a corporate officer you need to maintain oversight to ensure they follow company policies and conduct business legally and ethically.

You also need to provide resources and support the local office. Whether it is accounting, product management, IT, or technical support, make sure people at headquarters are responsive to the remote office's needs and do not consider them second-priority. Time differences can make this difficult, but it must be an equal priority for the headquarters staff to respond in real-time to remote employee needs. Otherwise, the local employees will feel second-rate and can quickly lose faith in the company. Despite all your other efforts, if the local employees do not feel supported by headquarters staff, it will devolve into an "us" versus "them" mentality that can severely impact your business.

The sales and support office also needs the tools to localize both their sales material and the product offering for their market. We go into detail about this in Chapter 18, Localizing Products and Services, so for now, let me just state that to succeed, you need to conform to the market as the market will not conform to you. If you do not provide the local team the tools to make modifications for their market, you will always be at a disadvantage because your competitors are giving their remote offices these capabilities.

Finally, as with the rest of your business, you must set clear goals and have the ability to measure results in real-time. Goals should include:

- revenue targets
- expense targets
- customer satisfaction metrics
- employee satisfaction metrics
- cash flow management goals
- market share goals
- measurement of other metrics such as ROI (return on investment), ROA (return on assets), DSO (days sales outstanding, a measure of how quickly customers pay), or others. The metrics you decide to measure should be similar to the ones you use to measure your overall business' health at headquarters.

Make sure you state these objectives and targets clearly, and have the right tools to measure them accurately and continually. You want to have the ability to easily pull reports at any time to see how your foreign sales and support offices are doing.

- Setting up a local sales and support office is often valuable, as it shows a strong commitment from you to the local market. If done correctly, it can be very profitable and professionally rewarding.

- Setting up an office in a foreign country is complex so have your accounting and law firms take the lead in the regulatory and administrative aspects.

- Have a well-thought out plan before entering a market. Think about both sales and support needs, including billing, technical, shipping and returns issues.

- Select a general manager to lead the remote office who has industry experience, can recruit and motivate staff and has excellent communications skills in your language. A local person has many advantages including fully understanding the culture and language.

- If you select a foreigner to run your office, make sure this person has extensively traveled internationally, is accepting of different cultures, willing to learn the local language, is a great communicator who gets along well with others, and quickly appoints a local as the clear #2 leader.

- The keys to successfully interacting with a foreign sales office are to communicate regularly, have weekly calls, give them freedom to structure and conduct business as they see fit, localize your product as needed, provide strong headquarters support, and set clear goals.

CHAPTER 9

Establishing an R&D Center

AS YOUR BUSINESS FLOURISHES, YOUR EXPANSION PLANS MAY need to extend beyond establishing sales and support offices in foreign markets. Certain countries may represent a significant opportunity if you plant deeper roots. Many large multi-nationals have succeeded because they established R&D, manufacturing, and extensive customer support centers in various foreign markets around the world. Such expansion provided them many benefits by leveraging local expertise in each market. The diversity of technical talent in other parts of the world can provide many advantages when developing new products. In this chapter, we will focus on what it takes to establish a research and development center in a new country.

Expanding your R&D capabilities beyond your home market provides many benefits, including:

- Leveraging the different engineering, medical, or scientific skill sets in other countries
- Increasing the company's daily R&D hours by having developers work on projects in multiple time zones
- More efficiently customizing or localizing your existing products for new markets
- Developing brand new products for your expanded market that can also be brought into your home market for an additional revenue stream

■ Creating a more flexible cost structure for your company as salaries vary throughout the world

To be effective, however, an expansion of R&D requires that your leadership team at headquarters is comfortable dealing with projects that are either jointly developed in multiple locations or completely developed in a remote physical office that they cannot closely supervise.

Considerations for Establishing an R&D Center

While there are lots of potential benefits in setting up a center in a new country, there are many issues that will require up-front planning. Some of these are procedural (such as legal, accounting and project management) while others are interpersonal (such as how to collaborate, share technology, and decide how individuals report to each other). Not addressing these matters can lead to a great expense in resolving them later on. To guarantee success, you need to make sure both your headquarters team and the new R&D team have the same understanding regarding objectives, processes, and the measurement and reporting of progress.

Like setting up a sales and support office, you may need expert advice to establish an R&D center. In fact, establishing an R&D center is much more complex than a sales and support office. In addition to the accounting and legal regulations mentioned in the prior chapter, such as establishing a legal entity for transactions, employment policies, taxation and banking requirements, there are many additional items you need to resolve.

The first is deciding how intellectual property is shared between locations. As different countries have varying policies for protecting intellectual property (IP), you should consult with an intellectual property attorney so you can create clear procedures on what is shared among countries. For example, at Atrua, with our China office we decided to share the source code for one of our ancillary product lines, but not for our main product line for fear of it being hacked by outsiders.

Next, you need to decide how new intellectual property will be created and its revenues shared. This can be tricky, especially if you ultimately license your IP to 3rd parties. Certain countries will make taxation claims on those license fees if the intellectual property was created locally. The United States is one country that makes these claims. So it is very important to understand taxation policies about IP licensing *before* you start development activities in the local market. Consult your accountant and/or attorney well in advance of kicking off any projects to ensure that you get complete guidance on how to best proceed. Better to know the implications up-front so you can model them into your business.

You will also need to research government policies towards establishing R&D centers before deciding on your final office location. Many countries and even individual cities offer tax and other financial incentives to establish a local R&D center there. The financial benefits can be substantial, so it is important to understand what is available before making a final decision on where to locate. Sometimes subsidies can greatly reduce your cost structure as they include multi-year tax waivers or even tax rebates for hiring local employees. Even if you have a good idea where you want to locate, do not be reluctant to negotiate better terms with local governments, as some are very aggressive in luring companies to set up development centers within their cities.

Note that in some cases, such tax incentives vary not just by country or city, but even according to specific zones within a city. To encourage development in certain parts of town, some cities vary their incentives based on the location of the office. For example, many cities in China have specified certain zones where they provide tax breaks to entice foreign companies to set up R&D or manufacturing centers in those areas. If you set up your R&D office in a different part of the city, those benefits will not apply. So make sure you investigate what each city is offering in different neighborhoods before picking a location within its boundaries.

In the last chapter, we discussed the importance of hiring the right person to run your international office. The same criteria apply to hiring your head of R&D. You want someone with solid and relevant industry experience, who can build a team, keep them motivated, and has excellent communication skills. Your head of R&D must be experienced in your technology, as you will have a hard time meeting your business objectives if he/she will be learning on the job. Since you are building a team, recruiting and retaining top talent must be job #1. So make sure the head of R&D is technically proficient, personable, and someone other engineers will want to work for.

Just like with local agents and general managers, the communication skills of your head of R&D must be strong, perhaps stronger. This leader must be able to communicate ideas and vision effectively in the local language and English, both verbally and in writing. This is critical if different offices are collaborating together on R&D projects, as miscommunications can lead to costly project delays. Specifically, schedules, technical specifications and overall project goals need to be well understood by all parties. Even if projects are being engineered separately, based on a shared core technology, being able to communicate technical details accurately is paramount.

Finally, keep in mind that your most proprietary and valuable company information is typically shared in the product development organization. Expanding this organization internationally creates a new set of IT systems risks that you need to mitigate or eliminate. There is no doubt that you must have a plan to protect your intellectual property via your IT infrastructure. The more locations you have, the more points of entry for aggressive network hackers and industrial spies to breach your proprietary data. Firewalls and other security measures you have implemented will need to be upgraded so that the remote R&D center can access all company information but outsiders will be blocked.

If you are establishing your first R&D center outside of headquarters, expect to make a good-sized investment to protect your network and data from external attacks. Upgrading existing equipment and software to implement the latest safeguard is likely necessary if you have remote locations. With technology advancing rapidly, this becomes an investment you should expect to make on a recurring basis as hackers will catch up with new protections. What is leading-edge network security today will most likely be obsolete in the next couple of years. If you are not sure what to do or implement, reach out to an IT consulting firm that can review your current topology and make recommendations for improvement.

How to Structure R&D Collaboration Between Offices

Once you've decided to open up new R&D centers, you must develop a strategy for determining what each center will do, and how they will work together. While larger corporations will typically have multiple centers doing core product research, smaller companies tend to keep the core research centralized, and have the remote R&D centers focus primarily on product customization or development work such as product line extensions and product enhancements. While there are many ways to decide how to split up development work among your international offices, a best practice is to come up with a structure that all locations will follow. As you decide the best way to set up your R&D structure, here are three structures I've seen and deployed successfully.

1. *Allocate projects by office.* While you maintain a centralized, core R&D function, you break out development projects on an office-by-office basis. This structure is the easiest to implement, and reduces potential miscommunications between offices as projects are segregated and handled within each facility. Thus, the amount of daily communications between offices is not as intense. For example, your US office can develop one line of products, while your Germany office develops a different line, and your Brazil office customizes one product and turns it into a new product line for emerging markets.

This kind of structure is typically deployed when leveraging different engineering skillsets from each market makes sense. The overall objective is to bring more products to market, developed with a different viewpoint than if they were all developed within one country. Another benefit is that this arrangement creates a more flexible company cost structure. In some countries, particularly in developing nations, engineering salaries are lower so those offices can focus their development efforts on activities that require more inexpensive entry- and mid-level engineers.

2. Have dispersed teams collaborate on the same product development projects. This is more of a vertical strategy, in which teams do different parts of a project. For example, in designing a new electronic device, your US team can develop the core product architecture and write the software algorithms, while your team in India can write the software drivers and develop the user interface, and your team in China develops the hardware and works with the manufacturer on making sure the product can be manufactured efficiently. Since all teams must work closely together, effective communications is critical with this structure to be successful.

Because of distances and time zone differences, all specifications need to be clearly spelled out. Frequent conference calls, even daily ones during critical stages of the project, are often needed. In addition, this structure may require more travel for face-to-face meetings. This collaborative structure is typically deployed when time is of essence and you can leverage multiple engineering skillsets from each market. It allows you to increase the number of R&D hours being spent on a particular project so you can bring your products to market faster.

3. Create a lead R&D center to develop brand new product lines. While the other R&D centers provide support, this center is tasked specifically with creating new products that can be offered either regionally or worldwide. In this environment, the new R&D

center is responsible for both core research and product development. The office will develop most of the technology internally and also be responsible for converting the technology into salable products. The new center is much more independent and self-sufficient, compared to the other structures.

Communications risks are minimized with this kind of implementation since everyone is in the same location. But the risk of developing a product that cannot be sold in other markets is greater. The reason is that the local team might end up thinking only about their home market as they define and develop products. This kind of structure is useful when the local market opportunity is very large, engineering skillsets in the country are broad enough to develop a complete product, and when you need to experiment with new product lines that may later be sold regionally or globally. The overall result of such an implementation is that you will expand your product lines via brand new offerings.

Example of Setting up an R&D Center

In previous chapters, I shared how my company, Atrua, set up a subsidiary in China. As you recall, Atrua developed security components for the mobile phone market. When we decided to set up a subsidiary in China, our goal was to create a center for sales and support of our customers' manufacturing efforts, but it was also to help develop new products. The sales and manufacturing support tasks and objectives were easy to define. As for product development, we had to decide what we wanted the office to do before we proceeded. We established the following goals for the R&D center in China:

- Expand our development capabilities so we could double our ability to release new products simultaneously. Our new China team would work with our core technology but develop a new set of products.

■ Reduce our cost structure. The engineers we were hiring in China had salaries that were about one-sixth of what our US engineers cost. By opening up the R&D center, our budget per product being developed was reduced substantially. This also benefited our expert US development team, as they could focus on more challenging projects.

■ Develop product line extensions, particularly for the very large China market. Most of our new sales opportunities were coming from Chinese customers. Many wanted a product that was a little different than what we were offering, so the China team would develop these derivative products to better suit local customers' needs.

■ Support our local manufacturing partners. Our semiconductors were manufactured and packaged in greater China. Supporting them from the US was challenging, so we wanted to have our development team work closely with our own manufacturing partners.

We began recruiting and hiring engineers. As we built up our team, we had to revise some of those initial objectives. Mixed signal semiconductor product development was still new in China, so we were not able to assemble the right team to develop a completely new integrated circuit. Our China team did well at supporting the US team, but they could not develop a completely new product. There were certain phases of development where they could assist, but not in others. So our goal of developing two products at once had to be abandoned.

However, we discovered that our new China team was very good at developing software drivers to support more products iterations. So we leveraged the local engineering skillset to provide more customer options for our existing product lines. This proved extremely beneficial as our China-based customers kept asking for more and more versions of our products.

In addition, our China office ended up providing outstanding manufacturing partner support. Not only did they embed some relevant expertise, but we now had a team in the same time zone, which enabled us to launch products faster since we eliminated time delays in working through issues associated with transferring an engineering design to manufacturing. So although we did not double our core product development, we were able to reduce costs, develop new product line extensions, and better support our manufacturing partners. This was a successful outcome for our company.

One last note regarding this example: we had two very different product lines, and for our main product line we elected not to supply our software source code to our China team. We were very concerned about hackers getting to our code. Based on the fact that we structured our R&D to allocate projects by office, it really was not needed for their tasks and we did not want to unnecessarily expose our intellectual property.

Hiring for the R&D Center

Soon after you have hired your head of R&D, selected your office location, and decided what activities and projects will be the responsibility of the local team, you will need to recruit your team. Hiring the right engineers and technicians is very important to your success. As mentioned, when you are building a team, recruiting and retaining top talent must be job #1. Seek engineers who are both technically strong and will work well with others in the office. However, it is very important to make sure they have the skillset and passion for the projects you will allocate to that particular office. The team must be engaged and happy to operate well together.

You also need to build a thriving culture in the office. Some engineers are very talented, but their personalities can clash with others in the organization. Try to gauge the cultural fit as you interview potential team members. Without the right office environment, you risk having a lot of employee turnover. Losing engineers is devastating to meeting your goals as it can lead to serious project delays, transferring engineers to projects where they do not have sufficient technology experience, and fractured collaboration on projects where remote teams must work together.

Next attribute on the list for hiring is trust. You and your domestic R&D team must trust the new overseas team. If trust is lacking, especially if people are collaborating together on projects, be ready for conflicts, constant project delays, and new products that do not meet your expectations. No one will give their best efforts if they feel they are not being trusted. To build trust, make sure the teams communicate frequently and are open about sharing both successes and challenges. The bottom line is, if you cannot grow to trust your international R&D team, you should not set one up in the first place.

I've found it most effective if you foster a continuous exchange of engineers. Having teams work together side by side once in a while is the best way to build trust. The exchange must be two-way, with engineers from both offices making visits. At Atrua, we would send US-based engineers to our China office for two-week assignments and the China team loved this as they worked hand-in-hand with their US counterparts. We also invited some of our most experienced China engineers to the US for one-month assignments where they got to work closely with the US team. Not only was the knowledge sharing invaluable, but the camaraderie and trust that developed was astounding.

KEY LESSONS

- Many multi-nationals cite having R&D centers in various markets throughout the world as a factor in their success, as they can leverage unique expertise in different countries.

- Expanding your research capabilities beyond your home market provides many benefits, as you can leverage different skill sets, extend your daily R&D hours, more efficiently localize products, develop new products that can be sold worldwide, and implement a more flexible cost structure for talent.

- The key decisions before setting up the center include determining how intellectual property will be created and shared, if you can qualify for financial and tax incentives, selecting the right head of R&D, and how to protect company secrets with your IT infrastructure.

- How to structure your corporate R&D is a critical decision. You can decide to split projects by office, have the teams collaborate on the same projects, or develop new product lines at the new R&D center.

- Other key considerations when setting up a center include how to recruit engineers, create a productive office culture, build trust between R&D centers, and implement a plan to exchange engineers on a regular basis.

CHAPTER 10

Product or Technology Licensing

Sometimes directly entering a market is not your best strategy. Perhaps the competition is too well entrenched that going head to head with them can be very costly. Or maybe the market is not yet ready for your product and the time it will take to generate market awareness is too long. Or possibly the laws make it difficult for a foreign company to succeed in the timeframe your business needs.

In these cases, one viable option is to license your product or core technology to either a local company in that market, or a global company already operating in that country. Licensing is a lower cost expansion strategy, but typically results in less control over how your technology is used by end customers. Due to the lower risk factor, this strategy often, but not always, offers you a lower reward as your revenue will be less. But on the positive side, when you license your product or technology, you often receive upfront payments and you get faster access to market information. You can also receive recurring payments on unit sales, but these will be lower than if you sold the product yourself. Note that some companies have successfully licensed their technology to gain a foothold in a market, only to enter it years later on their own.

Criteria for Selecting a Licensee

As with any kind of business relationship, selecting your licensee is critical. You will have to deal with your partner on a frequent basis, and share sensitive product information. Ensure the licensee is an organization you can trust. Is it someone you feel you can do business with for a long period of time? If you are unsure, or have hesitations, do not enter into an agreement with them, as you will always be second-guessing your partner's intentions. Like a marriage, you need to communicate effectively for the partnership to work. Licensing results in a complex business relationship, so find a partner you can get along with. As licensing contracts are usually very complex, always consult an attorney when structuring an agreement.

Look for a partner who is established in the market you want to enter. Don't give your license to help a new licensee make its initial entry in a country. After all, licensing deals require effort on your side in terms of sharing information and technology, and you will be allocating resources in order to be a successful licensor. These are resources that could be working on other projects for your company. Thus, a licensing deal should lead to quick market entry and revenue growth. If these don't happen quickly, you may never recover the expense of allocating resources to the project, or the loss of opportunities your resources could have alternatively produced.

Of course, make sure the licensee is not a direct competitor in this or any other market. You will likely have many meetings where product and marketing strategy are discussed. Having a competitor in the room for these types of meetings will become too uncomfortable and potentially risky for the rest of your business. Furthermore, you will be sharing sensitive technical information that can be useful to your competitor in other markets. You do not want to open the door to a competitor, especially one who competes aggressively with you in other markets.

You licensee should share common goals and values with you. It is detrimental to the rest of your business if your licensee positions your product or technology in a way that conflicts with the rest of your global marketing efforts. For example, if you license identification technology for child safety, you would not want your licensee to use it for purposes that your company would not agree with, such as online dating. Make sure you know how your product or technology will be used and in what form it will be sold before signing a contract. Furthermore, understand what other products the licensee offers, and in what market segments, to ensure they will stay true to their stated intentions.

Confirm also that your partner's overall business does not conflict with either your other product lines or doing business in other geographic markets. If they have products that compete with your other offerings, this can create market conflict for your product lines that are not being licensed. Alternatively, if your partner is very active in other countries where you sell the same product or technology, they can easily enter those markets and compete directly against you. Even if you add restrictions to the contract that limit where and how licensees can utilize your products or technology, there is always an inherent transfer of knowledge that occurs when two parties work together. This knowledge transfer can be used to compete with your other products lines or in other geographical markets. Make sure conflicts will not arise because of this agreement.

An ideal licensing partner is often strong in vertical markets you do not yet address with your products. Your licensee helps you expand your product's reach into segments where you currently have no presence. For example, if your primary market is electronics companies, a great licensing partner may be one who is strong in the auto industry. Another example is if you primarily sell to corporate customers, a great licensing partner would be one who focuses on selling to governments or consumers. In both instances, your standard product offering may not be well suited, but by licensing, your partner can modify it for that specific target market. Additionally, your partner would have strong brand awareness and relationships in these other verticals that would quickly ramp up sales volume that you may have never been able to access.

Common Licensing Strategies

Licensing is a very broad term, so let's narrow it down by defining the three most common strategies:

1. Technology Licensing. This is when you grant your partner the right to use your intellectual property to create its own products. Make sure you clearly define what technology you are licensing, as intellectual property encompasses many things. It includes your:

- patents
- software
- hardware designs
- tooling or manufacturing fixtures
- development processes
- any other know-how

There are many companies that successfully license their technology to third parties. One of the most well known in the technology industry is Qualcomm. They license their wireless IP to many companies, including makers of mobile phones, network infrastructure companies, and network operators. Their technology is used on most mobile phone systems from the back-end switches, to the transmission towers that send out signals, to the phones and tablets in consumers' hands. Qualcomm develops the technology and then licenses the rights for many companies such as Samsung and Verizon to use it.

Another good example of technology licensing is ARM Holdings from the United Kingdom. They develop designs for very efficient microprocessors and license their designs to most of the leading semiconductor vendors in the world. Nearly all mobile phones sold throughout the world have ARM's IP built into their core chipsets. In recent years, ARM's customers have also been expanding the use of their IP into other types of products such that ARM's technology is now used in a broad array of applications, including smart TVs, gaming devices, security systems, household appliances, and automobiles.

2. Product Licensing. This is when you license your complete product design to a third party, including aspects of your intellectual property such as patent rights or manufacturing processes. In this scenario, your partner will either replicate your product or they may modify it for their own particular needs. In a product license scenario, licensees will typically manufacture the end product themselves, or utilize their own third-party to manufacturer on their behalf. A good use of this structure is when your partner focuses on a different vertical market than you do, and the specification and feature requirements may differ.

For example, the requirements for electrical and mechanical components in automobiles are much more stringent to tolerances than for consumer electronics. So if your company focuses on consumer electronics, a licensing partner might be able to take your core product and adapt it for the auto industry in order to function under more rigorous conditions such as severe heat, humidity or vibration. Another example is if your partner seeks to sell your product to the medical field where regulatory certifications often require redesigns of products in order to obtain approval. Each of these three markets: consumer electronics, automotive and medical, have different product requirements (such as operating and storage temperatures) and certification requirements. A product licensee can take a product that was designed for one of these markets and adapt it for another.

3. *Private Labelling.* This is where your customer licenses your product 'as is' and sells it as virtually the same as yours. You take on the task of doing any customization of the product for your licensees, rebrand it, and either manufacture it or provide the modified software. Your customers then offer the products in the marketplace as their own under their brand. Companies often do a private label when their partner sells through different sales channel or has a strong presence in a geographic area they are not in.

This private label business is often referred to as an OEM business, which stands for Original Equipment Manufacturer. OEMs design and manufacture products and then offer the finished products to third parties who sell under their own brand. Many of my companies provided products via OEM relationships.

In some cases, an OEM may be requested to design a new or modified product for a customer. In these situations, the business is referred to as ODM, or Original Design Manufacturer. Many of the PC vendors in Taiwan are ODMs, because they design unique products for companies to brand and sell, such as HP and Dell. HP and Dell specify the products they want and the ODMs design and manufacture them.

Of the three structures for licensing, there is no single right or better strategy. It always depends on many factors including the type of product you have, the maturity of your market, strategic fit with a partner, and other things. You may even deploy multiple strategies with different licensees, depending on the range of products you offer and/or the uniqueness of your technology. As the following example shows, you can even implement more than one strategy with the same partner.

Example of a Multiple Strategy Licensing Deal

This example includes both product and technology licensing. I was running a business unit at Xircom, where we provided communication modules to PC vendors. Our focus was notebook computers and our main competitor, 3Com, sold competing solutions for both notebook and desktop computers. At the time, Intel was 3Com's main competitor for communication modules going into desktop computers. Thus we had a common enemy selling into the same customer base with different product lines. We saw a great opportunity in expanding our global market reach by licensing to Intel, a much larger company that was selling billions of dollars of components per year to PC vendors.

Our first step was to private label, or OEM, our existing product line to Intel. We customized the products so they were Intel-branded. They paid us upfront fees for customizing the products and they had to purchase the end products from our factory. We earned revenue both upfront and on an ongoing basis. In the marketplace, we gained lots of credibility because one of the greatest influencers in the PC industry was now reselling our products. So while Intel now had a direct product competing with us, our market share grew because larger customers had greater trust for the Xircom brand. There was some overlap in our sales channels, but the gain in distribution greatly offset that conflict.

Once that agreement was executed, we decided to expand our relationship by entering into a technology licensing agreement as well. We licensed our patents, software and hardware designs to Intel so they could develop a new line of products that included both their intellectual property as well as ours. As part of the agreement, Xircom would manufacture the products from this development effort, and both companies had rights to sell them. So we were able to leverage Intel's vast experience in semiconductor design to bring an innovative, new product line to market. This partnership proved beneficial to both companies as each of us gained market share. It was a very successful relationship that ultimately led Intel to acquire Xircom several years later.

Licensing Considerations

Licensing contracts are very complex. In addition to your typical contract terms, there are certain items that require detailed scrutiny. The first item that must be spelled out clearly is intellectual property protection. Your agreement must be clear on ownership rights, along with whether the licensee has any rights to sublicense the IP. If you will maintain ownership of the IP, the agreement must spell out that your IP is yours and you are just giving the other party rights to use the IP for the duration of the agreement. Sublicensing is when a licensee has rights to further license your IP to another party. Sometimes, you may grant limited sublicense rights. For example, you may give your licensee the right to sublicense for the manufacture of the product with your IP.

Intellectual property issues are more complicated when you are licensing technology. If the other party develops technology on top of your intellectual property, you need to clarify if you can use the newly developed technology since part of it is based on your IP. You also need to understand who owns any enhancements that have been developed. Are they jointly owned? If you use the derivative technology that has been developed, will you have to pay a license fee and enter into a new licensing agreement with your partner? There are many possible pitfalls with regards to intellectual property protection, so be sure to seek top quality legal advice to structure the contract so that your IP is protected.

Next, the agreement must be clear on what design work you are responsible for. In most cases, you will need to do some level of design work for your licensee. Make sure your contract spells out what you will do and how much you will charge for this work. Even if you decide not to charge for the work, detail what's included so that the licensee can't keep coming back for more and more customization that may utilize too many of your resources. A licensee can consume a lot of your team, if you let them. Unlike other customers, they need a much deeper knowledge of your products and technology. They will also ask a lot of detailed questions. If you do not proactively manage the relationship, your support costs can quickly escalate out of control.

All licensing agreements must include a clear time limit. You will need to determine if you are granting perpetual licenses or if they are for a defined period of time. It is always better to grant the license for a short period of time, such as one to three years. If the relationship is working out, the contract can allow for the license agreement to extend. However, given that your licensees will probably need to support their customers even after the contract ends, you may need to grant them some level of license that extends beyond the term. For example, if they can no longer manufacture and sell products with your technology, they will still need the authority to provide technical support and product replacements to their customers.

Another consideration is whether you will require a minimum sales volume for the license. Does your licensee need to produce or sell a certain number of units in order to either acquire the license or keep it for the duration of the term? All licensees will continue to need a certain level of support, but if their volume does not meet expectations, the relationship can end up costing you money. It is therefore important to understand what your ongoing support costs will be so you can decide whether you should enforce minimum volume levels.

For mature product categories, determining the minimum volume level for the license to remain active is usually easy to calculate. However, if your technology is new, or the market is still in its early stages, it can be difficult to estimate an acceptable volume level. You want your licensee to be aggressive in marketing and selling your technology, but if you set unrealistic targets, your partner can easily become demoralized and decide to abandon the effort. In such instances, a good strategy is to define an initial volume and then agree to have quarterly, semi-annual or annual meetings to review past success and agree on targets for the upcoming measurement period.

If you will continue to advance your technology, you will need to determine how to handle product updates. If you make updates to your product, do you have to provide customized versions for your licensees? This can apply to anything you update such as software improvements, hardware design improvements, and manufacturing process enhancements. There is a cost associated with providing product updates to your licensees, given that you need to allocate resources to do the customizations for your partner. So be sure you spell out how this will be handled.

For instance, will you charge for each update, thereby giving the licensee a choice on whether to accept it? Or will you automatically provide these updates for free? You could also decide to set a threshold where updates are provided at no cost if certain volumes are maintained, but a fee is charged if the volumes are not achieved. These are just some of the options to consider. The best way to determine how to handle product updates is to do a trial run where you release a minor update and see how much resources will be required to make that same customization for your licensee. The effort required should drive your structure on handling such situations.

When doing updates, it is also important to distinguish between small enhancements that improve existing functionality and adding product features that provide new capabilities. Enhancements typically are minor changes that improve the current operation or functionality of your product. The overall feature set of your product does not change; it just works better. New product features, on the other hand, add capabilities that give your product a new set of benefits in the marketplace. Distinguishing these types of updates will provide you maximum flexibility in negotiations, as you may want to charge a higher licensing price when introducing new product features.

Finally, it is advisable that you work into your contract a structure for progress meetings. Relying on an ad-hoc meeting schedule is too risky. If you do not plan and structure these meetings, chances are they will not occur. People get very busy and then meetings cannot be scheduled, or they are scheduled with the wrong people in attendance.

It is recommended to run face-to-face meetings with your licensing partners in order to have a complete picture of the relationship and its future prospects. At these meetings, review not only the product side of the agreement, but also how the business relationship is working for both sides. I've always preferred to have these meetings twice per year.

- Rather than directly entering certain markets, licensing your product or technology may be a better alternative. You can license your product or core technology to either a local company in that market, or a global company that is already operating in the country you want to enter.

- Licensing is a low cost strategy, with typically lower risk but lower rewards.

- To protect your company's interests, always engage an attorney when negotiating licensing contracts.

- Selecting the right licensee partners is critical. Seek those who are established in the market, share common goals and values, are not a direct competitor, do not conflict with the rest of your business, and ideally are positioned in a different vertical market.

- The three most common types of licensing strategies are technology licensing, product licensing, and private labelling.

- Licensing contracts are extremely complex. Items requiring special scrutiny include intellectual property protection, how design work is handled, time limits, volume requirements, product updates and review meetings.

CHAPTER 11

Joint Venture

SOME COUNTRIES HAVE UNIQUE CHALLENGES, SIGNIFICANT government requirements, or they are so large that entering on your own is either not possible or ill advised. For instance, in some industries, regulators will not allow a foreign entity to form a subsidiary in the country without a local partner. For example, a foreign airline cannot establish itself in the United States without a domestic partner that must own a majority stake in the venture. Moreover, while some countries may not have laws forbidding a foreign competitor, local business practices or entrenched competition may make it extremely difficult for a new entrant to succeed. In these situations, a joint venture, or JV, with a local partner is either your best choice or the only choice for market entry.

In a joint venture, two or more companies decide to form a new entity. Each partner owns a percentage of the ensuing company. The new entity will be a standalone organization driven by a set of goals determined by the owners. In addition to situations where a government mandate forces you to create a JV, you may choose to form one to:

- take advantage of a market opportunity that is so large, you cannot handle it effectively by yourself.
- benefit from a partner's market position, technology, or other unique attribute.

Before finalizing your market entry plan, consult with your attorney to see if any special requirements exist for your industry in that country. Joint ownership is common in many industries: oil and gas, utilities, transportation, and communications. Depending on the industry and country, you may only be allowed a minority stake, or only up to 50% ownership with your partner. However, if there are no ownership restrictions, you should seek a majority ownership position in any JVs you create. When you have majority ownership, you drive the strategic direction of the entity.

The Advantages of Joint Ventures

Joint ventures can provide many benefits to a company entering a new market, even if there is no government requirement that you form one.

1. *When entering a market through a JV, you can share the start-up and operating costs with your partner.* This can substantially reduce your upfront cost and ongoing investment in entering the market. Instead of bearing all the market entry costs on your own, your partner will absorb a percentage, typically commensurate with their ownership stake of the venture. If your partner is already established in the market, they already have an infrastructure in place that will also benefit your JV and reduce the total investment required over time.

2. *A local partner will also give you instant market credibility based on their existing reputation in the market.* For most companies entering a new country, the process of earning market credibility is difficult and lengthy. However, if your JV partner is well established, the new venture could receive a lot of attention from the media, ecosystem partners, and potential customers. Your prestige in the market will grow much more quickly, requiring less effort to achieve. In addition, recruiting local employees will be easier since your company will be considered more desirable to job candidates.

3. *Your JV partner has a better understanding of the market's needs.* If a partner wants to form a JV with you, it validates that there should be demand for your product. Anytime you can engage with a local partner, you benefit from their years' of experience in the marketplace. You also avoid many pitfalls by leveraging their history and expertise to help finalize your sales and marketing plan. Chances are that they have tried many go-to market approaches before settling on what works. You can bypass many tests and trials and more effectively get your product in customers' hands. The result is that their understanding of the local market will help you quickly ramp up sales.

4. *A JV should also enable you to receive stronger government support.* Regardless of your industry, if you partner with a local company, and create jobs in the process, the government will be much more supportive of any initiatives you roll out. Bringing your expertise, and possibly technology, into their country will be looked upon favorably, especially since a percentage of the profits will go to the local partner. This will result in stronger government support if you need to apply for any special permits or certifications. In addition, your chances of winning any government projects will drastically improve with a local partner involved in the process.

5. *A JV will provide the benefit of better scalability.* With an established, local partner, you can usually ramp up the business more quickly as your needs grow. This is an important advantage because companies often have to slow down their growth when they cannot find enough qualified people to meet the demand they have created. This is a conundrum because when you first establish a business in a new country, you do not want to overspend and build too large of an initial organization. However, growth could occur very fast and you then have to catch up by trying to hire quickly. With a JV partner, they should have resources available to quickly assist the entity and have a better pipeline to recruiting local talent.

Engage in Discussions before Forming the JV

Before engaging attorneys to draft a JV agreement, it is important that you and your potential partner clarify many issues. Each industry has its own unique set of business issues that need be negotiated, but let's review some common matters that all JVs need to determine even before they get to a contract.

First, what is the ownership structure? You need to come to an agreement on how much of the JV each party owns. Part of this is also deciding if the ownership structure remains fixed over time, or if it can change based on continued contributions of cash, technology, IP, or people. Agree on these issues before a contract is drafted, as the ownership structure of the JV will have an impact on many other terms within the agreement.

Next, determine how the JV will be staffed. Will each company contribute existing employees or will the JV contain only new, outside hires? In many cases, some employees come from the partners, and others will be newly hired.

Next is the question of who will lead the venture. Will it be someone from your company, your partner's organization, or a new hire? This person is key, as the day-to-day execution of the joint venture will depend on the background of the leader. If the leader comes from your JV partner, you run the risk that decisions might be based on objectives that conflict with your strategic goals and priorities.

You also need to define each party's rights in hiring new employees within the JV. This is especially important when selecting the rest of the senior management team. You want to make sure your company can provide input, and ideally have veto power, when the management team is selected. In the event of disagreements among the leadership, you want to have some rights in how the matter is resolved. If the JV head or its senior executives seek to steer the company in a direction you don't agree with, you also want the right to intervene. It helps to spell out a clearly defined process so that disagreements with leadership can be handled in a professional and expeditious manner.

Another issue is what responsibility will each party have in forming the JV. What amounts will be initially contributed? Consider not
just capital and resources, but also technology, training, process, and
so on. All these issues have a cost associated with them, so you need
to capture those expenses as they can affect the ownership percentage of each partner.

Next, determine if additional contributions beyond the initial
investments will be needed on an ongoing basis. For example, is
one party expected to keep contributing technology to the new
company? Ongoing contribution expectations are often overlooked,
which could lead to disagreements later on.

If the JV runs into financial or technical troubles, what is each
party obligated to do to support it? You cannot afford to make such
decisions later when the venture is in trouble, as one partner may
no longer be as committed to the enterprise. In developing a plan
for this possibility, also clarify the repercussions if one party does
not provide the obligated support. For example, will that party lose
some of its ownership stake? It is extremely important to agree in
advance about these matters if trouble occurs. Not all initiatives go
as planned, so having a blueprint for potential issues will save you
time, money, and stress in the long run.

Next you need to decide if the JV will have access to either party's sales channels or manufacturing facilities. If your partner's sales
channels are utilized, determine in advance the commission rate or
if other selling fees will be assessed. If you use your partner's manufacturing facilities, discuss the following issues:

- product markup, or transfer price, when goods are produced.
  You want to make sure the JV is treated fairly on pricing.
- manufacturing lead times for the JV's orders. You want to ensure
  your production runs do not get set aside for other customer orders that are more profitable for your partner.
- quality and product acceptance criteria. You need to agree on
  how quality will be measured and what are the acceptance

levels so the JV is assured of receiving product that meets your expected criteria.

You should also review and agree upon how you want to position the JV and its products. If you have different philosophies about positioning strategy, find out now before starting contract negotiations. An example of a common disconnect you want to avoid is your desire to position the company as an innovative technology leader while your partner wants to position the company as a price leader. You usually cannot be both. You have to agree to a single strong positioning strategy and try your best to fulfill it.

Related to this is your geographic positioning. While your goal for JV may be to enter just that specific country, your partner may view the joint venture as a way to expand geographically. So you need to decide upfront if the JV will be limited to the local market, or if you will expand regionally or even globally.

All these decisions affect the long-term aspirations for the business. If partners enter into a venture with different goals and objectives, conflicts will constantly arise. This leads to our last discussion item—how to manage conflict. Disagreements are inevitable, so you need to put in place a process on how they will be handled. If the majority owner has final say, then you should know that upfront. If the venture is 50-50, obviously you need to agree on a process to resolve a deadlock. For example, will all decisions be delegated to the management team and whatever they believe is best—or will the JV's owners have a say to either influence or veto decisions? Agreeing on both the goals and conflict resolution process are critical to the long-term success of any joint venture.

Example of Exploring a
Joint Venture—and Not Taking It!

I have previously discussed how my company Atrua set up a subsidiary in China that encompassed sales, manufacturing support, and R&D. To remind you, Atrua developed security components for the mobile phone market. Over time, our China business was becoming more strategic so we wanted to find ways to further solidify our dominant market share in the country while bringing down our manufacturing costs. One of our venture capital investors was a Chinese semiconductor fabrication company, and we asked them to assist us in finding a partner to form a joint venture.

As it turns out, many cities in China are aggressively enticing foreign companies to form joint ventures with local entities. We were introduced to a company in Wuxi, located about 90 minutes west of Shanghai, to explore forming a joint venture. The initial plan was to create a JV with each party owning 50%. We would set up a large office of a few hundred engineers, which would give us the manpower to aggressively introduce new products globally. The JV would sell the new products in China while providing Atrua a product line that we could sell in other countries. At the time, Atrua was manufacturing our components in Taiwan, so as part of the JV we agreed to switch fabrication in China, ideally in Wuxi.

Unfortunately, as we negotiated the JV, too many concerns surfaced that resulted in our walking away from the deal. In addition to requiring us to make a hefty cash investment, we were asked to assign some of our patents to the JV. This troubled us as we felt we would be contributing more than our expected share to the new company, and the risk of our intellectual property leaking into the market was too great. In addition, manufacturing options in Wuxi were not mature enough to produce our product with a high enough yield. As such, the benefits of having local manufacturing would not have been possible for at least a few years. Despite six months of negotiations, we opted to decline the JV because it no longer met our objectives. It is always better to walk away from a deal when the terms are not what you originally envisioned and you cannot negotiate what you need to meet your own objectives.

———

Negotiating Your Joint Venture

As the example demonstrates, international joint venture discussions are complicated. In addition to the issues you must solve in any joint venture negotiation, there may also be language barriers and cultural differences to overcome. It is so easy to get excited about getting a deal completed that you can lose sight of your overall objective. Don't let that happen. When negotiating joint venture contracts, keep a level head and don't be afraid to walk away, even at the last minute, if the terms are not right for your company. If not, you will pay for it later with lots of conflicts, stress, and possibly litigation. Make sure your original goals and objectives are achievable before signing the agreement.

While both parties enter the agreement expecting long-term success, always consider the consequences if the joint venture were dissolved at some point in the future. No one wants to plan for a break-up, but your contract must spell out what happens if the venture fails or falls apart. Too often, this is not detailed in the agreement, resulting in a process that is messy and potentially litigious. If you need help, consult and rely heavily on your attorney for advice because he or she will provide a much more objective view compared to your internal team.

The rule of thumb is that anything either party contributes to the joint venture must be spelled out in the agreement. So make sure all contributions that each party makes to the JV are specifically itemized in the contract. Do not sign a contract where issues are left to be worked out later. Here are three big areas of contribution where the contract must be specific:

1. *Cash contributions & withdrawals.* Be sure to spell out how cash inflows will be made into the JV—both the amount of contributions and timing of payments. You also need to plan for the future when the JV is profitable. Once it is generating positive cash flow, will the owners have the right to withdraw cash? If so, you need to

determine the type of withdrawal (such as a dividend), whether it applies to both parties, and the process for requesting and granting cash requests.

2. *Intellectual property contributions.* Spell out what rights the joint venture will have to the existing intellectual property of the owners. State whether the JV has to pay for these rights or if they will be granted at no cost. If intellectual property from one party is being used at no cost to the venture, the value of the IP needs to be agreed upon in advance and stated in the contract. In cases where the JV pays for access to the IP, you still need to agree on the value in advance, to avoid having the JV overpay for these rights later.

Of course, the newly formed company will most likely create its own intellectual property, so also be sure the contract states if the JV partners have rights to this IP. If yes, determine whether royalties need to be paid to the JV if each company uses any of the IP. Also, decide if there will be any restrictions on how this new intellectual property can be used by the JV partners.

3. *Ownership of assets.* The contract should state who will own the IP and other assets of the JV if the venture is wound down. Typically, it is joint ownership but this needs to be agreed in advance. It is important to agree on how to treat any value that has been created should you need to wind-down.

Ironically, another ownership issue to settle is handling of the employees. If the parent companies have contributed employees to the venture, will they have rights to take the employees back? If so, how will this be done? Is there then a risk that the JV could be understaffed? To be successful, any company needs a consistent employee base. Otherwise you run the risk that the newly formed JV will be at the mercy of one of the parent companies that can pull out or allocate employees as they see fit.

There are many potential pitfalls in structuring a joint venture as negotiating these issues can be extremely touchy. Be sure you hire an attorney with specific experience in structuring JVs *in your specific industry* and ideally within the country where you are negotiating. If your legal firm does not have this experience, then find a second firm to help your main legal firm with this particular contract. You cannot afford to have any business or legal issues overlooked, as they could substantially impact not only your JV, but also your entire business.

KEY LESSONS

- The desire to enter a joint venture may be driven by either government requirements or local market conditions.

- Depending on industry and country, you may be limited to a 50% share or minority stake in the JV.

- Joint ventures can provide many benefits including cost sharing, instant market credibility, better market understanding, stronger government support and scalability.

- There are many unique business terms that need to be decided before hire an attorney to draft your contract, including ownership structure, staffing, responsibilities, market positioning, overall goals and conflict resolution.

- Once the general business terms are agreed upon, engage an attorney with specific experience with joint venture contracts in your industry.

- All contributions to the JV need to be spelled out in the contract, both initial and ongoing contributions over the long term.

- Ensure a structure is in place for handling intellectual property and employees that come from the parent companies.

- Make sure there is a clear dissolution plan, including the handling of IP and other assets.

- Do not be afraid to walk away from the negotiating table if something is not right.

PART 3

FINANCIAL CONSIDERATIONS

CHAPTER 12

Cost Structure

REGARDLESS OF HOW YOU EXPAND INTERNATIONALLY, YOU NEED to create a comprehensive financial plan that provides you confidence in making the investment. This plan should detail your expected expenditures, forecasted revenue, and cash flow projections. Each of these items needs to be estimated as accurately as possible in order to create a realistic blueprint of this activity. Given that you may be dealing in multiple currencies complicates your financial modeling. When you are done with your financial plan, you should have your accounting firm review it for completeness.

To ensure you expansion remains viable once you enter a market, I recommend that you regularly measure your actual results against your original budget—preferably monthly. This allows you to make adjustments if needed to ensure your new venture remains financially on target. Of course, each situation is unique, and you can expect some surprises, so make sure you have enough flexibility in your numbers to account for variances. I often overestimate my expenses and underestimate my revenues just to give projections some leeway. I also assume cash collections will take longer and my cash payments will need to be made sooner. This way, if I get behind in my plan, I have some time to adjust and catch up.

In this chapter, we are going to focus on costs. I consider costs as the items in your financial plan where you have the most direct control. Your finance and accounting team is very well versed in your existing cost structure and how to plan domestically—and that should spillover into your foreign plans. However, as each country will likely have different expense items, you will probably need to do some homework to create a more accurate international projection.

Modeling Country Specific Costs

It is often worthwhile to hire assistance from a local accountant who is familiar with business in the new country to help you with modeling country-specific costs. Many countries impose fees and costs you may not be familiar with and that differ from your home country. Let's review a few of these.

1. *Regulatory expenditures.* Do not assume that regulation payments in your target country are comparable to what you pay in your home market. You need to find out the specific regulatory costs you will incur for your business within that country, including all licenses and various assessments that will be made. You need to determine if these fees are fixed or variable. Fixed fees are always more straightforward to model. Variable fees can be complex to model, as costs depend on whether they are based on revenue, assets, or some other measure. Sometimes you will have some fixed fees to be paid regardless of your activities, while others will vary based on some measure, such as revenue or assets. You also need to know how frequently these regulatory fees must be paid. If you fail to be compliant, you may be charged fines.

2. *Withholdings.* A government withholding—a sort of tax—may be levied on either a business transaction or the transfer of funds into and out of the country. If your target country has such withholdings, make sure you understand the conditions for the withholdings and what amounts will be withheld. How you classify sales or designate a funds transfer can sometimes determine if a withholding will be assessed.

In addition, when funds are being withheld, you may be able to recoup them by filing documentation with the government's tax agency. The timing of when you can file for a refund and the actual return of the funds is usually subject to strict guidelines. For example, you may need to file once per year within a certain 30-day window, or within 90 days of the occurrence of the withholding. If you fail to abide by the rules, you usually forfeit the entire amount of the funds. This is the most overlooked item when planning an international expansion and it can significantly reduce your initial working capital.

3. *Taxation.* When establishing your cost base, you need to understand how the country assesses corporate taxes, how they charge excise taxes when you purchase items, and the amount of payroll taxes you may need to pay. Each country has its own set of rules regarding these, of course. Some countries tax you not only on profits, but also on assets. In addition to projecting the actual tax rate and how it applies to you, find out if you can carry forward losses, and if there are exemptions you can deduct. Make sure your local accountant also fills you in on corporate tax policies at both the national and local level.

Regarding fees on assets, be aware that some countries actually assess a fee based on your assets within that country. Find out if your target country does this and if so, what are the fees and what assets are covered.

As for excise taxes, the most common one imposed outside the United States is called the Value Added Tax (VAT). Many countries throughout Europe assess VAT on all transactions as a percentage of the price. It is worthwhile to understand the VAT structure in your target market, specifically what purchases the tax applies to and the percentage. Paying VAT is not trivial in many countries. For example, if an item costs $1000, plus a 15% VAT, you're looking at $1150. A projected expenditure of $50,000 turns into $57,500 after VAT.

As in the United States, payroll taxes can be significant cost item. In the US, employees and employers must pay mandatory contributions to fund programs such as Social Security and Medicare. Many other countries do not have these same programs, but they likely have other worker-related programs that your company will be required to fund. Even if the burden of paying for these programs falls completely on employees, local business practices may force you to fund some of these expenditures. Talk to local HR or accounting people to make sure you understand these costs and can model them into your business plan.

4. Employee benefits. Your country may also impose other unique employee-related expenses and benefits, as we discussed in the Business Climate chapter. For example, Singapore requires employers to make a mandatory contribution to an employee retirement fund. In China, you must pay out an extra month's salary as a bonus every year. The United States has mandatory insurance programs, such as health care, for companies of certain sizes.

Expect most countries to have some expenses that expand beyond providing employee salaries. These employee policies need to be budgeted when creating your business plan. Personnel expenses are usually the greatest cost item in a budget, so speak with a local accountant to make sure you know what are the employee-related expenses associated with your target country.

5. Other fees. There may be other fees you could incur in a specific country. For instance, some local industry associations have strong clout within a country and require companies to pay a fee in order to provide their goods and services within that country. In some markets the fees may be optional, but not paying can blacklist you within the local industry. It is important to understand not only what is required, but also what is expected as you model your business.

Don't forget to take into account any professional services fees you will incur in your new market. As we said, you might need local legal advice, accounting services, and bookkeeping, and you might also incur fees to ensure compliance with the local reporting requirements, such as tax returns and financial statement submittals. Find out if your existing accounting firm can do this for you or if you will need to hire a local firm. If you decide to hire a local firm, first ask for a price quote on how much they will charge to manage this for your business.

If you elect to expand your existing domestic professional services firms to have them begin covering your international market, there could be extra "engagement" costs charged as the firm takes on the complexities of your international business. While local firms are often more cost effective, you potentially sacrifice the knowledge that your existing firms have about your business. Getting estimates from both your existing firms and local firms is the best way to compare fees and determine the most effective option for your situation.

To find good local firms to work with, check at your embassy's trade office, your local industry groups, and other multinationals that have established a similar presence. Not only can they probably recommend a good firm, they can also give you a ballpark for what market prices you should expect to pay.

Finally, be sure to count in any pre-paid expenses and other deposits that you may have to make. In some countries, for instance, you must pre-pay your office lease for the duration of the term. Other expenses, such as professional services and utilities may follow a similar model of prepayment. Credit policies, especially for new businesses, will also vary by country. When you first enter a country, you cannot assume that lenders will quickly provide you credit. Often, you need years of operating history in a country before credit is granted.

As you can see, it is a big task to understand all the unique ways business is conducted in the country you are planning to enter. If you don't plan and model your costs, you may discover large expenses that you were not ready to handle. I highly recommend working with an accountant to finalize your financial modeling. You might try doing a first draft of your costs internally, but then meet with an accountant that can help tighten up your numbers and fill in holes you left.

If your existing firm is not familiar with doing business in your target country, they should be able to research the market and assist you. If not, as I said, hire a local firm. In addition, talk to other businesses that operate in the country, ideally within your industry. Most are willing to share their experiences with you, which ultimately helps you more accurately model your cost structure.

Example of Financial Modeling

Here's a summary of how we modeled our business when Atrua set up our R&D Center in Shanghai.

We began by creating an initial plan based on many financial assumptions, and estimating higher costs to serve as a cushion to our business. We created a first draft internally, and then finalized the plan with our accounting firm. Based on our expected expenditures, the plan helped us recognize that opening up the office would be a good move, as the cost structure was low and the revenue opportunity was large.

We moved forward and hired a general manager for China. In addition to having all the qualifications we discussed in the chapter on R&D centers, he had recently set up an office for another US technology company, so he was up to date on estimating costs.

Based on his input, we further refined the cost structure of our financial model. We learned that there were cost items we were not aware of, but to balance that, he told us that some of the cash cushions in our expected expenditures were too high. So we revised our financial plan again. After looking at the updated, more precise numbers, we were still pleased, as we had originally estimated higher costs than what we would end up spending.

Our modeling process helped us learn a lot about costs in China with regards to regulatory issues, taxation, employee relations and benefits, and other fees we would incur due to the nature of our business. Although we did not know everything when we first started, it proved a good idea to be conservative with our initial financial assumptions. Then by asking a lot of questions, we were able to continue refining our cost estimates to the point where we had confidence that any surprises we might incur would be minimal.

KEY LESSONS

- You need to create a comprehensive financial plan that can provide you confidence that making your market entry investment is wise. This plan should detail your expected expenditures, forecasted revenue, and cash flow projections.

- As you enter your market, continue measuring your results and comparing them to your initial targets to know if you are achieving your potential.

- Expect some surprises when you operate your business and make sure you have enough cushion and flexibility to account for when they occur.

- Determine what regulatory fees you will need to pay, and if they are fixed or variable.

- Make sure you understand the local country's corporate and excise tax (VAT) structures, national and local government assessments, employment policies and pre-payment policies.

- Find out if your funds transfers or sales are subject to government withholdings.

- Many expense categories differ from one country to another. Speak with an accountant who understands the local market to learn the differences.

- Work with your accountant in order to forecast your compliance fees and finalize your financial plan.

CHAPTER 13

Forecasting Sales

ONE OF THE HARDEST THINGS TO DO IN BUSINESS IS TO forecast sales—*accurately*. No matter how much effort and research you put into it, you never know with certainty if and when your customers will purchase your product. Yet, forecasting is critical for managing cash flow and inventory. If you forecast too low, you may not be able to respond to your demand and customers may choose another vendor. If you forecast too high, you may build unneeded inventory, which potentially becomes obsolete. Just as bad, inventory ties up your cash.

It is also damaging to run your operating expense plan based on an overly optimistic sales forecast. How quickly you grow your staff and overall operation depends on your expected sales revenue. If you have a revenue shortfall, you will burn through more cash than originally forecasted, which can affect your ability to pay employees and vendors. Having to let go of employees because you can no longer afford them is stressful and difficult. Depending on employment laws, rapid reduction-in-force personnel changes may not even be allowed.

In short, I view forecasting as the one area in your financial plan where you have the least amount of control. There are so many external factors that affect your sales forecast, including economic market conditions, competitor activities and other priorities that may delay your customers' purchasing decisions. Despite this dilemma, you must try to make good assumptions and create the most accurate forecast possible. Moreover, your forecast should be updated regularly as you continue to learn more about prospective threats and opportunities. I recommend updating your forecast at least once per month.

Overcoming Forecasting Challenges

With years of experience, let me share some of the things I've learned about forecasting that can you help you overcome the lack of control.

First, admit that there is an element of psychology in forecasting accurately. Given this, make an effort to read between the lines as you try to understand what your sales people and their customers are really telling you. This is difficult, but in time you will get to know which of your sales people or sales channels are too optimistic and which are too conservative. Study the trends of their actual purchases compared to their forecasts so you can better calculate true product demand. Your skill at "deciphering" a forecast submitted from your team can be a real asset in effectively managing your business.

When you expand internationally, of course, the psychology of forecasting sales becomes even more difficult. Because of distance, your influence and recommended methodologies may not be as closely followed as in your home office. Remote sales organizations may think more independently than groups located at headquarters. Your day-to-day involvement is also less direct at remote offices, so whatever judgment factors you have used for domestic forecasting cannot be used for international forecasting. At the start, you will need to rely more on the forecasts submitted at face value. Over time, you will have a better idea on how to adjust the submitted data.

In my experience, the biggest challenges in international sales forecasting are due to culture. Different cultures have different ways of "seeing" things. Sometimes the differences are subtle, but other times they are quite obvious. Here is what I have observed first hand:

- Some cultures will seldom disagree with their boss or with head-quarters. If you are pushing for a higher sales forecast, there will be no pushback. However, when the results come in, you are likely to be disappointed. Confucian cultures, such as those in Asia, often fall into this category.
- Some cultures will always try to provide a lower forecast than they believe they can achieve. This gives them more comfort and a greater sense of success when they achieve their sales targets. Many European groups fall into this category.
- Some cultures will always provide you with an optimistic fore-cast that can only be achieved if the best-case scenario happens. Unfortunately, best-case results do not happen every month or quarter. I have experienced this with countries in the Americas.

These cultural challenges are as true for your employees as they are for your channel partners. They all follow similar patterns. The best way to neutralize these challenges is to communicate, communicate, communicate. The more you visit your foreign sales people and channel partners, the better you will get at understanding their cultural forecasting philosophy. Also being present and seeing what is going on first hand in a market will enable you to become a better judge of the true demand. If your only interaction with your sales resources is when you are on the phone listening to a forecast, do not expect to be able to make accurate adjustments to the submitted numbers.

Here are some ways to break though these cultural barriers so you can come up with an accurate forecast. First, use a soft approach when you begin the forecasting process. You may have a tendency to push for better results, but it may not work with your International sales teams, depending on the culture. Being a tough 'field general' at forecasting time is often not to one's advantage. If you demand and apply pressure, expect results that fall into the first or third category—your team will either superficially agree with your expectation or they will provide an overly optimistic forecast so they are not challenged.

Next, set up sessions to review the forecasts after they are submitted. These review sessions should be done within days of receiving the written forecasts so the thought process is still fresh in everyone's mind. Ask your international sales teams to present their forecasts to you, followed by a Q&A session. At these sessions, ask questions to figure out how your team came up with the forecast. Have them explain to you the process they used to develop the forecast, and not just their numbers. Ask lots and lots of questions. The more you probe, the better the accuracy of the end product.

Then track their forecast accuracy over time. This is necessary to accurately make adjustments to the initial forecasts. Keep a spreadsheet showing what forecasts were submitted and then tack on the actual results as they happen. Comparing historical forecasts versus actual results serves as a guide to plan adjustments when the team hands in future forecasts. As you follow this process with your international offices, you will start to see patterns that will help you refine the final forecasts.

Devote time in the field with your international sales teams. You and your headquarters team need to visit them frequently. When you go, get out with them into the field. Do not spend all your time in the office. You should spend more the 50% of your time out in the field visiting customers, resellers, and ecosystem partners. Meet as many customers and partners as you can, and ask a lot of questions about their businesses. The more you know about their businesses, the better you can assess the sales team's forecasts and make adjustments.

Finally, apply your own good judgment to any forecasts submitted. Do not take the numbers provided at face value. Based on information gathered in meetings, discussions with others in the organization, and site visits to customers and partners, you should adjust the estimates as you deem appropriate. The more information and questions you have asked, the better the adjustments you will be able to make. Ultimately, you are accountable for the results, so do not hesitate to revise any forecasts you receive from your sales teams.

Examples of Sales Forecasts in Different Cultures

Here are a few generalizations about cultures based on my experience in over 25 years of international business. As each culture is unique, your experience may differ, and some of the factors are due to the specific personalities and backgrounds of those involved. For example, in any country more aggressive sales people will have a tendency to forecast higher sales than less aggressive people. If your local sales team has worked for foreign companies in the past, they also may not follow the typical behavior found in their country because they have already learned to adapt to your culture. Nevertheless, I think these generalizations can prove useful as background if you are entering the market in any of these areas:

1. *Japan.* Early in my career, I would push my teams in Japan to increase their forecasts. They would do it, but at the end of each quarter, they always came up short. This was due to their culture of not pushing back if the boss pushed them. I learned and stopped pushing them, and their forecast accuracy improved quite a bit.

2. *Western Europe.* My teams here always seemed to provide the most accurate forecasts. If anything, they were conservative. Culturally, they took great pride in setting a number and then achieving it.

3. *Israel.* Here my teams would typically underestimate their forecast, and then exceed their numbers...but only by a little each time.

4. *Taiwan, Hong Kong, and Singapore.* In these regions, I would always receive very optimistic forecasts. While I appreciated the aggressiveness and confidence, these forecasts always required an adjustment before being entered into the financial plan.

- Forecasting sales is one of the hardest things to do, and it impacts cash flow and inventory. There is a saying that forecasting sales is art, not science. You will seldom be exactly on target with your numbers.

- This is the part of the financial model where you have the least control. It requires making a lot of assumptions, and then working as hard as you can to achieve those results. Lots of external factors impact your sales forecast, such as economic market conditions, competitor activities and other customer priorities.

- Because of distance, your forecast guidelines will probably not be followed as closely as your local team forecasts.

- The biggest challenges in international sales forecasting are due to culture. Sometimes the cultural differences are subtle, while other times they are quite obvious.

- To break through cultural barriers, use a soft approach for the fore-casting process, set up review sessions, and ask a lot of questions. Then track accuracy over time.

- Spend time visiting international customers, ask them questions, and adjust forecasts based on your own judgments.

- You need to make adjustments to the raw forecasts that are submit-ted. Ultimately, you are responsible so make sure you feel comfort-able with the revenue plan.

- In my view, it is better to under forecast and have a small backlog, than over forecast and have a potential cash flow crisis.

CHAPTER 14

Currency Risk

DEPENDING ON THE NATURE OF YOUR BUSINESS, CURRENCY RISK may be a factor impacting your financials. Currency risk happens when one currency fluctuates versus another. This can influence your day-to-day operations in a foreign country, as valuation changes can affect your internal costs as well as the selling price of your goods and your gross margins. When you consolidate your financials at a corporate level, currency fluctuations can also have an effect on your overall company profitability.

If the majority of your revenue and expenses are in the same currency, you currency risk is much more limited. For example, if you can conduct business in US dollars and pay the bulk of your expenses in US dollars, then you have avoided currency risk as it pertains to your financial statements. However, if the US currency appreciates in comparison to the local currency, your goods may become uncompetitive and too expensive for customers as they still pay for your product in the local currency. This may reduce the demand for your product, unless you decide to lower your prices. So no matter the situation, any time currencies fluctuate, there will always be some risk to your business.

On the other hand, consider what happens where your revenue and the bulk of your expenses are all in the local currency. In this scenario, your local set of financials will be relatively safe from currency risk. Everything is based on the local currency, so fluctuations between currencies do not have a bearing on your buyers. However, as the currencies vary, your overall company performance could be affected. The impact can be favorable or unfavorable depending on the direction of the currency fluctuation. If the local currency appreciates, your gross margin will improve when you convert your revenue to your home currency. Unfortunately, your operating expenses will convert at a higher rate, too. The opposite occurs if the local currency depreciates as your gross margins and operating expenses will go down when you convert your results to your home currency. (Note that these examples have been simplified as they exclude the impact of currency fluctuations if your costs of goods are paid in a different currency.)

The riskiest scenario is if your revenue is in one currency while the bulk of your costs are in a different one. Let's say that in Japan, your distributors pay you in US dollars, but your operating expenses are in Japanese Yen. Then you are always at risk because any fluctuation in either of the currencies will impact your financials. If the US dollar rises, then you benefit since your revenue stays consistent while your true operating costs go down. If the US dollar declines, then you are penalized because while your revenue stays consistent, your converted operating costs increase. The bottom line is that if the currency of your new foreign market differs from your home currency, you will encounter risk due to fluctuations regardless of how you transact business in the new market.

Considerations in Assessing Currency Risk

Let's take a closer look at how currency fluctuations might impact your business. Start with sales prices. Even if you sell in your home currency, sales prices are impacted by currency fluctuations if your goods are ultimately purchased in the local currency. At some point in the sales cycle, your pricing will be converted to the local currency. Someone will be taking currency risk when this happens because there is always a lag time between when they purchase in your currency, and the customer buys in the local currency. During that time, the conversion rate may have changed. If your channel partners have taken the currency risk, and if it turns unfavorable, they will ask to renegotiate their purchasing price with you in order to maintain their margins. If you do not make an effort to at least discuss this with them, they may stop purchasing from you because of the profitability risk.

Of course, if you sell in the local currency, you will feel the impact directly. Your channel partners and end customers will not feel the initial impact of the exchange rate fluctuation. However, as you consolidate your financials, all currency fluctuations will impact your profitability. If the local currency has devalued, the sales revenue will convert to less of your home currency. If the local currency has increased in value, you benefit as you will convert your revenue to a higher amount of local currency.

Due to currency fluctuations, if you sell your product through a distribution channel, you will need to account for "price protection." This means that you will compensate your distributor if the exchange rate turns unfavorable or if you change your manufacturer's suggested list price (you may do this to protect your margins if you sell in the local currency). Whenever there is an impact on what your distributor can charge its customers, there is a potential conflict since no distributor wants to sell your product at a loss. To maintain good relations with your sales channel, you can offer price protection if your distributor holds inventory in your product and the exchange rate fluctuates wildly.

Most companies do not like to go back and adjust pricing on invoices that are already closed, so if they decide to offer price protection, they either offer a discount on the next order or provide some additional product at no cost as compensation. I prefer offering a discount on the next order as it ensures that my company will get another purchase order. However, either method is fine. As long as your business has a consistent, or growing, level of sales, offering a discount on future orders or additional units at no cost should be acceptable.

Like sales prices, if your expenses are in the local currency you will feel the immediate impact of currency fluctuations when you consolidate your financials. If the local currency is devalued, when you consolidate into your local currency, you will see the benefit of the lower valuation. However, the benefit may be short lived as your suppliers may increase the prices they charge you. They will try to do this if a portion of their costs is in a foreign currency. In the long run, this may negate any cost benefits you have received when the devaluation initially occurred. On the other hand, if the local currency appreciates, you will see the negative impact as soon as you consolidate your financials. Unfortunately, you should not expect your suppliers to reach out to you with lower prices because of the local currency appreciation.

Another major area of impact of currency fluctuations concerns wages. Typically, your largest operating expense category is employee salaries. Any major shifts in the value of the local currency can have a major effect on your business. For example, if there is a large devaluation of the local currency, your employees' cost of living will increase. We live in a global world and even if your employees are paid in the local currency, they will feel the effect. Whatever goods your employees purchase for their families will become more expensive when there is a currency devaluation. This will influence their ability to maintain their current lifestyle. If this occurs, expect your employees to ask for raises to compensate for their more expensive cost of living.

A discussion of currency fluctuations is not complete without a conversation of grey markets. When you sign an agreement with a channel partner to sell your products, you will typically limit them to a certain territory. The territory can be a city, country and even a region, but you want to define where they can sell your products. These rules are meant to avoid conflicts where multiple channel partners try to sell product in each other's territory. Grey markets are those where distributors or resellers sell products outside of their authorized geography. They will typically do this if the demand in the other market is greater, or if they can make more money selling the product elsewhere.

If you sell product in the local currency in each market, you need to actively monitor the potential for grey market activities. For example, if one of the countries where you operate has a big currency devaluation, your channel partners' potential for margin will be higher selling into other countries. This is because the local currency is now worth less than other currencies. They can sell their inventory outside of their country in foreign currencies at a price higher than they could obtain in the local market. This will tempt them to try to sell outside of their territory to maximize their profits.

Even if you sell product to your distributors in your own currency, you still need to actively monitor for grey market activities. Let's assume your home currency is the US dollar (USD). As an example, if one of the countries where you operate has a currency devaluation, your channel partners' potential for margin will be higher selling into other countries. This is because they purchased in USD and if they sell in their local currency at a previously determined price they will make less money, since their effective cost will be higher when they convert to their local currency. Instead, if they sell their inventory to other countries in USD, they will earn more money.

Examples

Let's look at some examples I've encountered over the years in international business in trying to deal effectively with currency fluctuation.

1. *China.* Due to currency restrictions, I have always found it easier to conduct business in China in US dollars. Larger companies have offices in Hong Kong, which enables them to purchase in US

dollars. In cases where I dealt with a smaller Chinese company that did not have an external presence, a distributor or middleman was always available to purchase in US dollars and sell in renembi or Yuan. For a long time, China's exchange rate was fixed to the US dollar, so even though our in-country expenses were in the local currency, our revenue and expenses were pretty much shielded from currency risks. When the exchange rate was reset, we had to do a one-time adjustment to our plan. In summary, my China businesses were always easier to manage than other markets from a currency risk perspective because of the government's management of exchange rates.

2. *Japan.* Like most currencies, the Japanese yen trades freely on the open market. As a result, we were constantly subjected to its fluctuations. Unlike China, most companies, even very large multinationals, prefer to transact business in Yen. If business is done in USD, they do not want to take on the currency risk so most purchase orders are subject to adjustment based on the exchange rate. As my in-country expenses were always in Yen, there was no currency risk in matching revenue and expenses. However, if the dollar appreciated, we often had to lower our prices in order to complete sales. Having said that, I experienced some customers placing orders through their US offices in dollars, but if the Yen depreciated, the office in Japan would still ask for a price adjustment.

3. *Europe.* Most of Western Europe uses the Euro as their currency and the companies there prefer to transact in Euros. Since all our expenses in the market were also in Euros, this made our accounting easy. However, whenever the dollar started appreciating and goods became more expensive, I would get requests for salary adjustments. When dealing with European currencies, including the British Pound and Swiss Franc, significant currency changes typically happen over a longer period of time. This provides you more time to make adjustments to your business.

4. Mexico. Doing business in Mexico is far more complex because the currency is less stable than the others currencies discussed. The Mexican Peso experiences more rapid changes than these other currencies. When conducting sales in Mexico, we insisted on doing the transactions in US dollars. Our expenses were mixed, as many of the vendors would prefer to transact in dollars, but other expenses, such as salaries were in pesos. This led to a potential disconnect between cash inflows and outflows. In times when there was a big devaluation of the peso, we would offer either a salary adjustment or one-time bonus to employees.

Currency Hedging

As your international business grows, you may want to hedge your currency risk. This is a strategy to try to control the impact currency fluctuations have on your business. There is a cost to doing this, and you can never completely eliminate currency risk in international business. Hedging your currency is done by buying financial contracts that protect you in the event of a fluctuation in the currency. With hedging, you can lock-in an exchange rate for an amount of currency for a period of time, thus removing the currency risk over that timeframe. The downside is that it will cost you money to set up these hedges. Talk to your banker to find out what hedging options you can possibly pursue.

Since hedging contracts cover a specific period of time, most companies arrange annual or multi-year currency hedges to lock in a fixed exchange rate for that period. However, accurately forecasting sales and expenditures within a country is critical if you hedge, because you have to decide how much currency to hedge. If you hedge too little, then the hedge will not protect the portion of your cash flow beyond that amount. If you hedge too much, then you are paying excess fees, which could defeat the benefit of the original hedge.

For example, if you are hedging Euros and expect to generate 1 million Euros in cash flow over the next 12 months, you might opt to hedge 1 million Euros pegged to the US Dollar at a fixed exchange rate. You contact your banker who sets up the hedge for you at a fixed fee. Now if your business is very successful and you generate 2 million Euros in cash flow, only the first million will be protected and the second million will be subject to fluctuations. On the other hand, if your business does not meet forecast and only generates 500,000 Euros in cash flow, you will have ended up paying too much in fees charged by the bank. Your cash flow was protected, but the upfront fee you paid when setting up the hedge was higher than what your business needed.

Larger and more established companies typically use currency hedging because of both the amount of their exposed capital and the predictability of their cash flow streams. If you are conducting hundreds of millions of dollars of business in a particular currency, the cost of hedging that amount is minimal compared to the risk. Furthermore, if you can better predict your cash flow streams in a particular currency, the effectiveness of the currency hedge is much greater.

Smaller companies, especially when setting up operations in a new country, may find the cost of hedging too high if they cannot accurately project cash flow. If they can project cash flow with accuracy, hedging becomes an effective business protection tool.

- Doing business internationally adds a new element of risk to your company due to currency fluctuations. When setting up your business, you need to account for this risk, as the impact to your cash flow can be severe if currencies fluctuate wildly.

- If the majority of your revenue and expenses are in the same currency, you still have risk, but it is limited. Your risk is much greater if your revenue is in one currency while your costs are in a different one.

- Currency fluctuations can impact selling prices, price protection policies, employee salaries, and operating expenses.

- Currency fluctuations can create possible grey market issues with your channel partners who see greater profit in other markets if currency fluctuations occur to their detriment.

- As our world today is global, employee wages can still be impacted, even if you pay in the local currency.

- One strategy to minimize currency risk is hedging—buying contracts that guarantee your currency for a period of time. However, hedging has a cost and your forecasting needs to be accurate for it to be effective.

CHAPTER 15

Cash Flow Management

SUCCESSFUL INTERNATIONAL EXPANSION REQUIRES AN investment of a lot of resources, especially cash. You need to invest money when you start up the venture. As the venture expands, you will likely need to invest additional funds. Your plan is to see a return on your investment through profitability over time. But the time it takes for your local entity to reach profitability can vary. Managing your cash flow is thus an important item that needs to be closely overseen.

If you are either a small company or a rapidly growing one, cash flow management is even more critical. This is because the timing of your sales receivables does not always line up with the timing for paying your inventory and operating expenses. If customers delay payments but you must pay your costs, you can quickly deplete your bank account despite a favorable income statement that may show you are profitable. If you are growing rapidly, you run the risk of generating a lot of revenue but not having cash on hand to pay your invoices.

The most basic definition of cash flow is the money you receive from sales and other activities, referred to as your *inflows*, minus the money you pay out for expenses and other activities, referred to as your *outflows*. If in a given month you bring in more money than you pay out, then your cash flow is positive for that month. Alternatively, if you pay out more than you bring in, your cash flow is negative. If your operating cash flow is negative, then you must fund your business through other methods such as:

- depleting your savings
- borrowing money
- selling equity in your business
- selling assets

A Closer Look at Inflows

Let's drill down on the inflows portion of cash flow. Again, this is the money that your business brings in. It can include money from operations, financing activities and the selling of assets. Our focus is on operating cash flow, as the two other categories are typically one-time events that you may elect to do at the start of international expansion and/or at a later point in time.

Operating cash flow is what you manage on a day-to-day basis. Your main source of cash inflow from operations is through sales revenue. Anytime you sell something, you should get paid. Depending on your business, you will generate sales revenue in one or more of the following methods:

- *One-time revenue from a sale.* This is typical in businesses where physical products are sold, such as computers, clothing, or furniture.
- *Monthly recurring revenue.* This is common in services and software. Telephone, electricity, and online software services are good examples of recurring flows.
- *Licensing revenue.* If you license technology, know-how, legal rights, or other intellectual property, you generate licensing revenue.
- *Design services revenue.* If you provide any design services, such as engineering or manufacturing assistance, you could charge design services fees.

■ *Installation services revenue.* Anytime something is installed, there is the possibility to charge for it. For example, if I buy a washing machine, I can pay to have it delivered and installed.

Regardless of the type of revenue, you need to know when you will get paid in order to manage your cash flow. Depending on the country, the expectation of when customers pay may vary. While your accounts receivables are considered current assets because they should be easy to convert to cash, if your customers do not pay on time, you may not have enough cash available to pay your current bills. Unfortunately, this can lead to a business default. Thus, it is vital to understand when your customers typically pay so you can effectively manage your business.

There are two payment considerations you need to understand when conducting business in a new country. First is the *standard payment term*. In some cultures paying at the time of sale, or within a 15 or 30 day time period is standard. In others, though, they expect to delay payment for 90 or even 120 days. You need to understand the local culture before you model your business. Note that "standard payment term" is based on both the country and your specific market segment. For example, in Japan automakers expect to pay in 90 to 120 days, while computer manufacturers typically agree to pay in 45 to 60 days.

You can always try to enforce the same payment terms you grant in your home country but if they differ greatly from customary terms in the local market, your customers may dislike your terms and do business elsewhere. Or they may agree to your terms, but pay according to their own, disregarding your expectation. Even worse, if you try to enforce terms that are not typical within the country for your industry, you risk not winning business with prospective customers. In any of these situations, your cash forecast will be impacted.

The second consideration, *not getting paid in a reasonable time,* brings greater risk as it is harder to model in your financials. In some cultures, even if customers agree to 30 day terms, they may not pay for 60 or more days—and only if you continually bother them for payment. Many cultures honor the due date and pay on time; customers in Japan and Western Europe are very good at making payments when due. But I've experienced long delays in China, South America, and the Middle East. It is not that these customers try to single out your company, but this is the way business is conducted in their markets. Again, you need to understand this cultural habit so you can model your business to account for potential payment delays. Of course, if you are providing a recurring service, you have more control given that you can always shut their service off until payment is made.

When forecasting inflows you need to account for two items that may reduce your net cash received. The first is uncollectible revenue. Every time you sell and provide credit terms, there is the risk that your customer is either not able or unwilling to pay. No matter how hard a business tries to qualify customers, there will always be a small percentage of receivables at risk of not being collected. If you cannot collect, that loss of cash needs to be accounted for. If possible, find out what is typical for non-payment percentage in your industry in the new country. Then reduce your expected cash inflows by the same percentage.

The second item that could reduce your net cash received is warranty replacement costs. Every time you have to replace or repair a product, you will incur costs. This includes labor and shipping, and these show up as operating costs. If you replace product under warranty, you will also experience a reduction of salable inventory because every unit you ship out is one less unit you can sell. If you have less inventory to sell because of warranty replacements, your cash inflows will be lower. Determine the expected warranty replacement percentage and reduce your cash inflows by the amount of product that will no longer be available for sales.

Examples of Cash Inflows

Based on my experiences, here are cultures where you want to learn about your cash inflows and payment terms.

1. *China.* Most companies will agree to your payment term or ask for a slightly longer term. However, I've often found it necessary to contact the customer before payment is due to ensure it will be received on time. If you are not visible for collections, especially with smaller companies, you risk of not getting paid on time. It is best if you have someone on staff who speaks Mandarin or Cantonese and can make the calls to ensure there is no miscommunication.

2. *Japan.* Japanese companies of all sizes will typically try to negotiate a longer payment term. I believe one reason is that they have a more complex sales channel and receive customer payments later than what we experience in Western cultures. They will always push for more generous payment terms. However, whatever term is finally agreed upon, they will always pay on time, often on the exact due date.

3. *United Kingdom and continental Europe.* Companies in the UK and continental Europe will typically request 45 or 60-day payment terms. Most will pay by the due date. However, smaller companies may delay payment if they are having a cash flow problem, so it is important to assess the financial health of your customers before selling to them if you are counting on the cash flow.

4. *Brazil and the rest of Latin America.* I've found that if you extend credit to companies in Brazil or other Latin American countries, you will have to chase them down for payment. They ultimately will pay, but it takes effort to get payment. If you do not chase them, do not expect the payments to arrive. As a result, I often ask for payment up front to avoid this hassle.

The key point to remember is to communicate with your customers. Regardless of where they are based, business ultimately comes down to relationships. The more you visit and talk to customers, the more consistent they will be in paying. Yes, there will be times when customers have a legitimate reason to delay payment, but if you do not have a good working relationship, you will not be able to assess whether they really need the extra time or are just trying to delay settling their account.

A Closer Look at Outflows

In our chapter on costs, we spoke about all the various items you need to model for your new international business. Now we need to model when those expenditures will be paid out as part of your projection of outflows. To do this, you need to understand common practices in the country. While you should always ask for credit terms, understand that as a new company in the market with no credit history, this may not be a realistic option for you in the near-term.

Many of your smaller purchases, such as office supplies, are paid at time of delivery. Most of your larger purchases will have a clearly stated payment due date that you pre-negotiate prior to the sale. As mentioned, when you are new in a country, many vendors demand up front payment, which will impact your immediate cash flow. Over time, vendors may start to extend credit to you, but do not assume that this will happen. Only model payment terms when you know credit will be granted. For some expenses, such as office space or furniture lease, recall that you may be required to pay the full term up front at time of agreement.

The next outflow to model is employee costs, such as salaries and bonuses. In most countries, employees are not paid weekly or semi-monthly, but rather once per month. Find out what is the common practice or legal requirement in the particular country of your operation. You also need to consider bonus payments. As mentioned earlier in the book, some countries, like China, mandate an employee bonus. In other countries like India, employees expect bonuses and many will quit if they are not received. Research employee payment practices before modeling your business. Because these payments can be large, the timing of them is important when determining your cash requirements. In order to keep employees motivated, you should conform to local payment practices. Enforcing your home country practices can lead to high employee turnover.

Next, be sure to know the timing of paying government-mandated expenses. This encompasses everything from employee fees (such as retirement fund contributions) and employment taxes to regulatory fees, sales taxes, and income taxes. Each country has its own policies and not paying on time often leads to severe fines. Some of these local items can be quite complicated to determine, so consult a tax accountant who understands the local government fee market in order to ensure compliance.

When you are granted credit, be sure to pay on time so you can establish a good payment history in the new country. The more reliable you are, the more likely you will be able to negotiate favorable credit terms. Otherwise, you risk always having to pay upfront, which is bad for your cash flow management. Most local vendors in a new market do not care about your credit history in other countries because to them, it is not a guarantee you will behave responsibly in their country. So in many cases, you have to start from the ground floor and slowly build up your good standing with local suppliers.

- As the saying goes, cash is king! All businesses need to accurately forecast and manage their cash flow in order to succeed. When conducting business internationally, this can be tricky as local standards on both receivables and payables can differ greatly from you current business practices.

- Your main source of operating cash inflows is through sales revenue. Some sales items result in one-time payments, while others generate recurring payments.

- You must understand when customers in that culture pay in order to predict your cash inflow.

- You also need to understand common practices in a country in order to plan out your cash outflows. This includes payments for purchases, employee costs, and government mandates expenses.

- Do not assume you will be given credit when first entering a country. Be sure to pay on time so you can establish a good credit history in a country.

PART 4

GROWING YOUR INTERNATIONAL BUSINESS

CHAPTER 16

Visibility and Presence

IF YOU'VE EXPANDED YOUR BUSINESS INTERNATIONALLY, congratulations! You put a lot of hard work into your expansion plan, and perhaps you used this book as your guide. This section assumes that you successfully finalized your initial market entry strategy using any of the methods described in Part 2 of this book, "Market Entry Options." So now is the time to plan how to continue growing your business. After all, so much effort was spent on launching that you might as well aim for long-term success. No point squandering what you've already invested; let's aim for new highs.

As you are getting established, you will face many new questions. How do you make this business successful so it quickly contributes positively to your company's bottom line? You may have hired a local team to sell, but will that be enough? What activities and initiatives can you do from headquarters to help ensure success?

In this chapter, we will look at how to increase company visibility and your own presence within a market. We will not discuss local marketing activities, since the team you hired should have the expertise to accomplish this. Rather, our goal is to explore how to direct useful activities from headquarters that can assist your local team in marketing your company within the country. The activities from this chapter will augment what your local team is planning.

Building Market Visibility

Your financial plan most likely has a marketing budget assigned for the local team to build brand and product awareness. You have probably created a detailed line item list of things to do to make sure potential customers know you are in the market, and they understand the unique value your company's products will bring them. This is the minimum required to build presence in a market.

However, just hiring a marketing team in a new country and giving them a budget is not enough. In addition to that, it is your responsibility to be actively involved and further increase visibility and presence for your company. There are several methods I've used to do this.

1. Site visits. As I've stressed in this book, making frequent visits to the country is critically important. You, as CEO or senior executive, and your staff should plan to be on the ground working with the local team at least quarterly. This means sending one person from headquarters to visit your new office at least every three months. For more strategic markets, you should have a senior executive visit monthly. The more you are there, the more the local team will believe they are valuable to your business and the success of the company.

As stated before, when you visit the country, get out of the office. You should make appointments to see customers, potential customers, channel partners, ecosystem partners, industry associations, and even government regulators. Visit anyone who can impact your local business operations or can lead others to your company to generate revenue. Believe me, the more visibility you create, the more successful you will be. Another benefit of your taking the initiative to be visible is that your local staff will follow your lead. If they see that you are always networking to build the business, they will do the same when you are not there.

2. Press meetings. Next activity on your list during visits is to schedule press meetings. Local press is always receptive to meeting foreign executives, as they often want to better understand your local business plans as well as what you do in other countries. Your marketing team hopefully has relationships with some of the local press and can set up meetings for you. If you do not have a marketing team, or they do not have the right contacts, reach out to a small local PR firm, share your objectives with them, and hire them arrange press meetings. Holding an open house, where the press can come to lunch and learn about your company is often an effective strategy to make press contacts.

When you first establish your presence, focus on having press meetings, or even a press conference. This is the best way to introduce your company to the market, and get exposure without spending much money. You will find that journalists and bloggers often want to write about your company because you are newsworthy to them. After that, whenever you have a significant announcement, you can plan more press meetings. Significant announcements can be a new product introduction or announcing a strategic partnership or a significant customer win. I cherish establishing good relationships with the press because whenever they publish an article about you, it is free publicity! The added exposure often makes a difference, as you can experience local sales increases.

3. Speaking at industry conferences. Public speaking is another valuable tool to schedule as part of a site visit. At conferences, you can directly interface with many potential customers and ecosystem partners. Each country hosts numerous conferences throughout the year seeking guest speakers. Many of these events seek foreign executives to participate as it adds to their own caché. Presenting a talk or being part of a panel discussion are great ways to expand your company's visibility. You will be viewed as an industry expert, which helps position your company in a positive light. Either your marketing department or an external PR agency can research which conferences are most pertinent and work to get you onto the agenda.

If the language barrier is an issue to speak at a conference, ask a local executive to help you present or do a presentation on his or her own. You will always encounter colleagues who speak English who would be happy to engage in business discussions on your behalf or to help their own company. While your local executive generates interest by participating in a session, you can further develop interest in your company through one-on-one and small group dialogs throughout the event.

Ultimately, the more involved you are, the more receptive potential customers will be to do business with your company. Best of all, you do not have to create an advertising budget to visit customers and partners, schedule press meetings, or present at industry conferences—they are all mostly free!

Example of Creating Visibility

If you recall, AirPrime was making wireless modules for computing devices. We had originally hired a local agent in South Korea, and later set up our own sales office. Once we had our sales office, we established a partnership with a local company called QMTel, which also developed wireless technology. While they could have been seen as a competitor, there were many product and technology synergies between our companies. Working with their CEO, we formed a partnership to jointly develop modules specifically for the Korean market.

As we were getting close to signing the contract, we realized it was a great idea to host a press conference announcing the partnership. Our press event was a success; about half a dozen industry journalist attended and wrote about our new relationship. QMTel benefited by forming a partnership with a larger American company, and AirPrime benefited by publicizing our solid presence in South Korea with a local partner. Although we were both small companies, having a press conference with half a dozen journalists in attendance gave us a lot of exposure within that market.

From the event's publicity, we derived numerous specific benefits for AirPrime. Our credibility in the market increased, facilitating our ability to set up new meetings with target customers. One direct result was winning a prestigious contract to supply the world's first next generation 3G wireless products to one of the largest network operators in Korea, KTF. In addition, the press coverage resulted in my being invited to present at a wireless conference on Jeju Island in South Korea. This talk further increased our company's visibility in the market, and led to our generating additional sales leads.

How to Create "Presence"

Being visible in the local market helps you in dealing not only with outside parties, but also with your employees. I visited my remote offices frequently, knowing that it was important to ensure that local teams shared our company vision and knew they were significant to me. At all of my companies, the employees always seemed happy whenever I or other headquarter executives visited. At the end of my stays, they would often ask when I was going to return. Having the executive team visit always provided a sense of pride and unity to the organization.

I have noticed that a CEO or high-level executive being personally visible and providing a strong presence motivates local teams. They feel they belong and are part of the global company. Because of this, they want to do better and push themselves harder. Face time also helps reduce any of the 'us versus them' mindset that can so quickly happen with remote offices. Too often companies get bogged down in turf wars, as different groups want to push their own agenda. By having the most senior executives continually bridging the distance between offices, it is much easier to keep the company marching in the same direction as one entity.

In my own experiences, my companies have greatly benefited by creating remote employees who are more motivated and give greater effort. This was especially visible whenever the company was embarking on a project that required working late due to time zone differences. More people were willing to put in the extra hours to help their co-workers half way around the world, as they want to succeed together. A highly motivated work force also results in more open communication across the organization. The more people communicate, the fewer errors, politicking and redundant efforts, resulting in higher company output. The overall benefit is more efficient company performance and better communications.

Example of Creating Presence

This example concerns Atrua, maker of security components for mobile phones. When we set up our R&D center in China, we knew that we had to make a commitment to support the office. In a prior chapter, I mentioned that we would often exchange engineers on site visits. We also wanted to provide strong local support, so I would spend one week in Shanghai every two months to be with the team, visit customers, and talk to partners. In the months I did not visit, I made sure at least one other executive from headquarters went to Shanghai. We averaged more than one person from headquarters visiting our China subsidiary every month.

Just as I did at headquarters in the US, every time I visited the China office I would hold a company meeting at which I would update all employees about news at the company worldwide. I always emphasized how their work was benefitting the rest of the company. When I conducted company meetings in the US, I always had an open Q&A session where employees were given an open forum to ask questions. I was adamant about using the same process in all my remote offices, including China. Culturally, employees in China are afraid to speak up, so it took more effort on my part to get them to engage in an open dialog. But after a few meetings, we finally got to the point where some employees were comfortable asking me questions. This increased the value of my company meetings because we invited employee opinions and discussed issues of concern to them.

In addition to showing my presence internally, I also sought to provide more external visibility for the company. My general manager had good connections with the local media. So on many visits, we scheduled press interviews to garner more recognition. We hosted reporters in our office, visited them in their offices, and met them for coffee or lunch. We remained flexible about how to talk to them in order to maximize our exposure.

Along with our employee meetings and those press events, I also spent a good deal of time meeting face to face with customers, regulators, suppliers, and ecosystem partners during my visits. Customers and partners would often mention how comfortable they felt doing business with our company because of my frequent visits.

The end result was that we had extremely low employee turnover. We lost less than one engineer per year, which was atypical in a big city in China. Most companies experience much greater turnover as other foreign companies continually poach highly experienced engineering talent. Because of the efforts we made to keep our employees informed, motivated, and happy, we did not experience this phenomenon. I also believe the press interviews and employee loyalty helped us in securing our dominant market share in the country.

- Visibility and presence are very important to growing your international business. This applies both to external activities, such as dealing with customers and the press, as well as internally communicating and bonding with your local employees. The more your local team sees that they are valued, the better results your company will obtain.

- While you have a local marketing budget, it is your responsibility to be actively involved and further increase visibility and presence for your company.

- The best ways to increase your company's visibility in a country are to make frequent visits, schedule press meetings and speak at industry conferences.

- Your presence working with the employees in your local office leads to better communications and is critical to the continued success of your business.

- The more time you and your executives spend with the local team, the greater their motivation and productivity.

- The more visibility and presence provided by headquarters, the more driven the local team will be to succeed.

CHAPTER 17

Localizing Sales and Support

GLOBAL COMPANIES ACHIEVE SUCCESS BECAUSE THEY BRING A combination of global and local elements to each market they serve. Attributes like company positioning, product development philosophy, and corporate policy are standardized throughout the organization in all locations. These act as a common baseline for the organization so there is not a different company vision in each market served.

However, to maximize potential, successful companies localize how they structure their sales and support processes to adapt to how business is done in each country. Trying to enforce what works in one market without making any adjustments won't usually work in another country. The more competitive the market, the more flexible you have to be to compete. Local customers are more comfortable knowing that you understand their culture and needs. Otherwise, your company will be perceived as a foreign entity trying to push its way of doing business onto the local market. Unless you have a truly unique product, most potential customers will not accept that.

How to Localize Sales

Localizing your marketing and sales approach means more than just translating your brochures. It encompasses many decisions, including:

   1. *Product positioning.* While your overall company positioning should remain uniform on a worldwide basis, how you position
your product in each country should be localized for two reasons.
First, local customers may value your product's benefits differently;
second, your competitors may be positioned differently compared
to your home or other markets.

   Each country is unique and people tend to value distinctive aspects of a product differently. Some features may be more highly
sought after in certain countries, so if you do not make buyers aware
of them, they may neglect your product. For example, a refrigerator's energy efficiency is more highly valued in countries like Ecuador where utility rates are sky high, but not in the United States,
where storage space and the flexibility to reconfigure the inside
shelves and drawers are stronger selling points. Focusing on the
flexibility aspects of the refrigerator in Ecuador will not be met with
excitement, as what motivates your customers there is less power
consumption.

   Since your toughest competitors may vary from country to country, how you position yourself against them should also differ. In
some markets, there may be a lot of low cost local competition, so
to compete effectively you need to position yourself as a premium
foreign product. This is a great strategy in many emerging markets,
such as China and Brazil, where consumers value imported goods
and are willing to pay more. But in countries where you compete
with many foreign products and you use lower price as your distinction, you might position yourself as the best combination of quality
and price value. Many P&G products are positioned as premium
products in emerging markets; while in the US they are positioned
as providing quality at a good price.

   2. *Marketing strategy.* Your marketing strategy must be localized as well. The effectiveness of the many marketing activities
companies do differs from country to country. In some markets, traditional media such as print, radio and TV are most effective, while
in others, digital media and electronic billboards result in a better

ROI. For example, to reach consumers in countries where most people commute via public transit, such as in Japan and Western Europe, focusing your marketing on bus stop and metro billboards and social media is advantageous.

Keep in mind that your marketing also depends on your target demographic in each country. Younger people tend to favor social media and online, whereas older people are traditionally more receptive to print and television. In order to succeed, you need to understand what works best for your target demographic in that country. Once you understand the local marketing environment in the country, there are many decisions to make, including:

- Are print advertisements, such as newspaper and direct mail, effective to promote your product?
- Are TV ads an effective way to reach your target market?
- Will radio advertising work for your product?
- Should you invest in search engine optimization or spend time on Facebook pages?
- What about sponsoring local events such as sports?
- Do coupons and specials via text messaging work in that country?

Once you identify your primary target customer, and learn about how products in your industry are best localized, you can implement marketing programs that are most effective in increasing sales.

3. Sales pitch. In addition to determining how you will position your product and how to reach out to prospective customers through marketing, you may need to refine your actual sales pitch. A great sales pitch ensures you connect with your target customers at an emotional level. Companies often neglect how emotions affect buying decisions and instead focus on just the features of their products. As each culture is unique, various attributes of your product's features and benefits will appeal differently to customers in each country. For example, buyers of electronic products in specific countries will value differently features such as power consumption, safety ratings, user interface, compatibility with other devices, and even color selection.

You may also need to revise your sales pitch simply to comply with local business practices and regulations. For example, direct product comparisons are allowed in some countries like the US, but many countries limit what you can say about competitors' products. Regulations can change frequently as well, so you need to stay up to date. It is actually quite important to learn what you are allowed to say in the country before you start making sales calls. Consult a local attorney to guide you.

4. Sales collateral. The need to translate your sales materials into the local language is clear. But to effectively utilize your sales material, you need to go beyond doing a literal translation to ensure your collateral conforms to your product positioning and sales pitch in that country. In addition, a good translator will tell you that certain words and phrases do not translate well into the local language—the connotation or meaning is just too different. In many cases, American jargon gets lost in the translation. Be sure to utilize qualified local resources who understand your product category to ensure that your translations make sense and work in that culture.

Also be aware that even simple things such as your preferred color schemes and use of model numbers can have different meaning in some countries. For example, the number 4 is considered bad luck in many Asian cultures while the number 8 is considered lucky. If your collateral calls out numbers, avoid number 4 in Asia if possible. Red is a positive color in China, but too much red in your brochures will be seen as out of place. A color scheme that works well for you in Europe may need to be changed to appeal to customers in Asia. Remember, you need to connect with your customers at a deep emotional level if possible, so make sure your collateral achieves this goal by consulting with local marketing experts who know the cultural preferences.

5. Sales Partnerships. As you do business in each country, you need to seek out partners who can help you succeed in that particular market. Some global partnerships can be effective, but you may need to make adjustments in order to differentiate your company in a local country. As each country has its own unique way of doing business, see if there are any local partnerships that can help you succeed. As demonstrated in the example of AirPrime's partnership with QMTel in our last chapter, local partnerships can be very effective in positioning your company for greater success in a market.

6. Pricing. Most companies aim to have fairly uniform global pricing, but due to external factors it is not always possible. Several factors can impact your pricing strategy in each country, including import duties, transportation costs, taxes and regulatory fees, channel structure, and currency fluctuation. Any of these factors might cause you to increase your prices to preserve your profit margin, but you then have to weigh the impact on your competitiveness. If the market is saturated with many local players, you may need to price your product more aggressively than others to prevent yourself from being priced out of the market.

7. Sales organization structure and compensation. How you sell in a country might also need to be localized. If you sell direct, changes compared to your home office might be minimal since the sales process is the same. However, if you sell through distribution channels, and they are more complex in the country, you will probably need a different structure to compensate for the effect. This may mean having additional sales people who are focused on each layer of the sales channel.

As for sales people compensation, this too often needs localization. In some markets, like the US, you can implement programs that have a high commission potential compared to base salary. In other markets, such as parts of Europe and Asia, sales people expect to be paid primarily on base salary, with a small bonus component for sales success. Although you may be able to find good sales people in the US by offering 50% of their compensation in sales commissions, in other markets the best salespeople may require only 20% of their compensation in sales commissions. As a result, trying to implement a globally uniform sales salary based mostly on commissions may scare away many good sales candidates in other countries. Talk to local HR experts to understand what is considered an acceptable compensation plan for that country, and work within those bounds.

Localizing Support

Like sales, localizing support extends far beyond just providing resources that speak the local language. These are key issues to localize:

1. *Location of your resources.* The first question to answer is, "Where are your support resources located?" Ideally, you have support people in the country so they not only speak the language, but they also fully understand the culture and are available during business hours in that time zone. If this is not possible, the next best option is to locate support people at a regional office, so they are at least familiar with the nearby culture and in a closer time zone.

For example, many US companies establish a European-wide support center in Ireland. They staff it with a diversity of people who can fluently speak the many different European languages. This enables them to provide support in all the languages of their target customers. Such multi-lingual resources are easier to find in Ireland in comparison to the United States where most Americans do not speak foreign languages. In addition, the center in Ireland can more easily work normal European business hours as they are within one time zone from the majority of their market.

2. *Language capabilities.* Language issues can be tricky, however, in some countries where multiple languages are spoken or there are distinctly different dialects. For example, in China you need to have people who can speak both Mandarin and Cantonese.

In Switzerland, your team must speak German, French and Italian. In Spain, Castilian Spanish in Madrid differs from Catalan Spanish in Barcelona. Before you hire support people, assess what languages are expected for a support organization like yours, and then hire with this in mind.

3. Hours of support availability. In terms of support hours, this can also become a key issue. In some countries, like the United States, customers will expect 24x7 customer support, while in others, like Switzerland and Germany, you are fine with providing support only during normal business hours. You have to determine the standard for that country and provide the same hours of support, or better, if you want to differentiate yourself. If you try to provide fewer hours of support, your growth efforts will suffer. Many companies offer support during normal business hours, but have a process where support is available afterhours through another office, such as headquarters.

4. Customization. Next, you need to review whether the support tools your local support people use need to be customized to conform to the local way of responding to your customers. For example, how are issues logged and reported? What forms do customers need to fill out to get support? How do you communicate back to customers when problems need to be discussed or when a resolution is available? It is important that your local support teams are equipped with the right tools to be responsive to local customer expectations. Otherwise your global reputation could be damaged via negative comments posted on social media.

5. Types of support to offer. Another issue involves what types of support you will offer. Does your organization need to provide on-site support for customers or is phone support sufficient? If you provide email support, what kind of response time do you need to guarantee to keep customers happy? You also need to decide if you should provide live chat support over the Internet. There are so many different ways to support customers, so figure out what works best in that country and what your competitors are doing.

6. Interaction between support and development. You may also want to define a process for how local support people interact with product development teams if their feedback is required. If development is elsewhere, how will the feedback get to them? Another element of this issue is determining the escalation path that works best for your company to resolve complex customer issues. At what stage of a customer problem or complaint should engineering be brought in to solve the most complex issues?

7. Product returns. The next consideration is the product return policy. You may need to change your refund policy on a per country basis depending on customer expectations and local laws. When customers need to exchange a product for a replacement, you need to decide if you will provide a replacement in advance or only after you receive the defective goods. In markets like Japan, providing a replacement in advance of receiving the defective goods goes a long way to building customer trust. In many other countries, if you ship a replacement before receiving the defective good, the faulty product may never be returned.

Other issues of product returns that you need to consider include who pays for return shipping and how you handle out-of-warranty repairs. These are details that you must determine, though local laws and customer expectations may influence your policies. It can be useful to speak with your attorney and with channel partners before finalizing your support plans on these issues. With the prevalence of social media, providing an unacceptable return policy can quickly damage your reputation and future sales in the country.

8. Support structure. Finally, you will need to develop your support organization structure. How you sell in a country will determine the kind of support organization that you need. If you sell direct, you probably need a larger support staff to handle all incoming requests. However, if you sell through distribution channels, you may be able to structure it so that your channel partners handle initial support requests and only escalate calls to your company for issues they cannot resolve. If your channel partners agree to handle the initial support requests, make sure you provide adequate technical training, both at the start of your relationship and ongoing at periodic intervals, such as annual refresher courses. The better you train your channel partners, the less the daily support burden will fall back on your team.

Country Comparison Example

Here's an example that compares the differences between sales and support strategies for my company Atrua in China and the United States. As you recall, Atrua provided security components to mobile phone manufacturers.

- **United States.** At the start we had only a few target customers in the US such as Motorola, Palm, and RIM (which is technically in Canada), so we opted to have a dedicated sales team with people based in California and Illinois. We did not require any additional resources such as agents or sales reps, because we could easily reach out to all our target customers directly. Our marketing consisted of primarily doing direct sales with no need for advertising. Our main partnership strategy was to win over AT&T and Verizon as they would ultimately sell the phones that contained our security components. Our sales people drew a good base salary, but also had the opportunity to double their income based on commissions.

- *China.* At the time of entry in China, there were over 50 cell phone designers and manufacturers located in various parts of the country. In addition to our local China sales team, we deployed a regional sales director for Asia and utilized sales agents throughout China to introduce us to various manufacturers. For marketing, we did not advertise but were very active with press meetings and at conferences. Our partnerships were focused more on application developers, as the main mobile operators, China Mobile and China Unicom, did not subsidize phone sales to consumers (as is done in the US) and they were not even involved in selling the phones. Our sales people in China were compensated primarily through a base salary, with a small bonus component based on sales results.

As you can see, our sales approach had to be different in each of these countries. This is not unique, as most countries operate differently.

Now, let's look at how our customer support approaches had to differ.

- *United States.* Our customers (OEMs and ODMs) wanted 24x7 access to our engineers by phone and email. They also wanted periodic on-site visits. We accomplished this with our field engineering team that went out to see them, and we also had development engineers available on an as-needed basis, both for onsite meetings and conference calls.
- *China.* Here our customers also wanted 24x7 access to our support team, but primarily by phone. One key difference was that they wanted to have our support engineers onsite at their location through much of the product development and integration phase. They also wanted our support people onsite when they did their initial pilot manufacturing. Our China support strategy thus required much more face time and investment in our technical staff than our US support strategy. It even required hiring additional employees into our China support organization.

- You can often bring a combination of global and local elements to each market you serve. But localizing your sales and support strategy is critical to success.

- Localizing is done to conform to customer expectations and any legal requirements for how to sell to and support customers in each country.

- Most companies must localize how they structure their sales and support processes to adjust to doing business in each country.

- Localizing sales consists of many components, including positioning, marketing programs, sales pitch, partnerships, and pricing.

- Localizing support consists of many components including support people, tools, hours, types of support provided, return policy, and details such as shipping fees and replacement fulfillment.

CHAPTER 18

Localizing Products
and Services

WE HAVE ADDRESSED HOW TO LOCALIZE YOUR SALES AND support processes, so let's look now at localizing what you are actually selling.

Like your go-to-market process, what you offer customers may require customization in order to increase your product's attractiveness to potential buyers. After all, customer expectations vary by country. Sometimes the localization is simple and straightforward, such as changing the product color. In other cases, the localizing can be complex, requiring you to change integral aspects or features of your product. Without such localization, you will not be able to maximize your sales potential.

There are also instances when you need to localize your product in order to comply with country certifications such as safety and emissions. Without these modifications, you will not be allowed to sell your product in the country. This is especially true of electronics and communications products, as they generate emissions and interact with the country's electrical and telecommunications networks. To be safe, you should expect any product that requires electrical power to need some level of certification from a government agency. Do not assume that US or EU certifications will be accepted. Consult local authorities and test labs to see whether new certifications are required for your product to be sold in the country.

If you elect not to localize your product, or any of its associated services, you run the risk of alienating potential customers. This is especially true if your top competitors have a localized offering. While you may be very successful in your home market, customers in a foreign market may not be receptive to a product lacking characteristics that are valued locally. To become loyal buyers, they want to see your efforts to meet their expectations. For example, if you sell electronics products, your customers expect that the power adapter will be localized and the user interface translated into the local language. Even non-electronic goods, such as kitchen utensils often need to be customized (e.g., shorter or longer handles based on size of kitchen ranges, etc.). The more competitive the market, the more agreeable you must be to localize your product.

Areas of Common Product Localization

Depending on your product, there could be dozens of elements that need to be localized. We'll discuss a few of the most common:

1. *Manuals and documentation provided with your product.* Any user guides, whether online or on paper, must be translated into the local language. In fact, I would go one step further and state that any piece of paper included with your product should be translated, in order to appeal to the largest number of possible customers. While it may be okay to keep documentation in English for products targeted at large businesses, small businesses and consumers expect all information to be in their local language.

2. *Packaging.* It is also critical to translate your product packaging, especially if your product is sold at retail. You have to make it easy for potential customers to be able to read the features and benefits of your product on the packaging. In addition, you should explore making any necessary changes or updates to the look of your packaging to make it more attractive for a particular country. This

is especially true regarding colors. Certain color schemes are better received in some countries versus others. For example, green is not popular in Japan, France, or Belgium, but it can be frequently seen on packaging designed for Turkey and Austria. People from Islamic cultures react negatively to yellow. Europeans associate black with mourning and tend to prefer red, grey and blue. In the Netherlands, orange is the national color and therefore is often used to generate nationalistic feelings.

The sizing and amount of your product packaging may need to change as well. US retailers have more shelf space, but many countries have smaller stores with fewer shelves and need to pack in more products within a given space. Large packaging may find it difficult to earn a spot on shelves in those countries. Moreover, customers in some countries in Europe abhor excessive packaging and find it wasteful. They actually think less of your products because of this. Many European companies also emphasize recycling in their packaging so a product with non-recyclable packaging will be negatively received.

3. *Interfaces on software.* If your product includes software, or software is your entire product, you must translate and localize the user interface. This can be more complex than first envisioned, because if your have a lot of graphics with text, you often need to modify both. This requires working with the source files of your artwork and making the changes manually. Like packaging, the color scheme of your user interface can matter, too, as not all color combinations appeal to consumers in every country. Some colors, like black in Europe and yellow in Islamic countries, should not be the main background of your user interface.

Given that end users worldwide have become more impatient when using software, you want to make sure your user interface is easy to navigate and free from unnecessary clutter. This can be challenging, as some translations from English can be much longer in other languages, with more words to say the same thing. To see what I mean, go to Google Translate and write various phrases in English and see how they are translated into the language of your target country. Your menus also have to be natural and you want to minimize the number of clicks a user will need to complete an action. So in addition to translations, you often have to reevaluate how your entire software interface flows, and make adjustments to ensure your software is intuitive to local users.

4. Form factor. The physical look of your product is another element that may need to be localized. Making changes to your form factor can be complicated, as it often requires changing the tooling for manufacturing the physical components of your product. These changes might add several months to the schedule to bring your product to market, and they can involve significant additional expenses that must be budgeted. Form factor changes that might be required to make your product attractive in your target country include altering the color, shape, size and other attributes. For example, refrigerator makers need to change the form factor of their product by reducing the size if they want to sell their US-designed refrigerators in Europe. Many older homes and apartments in Europe do not have the space to accommodate large refrigerators. If you create electronic modules for appliances, you, too, may need to take the smaller-is-better requirement into account.

The choice of materials with which your product is made can also fall into question. Some materials are banned in certain countries, such as potentially toxic metals either on the surface or inside your product. Countries like Japan and those in the European Union have stricter standards for certain metals than in the US. Speak with a local certification lab to find out if any changes are required for your product to comply. And before finalizing form factor changes, do some informal (or formal) focus group testing on potential customers and channel partners so you can capture all the changes at once. Otherwise you may have to go through multiple design iterations to hit your new market's sweet spot.

5. *Functionality of your product.* Determine if there are any functions that need to be changed in order to either make your product work or be more useful for a given country. For example, if you have any device that requires electricity, you may need to change not only the power supply, but also other components to handle the different currents provided in various power networks throughout the world. Otherwise, an electrical spike can cause your product to fail, or even worse, injure the user. Countries are very strict about complying with electrical requirements and companies can receive substantial fines if they bypass these requirements.

Another example of a functional change is one we had to make at one of my companies, CloudTC. We designed our phone's display to be very bright, without the possibility of turning off the screen since our phone was constantly AC powered. We sold primarily to businesses with remote employees. In the US, where most people have their home offices separate from their bedrooms, this was not an issue. However, in certain countries, like Japan, this was an issue because some customers use their bedroom to serve as their home office and the bright light from the phone is a distraction at bedtime.

6. *Product Features.* You may also need to go beyond functionality to change or add product features for the local market. There could be good reason for you to add, delete or modify any existing features to gain approval to sell in a country or to make your product more competitive and attractive to that audience. For example, a lot of technology products need to remove various privacy features in order to be sold in China; if not done, the US government will not allow you to export to that market. As with the form factor advice above, be sure you speak to potential customers and channel partners early in the process so you capture all feature changes at once. Otherwise you may need multiple product development iterations, which will delay your product introduction.

7. *Accessories sold with your product.* As with product features, you may need to add, delete or modify any accessories either to gain approval to sell in a country or to make your product more attractive to potential customers. When I was at Xircom, we had to change our telephone cords in order to comply with country regulations and eliminate the need for an external adapter because the phone jack was different than the one used in the US.

Another example comes from what we learned in Japan about how end users physically carry their products. In that market and others in Asia, many portable products come with elegant carrying cases because customers enjoy the convenience and status of these. If you do not to include such a case, it will detract from your sales, especially if your competitors include one. Whatever your product, be sure to talk with potential customers and channel partners to assess what accessories you should include to maximize the appeal of your product.

8. *Product bundling.* A product bundle combines two products into one offering. This is common in many industries such as video games, where the system often comes bundled with some popular games. In the computer industry, some vendors bundle carrying cases with tablets or notebook computers. When deciding whether to create a bundle for a particular country, ask yourself the following questions:

- Is there an opportunity to bundle your product with another product or service, even if that second product is not from your company?
- Will bundling make your product more attractive to potential customers in this country?
- Will it give you instant market credibility?

Adding a third-party product can make your product offering more desirable. This is especially true if you are bringing in a new product category into the country. Also consider how creating a bundle could help localize your product and make it more attractive. If you piggyback your product on a well-known local offering, you could benefit from free brand awareness because of the other product's popularity. This is where understanding the local ecosystem and having contacts within it can help you structure valuable bundling deals.

Localization of Services

With many products, companies also offer value-added services such as installations and extended warranties. When entering a new market, these need to be evaluated to ensure they are appropriate for the local market. There are major variations in the expected level of service from one country to another. Study what is currently being offered in the market, and talk to potential customers and channel partners to devise a plan to localize your services for the country. Here are a few of the major concerns:

1. *Installation services.* If you currently offer installations in other countries, should you offer installation in the new market? This decision will depend on several factors including what is common in that country, whether you can find appropriate installers, if you can adequately support an installation, and whether there are any regulations that either allow or disallow you to install. For example, in some countries such as Japan, the channel partners expect to do the installations, so offering this service on your own will alienate them. In markets where installation is expected, going above and beyond what your competitors are doing is a good way to distinguish your company.

2. *Product configuration.* Does your product need to be configured before it is initially used or at some later point during its use? If so, you need to decide if you should handle this configuration internally or let customers do it themselves. In some markets, customers prefer their own product configurations, while in others they fully expect the vendor to be responsible. For example, many small American companies prefer to configure their accounting software

on their own, but in parts of Latin America, small companies expect their vendors to configure their accounts. Before you start selling products in a new country, you need to know if this responsibility will fall to you at any point during your product's lifecycle. You can sometimes charge extra for it, but on the other hand, it can be an additional cost you will incur.

3. *Integration with other products.* Will your product be used with other products? If so, how will you integrate your solution with these other products and services. Do you have to do the integration yourselves or will it be someone else's responsibility? What you decide could depend on what is expected or allowed in the given country. Also, as with product configurations, find out if this is an item you can charge extra to do, or if it will be an additional cost to you. Always look for ways to differentiate your company, so you are more memorable in the marketplace.

4. *Extended warranties.* Extended warranties are typically sold to prolong the warranty period of a product in exchange for a fee paid when the product is purchased. Find out if you can charge for an extended warranty, because not all countries allow it. Some government regulators feel that your standard warranty period should include the timeframe of the extended warranty. Before deciding if you should offer an extended warranty, check with an attorney if it is even possible.

Assuming you can offer an extended warranty, the question becomes should you? While selling extended warranties can increase your revenue, they can become risks for financial loss. For example, what if the normal operation in the country to use your product is at the extreme limit for how it should be used, such as using a machine for 16 hours per day when it is intended to be used only 10 hours per day. This could lead to many product failures during the extended warranty period. In some warmer climate countries, electronic products do not last as long because of the higher humidity environments, so an extended warranty could become very costly to your business. This is why it is worthwhile to stress test your product and know its operating limits before deciding on offering extended warranties.

Example of Localizing a Product

Here's an example where localizing a product was beneficial. Recently, I was running a company called CloudTC, which made smart office phones based on the Android operating system. We signed up a master distributor in Germany called TITAN Commerce. They agreed to work with us to offer the phone in Germany. In order to make the phone an attractive option for potential customers, we needed to localize the following:

- User manual: translate to German
- Software user interface: translate to German, including all the image files that had text.
- Functionality: we needed to modify our software so that it displayed German dialing strings when in use, and provided German ring tone cadences.
- Accessories: the AC wall outlets are different in Germany versus the US so we had to add a new adapter to the phone.

However, we did not have to change our packaging as the product was not sold in retail stores, and our box showed only our company logo. No localization was required for the form factor and product features. Bundling was not beneficial for this product, either. Because we entered the German market with a master distributor, we did not have to localize any of our support services. Instead, we trained our new partner and set up a close technical relationship where we made engineering personnel available to them during their business hours. Because of the localization we performed, our product was well received in the German market, resulting in sales that were double what we had forecasted had we not localized the product.

- Just as with localizing sales and support, you must also localize your products and services to the local market. This may require some customization in order to make your product more attractive to potential customers.

- If you elect not to localize your product you run the risk of alienating potential customers.

- The main elements to consider when localizing your product are manuals and documentation, packaging, software, form factor, functionality, product features, accessories, and bundling with other local products.

- You need to evaluate each of your services components for the local market including installations, configurations, integrations, and offering extended warranties.

CHAPTER 19

Networking and Localizing Yourself

So far in this part, we focused on what your company can do to broaden its presence in a country by expanding visibility and localizing how you sell your product and support customers. These are all critical components to growing your business internationally. But there is one further step that I believe is vital to localize: your personal actions as executive sponsor of internationalization and global expansion.

Ultimately, business is finalized when two or more people agree to work together. Despite all the advances in technology, it is personal relationships that drive business. People buy from people, so the closer the relationships you can form with potential customers, the greater your chances of success. While your local team is tasked with developing many of these relationships, your active involvement goes a long way in helping your company reach its growth goals. Companies with active senior leaders will be preferred over those that are not present.

We have already discussed the importance of visiting customers, prospective customers, and partners in a country. In addition to these activities, you should constantly be networking to learn more about your new market and expand your list of contacts that can help your business grow. If you consistently cultivate these contacts, they can prove to become significant people assets in future years. Likewise, you need to consciously work on localizing yourself, so other parties look forward to dealing with you instead of trying to find ways to avoid you.

Building Your Network

Networking is a vital part of building a business, regardless of location. The more people get to know your value proposition, the more opportunities you uncover for business. This applies not only to potential customers, but all types of possible partners we have discussed. Word of mouth and personal referrals are still two of the most efficient forms of generating new business. They are low cost methods to generate sales leads. When expanding internationally, having a large network of contacts becomes even more crucial given that you are not in town on a day-to-day basis.

There are many actions you can take to expand your network when building an international business. These are some of the most successful one I've used in my career.

As we said, make frequent visits to the country, as stronger relationships are built face-to-face. The actual frequency will depend on the opportunities in this market, as well as your overall global business. For large, strategic markets you should plan to visit monthly or quarterly, while for smaller markets one trip every six or twelve months may suffice. Even if your networking contacts will never become customers, spending face time within your industry's ecosystem will allow you to grow your network. The more people you are introduced to, the better your company's perception in the market. In addition, as you get to know partners, they will introduce you to other influencers and potential customers.

We have already spoken about presenting and being on panels at conferences. Unfortunately, getting a speaking engagement is not always easy, but even if you are not on the agenda, attending relevant conferences to network helps promote you and your company's offerings. People attend conferences to learn and meet others within their industry. It's not by accident that many of your potential partners will be at the same conferences and you can accomplish a lot by introducing yourself and starting conversations. Then during future visits to the country, you can continue building those relationships via face-to-face meetings.

Exhibiting at a trade show provides the perfect opportunity to meet potential partners and customers. They may come to your booth to seek you out, so having a senior executive from headquarters attending the show will be well received. Even if you are not exhibiting, just walking around a trade show as an attendee is valuable as other companies exhibiting are probably seeking new contacts as much as you are.

If you do not have a profile on the social network site LinkedIn, you should, as it is one of the best networking sites for business. When preparing to visit a foreign country, tap into LinkedIn to see if any of your connections have contacts in the country that would be valuable to meet. If so, ask for introductions. I have found that when the introduction is made and they know you are visiting from another country, people are receptive to taking a meeting. They recognize and appreciate that you have come from far away and are willing to listen. Many may be eager to learn from you as well. If the initial meeting is positioned as an information exchange, both sides gain something from the encounter.

As for Twitter and blogging, being active about your company or technology can be a great way to further build up your network. Anyone who follows you might be more willing to make an introduction leading to an important sale or partnership. While there is a lot of useless noise in social media today, it may still be worthwhile to put in some effort to promote your company whenever possible. Sometimes the best growth opportunities come from the most unlikely places, so experiment with many different methods to expand your network.

Tips on Maintaining Your Network

Once you have grown a network, you must remain active to keep the communications flowing, especially in dealing with international relationships. Unlike local contacts, you don't run into your foreign contacts at local establishments. It takes a conscious effort to maintain communication. When you go for onsite visits, prioritize who to see to maintain your top contacts. Book your meetings a few weeks in advance so that they can allocate time for you. If your schedule is too busy for a formal meeting, do a breakfast meeting or meet for a coffee. Casual meetings are often more effective in moving personal relationships forward.

When you garner visibility, your contacts become more willing to assist as you work on expanding your business. People have a tendency to support those they communicate with on a frequent basis. When you are back home, check in via email or phone on a periodic basis. Add their names to your calendar and set a teaser to email them and see how they are doing in their business. You can often get a heads-up on trends in their country by staying in regular touch. Be sure also to ask if there is any way you can help them. Mutual assistance is the best policy. They appreciate your effort and it builds credibility with your contacts.

One of the keys I have learned in international business is that follow-up is absolutely essential. If you say you are going to do something, make sure you do it! Serious business people don't like to deal with people who take an action item, but never follow-up. It leaves a bad impression, as that person is quickly seen as unreliable and less desirable as a business partner. To distinguish yourself, show that you always follow-up in a timely fashion. Even if you cannot offer a definitive response to an action item, just sending a quick note stating that you are working on it goes a long way to prove you have not forgotten. Everyone is busy, but using excuses are not going to cut it if someone is counting on you.

Finally, always make an offer to invite your contacts to your country and to host them while they visit. This is always considered a meaningful gesture in every culture. I've always found that if the person makes an effort to visit you in your country, the business relationship grows stronger. A deeper sense of trust is developed when you get to know each other in your home cultures. Reciprocating is a natural human gesture that tends to solidify your connection to people. When they visit, take them to the best lunch or dinner at your favorite restaurant, share food, and learn about each other's personal lives—these are activities that form a unique bond.

Localizing Yourself

Whenever you are in a foreign country, you need to make an effort to understand their point of view and respect how they operate. I call this process "localizing yourself," by which I mean not coming across as a narrow-minded foreigner who believes your way is always right, but rather making a conscious effort to understand and appreciate their cultural views. Being sensitive to the uniqueness of each culture shows respect and builds trust. Most executives can get short-term sales in a new country without much effort, but to cultivate a truly successful business, you need to develop a deep understanding of that culture.

Over the years, I've created a series of steps to localize myself. First, learn about the culture. Read up and study its history, customs, and the unique aspects of the culture. Assess how open the culture is to outside influences and if foreign executives are happily welcomed. See if there is anything in their country's history that could impact your ability to build a long-term relationship. With all the tools at your disposal via the Internet, it is easy to find written and video resources that can quickly educate you on the country.

In addition, learn how the culture typically negotiates and conducts business. We've reviewed many specific areas where understanding their approach to issues like negotiating, partnering, payments, and other things can be pivotal to structure a successful business venture.

Before my first trip to Japan around 20 years ago, I read two books—one on Japan's history and culture, and the other about doing business there. A country's history tells you a lot about how someone may perceive dealing with foreigners, while understanding the culture helps you appreciate the other party's point of view.

Knowing how business is conducted within the country helps you avoid making protocol mistakes that can severely detract from your ability to attract clients and successfully conduct business. Some countries, particularly in Asia, are very formal and protocol-based that if you violate one small part of etiquette, even without knowing it, your business negotiation can be doomed. Looking back to my first trip to Japan, these readings gave me the confidence to be immediately productive, and this has led to my doing a lot of business in that country over the past two decades.

Being adaptable and flexible when doing business internationally is a good rule to follow. You may be successful in your home market, but the tactics you use there often do not translate well in other countries. A few countries appreciate aggressiveness, but many others deplore it. You cannot be 'set in your own ways' if you want to succeed in international business. Instead, you must be willing to adapt to doing business the local way, and be flexible with how you approach situations.

Don't assume that countries in the same region are identical. For example, doing business in Taiwan is quite different from Japan. As I traveled directly from one country to the other, I was excited to challenge myself in how I needed to change my behavior in meetings in order for my trip to be a success. Doing business in Taiwan required my business style to be very direct and somewhat confrontational, while in Japan, I had to be more reserved and indirect in my negotiations. But I enjoyed the challenge as I found myself transforming my mindset during my plane rides from one country to the other.

Being adaptable and flexible does not mean compromising your integrity, moral beliefs, or violating any laws. Yes, you need to adapt but never do things you know are wrong. There may be times when you feel pushed to make a decision you know is not right. Remain strong and firm, as you take the high ground. You may lose a business opportunity, but you will always be respected. When it comes to integrity, morals, and laws, you need to remain true to your heart.

My final comment is what I refer to as "act global, not local." Throughout the years, I've encountered people who travel frequently to a country and start acting as if they were originally from there. They try to behave like a local person in everything they do. My recommendation is that is not a good idea. People who imitate a foreign culture can be viewed as acting in a phony way. I've always taken the approach to be global in my mindset. In my case, this means not acting like a local, nor like an American. Instead, I try to act as someone who is well versed in global cultures and is respectful of the local environment. I easily fit in wherever I am, but I never lose sight of the fact that I am a foreigner visiting their country.

Throughout my career, I was often complimented on how well I understood the local culture and how I was not like many executives from American firms. I recall being told on numerous occasions that competing executives did not listen, wanted things done their way, and would not embrace the local culture or even respect it. Customers found it hard to engage with such people, as they did not grow to trust them. Without trust, there is no foundation for a business partnership. Their lack of cultural flexibility helped me win a lot of business for my companies.

Example

There are many examples I might pick from to show how localizing yourself helps, but the one I want to share dates back more than 15 years. I have selected it because despite numerous changes of companies, I am still close to the people I met back then. I was running my OEM business unit at Xircom making communications adapters. We wanted to sell to the largest PC maker in China, a company called Legend, which was later renamed Lenovo. Back then, I did not have an office in China, but had a regional sales director based in Singapore. Through his contacts, we established a relationship with the team responsible for their notebook computer accessory products.

At the time, this particular team within Legend had never done business with an American company, instead preferring to work with vendors from China and Taiwan. In order to build their trust and secure the business, I often flew to Beijing to meet with them.

We developed a good working and personal relationship through business meetings, lunches, and dinners. Despite our product being more expensive than competing offerings from China and Taiwan, we won the business. It was a combination of my respecting their culture and my company's flexibility that proved the deciding factor.

During the sales engagement, I invited the team from Legend to visit our headquarters in the US. Because they were Chinese nationals, the process to get them here was not as simple as if they were from a European country. They needed to get written permission from the Chinese government to leave the country, and then apply for a visa at the US Embassy. To help with this process, I volunteered to prepare two sets of letters for them. The first was addressed to the Chinese government asking to give them permission to leave China and visit my company. The second was directed to the US Embassy in Beijing, asking them to grant a visa so my potential customer could visit my company. My contacts at Legend appreciated this effort and it worked.

I have maintained the relationship with my main contact at Legend over many years. We've both changed companies, but we still get together every time I visit Beijing. He often comes to the US and we meet for dinner here as well. Since I continue to do business with him, I still help with his business visas today. We have successfully done business together for over 15 years and have become close friends. We have even followed our kids' progress growing up over all these years.

KEY LESSONS

- As the executive sponsor of internationalization, you must take an active role in your company's global expansion. The more active you are, the more successful you will be.

- You should constantly be networking to both learn more about the market and expand your list of contacts that can help your business grow.

- To network effectively, visit the country often, attend conferences and trade shows, and be active on social media such as LinkedIn, Twitter and blogging.

- Actively work your network by visiting with your contacts, following up on action items, checking in frequently and offering to host in your country.

- To build trust, localize yourself by learning about the culture, being adaptable and flexible, and having a global mindset. Remember to act global, not local.

- Being adaptable and flexible does not mean compromising your integrity, moral beliefs or violating laws.

CONCLUSION

CHAPTER 20

Goods vs Services vs Software

THROUGHOUT THIS BOOK, WE HAVE PREDOMINANTLY WORKED under the assumption that your company provides a physical product. Let's discuss briefly any differences if you are providing a service, such as consulting or telecommunications, or are selling online software, such as Zoho or Xero accounting software. These are different categories of industries. Most of what we covered in this book can apply to all types of businesses. The processes for analyzing markets, deciding on best ways to enter a market, and growing your business are similar regardless of industry.

I focused on physical products because they require some special issues—such as import taxes, transportation costs, and inventory management—which are not applicable if you provide a service or software. Of course, if you sell pre-packaged software, you would need to manage the same set of items since you are selling a physical disk that includes your application. So when I refer to software in this chapter, I am talking only about downloadable software from the Internet or accessed for use via the web. This category is referred to as "software as a service" (SaaS).

There are only a few special issues that differ from selling goods vs. selling services and software. Here is a list of those:

- In the business climate chapter, the following items do not apply to services and software businesses:

- Transportation network under infrastructure
- Import/export duties and policies under regulatory
- Certain tax policies and incentives may only apply to companies making or selling physical goods

▪ In the competition chapter, it is worth noting that if your business sells services or software, the startup costs for a new company would be lower than one that makes and sells goods. This lowers your market entry costs, so the barriers to entry are theoretically lower in these industries. Both larger companies and start-ups are able to quickly enter the market to compete with you.

▪ The chapter on entering a market with a master distributor only applies if you are selling physical goods. The reason is that we defined a master distributor as one who takes title or ownership of a product. In the case of services and software, there is no physical good in which to take ownership. So while you may partner with a distributor in a foreign market who resells your services or software, the business model will be like a local agent, where your partner gets paid either a percentage of the sales revenue or a flat fee per sale.

▪ Throughout this book, and primarily in the Financial Considerations section, we talked about inventory management. This was prevalent in our forecasting sales, cash flow, and currency risk chapters. If your company provides services or software, then you do not have to worry about inventory carrying costs or obsolescence due to currency fluctuations.

▪ Finally, in the localizing products and services chapter, the following three items that you should customize apply only to physical goods: product packaging, form factor and accessories.

Services Businesses

If you provide services as your primary line of business, there are few additional items you need to be aware of prior to entering a new country. These are items not covered in the main body of this book, but may differ from how you operate in your home market.

1. *Professional certifications.* Find out if your company or certain employees need a professional certification to operate in the country. For example, if you provide accounting services, what kinds of approvals will your accountants need to obtain? This would impact both your hiring strategy along with your ability to relocate employees from other countries.

2. *Local environments with unions.* In many countries, certain services industries are unionized so when you establish a presence, your employees are legally allowed to form a union. In addition, some of your customers, partners and suppliers may be unionized, which could impact the hours they are available or the services they can provide. Find out if your particular industry is unionized in the country of operation you chose. If so, you will need to understand how this affects both your hiring and your company's ability to obtain customers. You also need to take into account the cost impact of unionized workers. I recommend you speak to a local attorney and human resources firm to strategize how best to prepare for unions.

3. *Citizenship requirements.* Some countries may have a requirement that either a certain percentage of your service employees be citizens of the local country or they may insist that a portion of the professional work force be local hires. While you may view this as protectionist, it may be a requirement and a cost to doing business in that country. This may affect your plans to relocate home employees to the new market. If so, your ability to grow your business may suffer if you cannot bring in senior people from other countries. You may also have to change your business expectations if most of the professionals in the country are less experienced, which is often the case in emerging markets.

4. Regulations. Find out the extent to which your industry is reg-ulated in the country including any professional services rates and fees you charge. Regulations can alter both how much you charge (revenue) and how much you have to pay employees (expenses). These fees can lower your revenue model and limit your compet-itive flexibility. If you have to provide certain minimum salaries to professional employees, it adds to your operating expenses and the time it will take you to reach profitability. Some countries, especially in parts of Europe, are much more regulated that the United States, so speak to a local attorney who understands your specific industry to finalize your plan.

Extra Information about Software Businesses

If you provide software as your primary line of business, the addi-tional issues you need to be aware of prior to entering a new country includes these.

1. Security requirements. Does your software have to meet any in order to be offered in the country? For instance, is there an en-cryption protocol that you must implement, or a software loophole that you must close to prevent third parties from remotely accessing the management interface of the software? Be sure you know what extra security requirements you will need to implement before of-fering your software. The potential fines for violating any of these security measures can be substantial. Worse, regulators will always scrutinize what you do moving forward, believing you intentionally did it. You may be surprised as to what is restricted in certain coun-tries, so have an attorney who understands software requirements verify compliance before you start selling.

2. Hosting. Does your software need to be on servers hosted within the country. Ideally, supplying your software via your exist-ing servers, even if located remotely, simplifies your market entry and requires less investment. This decision typically depends on the market segments you are servicing. For example, if you primary customers are banks, it will most likely be a requirement that customer records not be accessed or stored outside of the country. Most countries will not allow regulated institutions to store personal customer information outside of the country because of risk of theft.

The same usually applies to medical records, so if the healthcare industry is a target market for your business, plan to invest in hosting your software locally. Like bank information, medical records are personal and private and having this data stored outside the country is considered risky. If you need to add servers in country, you will need a resource plan in order to commence operations. This will increase your operating costs, as well as your hiring needs. Your network operations manager should develop this plan and submit the budget to you.

3. *Legal issues.* Find out if there are any laws that could adversely impact you in the event of a data breach. This is a very sensitive topic as software as a service is still relatively new, and most countries are not proactive, but reactive in implementing regulations. Typically, new regulations are created in response to a large data breach that is publicized in the media. So in addition to knowing the rules when you start offering your software, continue to monitor the regulations as they will evolve.

Each country will have its own set of privacy laws that you need to understand, along with the consequences of data breaches, and any mandated communication requirements in the event of breach. Some laws may carry substantial fines, while others may force you to stop offering your software until you can guarantee that the breaches have been cured. This is always a sensitive topic that requires working with a local regulatory attorney, both at inception and throughout the time you offer your software within the country.

KEY LESSONS

- Most of what was covered in this book applies to your business whether you sell a physical product, provide a service, or offer an online software application. However, some differences exist that will require you to modify planning and operations depending on your business.

- If you are not selling a physical product, the main items you do not need to concern yourself with are import taxes, transportation related topics, and any inventory management items.

- If you are providing a service, find out if there are any country specific professional certifications, industry-specific unions, requirements for hiring local employees, or pricing regulations.

- If you are providing an online software application, find out if there are any country specific software security requirements, server hosting requirements, or laws regarding data breaches.

CHAPTER 21

Summary

━━━◆━━━

EXPANDING YOUR BUSINESS INTERNATIONALLY CAN BE rewarding from both a financial and personal perspective. Financially, you can grow your business exponentially by expanding into new markets. The economies of scale from expansion can even help you be more profitable in your home market. Personally, the journey is fascinating as you can meet and work with people from many different cultures, some of whom may become friends for life. As you work with other cultures, your sense of appreciation of what they offer will improve.

Throughout this book, we have focused on building a blueprint that takes you from your initial desire to expand to:

- determining which markets to enter
- deciding on the best entry strategy
- developing financial guidelines for your business
- and implementing many strategies to grow your business

Once you get past the initial decision, your first set of choices revolves around deciding which country or countries you should enter. In Part 1 of the book, we went through the steps to:

- determine the market size
- understand the business climate

■ analyze the unique competitive market
■ evaluate potential partners and understand the ecosystem
■ leverage existing relationships to help you enter a market

In reviewing some of the high level points, remember:

■ Analyze each country separately. Do not lump them into a regional category at this stage. Each market presents its own unique opportunities and challenges that you will not completely see if you group countries together for your analysis.
■ Be realistic in determining what is the true addressable market for you in this country, and set realistic market share goals. Otherwise, you will fool yourself and be disappointed when your plan does not materialize.
■ Understanding the business climate in a country is a critical factor that needs to be part of your decision making process. Each country is unique, and not knowing the intricacies of doing business in a certain market, could lead to costly mistakes.
■ Make sure you study local, regional and global competitors, and do a SWOT analysis to assess your chances of success if you enter the market.
■ Find out if there are any potential partners that can help you get established quickly in a market. Usually others within the ecosystem are a good fit.
■ And finally, see what personal contacts you or the rest of your team have, who can help you analyze and determine if you should enter the market.

Once you have decided which country or countries to enter, you need to determine how to enter each market. Let's quickly review your various entry options we laid out in Part 2 of the book:

■ With a master distributor, you elect a partner who takes ownership of marketing and selling your products in the country.

- If you go the local agent path, your in-country partner acts as an extension of your team. Keep in mind you that you may want to have multiple agents based on vertical markets or geography.
- With a sales and support office, you are hiring your own staff to enter the market. While this is more complex, you have complete control of your operation.
- Going a step further, you can establish your own R&D center, which expands your sales and support organization to include engineering functions. Depending on your product and the specific market, this could be a very profitable route.
- In some instances, licensing your product or technology can provide you a very good return without much expense or risk. Depending on your product, the business climate and competitive environment, licensing may be your most prudent option.
- And finally, you could decide to form a joint venture with a local or regional company in order to attack the market. If you enter into a JV, make sure the partner brings a lot of value to the business so that $1 + 1 = 3$.

As shown in various examples, you can enter the market with one method, and as your business evolves, expand your presence using other methods. For example, you can start with a master distributor or local agent, then expand to setting up a sales office to then establishing an R&D center or even enter into a joint venture.

In order to set goals, devise your execution plan and measure your progress, you need to understand the financial impact entering a new market will have on your overall business. The items we focused on in Part 3 of the book include:

- Make sure you understand all the unique costs that you might incur when doing business in the country. Each country has its own environment, so expect some differences in cost structure from market to market.
- Accurately forecast sales, being aware that cultural differences can make this difficult at first. The key to getting to accuracy is

to constantly communicate with your team and visit customers often.

- Understand and plan for currency risks. Remember, if your revenue and income are in different currencies, your risk is much greater. If this is the case, determine if hedging is a good strategy for your business.
- And finally, ensure you are managing your cash flows so that you do not run out of money. Not only is this a challenge during the startup phase, but when you are growing rapidly, your inflows may not match your cash outflows. Also, make sure you understand what is the expected paying process in the new country.

In Part 4, we examined in detail what to do to continue growing and expanding. The road to get established is tough, but making your business successful for the long-term requires continuing effort and thought. While there are lots of things that need to be done on an ongoing basis, we focused on the following issues in this section:

- Establish a plan for consistent visibility and presence. Not only is this important for winning customers, but also for keeping your in-country team motivated.
- Localize your sales and support efforts. There is more involved than just translating what you currently have. Each market is different and will require its own plan in order to maximize your sales.
- Localize your product and services. Determine what customizations or variations you have to make to create an attractive offering that resonates with customers at an emotional level. Also understand if there are any product changes that need to be made to comply with local regulations.
- Network and localize yourself. As the sponsor for internationalization, you will play a key role in shaping your global business. Remember to learn about the culture, visit frequently and to act globally.

I hope you have found this book to be useful as you plan your business expansion. I have provided two appendices to help you further. The first is a detailed list of questions for each of the book's chapters to make sure you are not overlooking any items. This makes it easy for you to review what you need to ask yourself and/or your professional services companies (lawyers/ accountants / HR and so on). Use these lists of questions to make sure you are properly planning your expansion. It is always better to 'over prepare' than not be fully informed when making key business decisions that can greatly affect your future. Treat these questions as a series of checklists to review as you finalize your international expansion plan.

The second appendix is a brief list of online resources where you can reach out and find answers to many of the country specific questions you will uncover during your journey. This is just an initial list. Conduct your own Internet searches to find other resources that can help you:

- Research each market.
- Find local resources, such as accountants, attorneys and trade groups, who can provide valuable data.
- Determine potential partners and sketch out your ecosystem for that country.
- Look up financial and legal regulations.
- Develop a list of conferences and trade shows to attend.

APPENDICES

Questions to Consider When Expanding Internationally

USE THIS SET OF QUESTIONS FOR EACH CHAPTER AS A CHECKLIST of issues you need to consider when evaluating your options for expanding internationally. This list will also come in handy when you are meeting with any legal and accounting professionals you might need to hire for consulting.

Chapter 1: Opportunity and Market Sizing

- What regions are you considering for expansion? Why?
- Within each region, which countries are you considering? Why?
- What is your plan to research each country?
- Who can you consult with for additional input in your market research?

Chapter 2: Business Climate

Economic Conditions:

- What is the economic growth rate (GDP growth rate) in that country?
- What is the GDP per capita?
- What is the unemployment rate?
- What is the GDP forecast for the next several years?
- What is the unemployment forecast for the next several years?

Infrastructure:
- Are utilities generally available within the country?
- Is there a robust transportation network?
- Is high-speed Internet readily available?
- Is the country easy to reach via air transport?

Regulatory:
- Are prices regulated for your particular type of product in the country?
- Are the importing and exporting guidelines clear?
- Do you need any specific licenses? How easy are they to obtain?
- Does the legal system have due process? Can you succeed in the local courts?
- Is intellectual property respected and protected? What recourse do you have if violated?
- Are there any other regulations you need to be aware of?

Employment Policies:
- What is the policy for hiring employees?
- What is the policy for terminating employees?
- Are there government-mandated employment costs?
- Are there any local business practices or traditions you will need to respect?

Tax Policy:
- How easy is it to move money in and out of the country?
- Are there any government withholdings if you try to move money out? If so, what are they?
- What duties are assessed when you import products?
- Are there any export taxes due to ship product out of the country?

Sales Channels:
- Sketch out how products similar to yours are sold in the country.
- Can you sell directly to end customers?
- Do you have to go through a distributor?

- Can you sell directly to a reseller?

Receptiveness:
- How receptive are customers in that country to purchasing products like yours from a foreign company?
- Any there any issues or concerns from customers regarding products from your home country?

Chapter 3: Competitive Landscape
Types of Competitors:
- Who are your global competitors? How should you compete against them?
- Who are your regional competitors? How should you compete against them?
- Who are your local competitors? How should you compete against them?

Create a Company Level Competitive Matrix, including:
- company size (global and local)
- existing market share (global and local)
- advertising/marketing expenditure (local)
- distribution channels (local)
- customer support responsiveness (local)
- lead-time in fulfilling orders (local)
- flexibility in payment terms (local)

Create a Product Competitive Matrix, including:
- Price comparison
- Feature comparison (relevant features for the specific market)
- Listing of key benefits
- How do your competitors position their products?
- What kind of marketing do they do?
- How do they sell?
- How do they support customers?
- List any unique relationships each competitor may have.

SWOT Analysis:
- What are your company's strengths in this market (be honest)?
- What are your company's weaknesses in this market (be honest)?
- What are the realistic opportunities in this market?
- What are the realistic threats in this market?
- Do a SWOT analysis for your main competitors

Chapter 4: Possible Partners and Ecosystem

Possible Partners:
- List companies that can benefit from offering your product.
- List companies that can benefit from integrating your product or technology into theirs.
- Rank potential partners based on which gives you the most credibility, access to sales channels, and the best understanding of market.

Ecosystem:
- Sketch out how your industry ecosystem works within the country.
- What partnerships within the country can help you succeed?

Chapter 5: Leveraging Existing Relationships

Relationships: Have you reached out to:
- Your existing partners?
- Your suppliers?
- Your customers?
- Your investors?
- Your personal network?

Additional Assistance: Have you reached out to:
- Government agencies?
- Trade offices?
- Industry trade groups?

Areas of Guidance:

- What city or cities should you move in to?
- Any potential tax breaks?
- How will you hire local employees?
- Have you identified critical local suppliers?
- Where will your office be located?

Chapter 6: Master Distributor

- Will the Master Distributor take title to goods upon delivery?
- In what currency will the Master Distributor pay?
- Will the Master Distributor hold and own inventory? How much?
- Will the Master Distributor handle customer support? What training is required?
- What are payment terms with your Master Distributor?
- How will customer returns be handled?
- Will the Master Distributor localize the sales collateral?
- Will the Master Distributor dedicate resources for sales and marketing? How many?
- What is the pricing between you and the Master Distributor?
- Is the Master Distributor offered many bonuses for selling other products they carry? Will this cause them to focus on other products and not yours?
- Does the Master Distributor insist on exclusivity?
  - What is the time period?
  - What is the volume commitment and over what period of time?
  - What is the investment the Master Distributor agrees to make to promote and sell your product? Over what period of time?
  - Will the Master Distributor agree to not carry competing products?
  - What are payment terms in exchange for exclusivity?

Chapter 7: Local Agent

- What is the industry experience of the agent?
  - Local competitor experience?
  - A large target customer?
  - Sales channel partner?
- Is the agent a local person?
- Is the agent technical? If not, does he or she have a technical partner?
- How well does the agent communicate verbally in your language? What about in writing?
- In what vertical markets is the agent strongest?
- With which target customers does the agent already have relationships? At what levels within these companies?
- Does the agent require a monthly retainer? How much?
- What is the commission structure for the agent?
- Should you seek multiple agents in this country?
  - By product line?
  - By vertical market?
  - By geography?
- What is your communication plan with the agent?
  - Have you set up weekly calls?
  - What kind of status reports will be provided?
  - How often will resources from headquarters visit to support?

Chapter 8: Sales and Support Office

- What are the legal requirements to set up an entity?
- What are the employment policies?
- What are the taxation requirements?
- What are the banking requirements?
- Where will customer support be handled?
- Who will be your top executive in the country?
- If executive is from the company:
  - Has he/she extensively traveled and conducted business internationally?
  - Is accepting of different cultures?

- Speaks the local language? If not, willing to take classes?
- A good communicator?
- Gets along well with others in the office?
- Willing to appoint a local strong #2?
■ If you hire locally:
  - What industry experience does the candidate have?
  - Does the candidate have experience building teams? Motivating them?
  - How well does the candidate communicate verbally in your language? What about in writing?
■ What are your office space options?
■ Is headquarters ready to:
  - Communicate often and openly?
  - Give the local office freedom to operate?
  - Provide the support resources needed to succeed?
  - Provide the tools so the local office can localize sales material? What about the product?
  - Set clear goals for the local office? Have the right tools to measure performance?

Chapter 9: Establishing an R&D Center
■ What are the legal requirements to set up an entity?
■ What are the employment policies?
■ What are the taxation requirements?
■ What are the banking requirements?
■ How will intellectual property be created?
■ How will intellectual property be shared?
■ Are there any tax or other financial incentives for setting up the R&D center in this country? In which cities and/or zones?
■ To hire your head of engineering or R&D:
  - What industry experience does the candidate have?
  - Does the candidate have experience building teams? Motivate them?
  - How well does the candidate communicate verbally in your language? What about in writing?

- What improvements will you need to make to your IT infrastructure to support the new R&D center?
- How will your R&D centers operate:
  - Splitting up projects by office? Which ones will the new office be responsible for?
  - Collaborate on the same projects? How?
  - Develop brand new products or product lines?
- What is your recruiting plan for this office?
- What kind of office culture are you seeking? How will you maintain it?
- With what proprietary information will you trust the new office?
- Do you have a plan to exchange engineers on a regular basis?

Chapter 10: Product or Technology Licensing

- Is your potential licensee:
  - Established in the market? To what extent (market share, channels, revenue, sales people, etc.)?
  - A competitor? If so, why do they still make sense as a licensee?
  - Share common goals and values?
  - Conflict/compete with other product lines you have?
  - Do business in other geographies that you actively sell into? Which ones?
  - What vertical markets does this licensee sell to?
- What kind of license are you seeking with this partner:
  - Technology license? If so, what will you license to them? What help will they need from you initially, and on an ongoing basis?
  - Product license? What help will they need from you initially, and then on an ongoing basis?
  - Private label? What customization will they need from you initially, and then on an ongoing basis?
- How will you protect your intellectual property?
- Can the licensee sublicense? To whom?
- Do you have rights to any IP the licensee develops that is on top of your IP? What royalties, if any, will you have to pay?

- What is the scope of the design work you will need to do? How much will you get paid for it? How will additional work be charged?
- How long is the license for? How can the agreement be extended?
- Will licensee need to produce or sell a certain number of units to maintain the license?
- Do you have to provide customized versions of your product updates? In what time frame?
- How will product updates be handled? Will you charge for them?
- Can you distinguish between product enhancements and new features?
- What is the structure for progress meetings?
- What are the upfront and ongoing license fees the licensee will pay?

Chapter 11: Joint Venture

- Is a joint venture required by the government or other entity in order to enter this specific foreign market?
- Are there government incentives to form a joint venture?
- If the joint venture is opportunistic:
  - Is it market opportunity related? How?
  - Is it due to benefits your partner would bring? Be specific on listing these benefits.
- What are the cost sharing advantages of this joint venture?
- How will you gain market credibility through this joint venture?
- Will you have a better understanding of the market need? How?
- Will the joint venture result in stronger government support? How?
- How will the joint venture be able to scale for growth?
- What is the ownership structure of the joint venture? What percent will you own? Can that change over time? How?
- How will the joint venture be staffed?
- Who will be the leader of the joint venture?

- If there is disagreement with the leadership, what are your rights to make a change?
- What will each party initially bring into the joint venture? What about on an ongoing basis?
- What will each party be responsible for as the venture moves forward?
- How will the joint venture position itself in the market?
- Will the joint venture be limited to the local country or can it expand beyond its borders? If so, to where and under what terms?
- What are the high-level goals of the joint venture?
- How will conflicts within the joint venture be managed by the investors?
- What is the dissolution plan? Make sure it is specific with regards to IP, assets and liabilities.
- What are the contributions each party will contribute to the venture? Have detailed lists.
- How will cash inflows and outflows be managed?
- Does the joint venture have rights to either party's existing IP? Under what terms?
- How will intellectual property created by the joint venture be treated? Do the investors have rights to the IP? Under what terms?

Chapter 12: Cost Structure

- What are the regulatory costs you will incur for your business within the country?
  - Are the costs fixed or variable?
  - Are they based on revenue, assets or other measures?
  - How frequently do you have to pay?
- Will you be subject to any withholdings?
  - Under what conditions?
  - How can you recover these withholding costs?
- What is the corporate tax rate structure?
  - Can you carry losses forward?
  - Will you be eligible for any tax exemptions?

- What is the VAT percentage?
  - Will you pay VAT or any other excise tax on purchases? If so, for what items?
- What employee related expenses will you incur in addition to salary?
- Any assessments on assets? Under what conditions?
- Are there any industry association fees you need to pay?
- Can your existing firms handle professional services? At what cost?
- If you need to hire local firms, what costs will you incur?
- What expenses will you need to pre-pay as you establish your business?
- What are the compliance requirements?
  - What forms need to be filed?
  - When will these forms need to be filed?
  - How will file these forms for you?

Chapter 13: Forecasting Sales

- What is the local culture like when forecasting? Is it conservative, optimistic, non-confrontational, or other?
- Are you using a soft approach to get an accurate forecast?
- Have you set up review sessions to understand the submitted forecast?
- How has the country's forecast vs. actual results tracked over time? Chart the accuracy over time to help you apply judgment factors.
- How often do you visit customers in the country?
- Have you revised the forecast based on your judgment?

Chapter 14: Currency Risk

- In what currency will you generate sales?
- In what currency will you incur and pay most of your expenses?
  - Breakdown expenses paid in local currency versus other currencies.

- Estimate the impact to your business if the local currency appreciates:
  - Impact on sales prices?
  - Will you need to provide price protection?
  - Impact on employee salaries?
  - Impact on other operating expenses?
  - What are the possible grey market implications?
- Estimate the impact to your business if the local currency depreciates:
  - Impact on sales prices?
  - Will you need to provide price protection?
  - Impact on employee salaries?
  - Impact on other operating expenses?
  - What are the possible grey market implications?
- Hedging currency:
  - Can you accurately estimate cash flow for the next 1, 2 and 3 years?
  - If so, is hedging worth it for your business? Will you do it?
  - What amounts will you hedge?
  - Which banks will you approach?
  - What are the costs for the hedges? Any other bank conditions?

Chapter 15: Cash Flow Management

- What are your monthly cash flow projections over the first three years?
- How will expansion be initially funded?
- If you are in a negative cash flow situation, how will you fund the business:
  - For how much of a deficit can you rely on savings?
  - If you need to borrow, from what source and under what conditions?
  - If you need to sell equity in your business, to whom and at what valuation?
  - If you will sell assets, which ones? How much do you think you can get for the assets?

- Sources of cash inflows:
  - How will you generate revenue?
  - Any monthly recurring revenue?
  - What percent of revenue do you forecast needing to write off as uncollectable?
  - What percent of revenue will you need to set aside for warranty costs?
  - What payment terms do you think you will be able to demand?
  - Realistically, what payment terms do you think your customers will honor?
- Cash outflows:
  - Can you get payment terms for larger expenditures? If so, how long?
  - If you must pay up front, for how long? What payment terms can you get once you establish a good payment history?
  - Which expenditures will you be required to pay for the full term upfront?
  - How often will you have to pay salaries?
  - What bonus plan should be modeled?
    - When will government-mandated bonuses need to be paid?
    - When will you pay other bonuses?
  - How often will raises need to be given? What are the expected salary increase percentages?
  - What government-mandated fees will you have to pay?
    - What employee fees will have to be paid, and when?
    - What employment taxes will have to be paid, and when?
    - What is the timing for paying regulatory fees?
    - When will sales taxes need to be paid?
    - When will income taxes need to be paid?

Chapter 16: Visibility and Presence
- How frequently will you visit the country?
- How frequently will your other executives visit the country?
- Are you engaging with all your employees when you visit?

- Every time you visit, are you meeting with customers, potential customers, channel partners, ecosystem partners, industry associations, and regulators?
- Who are the press contacts you want to establish relationships with?
- How often are you scheduling press meetings?
- Do you have any significant announcements that merit a press conference?
- What industry conferences should you participate in?
- Can you get speaking slots at industry conferences in the country? How?
- What are you doing to ensure the in country employees feel they belong and are part of the team?
- Is there good collaboration between employees in the country and headquarters?
- Is there an open communication channel between the in-country employees and management at headquarters?

Chapter 17: Localizing Sales and Support

- How are you localizing sales:
  - What is your local product positioning?
  - What marketing programs will you implement?
  - What is your sales pitch for this country?
  - Have you customized your sales collateral taking into account your local positioning and sales pitch?
  - Who are local partners that can help you succeed?
  - What is your pricing strategy?
  - How will your sales organization be structured?
  - What is the sales compensation plan?
- How are you localizing support:
  - Where will you locate your support resources?
  - What customized support tools will you need?
  - What is the process for local support to communicate with engineering?

- In what languages will you offer support?
- What will be your in country support hours?
- What types of support will you offer?
- What is your return policy for the country?
- How will you structure your support organization?

Chapter 18: Localizing Products and Services

- How are you localizing your products:
  - Have you localized paper and online manuals? What about other documentation?
  - Have you translated your packaging?
  - Do you have to change the color of your packaging?
  - Any other changes required in customizing the packaging?
  - Have you localized the software?
  - Any form factor changes required?
  - Any changes required in product functionality?
  - Any features that need to be added, deleted, or modified in the product?
  - Do you have to change any of the accessories that ship with your product?
  - Are there any product bundles that you can do in-country to make your product more attractive?
- How are you localizing your services:
  - Should you offer installation services in this market? If so, how?
  - Should you do product configurations for your customers in this market? If so, how?
  - Do you need to integrate your product with other products or services? If so, how?
  - Should you offer an extended warranty? Under what terms?
  - Have you tested your product to ensure the extended warranty will not be too costly?

Chapter 19: Networking and Localizing Yourself

- Networking methods:
  - How frequently are you traveling to the country?
  - What local conferences can you attend?
  - What local trade shows can you attend?
  - Are you networking on LinkedIn?
  - Are you active on Twitter?
  - Are you actively blogging?
  - How visible are you with your in-country contacts?
  - Are you following up all your action items?
  - How often are you checking in with your contacts via email? How about by phone?
  - Have you offered to host your customers and contacts in your country?
- Localizing yourself:
  - What is your plan to learn about the culture?
  - In your discussions, are you being adaptable and flexible?
  - Are you approaching your business with a global mindset?

Chapter 20: Goods vs Services vs Software

- If you are providing services:
  - Are any professional certifications required?
  - Are unions common in the country for your specific industry?
    - How do unions impact your ability to hire?
    - If your employees elect to unionize, what will be the cost?
  - Is there is any requirement that a certain percentage of professionals be local citizens?
    - If so, is the local talent experienced enough for you to meet your business objectives?
  - Are there any regulations that impact the prices you can charge?
  - Are there any regulations that impact the salaries you can provide employees?

- If you are providing online software:
  - Are there any country specific security requirements?
    - Are there any security protocols you need to implement?
    - How are software loopholes treated?
    - Any other specific requirements?
    - What are the repercussions if you do not comply?
  - Will you be required to host your servers within the country?
    - If so, what is your plan to implement?
    - Will you have to hire another resource to manage?
    - How much will local hosting cost your business?
  - What are the laws with regards to a data breach?
    - What are the repercussions if there is a breach?
    - What are the communication requirements in the event of a breach?
    - Is there a set time for you to cure a breach? How long?
    - Do you have a plan in place to continue monitoring the laws so you understand any changes?

Resources for Expanding Internationally

Global Trade Resources:
World Trade Organization (WTO)
www.wto.org
Regulates trade and tariffs worldwide. Formed as successor to the General Agreement on Tariffs and Trade (GATT).

International Chamber of Commerce (ICC)
www.iccwbo.org
Promotes international trade, investment, and the market economy system worldwide.

Federation of International Trade Associations (FITA)
www.fita.org
450 association members dedicated to the promotion of international trade, import-export, international logistics management, international finance and more.

Listing of International Trade Shows:
www.expodatabase.com/international-trade-shows/

In Country Resources:
Each Country has its own Chamber of Commerce and some have Trade Associations or Trade Councils that promote doing business

with the country. Some are government agencies while some are independent. Best method to get contacts is to do an Internet search. Here are examples of some of the resources for a few countries:

United States:
Export.gov
www.export.gov/index.asp
Managed by the International Trade Administration in collaboration with several US government agencies. This is the official US Government resource for American companies looking to expand internationally. In addition, this website contains links to many partner agencies that can assist you:
www.export.gov/about/eg_main_016802.asp

US Chamber of Commerce
www.uschamber.com
Federation of businesses, chambers of commerce, American chambers overseas, and trade and professional associations.

Australia:
Austrade: Australian Trade Commission
www.austrade.gov.au
Export promotion agency of the Australian government.

Canada:
Canadian Chamber of Commerce
www.chamber.ca
Working to create a climate for competitiveness, profitability, and job creation for businesses of all sizes in all sectors across Canada.

Japan:
Jetro (Japan External Trade Organization)
www.jetro.go.jp/
JETRO is a government-backed organization that works to promote mutual trade and investment between Japan and the rest of the world.

The Netherlands:
Dutch Foreign Trade Agency
www.hollandtrade.com
Official information about the Dutch economy and business opportunities in the Netherlands.

Norway:
Bedin
www.bedin.no
Norwegian Ministry of Trade and Industry site providing resources on establishing and running business enterprises in Norway.

Romania:
Chamber of Commerce and Industry of Romania
www.ccir.ro

Singapore:
www.sicc.com.sg
Open to all races and nationalities with business organizations in Singapore.

Sweden:
Swedish Trade Council
www.swedishtrade.se
Swedish Trade Council assists Swedish companies in doing business abroad and help foreign companies to find good partners in Sweden.

United Kingdom:
British Chambers of Commerce
www.britishchambers.org.uk

Notes

Notes

About the Author

ANTHONY GIOELI has over 25 years of experience managing fast growth high technology companies, specializing in building and leading global organizations. He has served as President and CEO of three US-based technology companies: CloudTC, Inc., Atrua Technologies, Inc. and AirPrime, Inc. Two of the companies (CloudTC and AirPrime), were acquired by foreign corporations, and the third generated over 80% of its business overseas.

Anthony also served as a division General Manager at Xircom, and as Vice President of Sales, Marketing and Business Development at several companies in the technology industry that were headquartered in Australia, Europe and North America. In his most current position, he is CEO of a company based in Switzerland. Earlier in his career, Anthony worked at large multinational corporations including AT&T, Compaq Computer Corporation (acquired by Hewlett Packard) and IBM in various roles in engineering, marketing, finance, and sales.

Throughout his career, Anthony's focus has been on international business. Some of his activities have included setting up an R&D center in China; opening up sales and support offices in Belgium, Germany, Japan, Singapore, South Korea, Taiwan, and the UK; establishing joint development agreements with companies in Bulgaria, India, Romania, South Korea, and Taiwan; and forming strategic partnerships with companies in Africa, Asia, Australia, Europe, North America, and South America. Anthony's educational background consists of earning a Bachelor of Science in Electrical Engineering from New York Institute of Technology and an MBA in finance from the University of Southern California.

15474999R00138

Made in the USA
San Bernardino, CA
26 September 2014